UX-6000

UX−6000

Battle of the Death Sub's Secret

PETER W. SCHNEIDER

Andover Press
Andover, New Jersey

Publisher's Cataloging-in-Publication
Schneider, Peter W.
    UX–6000 : battle for the death sub's secret /
    by Peter W. Schneider, Michael Duffy, Roger N.
    Pierson --1st ed.
        p. cm.
    1. World War, 1939-1945--Naval operations--
    Submarine--Fiction. 2. World War, 1939-1945--
    Naval operations, German--Fiction. 3. World War,
    1939-1945--Naval operations, American--Fiction.
    I. Duffy, Michael, 1952- II. Pierson, Roger N.
    III. Title
    PS3569.C522388U93 2001   813.6
                        QBI00-500113
ISBN 0-9703512-0-8
SAN: 253-3243

10 9 8 7 6 5 4 3 2 1

PROLOGUE
1 March
1945

Bremerhaven, Germany—0610 Hours

Dawn. U-boat Captain Heinz Dorfmann turned his head toward the coming light and the danger it brought. The first faint rays of the rising sun reflected off the bottom of the low cloud layer, and he tensed as his black German submarine became visible. He knew the brightening sky would quickly fill with American war planes. It was time to go.

The captain felt the gentle rolling of his war vessel under his feet as the light chop of the cold North Sea water moved the U-boat against the straining ropes. He barked an order toward the heaving deck. The crewmen quickly released the U-boat and tossed the heavy wet ropes up onto the tie up stanchions.

Dorfmann thrust out his right arm in a stiff Nazi salute toward the small group of black uniformed officers standing on the bomb-cratered concrete dock. No military band would honor this departure; no crowd of well-wishers would wave and shout their support; no newsman would record what posterity should know. Those happy days were gone. Only General Schmitt and two staff officers would witness the beginning of this dangerous and vital mission.

The captain turned away and shouted his order to move ahead slow. He watched as the rounded steel bow began to thrust the dark gray water aside. He ordered a north northwest course, away from Bremerhaven and their fatherland, toward the still black sky of the open sea.

1

After shouting down his order for full speed ahead, he braced himself for the surge of acceleration as the U-boat raced for deep water. In the open seas, he hoped to be safe from the revealing light of day and the prowling British destroyers hunting the sea. With a final shiver in the frigid winter air, he shouted the order to dive.

The captain drew comfort from the skilled movements of the crew, the clanking sounds of hatchways being closed and dogged down, the diesel engines shutting off and their air induction valves closing. Even the creaking of the metal hull as it strained against the weight of the icy water now surrounding the U-boat reassured Dorfmann.

He looked about at the faces of the officers and crew. They had been together for only a short time. Too short to accomplish thorough training, the captain mused, but hopefully long enough. If only there weren't so many boys. Unfortunately, grown men weren't available anywhere. Germany was short of everything these days, especially experienced submariners.

The experts, those black uniformed generals spending the war well-fed in cozy bunkers, blamed it on the drive into the fatherland, on the Allied armies—fat on American wealth flowing across the Atlantic—and, of course, on the Russians entrenched on the east side of the Oder River. Everyone, it seemed, was threatening to cross the Rhine. Little remained to stop them.

By now it was painfully obvious that America was the adversary Germany must weaken. Yes, Dorfmann told himself, America. And I am just the man for it. Beneath his feet he could almost feel the awesome weapon waiting below. A weapon of terrible destructive power. A perfect gift for the arrogant beast America. Its use would almost certainly kill hundreds of thousands of their citizens. It might even paralyze the enemy's war effort. Yes, how sweet that would be! Hold them back long enough for Germany to recover its fighting strength. The war must continue, the thirty year old captain thought. It must! Ah, but if only there weren't so many boys, so many boys.

With the course now set and the submarine cloaked in the

dark waters of the North Sea, the captain had time to reflect on the meaning of the general's final words. Spoken with a voice choked with emotion, the high ranking officer told him of how he and his aides planned to kill themselves before allowing the Allies to capture them. Proud words. But tears streaked the old man's face, and Dorfmann saw defeat in his eyes. Dorfmann could not think of defeat. Not now. He clicked his heels, saluted his superior, and the two men clasped hands.

Dorfmann looked at the envelope the general had given him. He didn't need to read the contents. He already knew what the written orders inside the envelope would say—the mission of the U-boat might well decide the fate of the fatherland and of Adolf Hitler. It might well change the course of the war. And now the enormous responsibility was in his hands. His. His and his crew's.

The general had been like a close friend to the captain. He had helped the young man to become a combat pilot in the Luftwaffe, a career that the young man from Pegnitz had always wanted. But bullets fired by an American P-47 Thunderbolt changed everything. One crushed the bones in his left arm. A pilot needs two good arms, if he hopes to survive. And Dorfmann considered himself a survivor.

But now it was time to put away both the envelope and the dear face of General Schmitt. It did no good to think of the families that had been lost to the thunder of Allied bombs. Nor did it help to remind himself of the truth in Schmitt's eyes—they would never meet again.

Dorfmann looked up at the bright bare bulb above and sighed. Perhaps I could manage a cup of coffee, he thought, and a few minutes rest. He stepped to the small mirror on the bulkhead of the officer's quarters. He stared at the reflection for several minutes. The face seemed unfamiliar. He couldn't remember getting so old. The look of resignation, of desperation, was unnerving.

He lay down on his personal bunk, a true luxury aboard a U-boat, fully enjoying not having to "hot rack," that is, to share a bunk like the crew did. He covered his eyes with his forearm. Must focus on the job ahead, he thought.

The news of the deaths of his wife and children had depressed him deeply. This assignment would fix that. He had the chance to kill the American swine responsible for destroying his family. The thought buoyed him. His hatred of this enemy gave him the strength to drive this powerful weapon deep into the Americans' hearts. It would be both his and Germany's revenge.

He didn't need convincing. But he knew that his men did. So he gave the same old, tired speech to the crew. Those well-worn patriotic words and phrases driven by Doctor Goebbels into the hearts of the German people. Duetschland, Deutschland, Deutschland! He cringed when the young men, mere boys, had cheered the words. So far, so good.

But then he glanced toward the old, experienced men. They were not cheering. They stared back at their captain with a shallow, hopeless look. Their faces bore the truth. They knew. They knew these youngsters would not celebrate another birthday—none of them would. The powerful Allied anti-submarine forces were out there waiting. They knew the reality. U-boat missions were now suicidal. They would not be coming back.

But if the mission succeeded—it would be worth it.

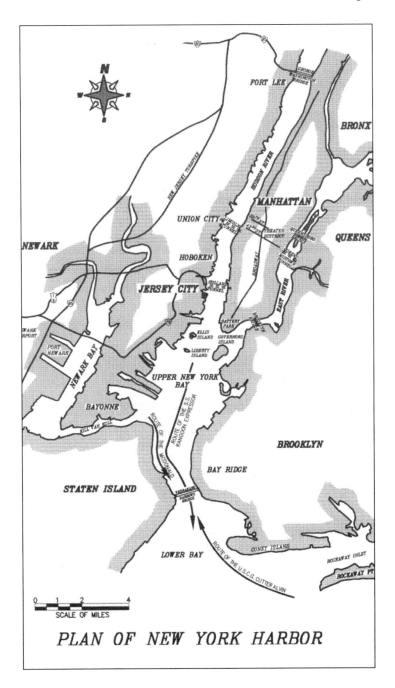

PLAN OF NEW YORK HARBOR

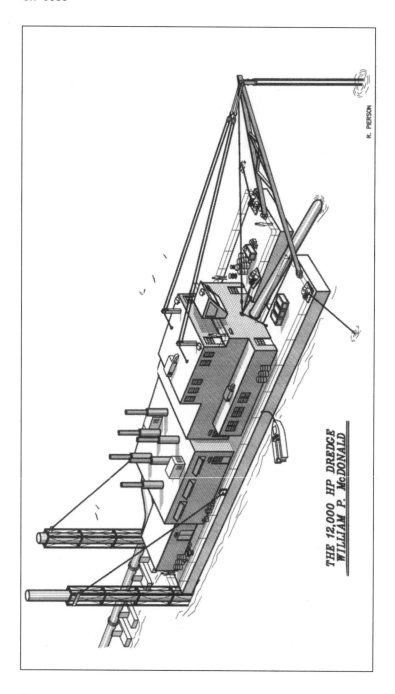

THE 12,000 HP DREDGE
WILLIAM P. McDONALD

R. PIERSON

U.S. Coast Guard Headquarters, Governors Island—1510 Hours

U.S.C.G. Lieutenant Commander Robert Scott sighed and leaned back in his swivel chair. He looked up at the ceiling and rubbed his tired eyes. Damn this paperwork. He was in charge of accident investigation and harbor safety, but the endless paperwork was beyond endurance. It was the bane of all police organizations, and the U.S. Coast Guard was no exception. He hated doing it.

The telephone rang, and he grabbed for it, a slight smile appearing on his face. Maybe something new, he thought, laying down his ballpoint. I'd do anything for a chance to get the hell away from this desk.

"Commander," his boss, Captain of the Port, Ronald Peters, began. "Port Authority just called. That dredge from Texas has hit something. Go out and find out what's going on. Report back to me within the hour."

"Aye, Sir," Scott replied.

Scott needed no prodding. He lifted his officer's hat from the shelf and almost trotted for the Governors Island boat slip. He strode quickly toward the waterside, his thoughts turning to the task ahead and his jurisdiction. As the bi-state agency in charge of maintaining the harbor, the Port Authority called on the Coast Guard for just such assistance. He knew dredging was necessary to keep the shipping channels open. Important work that must not be delayed. And it was work in the open air.

So the phone call was routine. Potential hazards to navigation fell under U.S. Coast Guard jurisdiction. Dredges hit buried objects all the time, Scott thought, probably another junk car that fell off a barge. Reaching the dock, Scott quickly stepped into the waiting boat.

Aboard the U.S.C.G. Bayliner Ciera—1515 Hours

The afternoon sun had cooked the boat's vinyl seat cover to a skin-searing temperature, but Scott didn't seem to notice. Actually, he thought, the heat felt good. The boss kept the office colder than Scott preferred, a situation he was certain caused his sinuses to plug up. But out here on the water Scott knew he could relax and enjoy the ride, pleased that his regularly assigned coxswain was at the helm. He tapped his foot to a Phil Collins hit playing on the boat's sound system. He and the coxswain, it seemed, both enjoyed soft rock music.

Scott relished the feel of wind across a fast moving bow on a sunny day. His assignment to the New York Coast Guard station provided him frequent reason to be out in one of the world's busiest harbors. A responsibility he was proud that had been entrusted to him.

He never tired of the parade of great and the not so great ships as they came and went through the Narrows from the restless ocean beyond. Carrying cargo of all kinds to and from the port, they flew the flags of many nations and added, for Scott, a glamour that most other work lacked. Even the countless small motor and sail boats, darting and bobbing about the slow moving large vessels, brought a clutch to his throat. Overhead, the air suddenly filled with flapping white wings as seagulls searched the water for food, and he felt instantly at home.

The huge hydraulic dredge loomed ahead as the waters of the upper bay steadily slipped below the Coast Guard boat's hull. The ride gave him time to reflect on the tales he had been hearing ever since the *William P. McDonald* had arrived.

Gossip traveled fast around the harbor, especially juicy gossip. The stories of the rowdy crew of this dredge were becoming legend. Their exploits in the whorehouses and bars along the Jersey side of the Hudson were without equal. But the most titillating gossip concerned the assignment of Sherry Edwards to supervise the dredging.

She was young, beautiful, an engineer, and – most importantly – impervious to all the silly gossip about her being the only woman with all those sex-crazed crewmen on the dredge. But, boy, did it make tongues waggle! He didn't believe any of the stories, of course, but the rumors persisted. Still, he wondered, why would any woman subject herself to being alone with such a difficult male crew?

He remembered his last encounter with her. She had seemed very warm and receptive at the Port Authority Christmas party. He thought back to how she seemed almost to cling to his side. He certainly didn't object. Her beauty, her voluptuous body, her wonderful scent, all were intoxicating beyond any other women he had met. And it didn't hurt that she was an engineer.

Long separated from his wife, he decided to ask her for a date. She brightened, seemed ready — almost eager — to go with him, but then her look grew serious, and she asked about his marriage. When he said that he and his wife had separated, she suddenly seemed cold and pulled away. He never found out why.

The sudden reversal of the engine followed by the gentle bump of the bow against the steel side of the dredge brought Scott back to reality. Well, he wondered, if Sherry's aboard—I hope she's not still pissed.

One of the crewmen of the *McDonald* was waiting at the boat tie-up area at the rear of the dredge as Scott climbed aboard. A very rough looking man, Scott thought, a bit like a pirate. A slight beguiling smile was his only greeting. These construction crews never seemed to like anyone in a position of authority.

"Hey Tiny," the man spoke into the intercom. "That Coast Guard guy is here."

"Yeah, okay," the dredge captain's voice came back. "Send him up to the control cab."

9

Aboard the dredge *William P. McDonald*—1530 Hours

While Scott found his way to the dredge captain, Sherry, at the front of the dredge, tracked the points of contact with the object. Beside her, the dredge's day operator, Charlie Weavers, continued moving the huge machine toward the Verrazano-Narrows Bridge. The graph paper chart on her knees soon took on a leopard's look. Charlie laughed at her drawing. He said it reminded him of connect the dots from kindergarten.

Sherry found Charlie's stories of Captain Harris and his crew and their many adventures interesting but more detailed than she wanted to know. But then, Charlie was a talker. He had a lot to tell, she thought, because he'd been the dredge operator for many years. It was obvious that he was proud of the dredge's captain and admired his tough guy image.

Now he was talking about the dredge captain's early days as a company troubleshooter. Once their captain had to fight a group of armed thieves stealing the company's property. Charlie had watched as the dredge captain shot down four of the robbers despite their bullets hitting him several times They'd fought more than a few fist and gun battles. So the dredge captain had been a troubleshooter. Wasn't that just another name for hired gunman, Sherry wondered?

She looked up as Charlie paused to relight his pipe. He picked up a large box of kitchen matches and struck one on the box. When the match flared up, the acrid smoke smarted in Sherry's nostrils as he sucked the flame down into the tobacco. The aroma of the smoke from his tobacco was pungent, but the air conditioner ventilated the cab every few minutes, keeping the smoke from building up. His half-empty cup of chicory-flavored coffee still steamed on the small shelf to his left, the vapor slowly rising toward the vent at the top of the control cab.

"Charlie, you smoke too much," she said as she reached down for a small ruler on the floor and placed it on the plotting surface. Charlie laughed at her comment and kept puffing. She measured that the dredge had moved about one hundred and fifty feet along the sunken object.

Charlie looked over Sherry's shoulder at her drawing and said, "You know what, missy? That looks like a submarine." He started laughing again and blew a cloud of smoke toward the windows.

"Oh, my God!" Sherry gasped. "It does at that! Whatever would a submarine be doing in New York Harbor buried in the mud?"

"You got me."

The captain of the dredge, Russell Harris, thrust open the door in his usual forceful way. "Well, Edwards," he said coldly. "Have you got an answer yet?"

"Tiny," interjected Charlie, using the nickname the dredge crew had given to Captain Harris. "We done dug up a real honest-injun submarine!" He laughed again. He was really enjoying this big surprise, Sherry thought.

"Have you gone nuts?" demanded the dredge captain.

"Well, take a look at Sherry's drawing, and *you* tell *me*."

"You're both crazy."

Sherry popped to her feet. "I may be crazy, but this data isn't."

She thrust the graph at the huge man. As he studied it, Sherry felt herself stiffen at the close-up look of his scar-covered face. And then the face, that Charlie had just told her was that of a killer, shifted his gaze to her.

He scrutinized her with the same intensity he just used with the graph. Was he trying to stare her down? Was this a macho thing? Sherry felt her stomach tighten and her throat close, but she held herself still, kept her green eyes focused. Then, from deep in those eyes, she sensed something — a contradiction. The hard penetrating stare betrayed itself with soft brown eyes. She stepped back. She knew that look, had dealt with it since she was a teenager. Desire. A desire for her.

Only when he turned away to look out the window did she allow herself to relax. Whew, she thought, with relief. She took in the massive breadth of his shoulders and said to herself, "You turned away first, captain. Makes you almost cute." Then she noticed that her hands were shaking.

A moment later, Scott, stepping through the control cab

door, found himself facing a giant of a man. An unfriendly, intimidating giant at that, a man tall enough to have to stoop through a door. Being just under six feet tall, Scott was a big man himself, and his 180 pounds of hard muscle made him seem even larger, but he wasn't used to leaning back to see another man's face.

Scott extended his hand in greeting and was met with a cold, hostile stare. The silence made Scott wonder what the hell's wrong with this jerk The impasse was finally broken by another voice as Charlie introduced himself and extended a much more inviting hand. Scott was thankful for the friendly smile and the life in Charlie's gray eyes. The man's large white full beard and mustache on his weather-beaten face gave the old dredgeman the look of a department-store Santa.

Scott was pleased to see Sherry standing alongside Charlie, her light auburn hair flowing out from under her construction hard hat. Her face was just as he remembered — beautiful. Scott matched her slight smile with his own as he clasped Charlie's outstretched hand.

"Well, Commander," said the dredge captain at last. "You damn well better straighten out this damn mess!"

"That's why I'm here, Captain," Scott replied.

The dredge captain pointed at Charlie and Sherry. "These fools think we've run into a submarine."

"Take a look at my plots, Commander," said Sherry. "It has the right shape for a sub whether a certain man likes it or not." She returned Harris's scowl.

Scott studied the plots for several seconds and then said, "It sure looks big enough, but a submarine this far up in the harbor—ridiculous! I know the sunken wreck records of New York Harbor by heart. Nothing like a submarine has ever been reported. Ever. But then, no one had ever dredged below 45 feet before."

"Listen, Coast Guard man!" the dredge captain barked while pointing his finger at Scott's chest. "I don't give a damn if it's a submarine or a can of beans—it's in my damn way and it's costing me money by slowing down this dredge. I expect you to clear it out of my damn way and I don't mean next week. You hear me!"

"Take it easy. We'll get to the bottom of this, I assure you." Scott spoke with confidence and authority. "I just don't see how it could be a sub, but if it is—this could be a major problem."

"Any chance it could be a sunken cabin cruiser?" asked Sherry.

"No way, missy," chuckled Charlie. "Any sunken small boat would done been cut to pieces by that cutter head. Remember that fifty-six-foot sailboat we hit down in Miami last year, Tiny? Chopped it up into a million pieces and spit it out the back."

"Yeah," answered the dredge captain. "I also remember it took two hours to unplug the slurry pump." He turned to Scott. "All right, let's talk money. Who's going to pay for my lost time? And if I have to drag this dredge back for a recut, who's paying for that?"

"I can't answer that," Scott replied. "Your contract with the Port Authority should cover that sort of question."

"Well, you listen to me, mister! It costs the company over twenty thousand dollars a day to operate this dredge. If my boss sends one of his henchmen up here from Galveston to climb on my back about it, you can bet some S.O.B. is going to be pounded real bad!"

"Now calm down, Captain. Let me call my boss and start things rolling," Scott said, while thinking — what's this guy's problem?

"You could use the phone in my office, Commander," suggested Sherry.

As the door closed behind him, Scott thought he heard the dredge captain comment to Charlie that he'd be damn glad to get both those pretty faces off his dredge.

Sherry and Scott hurried toward the rear of the dredge where they could talk freely. He thought, as she took the lead, she's wearing that perfume I remember from Christmas. Walking along the catwalk, the metallic clink of their steps bouncing off the green walls, Scott remembered the stories of how she had had to fight to get this job. He knew that the bosses at the Port Authority definitely would have preferred a male engineer. They had done little to hide their true feelings.

But Sherry Edwards's expertise and record had won her the job. Scott had to wonder why she pressed so hard to get assigned to such a macho place. A man probably would have a lot less trouble getting along.

They stopped at the engine-room door and put on the oversized muffs for hearing protection from the roar of the big diesel generators. Sherry pushed the heavy door open and the engine room's pounding cacophony hit their ears anyway.

The six huge engines were running at nearly full throttle to produce enough electricity to power the massive slurry pump and other dredge machinery. Walking past the first diesel, Scott saw the engine crew servicing the next one. The mechanics saw Sherry and stopped working to leer. Scott chuckled at how she looked right through them.

Scott could see that Sherry had obviously selected an ill-fitting construction outfit, but it didn't seem to make any difference. There was no way to hide that figure. The men's eyes seemed to strip away her attire. If those mechanics had seen Sherry in that tight green dress she'd worn at the Christmas party, Scott mused, they would have lost their minds.

But Scott still had to wonder — why, pretty lady, do you hide your figure, yet allow that gorgeous hair to flow out from under your hat? Do you know what it does to us? But the natural way she walked in front of him told him she didn't. She was unaware of her conflicting messages.

They quickly crossed the engine room and reached her office. With the heavy metal door closed, they could at last remove their hearing protection and enjoy some relative quiet.

"Whew," Scott said. "That Captain Harris is one tough bird. Is he always like that? How have you managed to deal with him?"

"He hasn't beaten me down yet," she answered. "I wanted this job to show my bosses that I can handle any type of work that the Port Authority needs done. I can't get ahead if I duck out whenever a job gets tough. I'm a lot stronger than most men think. But it's not too bad. I'll bring these guys around eventually."

"Good for you. How tall is that man?"

"Charlie tells me that Harris is over six foot-ten inches tall. Can you imagine it? The crew calls him 'Tiny'."

"Tiny, huh. He must weigh at least 300 pounds."

"Charlie says 320. But don't think he's soft. He's a serious weight-lifter. Charlie claims the captain is all muscle. He can lift a 400-pound barbell over his head."

Scott shook his head in disbelief. He reached for the phone and dialed Coast Guard headquarters on Governors Island.

"Captain Peters, this is Scott. I'm on board the *William P. McDonald* and there is a real problem here. They've hit a very large object about fifty feet down, and it's definitely interfering with the operation of the dredge."

"What do you think it is?"

"Really don't know. Could be a barge or an industrial process tank," he hesitated. "Maybe a sub."

"A sub? That's crazy. Impossible!"

"I know it sounds crazy, but Sherry Edwards's plotting sure has the right shape for it. I'd like to do a magnetic-sonar survey."

"Approved. I'll have Chief Morris report to you immediately. Get your results to me as soon as the data is complete." Peters cleared his throat then continued. "I must remind you that it is imperative that nothing delay this dredging project. The Japan-Athens Shipping Company contract depends on that channel being ready in three weeks, or else they'll transfer operations to Baltimore. Then thousands of jobs would be lost. That is unacceptable."

■ ■ ■ ■

Ninety minutes later Chief Petty Officer Morris climbed aboard the dredge carrying data from the completed survey. He located Scott talking with Sherry Edwards in her office.

"It's a sub all right!" Morris exclaimed. He laid the plot down for Scott to study.

"Incredible! But whose?" Scott asked.

"How long do you think it's been there?" Sherry asked. "Is it a U.S. sub?"

"Slow down," said Scott. "Let's think this out. We might answer the question of *who* it belongs to if we could figure *when* it got buried in the mud."

"That's pretty obvious, Commander," replied the chief. "This area has been used as a dredge-spoil dump ever since the forties. This part of the channel was last kept clear during the Second World War. The Army Corps of Engineers started filling this area around mid-1945. So the sub must have been here before then."

"You're suggesting that the sub would have to be a World War II model. But I don't remember anything that looked like this back then. Look at the conning tower. Looks more like a nuclear sub. See—it's streamlined."

"That's right. Now I remember! There was one type of sub built in World War II that was streamlined. The German Type 21!"

"Are you guys crazy?" asked Sherry. "A German sub buried here undetected for fifty years? Unbelievable!"

"We can't answer all these questions now," replied Scott as he reached for the phone. "Let's talk to headquarters."

Sherry and Morris whispered excitedly as Scott talked with Captain Peters. He hung up the phone and turned toward Morris.

"We're to meet with the boss at 0900 hours tomorrow. So, for now, proceed back to base with your launch. I'll follow shortly." Then to Sherry he added, "I'll call you after the meeting with Captain Peters."

"I'd appreciate that. But if you don't mind, I'd like to catch a ride into town with you now so I don't have to wait for the Port Authority service boat. It's always late."

"Sure, no problem."

"Let me leave a note for George. His shift starts when I leave, so he'll continue to plot the points of impact. They run this dredge around the clock, you know." She shuddered at the thought of her assistant. She didn't really trust him. Lately, he had the annoying habit of prying into her affairs.

"Can we go now?" she asked.

"Sure. After you."

Aboard the U.S.C.G. Bayliner—1720 Hours

Scott released the tie lines and the coxswain eased the throttles forward. Quickly the Bayliner Ciera began cutting through the murky brown water that surrounded the dredge. He liked this motor launch better than the more spartan standard issue forty-one foot launch that the Coast Guard normally used. Scott rubbed his hand along a small tear in the vinyl covering. Gotta get that fixed, he thought, wouldn't want the boss to think I'm not taking care of this prize.

The launch had belonged to a drug dealer who was caught carrying cocaine inside the upper bay. The Coast Guard had seized the craft and assigned it to Scott. He enjoyed the comfort, and he especially liked the ability of the craft to maneuver in tight places when he had to carry out his duties investigating accidents.

As he sat next to Sherry, he found himself wondering once again about Sherry's choice of career. It had been Sherry's hard work in convincing the public to allow hydraulic dredging to proceed that had put the channel widening project back on schedule and within budget. It had been a tough battle with the environmentalists and shellfish interests who feared pollution would be stirred up. Yet she had pulled it off. It was good luck for the Port Authority, he mused. But it caused her to deal with hard men like Captain Harris.

Out of the corner of his eye, Scott could see Sherry glance surreptitiously in his direction. Her green eyes seemed to express interest as did her slight smile. When he turned his head to face her more fully, she quickly looked away toward some harbor scene. An interesting game, Scott decided, kind of fun. What's she up to?

His rugged good looks and easy manner had served him well with women, and he never had trouble getting dates. But now, sitting next to Sherry, he felt almost shy. Maybe it was her strange behavior at the Christmas party eight months ago. Scott was still troubled by that first failure. He had no clue what he'd done to piss her off so.

"Sherry," he said, turning toward her. "Could I ask you something?"

"I've been expecting your question," she answered. "You're still wondering why I was so moody toward you last Christmas."

Scott smiled. "So, you're a mind reader on top of all your other talents."

"I apologize. I like you very much, Bob, but I just felt we weren't right for each other back then."

"You seemed receptive to me at first and then suddenly got mad."

"I don't wish to discuss it. I'd like to remain friends. Please don't pursue this any further." She turned away and looked out across the harbor.

"Sorry. I didn't mean to upset you. I mean, I'm in another relationship now anyway."

Without looking at him she said, "That's nice."

Scott could only stare at her, a quizzical expression on his face. Her answer seemed to be no answer at all.

Long Island, N.Y.—1820 Hours

After he'd dropped Sherry off, Scott drove toward Nassau County on Long Island. If I hurry, he thought, I can still beat the train and pick up Brenda. He parked his Oldsmobile Regency in the lot and hurried to the station platform as the 6:33 was just pulling in. He waited, anxious for her to emerge.

His marriage of 18 years had come to an end and Scott had developed a new relationship with Brenda Mason. She was the cousin of Scott's best friend who'd introduced them. Scott was not impressed at first—Brenda seemed plain. He took her out just to return his friend's favor, but had no thought of pursuing a relationship.

But then it happened. Her brightness, cheerfulness and honesty worked on him, drew him closer. He awoke one morning and approached the mirror to shave. As he stared at his own light brown eyes—it hit him. He loved Brenda. And it was not a love borne of Cupid's measly arrows. No, sir. This felt more like a laser guided bomb! He simply could not turn away from her. Could not. Brenda was, well, special — more than any other woman.

He was unsure if she had caught the train, but soon caught sight of Brenda as she stepped onto the platform. Sudden pounding in his chest accompanied Scott's broad smile as Brenda moved toward him. She was dressed in a sleeveless, tight-waisted, knee-length dress. Her white pumps contrasted with her dark hair and eyes.

"Hi, Bob," she called as she saw him.

"Brenda! I've been thinking about you all day." He opened his arms to receive her embrace.

"I'm sure glad to hear that," she responded with a big smile and a light laugh. "I've been thinking about you, y'know." They swayed for a minute enjoying their hug.

"Hungry?"

"Sure. Are you planning to cook, or are you coming to my apartment so I can properly take care of you?"

"Let's just grab a bucket of chicken. We can take it out to the yacht club and share it with your cousin. I promised him I'd help him varnish the main cabin. OK?" Scott leaned down to kiss her full red lips on her upturned face. A kiss that lasted several minutes. She finally laid her head against his chest and sighed in contentment.

"OK," she replied. "When are you guys going to finish working on that boat?"

"We're getting there. Takes a lot of effort to restore a 40 year old cabin cruiser. Be like new in a few more weeks." Scott clasped her hand and they began walking toward the car. "We'll be going out for a ride this week-end, if that new manifold gets here."

"That sounds like fun. But, let's leave some time for us. I want to spoil you with lots of loving care."

"Think I deserve that?" Scott chuckled and squeezed Brenda's arm. He reached down and pulled the car door open.

"Sure. Especially after what your ex-wife is trying to do, you know." Brenda slid onto the car seat.

"Not ex-wife yet. The divorce isn't final for several months." Scott closed the door and moved around to the driver's side and got in. Brenda moved beside him as he started the engine.

"Is she still trying to evict you from your house?"

"Yeah. Even though she moved out months ago. The real estate people have convinced her that the house will sell easier if I'm gone." Scott pulled the car out onto the highway and headed toward Manhasset Bay.

"I'll do anything I can to help you through this. You can still move in with me."

"Thanks. I may have to, but I'm concerned about appearances. The Coast Guard brass doesn't like officers living with a woman without the sanction of marriage."

"Seems that everyone is against your happiness."

"Except you."

"I love you so much. I hate to see you suffer."

"Your love is what sustains me. Just have faith. We'll get through this somehow."

Fifth Avenue, Manhattan—2000 Hours

The block-lettered sign in front of the hotel ballroom announced that the National Businessman of the Year dinner would begin at eight p.m. Douglas Erickson, chairman of one of America's largest trucking companies, stopped in front of the large gold framed mirror by the ballroom door and straightened his tie. He was still a good-looking man, he thought, even if he was pushing seventy-seven years. This was to be his night. He deserved this award.

The uniformed usher pulled open the oversized door and Erickson walked into a warm crowd of fellow businessmen and powerful political leaders. To his left he noticed that the Mayor of New York had monopolized the governor's ear in a serious discussion, most likely concerning the new state budget. They were surrounded by a large group of state legislators and at least half of New York's congressional delegation. The talk seemed more heated than Erickson expected at this hour. The free flow of alcohol had obviously lubricated tongues to the point of affecting civility.

Erickson felt a tug on his arm as he moved into the group. His old friend U.S. Senator Samuel Tifton wanted to introduce him to several of the well-dressed men standing nearby.

"Doug!" the senator said. "Come and meet some of my colleagues. Congressmen, our guest of honor tonight. National Businessman of the Year, Doug Erickson!" Erickson smiled in response to the impromptu applause. "More than that, he's my old army buddy from the big war. He was my executive officer back in the O.S.S." The senator quickly started into a couple of old World War II stories. Not again, Erickson thought, can't he forget this stuff. There are a lot of things I'd just as soon wish never had happened.

The senator had been a U.S. Army major, and Erickson had been a captain in the Office of Strategic Services. Of course, they won the entire war on their own. Okay, the senator admitted, we did have some help. Erickson had to suppress his chuckle as the senator embellished his role in saving the world. Tifton's ego was about the size of a 747, Erickson mused, a real showboat too. But, then, that was what had driven him to become one of the most powerful members of the U.S. Senate, Chairman of the Senate Intelligence Committee. He was one of three men to whom the C.I.A. must answer.

Erickson's thoughts were interrupted when he felt his sleeve tugged a second time. He turned to his left.

"Bernie!" Erickson said. "How's the Attorney General of the great State of Georgia. Been too long since you've been up north. Heard you rolled up quite a vote last year."

"Doug," Stan Bernard replied quietly. His face was a mask of serious concern. "Come quick. We've got a big problem." Bernard dragged him toward a rear exit.

"Let go of my arm, Bernie, or I won't take another step."

"Mikelovich is here." Bernard pushed through the door.

"Mikelovich! Are you mad?" Erickson's question was answered as they turned into the rear hall and came face to face with a strongly built stocky man of about forty. A man Erickson had no thought of seeing this night. "What are you doing here? Couldn't you have called on my cell phone?"

"I hear from informant," the unwelcome man answered with a thick Slavic accent. "News no good." He struck his hand on his leg. "Cell phone not secure."

"Okay, fine. What is it?"

"Coast Guard called in already," Mikelovich continued.

"Already for what? You mean....Not the...."

"The sub?" Bernard gasped.

"Shut up, Bernie!" Sweat began to flow on Erickson's face. He nearly dropped his empty cocktail glass. But then he quickly regained his composure. Can't appear scared in front of these men. "This is a disaster. We've got to stop them."

"I agree," Bernard responded. "The Coast Guard will not stop until they figure out who we are. There's no statute of limitations for what we did. We'll be exposed. Ruined."

"Tonight of all nights." said Erickson. "I've got to go back in there and sit at the head table to receive my award. Right in front of the governor and everybody. How am I going to keep a smile on my face?"

"Shall we tell the senator?"

"No! Dear God, no. He's standing next to the mayor and the police commissioner. I'll brief him after the dinner. If I'm still able to speak."

Erickson could only stare at Bernard and wonder if his former first lieutenant had the strength to handle what must now be done. Bernard was two years younger than Erickson, a bit shorter, and noticeably heavier. He had been very squeamish about killing another human being during the war and Major Tifton had often referred to Bernard as "the weakling."

Erickson felt that Bernard looked fit despite his obvious nervousness. But then, he had a right to be nervous with this news suddenly hanging over all of their heads. Still, his eyes looked clear and his face was determined. Erickson relaxed, thinking that Bernard would be able to do whatever he must. After all, his head was on the line too.

"There's only one thing to do," Erickson said, taking charge. "Mikelovich, you are to prepare your soldiers to carry out the demolition plan immediately."

"Need much dynamite," the Russian responded.

"I will arrange the shipment as we discussed. You should have done this last week when I told you, dammit."

"Couldn't. Dredge people show up, and they would've seen us. Besides, you said sub was supposed to be closer to shore and dredge wouldn't hit it."

"I told you to go ahead. You fucked up. Don't try to blame this on me. Now, get it done, damn you!"

"What about dredge people?"

"Blow them to hell along with the sub. Now move!"

Erickson and Bernard could only watch as Mikelovich quickly walked to the rear door and disappeared.

"Damn him," Erickson finally said. "If he hadn't fouled up that first attempt to blow the sub, we wouldn't be in this fix."

"It wasn't his fault," Bernard responded. "Nobody could have predicted that mud slide burying those divers. Completely unexpected."

"That's what we pay him for. To deal with that sort of situation. He blew it. I've got a good mind to look for a better group of mercenaries."

"There's no time."

"Let's get inside. Try not to look like a criminal in front of all those law-abiding citizens. We'll get together with the senator after I get my plaque."

TWO
Thursday
6 August

U.S.C.G. Headquarters, Governors Island—0810 Hours

Scott placed the telephone handset back in its cradle and leaned back in his chair. He stared at the ceiling for several minutes as he drummed his fingers on the armrest. He felt empty, drained. The phone call had been expected, but he was still unprepared for the news.

The divorce court had ruled in his wife's favor—he must vacate the house by tomorrow. Damn! What to do?

He looked down at the corner of his desk. How many years had the picture of his wife sat there—seemingly watching him—eighteen? Eighteen years? She had been so beautiful. He smoothed his sandy colored hair back with his hands.

Now it had all come down to this—a slugging match between lawyers. The emotional and financial drain on him had been devastating. He couldn't think—couldn't concentrate now on his work. His boss, Captain of the Port Ronald Peters, had been understanding of the situation. Peters had protected him from criticism when things first soured and Scott failed to complete some work assignments. For a while it looked bad.

Then Brenda entered his life. His interest in living, in his work returned as her love strengthened him. He regained his enthusiasm, and his work returned to normal. Now, this. The final nail. Well, he thought, can't put it off any longer. Time to hoist anchor and drop it someplace else. At least Brenda will be pleased.

38th Street, Manhattan—0820 Hours

Across the harbor in his top floor Manhattan office, Erickson leaned back in his dark blue high-back chair and stared at the ceiling for a moment. He had slept little. The strong sunlight streaming through the large glass window wall barely kept him awake. He and his small group of associates now faced a situation, and that was more than enough to keep him wired. The sunlight lit the right side of Senator Tifton's face as he tapped on the armrest of his chair.

"God dammit, Doug," the senator finally said. "You assured me that the fuckin' boat would be blown up last week. I did my part by sending those two divers. Now this!"

Erickson tensed in his chair under the senator's angry response to the news that he had delayed telling until now. He was in need of a very large drink, but now was not the time. They must be sober to deal with this.

"Mikelovich failed us," Erickson finally responded.

"That miserable Russian bastard! I never liked using him." The senator swung his hands violently into his chair cushion.

"He and his men have done several other jobs for us without trouble. That mud slide couldn't have been predicted."

"The divers are both still down there?"

"Yes."

The door to the spacious office opened, interrupting their dialogue as Bernard and Brogano entered. They were expected.

"About time," Erickson snapped. "Where's Ledbetter?"

"On the phone," Stan Bernard answered. The two arrivals sat at opposite ends of the couch facing the large dark mahogany desk, the centerpiece of the luxuriant office.

For a moment, no one spoke. The silence was broken only by the senator's continued tapping. His presence seemed to intimidate the others. But, then, he had always intimidated them. Ever since he had been their army commander during World War II. None of them, Erickson thought, had ever been able to say no to the S.O.B. He loved Tifton back then, but now

Erickson felt resentment. Now, that unquestioned loyalty over the past fifty years might just cost them all their lives.

"When will Mikelovich be ready to detonate the bomb?" the senator asked.

"Tomorrow night," Erickson replied. "I just set up the dynamite shipment for this evening. Mikelovich's men will hijack the truck tonight. They'll need tomorrow to rig the bomb."

"Don't let anything screw this up! If this fails, our necks will be worthless. I'm not going to surrender—dammit!"

"I don't see this," Stan Bernard broke in. He held his hands between his legs. Trying to hide his liver spots, Erickson thought contemptuously.

"See what?" Vince Brogano asked from his end of the couch. He stared at Bernard, who was squirming uneasily at the other end. Erickson and the senator both glared at Bernard, which only increased the small man's discomfort.

"Even if the cops get inside the damn sub, what are they going to find? We cleaned up very carefully. How they going to tie the thing to us anyhow?"

"Do you want to take that risk?" the senator asked. "I sure don't. Too much chance they might find something. You're an experienced prosecutor, Stan. You know how effective crime labs are today. A few hairs. A fiber. They just might make a connection. And what if... what if they trail the cargo?" The opening of the door interrupted the senator as Rolland Ledbetter, ashen-faced, joined the group. "Rolland! What's wrong?"

"The cops have found one of the divers," the former navy commander answered. "About ten minutes ago."

"Shit! This nightmare is going right to hell! What do you know about these cops? Any way to get to them?"

"It's not the harbor police that worry me. It's the Coast Guard I'm sweating. This Commander Scott and his boss are real persistent investigators. They won't stop until they uncover every damn fact."

"Then we'll just have to stop them. Your son Jerome is still in naval intelligence. A captain, isn't he? Call him. Tell him to prepare a request for the President's signature to assign the New York station to Navy control, with himself to take command. With your son in charge, I'll be able to control this investigation."

"What if the President won't go along?" Vince asked.

"Then we'll just have to kill the bastards!"

"How are we going to do that?" Bernard asked. That nervous twitch had come back, Erickson noticed. He remembered how Bernard always had that twitch on his face when he got scared. "Look at us. We're relics. None of us is going to see seventy-five again. Christ, I can barely make a fist—my arthritis is so bad."

"Shut up, Stan! There are other ways to fight them. We may be old, but we all have money and plenty of political power. If we have to, we'll hire an army of mercenaries to do the fighting." The senator stood up to his full six and a half foot height. His facial skin was surprisingly free of creases and blemishes. Those hard gray eyes, still penetrating.

"I want nothing to do with murder!" former commander Ledbetter said. "After all, I only arranged the transportation. You two pulled those triggers!" His aged gnarled finger pointed to Erickson and the senator.

"You think the Coast Guard is going to give a damn?" the senator shouted. "If I go down, everybody goes down. Think about it, gentlemen. This scandal could destroy our families, our fortunes—everything. We are going to do whatever it takes. There is no further discussion—period!"

U.S.C.G. Headquarters, Governors Island—0845 Hours

Scott looked up as the door to his office opened. Chief Morris, carrying documents, entered and placed the material in front of Scott.

"Look, sir," the chief began. "Here are the old harbor charts from the forties. It's just like I remembered. That part of the channel was kept clear until August of 1945. At that time the Corps of Engineers said it wouldn't be needed anymore since the Brooklyn Navy Yard had no plans to build any more big battleships. So they decided to fill that part of the channel where the sub is with mud from the rest of the channel. It's been full of mud until now."

"So the sub had to be there *before* August forty-five."

"Right, and prior to 1942 that part of the channel had never been excavated. The government opened that area in 1942 when it decided to build the Montana class battleships at Brooklyn. Therefore, the sub had to have sunk there between June 1942 and August 1945."

"But the USS *Montana* was never built."

"No, sir, but it was planned. It was to be bigger than the Iowa class battleships. The Corps of Engineers went ahead with the channel-widening project before the navy decided not to build the *Montana.*"

"Good work, Chief. Let's take this to the boss and see if he can make some sense out of it."

Twenty minutes later Scott and the chief laid down the charts and magnetic-survey plot on the captain's desk. They explained in detail what they knew so far.

"So, have you thoroughly checked all the records to see if any submarine wrecks were reported inside the harbor back in the forties? Any sub attacks?"

"Yes, Captain," Scott answered. "There are no reports. If Chief Morris is right about this being a German Type 21 submarine then it may still have torpedoes, fuel, and ammunition on board. We need a real expert to help us identify this sub and determine the best way to deal with it."

"Agreed. Anybody in mind?"

"Harold Davidson. He's been working at the Submarine Building Company in New Haven since he retired from the Navy."

"Yes, I remember Davidson. Red and I were close friends. Let's call and see if he's available." He stabbed numbers on his desk phone and pushed the speaker button.

A few minutes later, Davidson's voice was heard.

"I've got Bob Scott and CPO Morris here with me," Peters

said. "We're calling because we've got one hell of a mystery down here."

"Mystery?" Davidson responded.

"Scott and Morris believe they've found a German Type 21 submarine buried on the bottom of the upper harbor."

"What are you guys drinking down there? That's impossible! Every single Type 21 was accounted for after the war. Every one! We know where every sub went down, and they're still there. Not one of them is in New York harbor!"

"Well, we've got a magnetic-sonar-survey plot of one, and it's on the bottom of the upper bay."

"There has to be some mistake. I'd like to see your data."

"I was hoping you would. I'll have Chief Morris fax the plot up to you right away. We'll also send up the computer record on the Defense Internet. You should have everything in a few minutes. Now, do you have any thoughts as to how we can confirm this find and what to do if it is a Type 21?" A wave of Peters's hand sent Morris to the communications center.

"You'll have to send divers down before you can be sure. The Type 21 had a number of very distinctive features that will make your identification certain."

"I had the same thought. Call us back as soon as you've studied the data, will you?"

"Will do. Better tell Scott to stick to chasing drunken weekend sailors. He's losing it."

"Okay, Red," Peters and Scott both responded with a laugh.

Captain Peters cut the speaker off and looked at Scott. "How bad is the water out there? Could a diver see anything?"

"The dredge does have the mud stirred up, but conditions will improve as the cutter head moves down channel. By tomorrow the water will be clear enough for someone to dive."

"Call Sherry Edwards and find out where the *McDonald* will be tomorrow. Advise her that we're going to send divers down tomorrow if the water clears enough."

Scott reached for the phone.

Just then Chief Morris returned. "The plot's on its way, Captain," he said as he closed the door behind him.

"Chief," said the captain, "contact Search and Rescue. Tell them to provide two divers for tomorrow and get the motor launch ready for diving operations. While we're waiting for Red to call back, we might as well take a look at some of these other reports."

At 9:45 a.m. the secretary called over the intercom, "Captain Peters, Mr. Davidson calling on line three."

"Well, wild horses couldn't keep me away now," Davidson began. "The data is unbelievable. Everything logical says you should be wrong. But damn if I don't believe you're right. The data definitely shows it to be a Type 21 lying on the bottom with a thirty-two-degree list to starboard!"

"I guess the Germans miscounted," joked the captain.

"It's mind-boggling. Have you decided to dive for a visual confirmation?"

"Yes. We're planning to go down tomorrow if the water is clear enough and the weather cooperates."

"I want to be there."

"Good. With your expertise, you can advise the divers what to look for."

The intercom came to life as Peters hung up the telephone. He picked up the receiver again. Scott and Chief Morris waited until Peters again hung up the telephone and looked up at his two subordinates.

"That was the harbor police. A body has been found near the dredge. Check on it and see if it has any connection to the sub. Sounds a bit strange."

U.S.C.G. Boat Slip, Governors Island—0920 Hours

Chief Morris stood by the gangway to the 41-foot-long motor launch waiting for Bob Scott to arrive. He was a career chief petty officer who had given his life to the Coast Guard, a decision he was very satisfied with. About fifty years old and below average height, he was a strong man fighting a tendency to gain weight. He leaned down to rub his knee. "Damn," he muttered. "Getting old is a rotten pain."

The Morris family had a long and proud history with the Coast Guard. The chief's father and grandfather had both served, the grandfather having been enlisted in the former Revenue Cutter Service before it became the Coast Guard.

The New York station was part of the Coast Guard's largest base and was located on Governors Island. With some four thousand personnel—plus families, dogs, and even parakeets—the island formed a unique community, free of the problems and crime of the surrounding city of New York, yet only a brief ferry ride to Battery Park at the southern tip of Manhattan Island.

Now, in the summer of 1995, rumors were circulating that the Department of Transportation was considering the closing of the base and transferring all personnel to other Coast Guard installations. Chief Morris and most of the other older senior chiefs were not pleased with the rumors. This wouldn't be happening if the Coast Guard was still a part of the Treasury Department, the old Treasury hands were heard to say.

■ ■ ■ ■ ■

Morris greeted Scott as he boarded the motor launch.

"Okay, Chief," Scott said. "Let's head to the *McDonald.*"

Scott turned to look over the bow of the launch in the direction of the dredge some five miles distant. The murky water in the harbor was relatively smooth in the warm sunshine. The efforts of the city and state to clean up the harbor had improved the smell a lot. Scott was glad for that as he remembered the odorous, not-so-good old days. The traffic was not heavy, and the launch was able to travel at nearly full speed.

Settling back into the captain's seat, Scott thought of his father, who had urged him to consider a naval career. But Scott didn't care for the rigid military discipline. Navy life would be just too confining, he had told his Dad. But Scott did enjoy working on and around the sea.

The Coast Guard was a better choice for him. He liked the informality of the service. Even the lowest-ranking member of a cutter's crew could call his captain by his first name. Try that in the navy, he thought with a slight chuckle as he raised his binoculars.

A bit more than a mile behind the dredge, the ferry boat pier on the north end of Staten Island poked out of the water. Scott could see the routine arrival and departure of ferry boats. Nearer to him, the huge dredge staggered like a drunken sailor between its left and right anchors raising and lowering its long vacuum cleaner nozzle as it sucked in tons of mud and water. The *McDonald's* workboat, a small tug with a derrick on the bow, came into view near the right anchor. Like a child helping its ponderous mother, the workboat darted to and fro as it accomplished its many chores.

Scott refocused his glasses to view the harbor police boats tied up at the dredge. A thousand questions flooded his mind. Why would a body suddenly appear near the submarine? A simple coincidence? It couldn't be a body from inside the sub. After fifty years, any such body would be decomposed. A few minutes later the launch moved alongside the dredge.

Aboard the dredge, *William P. McDonald*—1015 Hours

Scott dashed to the front of the dredge where Lieutenant Branson, the NYPD Harbor Policeman directing the operation, quickly briefed Scott. They watched the medical examiner cut the body out of the diving suit.

"Is this related to the sunken wreck I'm investigating?" Scott asked.

"Can't say, Commander," Branson replied. "I believe the body was being held down on the bottom until the dredge cutter broke it free. The medical examiner's preliminary time of death will take at least a week. Maybe more. The cold water slowed the deterioration of the body, so we should get good fingerprints. Look here. You can see where the air hose was freshly cut."

"So, he drowned?"

"No, sir. Not with a bullet hole in his face. This was murder."

"Murder!? Now I really am suspicious. There must be a tie-in with the wreck. We've got to get a look down below. Any chance of getting divers down today?" Scott knelt down to examine the bullet hole in the diving helmet's glass pane.

"No. The mud is just too stirred up. Visibility is zero."

"Understood. We will send a diving team down tomorrow morning. I'll let you know if we find anything."

Branson shook his head side to side. "That won't be necessary. My police divers will be down at first light."

Scott and Chief Morris continue to watch the police investigation for several minutes. No stranger to death, Scott felt chills when he looked at the fully exposed body of the dead diver as it lay on the deck. The body bore many scars, including what appeared to be old healed bullet wounds. He might have been a soldier, Scott thought, or a gangster.

The sound of the zipper closing the body bag returned him to reality. He decided that the investigation of this murder would be within the jurisdiction of the harbor police, and not really his. So he told himself to keep his focus where it belonged — on the submarine.

"Please keep me informed, Lieutenant. I want to know why he was down there. This could be involved with my investigation of the wreck."

Aboard U.S.C.G. Motor Launch—1030 Hours

The ride back to Governors Island gave Scott time to think. He sat back and rubbed his eyes. Tired. These last two days had been so full. As much as I need sleep, Scott mused, I won't tonight. I'm not going to let a little thing like exhaustion keep me from Jill Engles and Alan Hillerman's big dinner party. Jill has so much energy and keeps everybody laughing. Hillerman had been Scott's best friend for many years, but now that his girlfriend Jill and Brenda had become so close, they had grown even tighter. The four of them had become, for lack of a better word, a circle. Yes, Scott thought—a circle, surrounding me with love and support.

As my marriage disintegrates, it's good to have something to keep me afloat. So I guess they're my family now. God, what would I do without them?

U.S.C.G. Headquarters, Governors Island—1340 Hours

Scott set his nearly empty water glass down on the small refreshment tray at the corner of U.S.C.G. Captain Peters' big mahogany desk. The Captain's office furniture was unusually plush compared to the more standard metal desk and chairs issued to Coast Guard stations. Peters had managed to "liberate" the furniture from the First Army Headquarters when the Defense Department transferred the soldiers from Governors Island.

"Anything more on the dead diver?" Peters asked. He lowered his arms from the back of the high back chair onto the armrests.

"No, Sir," Scott answered. "It's probably just a coincidence."

"All right. Stay in touch with NYPD. But now, I have something more. About an hour ago, I had another conference with the submarine experts in New Haven. This is very confidential and damn scary."

Scott looked at Peters with raised eyebrows. Peters's expression was very unusual for a man Scott always thought to never show fear.

"There was an unconfirmed report right after the end of WWII," Peters continued. His voice was low and blue eyes piercing. "An S.S. General Schmitt was captured in Hamburg, but he managed to shoot himself before his gun could be taken. While confined in a hospital, he told of a secret U-boat mission to attack New York City with a weapon of mass destruction. The general said the U-boat was last heard from when it entered this harbor in 1945."

Scott sat open mouthed, staring at Peters, the metronomic ticking of the brass ship's chronometer now the only sound in the room. For a moment, he couldn't speak.

"A weapon of mass destruction?" he said finally. "Do you mean a nuclear bomb?"

"No one knows. Schmitt died before the interrogators could get any more information. An O.S.S. team was sent to search out further data, but found nothing. So, the report was dismissed and forgotten about until our phone call. The experts in New Haven believe there may be two possibilities.

"The first is a radiation bomb. The Germans did not develop a working nuclear bomb, but did have research reactors during the war. New Haven thinks the Germans could have taken the spent highly radioactive fuel and mixed it with TNT. When exploded, a radioactive cloud would result contaminating a hundred square miles, maybe more. Thousands would have died from radiation sickness and a vast area of the city would have been rendered unusable."

Scott felt a bit queasy, his mouth dry. He reached for a full water glass as he stared at the captain.

"The second," Peters went on, "is nerve gas. The Germans had stock piles of nerve agents at the end of the war. They may have loaded many tons on board the U-Boat with plans to release it. God knows how many people could have been killed."

"But if this sub is that U-boat?" Scott asked. "Why didn't the crew set the weapon off?"

"Have no idea. We have to assume the possibility that this sub is the U-boat containing the awesome weapon, and that the weapon may still be on board. Bob, you must find a way to get inside the sub and determine if this report is true. If this weapon is there, then we'll bring in experts to neutralize it."

Why me? Scott thought as he stared at his captain. This is beyond any experience I've ever had.

"We must resolve this quickly," Peters resumed. "Cargo ships are getting bigger every year. Eventually, some monster ship is going to collide with the sub. Such an accident could set the weapon off. We could be facing thousands of deaths, maybe all of Staten Island. I have been informed that the *Samurai of the Great Seas* sailed from Osaka this morning. This will be the largest ship to ever sail into this harbor. The sub must be dealt with before that ship arrives. You've got two weeks."

Scott rose slowly from his chair as he continued staring at the captain. His knees didn't seem to want to work.

"I'd like to brief Chief Morris about this."

"No. This information is restricted to you, me and Davidson. That's all Commander."

Truck Stop, Westbound Route 80, New Jersey—2030 Hrs

The overhead loudspeakers at the Interstate 80 diner blared a monotonous mix of rock and country tunes. Two fluorescent tubes in the ceiling flickered their final claim to light. None of this seemed to matter to the row of truck drivers seated at the long counter. Their attention seemed focused on filling their stomachs before returning to their travels.

The darkening twilight left the trucks in the parking lot difficult to see through the front windows of the restaurant. The proprietor, standing behind the cash register alongside the window, knew every idling behemoth by sight as well as their usual drivers. The men and their vehicles were regulars at the west Jersey truck stop, and this night was typical.

This knowledge caused the proprietor to take immediate notice when the headlights of a huge Peterbilt truck unexpectedly came on. He swung his head to look down the counter to see if the truck's driver had left the restaurant. He hadn't.

"Scooter!" the proprietor called out. "Your rig is moving out!"

"What the hell!" the driver yelled in surprise. He nearly fell over his feet jumping from his seat. He ran to the restaurant door only to see his assigned vehicle smash into a lamp post in its haste to leave the parking lot. "Call the damn cops!"

"I'm dialing already."

The angry driver could only stand and watch the rapidly

moving rear lights of his truck as whoever was at the wheel drove toward the eastbound side of Interstate 80. Several other drivers—no strangers to hijacking—joined him.

"Rotten luck," one of them offered. "You sure you had the doors locked?"

"Hell, yes," Scooter answered. "Security latches were on, too."

"Where was your guard?" a second driver asked. "I thought you always carried a guard with you?"

"Yeah. He couldn't make it tonight, and the boss said he didn't have anybody to spare. So, I had to make this run alone."

"You packing dynamite again?"

"Yeah. More than twelve tons. Them miners is gonna be some pissed when I don't show up with that damn stuff. Mighty pissed."

THREE
Friday
7 August

U.S.C.G. Headquarters, Governors Island—0810 Hours

Lieutenant Commander Scott entered Captain Peters's office, where ex-Commander Davidson, a former U.S. Navy sub captain, and Chief Morris were just sitting down at the conference table. Scott gave his old friend Davidson a smile. They had met at the Coast Guard Academy when Davidson had taught a course in submarine detection. They had taken an immediate liking to each other, and had come to enjoy boating and fishing together. His strongly reddish hair had labeled him with his nickname—Red.

"Chief, when are the divers due to arrive?" Peters asked.

"No later than 0900 hours, sir," Morris answered. "We've got everything just about ready."

"Who's coming over from Search and Rescue?"

"Lieutenant JG Hampton and his master chief petty officer. They're two of the most experienced divers in the Coast Guard."

"Equipment on board?"

"I've had the seamen load the motor launch with four sets of scuba equipment and a dozen reserve tanks, and I've put on a high-pressure-washing pump system so the divers can clear away the remaining mud and get to the actual hull of the sub."

"Red is suggesting a hot tap so we can test the air inside—assuming the boat is not flooded."

"We can also send a small video camera through the tap-hole for a first look," Davidson added.

"Can Hampton handle that?"

"I doubt it, sir," Scott answered. "That's a very specialized welding job. However, there are welders on the *McDonald* who probably can do it. American Harbor and Dock Company does a lot of underwater work on pipelines and oil platforms. I'm sure they do hot taps often."

"Call out to the *McDonald* and see if they can handle the tap," Peters ordered.

"Yes, sir," Scott answered. He reached for the telephone and called Sherry Edwards. Since the dredge was under contract, the Port Authority's approval for any use of the dredgemen had to be approved by that agency. He explained what was needed, got the answer he wanted, and turned to the captain. "Miss Edwards will talk to Captain Harris and get back to us, but she's certain that they carry the necessary equipment on board the dredge. She knows that the two welders are certified for underwater welding."

"Then they should be able to help us—assuming the sub is not flooded."

"Hampton should be able to answer that question fairly quickly," Davidson replied. "The sound of a flooded sub is an obvious *thud*, while a dry boat will give a lighter *clink* sound."

"Tell Hampton to do that check right off so the welders can get to work."

"Captain," Scott said. "Miss Edwards says that some of the Port Authority staff are pushing the idea of reburial in a deep trench adjacent to the present site without going inside. How should I deal with that after the information you received yesterday?"

"Tell them no decision has been reached. The disposition of this matter will be made only after a board of inquiry. Our job now is to gather all of the information that we can for that review. I would not want to rebury until all weapons have been removed. I can't believe that Port Authority management would favor having a submarine in the middle of a busy ship channel still filled with all sorts of explosives and possibly other things."

Peters continued, "Some other news. Lieutenant Branson called about twenty minutes ago. The police divers have already been down near the sub. They found the other end of that murdered diver's air hose. It had been tied to a weight to hold him down on the bottom. But still no evidence as to why he was there."

The men in the large office looked at each other, but didn't speak. They didn't need to. Scott knew what was going through their minds—this was too suspicious not to be tied to the sub.

U.S.C.G. Utility Motor Launch—0900 Hours

Scott arrived at the Coast Guard boat dock and found the divers on board and the Coast Guard crew ready to get under way.

The divers appeared to be in excellent physical shape. The master chief, the older of the two men, had a bald area at the top of his head and sported a large tattoo on his left upper arm. Lieutenant Hampton, on the other hand, was taller and more slender, with a full head of brown hair. He bristled with enthusiasm for the work ahead.

"Commander," Lieutenant Hampton said to Scott. "What do you want us to look for?"

"Fortunately, we have one of the world's greatest authorities on submarines with us today to answer your question. Former Commander Davidson will brief you."

Davidson smiled and waved a hand dismissively at the designation. He braced himself on the rail as the motor launch got underway. Then he said, "If the magnetic-sonar survey is correct, you should look for three features that were specific to the German Type 21 submarine. First, look for the antiaircraft mounts on the top of the conning tower—now called the sail. The Type 21 carried either a twenty-millimeter automatic cannon at each end of the sail or (on later versions of these boats) a thirty-millimeter automatic cannon. Here, I've brought along some old photos to show you."

He handed over a manila envelope. Hampton removed the photos, and they all crowded around him to look at the pictures.

Davidson continued, "Second, look for the snorkel just behind the periscope. However, both the Soviet Whiskey class and the French Narvel class mounted their snorkels that way, so it's not as positive as the gun mounts.

"Third, check for the boat's identification number, which should be near the rear and top of the sail. You'll almost certainly have to clear away mud, so take the nozzle hose down with you."

"Also," Scott added, "we want you to tap the hull first to see if the boat is flooded or dry. We need that real quick to make the decision as to whether or not to try a hot tap."

"Okay," responded Hampton. "Let me help my chief with the gear." The lieutenant then moved to the other side of the motor launch to aid the crew with the final preparations of the diving gear.

As the launch moved toward the site of the submarine, Davidson and Scott turned to look out over the rail at the harbor traffic. The weather was cooperating, with warm sunshine and light winds. The men watched a flock of sea gulls following a barge loaded with garbage on its way to the disposal area. They pinched their noses when those light winds shifted.

"Have you guys told the Navy about this find yet?" Davidson asked.

Scott laughed. "I'm afraid that Captain Peters is not on speaking terms with the Navy."

"Sounds like your appropriation must have gotten cut again."

"It's a bit more than that. Captain Peters still resents the way the Navy tried to blame him for that destroyer accident several years ago. Turned out that the Navy's own captain had been at fault."

A short time later, the launch rounded the front of the dredge and Scott could see the *McDonald*'s workboat waiting at the sub's location. The motor launch pulled up alongside. The white tie ropes glinted in the bright sunshine as they arched across the water.

Scott waved hello to Sherry in the workboat as the two craft came together with a clunk. Standing alongside her was the *McDonald's* first mate, J.D. Simmons.

"Sherry says we're to stand by until you find out if the sub's full of water," J.D. said as he and Sherry crossed over the railings to board the Coast Guard motor launch.

"Right," answered Scott. "Hang tight while I get these guys started." He turned to watch the two divers getting ready to go over the side. They dropped off backward so that their air tanks hit the water first. The splashes were almost simultaneous.

Seconds later, they disappeared from sight in a column of bubbles. Powerful kicks of their flippers would drive them along the buoy line down to the anchor that had been set by the survey boat.

Morris reached for the microphone on the sonar communication link, an ultrasonic underwater radio capable of reaching divers a full quarter mile from the launch. "Lieutenant," he called, "can you hear me?"

"Yes," came the distorted voice, through the throat microphone, mixed with the sound of gurgling bubbles.

Morris answered with a laugh. "I know these sonar phone units sound funny, but we didn't want you guys getting tangled in the wreck with telephone wires."

"Right, Chief. Have your boat in sight. We'll work down the sail toward the deck. Tell Commander Davidson there's an automatic cannon right where he expected. Whew, mud all over. Okay, measures thirty millimeters. Hang on. Moving down the sail. I can confirm we're on the bow end of the boat. Man, is this thing listing to starboard! Makes it hard to move along the hull. We're using the washer to expose the pressure hull. We'll try a hit in a minute. Hang on. We've just hit the hull and it sounds dry. Did you get that, Chief?"

"Yes, Lieutenant. Commander Davidson wants to know where you are on the hull."

"About twenty feet in front of the sail and about ten feet down the port side, which is the top right now due to the list. Most of the pressure hull is behind the outer casing, so we can only hit a few spots through the vent holes."

"Can you work down the side to see if the lower part of the boat is flooded?"

"We'll try, but with all the mud it's going to be tough."

Scott motioned to J.D. "It's dry at the top. Let's go ahead with the tap. Tell the divers they'll need to cut away some of the outer casing to get to the pressure hull. I'll have Hampton show them where."

J.D. directed Cracker and Curly, the *McDonald* welders who would do the hot tap, to put on their metal hard-hat diving helmets, locked them onto the inflatable yellow rubber suits, then had them stand on the diving platform. With a squeak and a rumble, the platform lowered the two divers along with their air hoses and tools into the turbid water. The regular hard-hat diving suits would give them a constant air supply, through hoses from the boat compressor, that would allow them to remain down for a longer period.

The two Coast Guard divers, who were already down, needed freedom to move about the submarine; having to drag air hoses around might accidentally tangle them in the wreck.

While they waited for events below to proceed, Scott glanced over at Sherry. She was holding a notebook and pen to take notes for those endless daily reports to her Port Authority bosses. She glanced back at Scott with a surreptitious movement of her head, a slight smile on her face. That little game again, Scott thought remembering their boat ride of Wednesday. Even her handwriting is beautiful. She's so damn friendly today. What's she up to?

A few minutes later, the voice of Lieutenant Hampton came over the sonar communications link. "Have hard-hat divers on the boat. I'm going to get them set up and then we'll move to check rear of sail."

"Roger, Lieutenant," Morris answered.

"Okay," Hampton responded. "We've got the underwater

lights set up. They're lighting the cutting torch now. We're headed toward the stern."

Cracker knelt down and directed the hot flame, which was protected inside an air bubble, against the cold wet outer steel casing of the submarine. He needed to expose enough of the inner pressure hull so that a valve could be welded to the metal. Curly could then hold the valve mounted on a short length of pipe against the hull while Cracker brazed the pipe permanently to the hull.

As the hard-hat divers worked, Lieutenant Hampton continued to survey the submarine.

"We're at the rear of the sail," Hampton announced to the group above over the sonar. "Confirming that there is another thirty-millimeter automatic cannon at the top. We're going to wash to try to find some number."

"Understood, Lieutenant," Morris answered.

A few minutes later Hampton's voice came again. "Well, we got what looks like a number. It's pretty beat up, but I think it's UX-6000."

"What?" Davidson exclaimed. "The Germans never used any such number. They must have it wrong. Have them verify."

"Lieutenant," Morris asked, "please repeat."

"UX-6000."

"That's ridiculous!" Davidson said firmly. "It's got to be a mistake!"

"Lieutenant," Morris said in the mike, "you should be starting up. We figure you're down to about ten minutes of air supply."

"We're coming up."

Scott looked at Morris with a grin and said, "It looks like our submarine expert is about to have major stomach distress."

Morris chuckled.

"Well, you characters can laugh all you want," Davidson responded, "but no matter what you may think about the Nazis, they kept meticulous records. When Germany surrendered in 1945, Admiral Karl Doenitz handed over every record, every list, every document concerning the submarine branch of the navy.

"Every scrap of information was checked. Nothing was left in question. No UX-6000 exists on any of the German navy's records! Preposterous!"

Preceded by columns of bubbles, the two divers surfaced alongside the boat. Morris and the Coxswain went to help them aboard as Scott and Davidson joined them.

"Lieutenant," Davidson began, "is there any possibility that you could have misread that number?"

"Maybe, but I'm pretty sure. What about you, Master Chief?"

"I read the same thing. Maybe the X means it's some kind of experimental boat. I remember the Germans tested a chemical engine for subs during the war."

"Yes, the Walter hydrogen peroxide turbine, but it didn't work very good. That's when they went to the Type 21, Chief."

"I'm afraid I've no other ideas, sir."

"Commander Scott," said Hampton, "we'll be ready to go down again shortly. What would you like us to do this time?"

"We need a way in, Lieutenant," Scott answered. "You need to clear off the hatches to see if any of them work."

"After fifty years, sir? They'll be so rusted, I wouldn't hold out any hope."

"Red, can you brief us on the hatch locations?" Scott inquired. "Maybe we can break one of them loose with hammers."

"There are three possibilities. One is the loading hatch over the torpedo room near the bow. Then there's the top hatch on the sail, and also the escape hatch on the sail near the deck. But the only one you might be able to go through underwater would be the escape hatch since it's equipped with an air lock. The other hatches could be opened only on the surface."

"We'll check 'em out," Hampton promised. The two divers finished changing to fresh air tanks. They then checked out their regulators and pressure gauges.

■ ■ ■ ■ ■

Below the surface, the hard-hat divers wrestled the large pneumatic-powered hot tap drill into position and bolted it to the top of the valve, preventing water from entering the pipe when the valve was opened. Cracker turned the hand wheel, pushing the drill bit through the open valve, and started it turning to cut a hole through the submarine's hull.

A vast column of bubbles enveloped the divers until the drilling ended. Curly began removing the bolts as Cracker pulled the drill bit back up through the valve and then closed the valve. With the hot-tap drill unbolted and pulled away, the divers were ready to connect the hose to the waiting valve.

■ ■ ■ ■ ■

Above, Scott and the others watched a nearby TV news boat approaching, while Morris used the sonarphone. Scott remembered Captain Peters's order to keep this investigation confidential. He reminded the others not to answer any questions. A few minutes later, the chief called out to Scott, "Commander, the lieutenant says the escape hatches are totally jammed. No possibility of opening them. They're going to check the top hatch next."

"Well, I'm not surprised," Davidson commented. "After fifty years—no way."

"Even if one of the other hatches works," Scott reasoned, "without an air lock we can't open them without flooding the boat."

"How about building an air lock and taking it down and welding it on?" Sherry suggested.

"Hmmm, what do you think about that, Red?"

"That could be done, but the boat's at such a list it would be awfully tough."

"Commander," Morris called out, "the lieutenant says the top hatch is rusted shut even worse. They're going forward."

"Okay, Chief," Scott answered. Turning back to Davidson, he continued, "Suppose we put a large-diameter pipe all the way from the surface to the top of the hull, weld it on, pump out the water, and then burn a hole big enough to climb through."

"You mean like a caisson?" Sherry suggested.

"Right. It would be like a sixty foot tunnel through the water that a man could climb down through to the sub without needing diving gear."

"Hell of an idea," said Davidson. "Can we do it?"

"Sure," J.D. answered. "My crew could handle a job like that. We deal with big-pipe and underwater welding all the time."

"What size pipe would we need?" Sherry asked.

"Well, big enough for a couple of guys to stand on the sub in and be able to work," J.D. answered.

"Not really," Scott joined in. "Suppose we put a box at the lower end to sit on the hull. Then the pipe could be just big enough for a man to climb through."

A change in motor noise alerted the group on the Coast Guard boat that the TV news boat was moving away, heading toward Port Newark.

"Commander," Morris said quietly, "they might come back later with their own divers. They could follow our marker-buoy anchor line right down to the sub. I'd like to move the buoy about a hundred yards down the channel to foil that."

"Good idea, Chief. Only let's make it two hundred yards."

"J.D.," a deckhand called from the workboat, "Cracker says they're through drilling and are ready to send the drill back up!"

"Okay. You pull the drill up and hook on the pressure hose so we can get that down to Cracker."

"Commander," Morris called, "Lieutenant Hampton says the forward hatch is rusted beyond hope. They're going back to help guide the hose down to the hard hats."

"Understood. We're going to have to burn our way in, Sherry."

"Yeah. Let's start getting the stuff together. Let me get my cellular phone."

She placed her notebook on the deck.

A few minutes later, Sherry confirmed that a used water tank—six feet in diameter by ten feet tall—was available at a salvage yard in Bayonne. She explained how she planned to cut the bottom off and shape the tank to fit the pressure hull so that it could be welded to the submarine. She picked up her notebook and made a quick sketch showing how a thirty-six-inch-diameter pipe would rise from the top of the tank to the surface. The water could then be pumped out, allowing the welders to cut a large hole in the submarine's pressure hull.

"Sounds great," Scott responded. "Where can we get the thirty-six-inch pipe?"

"That's easy," J.D. answered. "We use that size pipe to carry the mud slurry from the dredge to the spoil dump area. We have several pieces of spare pipe on the dredge."

"How will you handle the weight to get it set for welding?"

"We can use the front derrick on the *McDonald*. When we disconnect the cutter head, the dredge becomes a floating crane." He drew a quick sketch showing how the weight of the cutter head hung from the derrick's big hook.

"Okay. Now all we have to do is convince all the bosses. Sherry, is the land connection still working for your phone? I'd rather not use the cellphone to explain all of this to Captain Peters. Somebody might listen in."

"The phone should be working, but Charlie says the dredge'll be too far out tomorrow."

"That's right, Commander," J.D. agreed. "We have to relocate the discharge point tomorrow, and we won't be able to reach the land lines once that happens. All communications will be by radio phone after that."

Just then Chief Morris interrupted. "Commander, the hose is hooked up to the tap. We're ready to open the valve."

"Proceed," Scott ordered. Morris lowered a vacuum bottle down the hose and, once it was inside the sub, remotely opened the valve, allowing the fifty-year old stale air to be sucked into the bottle. Seconds later, the valve on the bottle was closed and the bottle pulled back up the hose for gas analysis.

Scott and Davidson lowered the video camera down the hose and switched on the lights and the VCR. Everyone crowded around the television screen where it sat on the deck. "What a mess," Morris commented. "Where are we looking?"

"This should be the galley and dayroom," Davidson answered. "Because of the list, everything loose has slid to the starboard side: oh good God! Bob, can you refocus? It's bones—bodies—skeletons!" The bodies were only partially covered with flesh and bits of rotted clothing. They were mostly bared bones.

"Well, now we know that the crew didn't escape," Scott said.

"It's a tomb," Sherry whispered. Scott could see that her eyes were transfixed on the screen and filled with horror—yet obviously fascinated with the scene.

"Chief," Scott said to Morris, "see if the analyzer is done. Maybe we'll learn how they died."

Scott slowly turned the camera revealing a scene of debris and death as his companions watched the screen. No one spoke, but their horrified and tensed expressions said enough.

A few minutes later, Morris announced, "There's almost no chlorine present."

"Then the battery compartments must be dry," Davidson reasoned. "If the salt water had gotten in and shorted the batteries, then chlorine would have formed. What about CO_2 and oxygen?"

"CO_2 is high, and oxygen is low. There are also several sulfur compounds. It's not breathable."

"Well, I don't see any option, Red," Scott said, being careful that no one else was listening. "If the crew didn't escape, then there's every reason to believe the boat's loaded with munitions and possibly a weapon of mass destruction as your assistants told us. We've got to board her and remove the explosives before the boat can be reburied."

"I agree. I say it's time for us to meet with Captain Peters."

Scott switched off the video equipment and pulled the camera back up the hose. "J.D., have your divers close the valve and disconnect," Scott ordered. "We don't want to leave any signs of what we're doing if those news people come back. Have them pack mud over the valve to hide it."

Morris and the Coxswain finished hauling in the marker buoy and its anchor. A short time later, they dropped it back in the water some distance from the submarine to confuse the media.

Mercenary Hideout, Queens, N.Y.—1830 Hours

"Not much of a supper," Mikelovich grumbled. "That stupid Romanian cook. He made the cabbage soup too salty."

He tasted his food and then the phone rang. He rose and walked across the mercenary army's hideout to the table against the concrete block wall. He grimaced a bit as he walked, a bullet fragment lodged near his spine constantly reminding him of his tour with the Soviet Army in Afghanistan.

"Yeah," he said into the handset. He waited for a voice to come from the caller.

"The sub's location has been marked with a yellow and orange buoy," the voice finally told him. Mikelovich recognized the caller by his high pitched whine — the paid informer from the dredge.

"Coast Guard gone?"

"Yeah. Nobody's around."

A quick click in Mikelovich's ear ended the communication. Nothing more had been needed. Mikelovich replaced the handset into the cradle and turned to face several of his men.

"No more bad food. We go," he said.

FOUR
Saturday
8 August

Aboard the dredge, *William P. McDonald*—0200 Hours

The dredge's night shift operator, Smitty, put his coffee cup down and reached for the winch control lever to change the direction of the cutting head. It was nearly two in the morning, but the floodlights enabled the dredging to continue all night. Smitty liked the solitude of the night shift with most of the crew asleep. Only he and one of the dredge's engineer's, Bear, were awake, with Bear watching the engines.

Smitty's sharp eyes caught the strange sight of a large cabin cruiser running without lights emerging from the darkness. The cruiser was visible for just a minute as the craft passed through the dredge's flood lit area. It disappeared from sight as it moved up channel.

Smitty followed the event with a quizzical look.

"Now, just what the hell is that all about?" he muttered. "Well, screw them idiots. Running without lights. Dumbasses for sure."

He turned back to the control board and reached for his coffee. A quick sip and he replaced the cup on the shelf. He then moved the winch control lever once again.

At about two thirty, the coffee cup suddenly flew into Smitty's lap, and a loud explosion shook the dredge violently. A few seconds later, the dredge leaped up and jumped to the left as if by a giant kick. Smitty hit the emergency stop.

A minute later, Captain Harris, followed by J.D., burst into the control cab. "What the goddamn hell was that!" Harris demanded.

"I don't know, Tiny," Smitty answered. "Something blew up, I reckon."

"No shit!" Harris growled.

A moment later, Bear was on the intercom.

"Is everything all right down there?" Harris shouted back at the engineer.

"Yo, but everything just went off line. We on battery power now."

"Get everybody up and search for damage. J.D., get Bulldog and run the workboat down the discharge pipe and see if we're okay."

"Right," J.D. answered and left the control cab.

Bear hurried to the crew's quarters and found them up and wondering what had happened.

"I've had wake-up calls before," said Cracker, "but what the hell was that?"

"Hey, d'engines issa down!" said Frenchy, the dredge's chief engineer.

The crew pulled on pants and shirts in the dim light of the emergency batteries.

"This is a damn poor way to treat company," came a voice from the murk.

"Hey, Kendall, when did you guys get here?" a crewman asked.

"Yeah, who let you river rats on board?" Curly called out.

"J.D. said you guys couldn't handle this job without us," Kendall responded. He and his assistant had been sent from Galveston to help install the caisson pipe.

Captain Harris came through the door. "All right, damn it, let's go! Cracker, you and Curly get below and check for leaks, pronto! You deckhands get on deck. Find out what we lost overboard and get the rest of the gear tied down."

The dredge captain was interrupted by the sound of the workboat engines starting up. Harris knew from the engine sound that Bulldog, the workboat's operator, and J.D. were speeding up channel to inspect the slurry-discharge pipeline.

"Charlie, are you hurt?" Harris asked.

Charlie, who was sitting on his bunk holding his head, said, "I done got throwed on the deck, Tiny. I don't think it's serious."

"All right, take it easy. I'll have J.D. take a look at you when he gets back."

Charlie nodded and continued to rub his head.

"Where's them damn mechanics?" Harris demanded.

"Ah, they picked up a coupla broads at the bar and went off to shack up," Curly answered.

"Damn! Them dickheads picked a lousy night to pull that stunt. Cookie, get up to the galley and make some coffee."

"Yes, suh," Cookie replied with his thick southern black accent.

"Frenchy, get us some power."

"Yeah. Come on, Bear, we try'n crank up number three."

Harris went to the stairs leading up to the control cab. "Hey, Smitty! Call them slime-bucket Coast Guard assholes and tell 'em that their fuckin' toy boat just blew up!"

"No can do, Captain. Don't you remember—our battery-operated ship-to-shore is out! Galveston ain't sent that spare yet!"

"Christ, that's right!" Harris turned toward the engine room and shouted, "Frenchy, I need power now, goddammit!"

"Yeah, yeah! Keep you big stuffed shirt on, we getting it!"

Aboard the workboat, 450 yards up channel—0218 Hours

As Bulldog moved the workboat up the channel, J.D. aimed the searchlight, its powerful beam stabbing into the darkness along the slurry pipeline. The pipeline sat on pontoons that floated each of the forty-foot-long sections. As the workboat passed over the sunken submarine, the light revealed several pieces of the floating pipeline drifting out into the channel mixed together with considerable flotsam.

"It's round-up time, Bulldog!" J.D. called out. It was broken in at least four places. J.D. looked over his shoulder and saw that the lights were back on aboard the dredge. "Try calling Smitty again." Other lights appeared moving rapidly across the water toward the workboat. Must be the cops, J.D. figured. The explosion must have woken up everybody for miles.

"Bulldog calling Smitty. Smitty, you there?"

"Yeah, Bulldog," came the answering call. "We're back on now. What's it look like?"

"She's a-busted. Me and J.D. are headed back. Tell Tiny we're gonna need help to get the stuff hooked together again."

A short time later, using the workboat as a tug, the sections were towed back in line and temporarily roped together. "Ain't this fun," J.D. joked. "Playing cowboy in the middle of the fuckin' night!"

The crewmen climbed out onto the floating sections and rebolted them. The night air was filled with the sounds of pneumatic impact wrenches and splashes as broken parts were discarded. After an hour, the pipeline was reconnected and ready for operation.

Nassau County, Long Island—0320 Hours

The jangling phone in Brenda Mason's apartment seemed a long mile away to Scott's sleep fogged brain. A very sleepy Brenda managed to answer. "Hello," she said, barely awake. Then, with a yawn: "Bob, some captain wants you."

"Scott here," he answered, quickly awake.

"Bob," U.S.C.G. Captain Peters began. "Sorry to have to track you down, but about an hour ago there was a powerful explosion at the site of the sunken Type 21. She may have blown up. I sent two patrol boats out to the area. They're reporting that the marker buoy is gone and considerable floating debris has been seen. Fortunately, there haven't been any reports of casualties."

"Are they sure they were at the site of the marker buoy?"

"I had our people measure down from the *McDonald*'s position. It's four hundred fifty yards up channel."

Scott laughed and answered, "Then it can't have been the

sub, sir. Chief Morris and I secretly moved the marker buoy two hundred yards up the channel to prevent those news people from sending divers down to find out what we were doing out there today. The boat's only two hundred fifty yards behind the dredge."

"What! Then if not the sub, what the hell blew up?"

"Right now I don't know. Red and I will go out to the dredge at first light."

"All right. I told Morris to get Lieutenant Hampton and his chief to join you to go down for a look. Morris will have the motor launch ready at 0700 hours."

"Yes, sir. We'll get to the bottom of this, I assure you."

Scott passed the phone to Brenda and closed his eyes, his mind whirling with questions.

"Bad trouble? Do you have to go?" she asked. "I hope you can stay—you need proper sleep."

"I assure you," Scott said softly, still preoccupied, "this is very unusual. Go back to sleep. I'll be right here."

As Brenda turned her back to him and slept, Scott stared into the darkness.

He had much to think about. Only a few hours earlier, he had been at a lawyer's office with his wife. A heated argument had brought what little communication remained to a sudden final end. She even admitted living with another man. Scott already knew that. She said she had accepted a new love because Scott was never with her even when he was at home. His mind was always a thousand miles away. She refused to relent on her demand that he move out of the house they jointly owned.

There was no more to be said. He brought a couple of suitcases to Brenda's apartment.

Now this explosion near the submarine. What the hell will happen next?

U.S.C.G. Boat Slip, Governors Island—0650 Hours

Scott hurried to the Coast Guard dock early the next morning at first light. Morris and the Coxswain were nearly ready to leave. Davidson and the divers boarded a moment later.

The motor launch's bow was soon cutting through the green gray water. Scott was relieved to see in the distance that the dredge seemed to be working normally. The early hour and harbor police boats were preventing the media boats from direct access although a news chopper passed overhead.

"From the newscasts, I was afraid that the *McDonald* might have been damaged," Davidson said.

"Well, you can bet that if it was, Captain Harris would bite my nose something awful," Scott replied.

Rounding the dredge, they reached the submarine site and prepared the divers. Two splashes and Lieutenant Hampton and the master chief disappeared quickly from sight.

"Are you sure that we're in the right place?" Davidson asked.

"Yes. You can tell from that jetty over there and those apartment buildings on that side. Morris and I plotted the location before we moved the marker buoy."

"Commander!" Morris called out. "Hampton reports the boat's still there and everything looks like it did yesterday."

"Have them tap the hull and see if it's still dry!"

A few minutes later, the chief called out again. "He says it sounds dry, Commander!"

"Great. Tell Hampton to swim downstream two hundred yards to the explosion site and take a look. Let's move the launch down there, too!"

"What was that, Lieutenant?" Morris asked. "Say again." A moment passed, and the chief's face turned ashen as he listened to Hampton's voice. He turned toward Scott. "My God, Commander. They've just spotted another dead diver! With a cut air hose. They didn't see him yesterday. Hampton thinks the body could have been buried in the mud and washed free by last night's blast."

For a moment, Scott just looked at the chief.

"Unbelievable!" he finally uttered. "Now there's no doubt that the first body we discovered Wednesday is tied to this boat.

Call Branson. This is a job for the harbor cops. Don't touch the body. Let's get on with our investigation."

■ ■ ■ ■ ■

"I was expecting to see debris, Chief," Davidson observed as the launch reached its goal.

"Captain Peters had the patrol boats pick up most of it last night, sir," Morris replied. "He was afraid it might drift away. They've got it back at Governors Island."

About fifteen minutes later Morris finally called out, "The lieutenant says they found a big hole blasted in the bottom. They're bringing up some debris."

"Red," Scott said, "I'm convinced this was no accident, especially since we found the second dead diver. Somebody brought a big bomb out here last night and tried to blow up the sub. If we hadn't moved that marker buoy, they would have succeeded!"

"This was deliberate? Who would have known about the sub? Why would they blow it up?"

"I don't know, but something is going on. I've had a strange feeling about this whole thing since we saw those dead crewmen yesterday. It just doesn't add up. Now this blast business and this dead diver. Somebody does not want us to go on board that sub. Why? I don't know."

"That's some crazy idea!"

"I know, but I've got a definite feeling about it."

They were interrupted by the divers' resurfacing, each carrying twisted pieces of metal. Scott and Davidson examined the salvaged pieces.

"I think it's a propeller blade off a high-speed screw," said Davidson. "The type used on large cabin cruisers."

"Uh-huh, and this is a valve cover for an inboard marine engine."

"We found those outside the crater," the master chief said. "One hell of a hole down there."

"Got any idea what it would take to do this?" asked Scott.

"At least eight, maybe ten tons of explosives," answered Hampton. "My best guess is a whole boatload."

"But how did it get there?" Davidson inquired.

"I don't know, sir," replied Hampton. "All I can say for sure is that the explosion occurred on the bottom. Underwater, not on the surface."

"Somebody filled up a large cabin cruiser with explosives," Scott elaborated, "and brought it out here. Scuttled it right where they believed the sub to be and set it off, hoping to destroy the sub."

"That's crazy, sir!" exclaimed Morris.

"I agree, Commander," said Hampton. "That's definitely what it looks like down there."

"My God, sir," Morris said. "If we hadn't moved that marker buoy, the sub would have been destroyed. What could be on the sub important enough for somebody to take such an action."

I can't answer that, chief," Scott replied. "Let's get to the dredge. Call and tell Captain Peters that everything is as I suspected."

Aboard the dredge *William P. McDonald*—1040 Hours

Sherry Edwards, dressed in her normal work uniform, stood at the rear of the dredge as the launch arrived and tied up.

"What did you find out about last night?" she asked.

"I'll tell you later," Scott answered. "Did the dredge suffer any damage?"

"It did. I've already been chewed out by Captain Harris. Now it's your turn."

"What happened?"

"The crew got banged up pretty bad. Charlie has his head wrapped like an Arab sheik, and old Cookie can hardly walk. The left pivot pole is bent. Some of the deck gear went overboard. They were shut down for over an hour. Everybody is damn unhappy. Enough?"

"Well, let's go face the storm," Scott said as Sherry led him and the others to the dredge captain's office.

Harris looked up as they entered. Scott could see that his eyes flamed with anger.

"I want an explanation, Commander," Harris demanded. "We went through hell last night!"

Scott explained what they had discovered and shared his suspicions that it was a deliberate act.

"That's crazy!" Harris retorted. He swung his fist against the desktop.

"Captain," Scott went on, "did any of your crew see anything last night before the explosion?"

"Smitty told me he saw a big cabin cruiser and a speedboat head up the channel just before it happened."

"That's the answer, Captain. But *who*? and *why*? are the big questions."

"Screw the questions. Are you people going to arrange protection?"

"Yes. You can count on it. Now that this threat has become known, both the Harbor Police and the Coast Guard will be patrolling the area continuously."

"Do we go ahead with the plan to board the sub? I've got everybody standing by."

"Yes, as fast as possible."

"I don't like it, but okay. I'll get things under way." Harris got up and left the office to start the work.

Scott told Morris to take the two divers back to Governors Island and make a full report to Captain Peters. As the motor launch roared away, Davidson briefed J.D. and the welders on the shape of the cut that would allow the old water tank to join the hull of the submarine with a tight fit.

The sound of the workboat's diesel announced that Bulldog had arrived from Port Newark with the tank strapped to the service barge. By noon the welders were busy burning the bottom of the tank in a shower of hot oxidized iron sparks.

■ ■ ■ ■ ■

Scott was in the dredge's galley when Chief Morris came in. "Anything from the boss?" he asked.

"Yes, sir. Captain Peters was very pleased with your report. He was busy fending off the press, though, and didn't have much time to talk."

"How bad is it?"

"The captain said that he's heard from all the networks, dozens of newspapers and radio stations, but he seems mostly worried because our real enemy must have heard about this."

"Our real enemy?" asked Captain Harris. "Who, the jerks who caused that explosion?"

"The U.S. Navy," Scott answered with a laugh. "Captain Peters has no love for the far out sailors."

"I've had my problems with them jerks, too," said Captain Harris with a grunt.

"He wants us to refer the press to him when they show up with questions," the chief continued. "He's using a cover story that we're dealing with an old water tank that fell off a barge years ago. He's saying that the explosion was a barge accident unrelated to our dredging project."

"Do you think the press is buying it?" Scott asked.

"I don't know, sir. The news broadcasts will soon answer that question."

"Okay. Let's push on."

"We'll have the caisson ready to install by tomorrow morning," said Harris. "Kendall and his assistant are scheduled to cut away the outer casing tonight. With luck, we'll be able to cut the hole into the sub Monday morning."

"Good. Let's see how the assembly is going."

They headed out of the galley to the service barge, where Davidson watched Cracker and Curly burn the top off the old tank. The odor of hot iron hung in the nearly still air, air heavy with humid heat that caused sweat to roll down the welders' faces.

The bottom of the tank had been cut and shaped to fit the curved pressure hull of the submarine. After checking it three times, they were certain that the fit would be nearly perfect. Once the 36-inch diameter pipe was connected to the top, the assembly would appear to form a sort of upside-down funnel.

"How much will it weigh when they're done, J.D.?" Scott asked.

"I estimate about ten tons, but that won't be any problem," J.D. said. "The front derrick can handle four times that much."

"Good. When do you plan to stop dredging and remove the cutting head?"

"You know Tiny, Commander. He'll keep dredging until the last possible minute. We'll be dropping the front assembly tonight. Then we'll swing the dredge around and push her into position over the sub just as the caisson is finished."

After first going over the final part of the plan with J.D., Scott and Davidson prepared to leave for the day. It was getting late. They watched Charlie as he pushed the lifting winch control lever to raise the cutter-head assembly in preparation for removal. The air was filled with the chatter of impact wrenches as the crew disconnected the slurry-discharge pipeline to allow the dredge to be moved up channel. Scott felt satisfied that the work was being aggressively pursued.

Lower Manhattan—0810 Hours

Sherry drove through the Holland Tunnel, emerging into very light early morning traffic. The tires made splashing sounds on the wet streets after an early morning rain. The sun peeking from behind gray clouds gave hope of improving weather later in the morning. She continued on toward Battery Park, confident that she would arrive at the ferry landing on time.

Meeting the Coast Guard motor launch was a pleasant change from her normal routine of driving to Port Newark to board the Port Authority's service boat. She looked forward to riding with the Coast Guard. Maybe I'll get more information about that explosion, she thought, and maybe learn what Scott thinks is on board the sub.

She parked her Honda at the fire boat station and quickly walked past the historic masonry fort that once held muzzle loading cannon that gave the park its name. Replacing the cannon, sadly, homeless people slept or panhandled in their efforts to survive. She tried to ignore them by looking past their well practiced begging poses but did finally give a dollar to one very shabby old woman.

Finally the Coast Guard boat came into her view, just beyond the Circle Line ferry. She moved through the long lines of tourists waiting to board the ferry to Liberty Island and finally reached the seawall next to the motor launch.

She jumped down from the seawall into the Coast Guard

vessel, the wind snapping her earth tone Dickies work ensemble as her light brown engineer boots struck the deck. Her usual smile and sparkling eyes were infectious as the men responded with their own looks of pleasure at her arrival.

"I hope the *McDonald* will be able to set the caisson pipe today," Davidson commented as the launch moved quickly down the channel.

"You can see that the dredge is positioned over the sub's location," Scott answered, "so it appears they're on schedule."

"I got a call from George just before he came off the night shift," Sherry offered. "He said that everything was okay then. Have you guys come up with any more information about what's behind that explosion? What's down inside the sub that's so important?"

"We don't know any more yet," Scott answered. "I'm convinced that somebody awful important is behind this. Why? I just don't know. I can't tell you anymore right now."

"Well, it looks like the weather is going to cooperate after all," Davidson commented, changing the subject. "That's a big help since the positioning of the caisson pipe is so critical. Rough water would really foul up things."

"That's for sure," Scott agreed. "And I sure hope that your idea will work, Sherry."

Sherry replied, "It should. It's basic static mechanics. J.D. said he liked it."

Sherry's rigging plan required a secure vertical suspending point to hang the caisson from along with three winch lines to drift the heavy pipe horizontally in any direction. They would make the suspending point by locking the dredge into a fixed position, using its rear pivot poles and forward swing winches to hold the derrick hook exactly over the point of contact. Then three separate horizontal cables would be stretched from the two front corners of the dredge and from the workboat to the pipe so that winches could pull the pipe in any direction.

She noticed the men grow suddenly nervous and silent. "Hey, guys," she said. "Lighten up. It'll work. Really. At least, I think it will."

"That's reassuring," Davidson said.

Aboard the dredge, *William P. McDonald*—0840 Hours

Scott felt a mood of apprehension hanging over the crew as they joined J.D. and the others at the front of the dredge. Scott asked him when the caisson pipe, which lay on the service barge, would be hooked to the derrick and lifted off.

"We're going to hook the top as soon as the workboat gets the barge set at the front of the dredge. I'm having Cracker and Curly suit up to go down right after we splash it off the barge. Kendall and his assistant finished cutting the outer casing a couple of hours ago. I've got them sleeping now, so they can take over later."

With the service barge in place, two crewmen, grunting and groaning from the effort, attached the heavy chain to the lifting hook. The derrick then raised the pipe as high as it could, but the large end of the caisson still rested on the barge. Sherry had expected this, and she directed the crew to roll the rest of it off by pumping the barge's fuel oil to the port side until the barge listed. Once that balance was achieved, the pipe rolled off the barge, splashing heavily into the water. After a moment, it settled into a vertical position, hanging from the hook. Scott and Sherry joined in laughter as a flock of seagulls had to take flight when their perch suddenly disappeared from beneath them.

Davidson shouted gleefully. "It worked just like you predicted, Sherry."

"Okay, you wise guys," Sherry answered with a smug smile. "Now maybe you'll believe I know what I'm doing."

"How about we wait on that until we see how your triangular alignment works," J.D. answered patronizingly.

Sherry glanced over her shoulder and gave him a just-you-wait-and-see look.

But she couldn't gloat for long. She had to point out where the cables had to be connected to the three points on the caisson pipe. Each cable was three-quarters of an inch thick and connected to a power winch at the two front corners of the dredge and to the rear of the workboat.

Bulldog pushed the workboat's throttle forward, and with

a roar of diesel exhaust it pulled away from the dredge. The two power winches balanced the force from the workboat in a mechanical tug of war, holding the workboat and the pipe in a fixed position.

The welders, wearing their yellow hard-hat diving suits, stepped on to the lift platform to be lowered down to position the caisson pipe and weld it to the hull of the submarine—the most critical part of the job. The three cables had to be moved very precisely to shift the bottom of the pipe a few inches at a time until the fit was exactly right. The divers, using under-water lights and a telephone line, would call for corrective moves.

Charlie, sitting in the control cab of the dredge, had the best view of the ship traffic and was the first to spot trouble. He immediately called J.D. on the walkie-talkie.

"Hey!" Charlie's voice came from the radio, "look up chan-nel! What's that dad-burned steamer doing?"

Everyone turned to look.

"What the hell!" Scott shouted. "She's headed right at us!"

"Got to be doing fourteen knots at least!" Davidson yelled.

"Chief! Get the launch started! We've got to turn that ship fast!" August heat or not, Scott's blood suddenly ran cold.

They raced to the launch, shouting for the coxswain to start the engines. Chaos gripped the dredge as the crew started locking the equipment down.

Aboard U.S.C.G. Motor Launch—0915 Hours

The coxswain threw the throttle wide open and had the launch moving at full speed seconds after Scott and Morris leapt aboard. Scott frantically grabbed the Morse code lamp, aimed it at the bridge of the huge steamer, and began flashing "turn to port" over and over.

"She's still turning starboard, sir!" shouted the chief.

Scott grabbed and raised the flare pistol. The flare rose above the motor launch, its red flame bright against the sky arcing toward the oncoming steamship, now less than half a mile from the *McDonald*. Sweat poured down his face at thoughts of the impending disaster. Collision was only two minutes away.

Suddenly the 600 foot long steamer ship began to turn to port. The turning radius was wide; if collision could be avoided, the ship would brush by the dredge at a distance of less than a hundred yards.

Scott knew that even if the ship had reversed her engines, the remaining half mile would be too short to stop in time. Slowly, the big ship turned to port, and Scott saw that collision would be avoided. He mopped the sweat from his face. But the speed of the ship was not slowing and he could see that the bow wave would hit the dredge hard.

"Chief!" Scott shouted. "Call Charlie! Tell him to warn everybody to hang on tight!"

Scott watched helplessly as the ship passed the dredge, its bow wave moving outward across the otherwise calm water.

Aboard the dredge, *William P. McDonald*—0938 Hours

As the bow wave hit, the dredge suddenly pitched up. A second later the wave struck the caisson pipe, pushing it to the left. The sudden position change overloaded the cable, snapping it with the sound of a rifle shot. The broken end of the cable whipped back toward the dredge at close to the speed of sound. Tim Collins, one of the dredge's deckhands, stood beside the winch, frozen in fear. No time to move. The cable struck him hard, nearly severing his left leg. He screamed and fell heavily, spurting blood.

Sherry realized instantly that an artery in Collins's leg was severed. He would bleed to death in minutes. She ran forward, knelt on the hard metal deck, and pressed her hands on the gaping wound to stop the bleeding. Collins' face was white. He was rapidly going into shock. The warm, sticky red liquid ran over Sherry's hands. She yelled. Seconds later, J.D. leapt over a cable reel and reached her side.

"J.D!" Sherry cried. "I need a tourniquet!"

"Hang on, girl," J.D. responded as he pressed the transmit button on his hand radio. "Charlie, call for a medevac chopper—*now*!"

Captain Harris and a crewman reached the scene of blood and pain.

"It's bad, Tiny," J.D. said with fear in his voice.

"You, give me your belt for a tourniquet," the dredge captain ordered the shaking crewman. "Move—now, dammit!"

"The chopper's on its way," Charlie called down.

Harris and J.D. fashioned a tourniquet from a metal rod and the belt. The blood flow stopped.

Sherry removed her blood-soaked hands. She looked at the dredge captain with pain in her eyes, her dripping hands held stiffly away from her blood splashed beige work suit.

"Captain," she said with a tight throat. "He's got to get to a hospital now."

"I know, but thanks to you, he's got a chance." Harris's voice cracked. "Get cleaned up. You're covered with blood." As she rose to walk away, the dredge captain briefly looked at her, a speculative look on his hard face.

Aboard U.S.C.G. Motor Launch—1005 Hours

The coxswain pushed the Coast Guard motor launch to its limit. Scott continued flashing Morse code at the bridge of the speeding ship. "*SS Rangoon Expresser*: You are ordered to stop immediately." He repeated the message over and over. The coxswain swung the launch back and forth across the ship's bow, a dangerous maneuver.

"The cutter *Alvin*'s on her way, Commander," the chief shouted. "She'll be here in ten minutes!"

"Tell her skipper to be ready to fire into this idiot's bridge if he doesn't stop, by God! Remind him that I'm the acting Captain of the Port today. And call Floyd Bennett heliport! I want an armed chopper—ASAP!"

"Aye, sir!" Morris shouted back as he headed for the radio.

The steamship passed through the Narrows at a speed of

fifteen knots with the Coast Guard motor launch a few yards in front of its bow. Finally, two miles below the Verrazano-Narrows Bridge, the ship began to slow and come to a stop. Scott looked skyward for a moment with relief that the mad race was over.

"Thank God!" Scott said as he saw the armed helicopter approaching from the east. "Things were about to get real ugly!" His shirt was soaked with sweat. For several minutes, he had even forgotten the humid August heat.

"The *Alvin*'s turning this way, too, sir!" the chief shouted.

Scott could see the 110-foot cutter moving up the shipping channel at high speed, a high bow wave curving away on either side. "Call her skipper and tell him to send us an armed boarding party as backup! Have you been able to raise this idiot steamship captain on the radio?"

"No, sir."

Scott sent another Morse code message toward the bridge of the steamship. "SS *Rangoon Expresser*: You are to drop your pilot's ladder and prepare to be boarded."

The pilot's ladder came down. As the coxswain maneuvered the launch toward the ladder, the *Alvin* arrived alongside the steamship. The cutter's automatic twenty-five-millimeter cannon was swung out, the gun crew at its station. Just let somebody try something now, Scott thought.

"Chief," Scott called out, "get our side arms!"

The chief nodded, and a moment later he and Scott strapped on their standard-issue nine-millimeter semiautomatic pistols. Morris tied the launch to the ladder landing, and he and Scott hurried, with clanking steps, up to the steamship's deck.

Aboard the *S.S. Rangoon Expresser*—1020 Hours

Disregarding the customary request for permission to come aboard, Scott brushed past the ship's officer at the top of the ladder without a word. The man backed away with a surprised look on his face but kept silent. Scott was furious. He and Morris headed immediately, at a fast walk, for the ladder to the main bridge.

Scott was surprised to see his good friend, Terry Watson, one of the New York Harbor Pilots, at the helm, acting as temporary captain of the vessel in the harbor. The regular captain of the steamship stood beside him. Both of them were breathing hard and wiping sweat from their strained faces.

"Terry!" Scott demanded angrily. "What the goddamm hell is going on here?"

"Slow down, Commander. We've been going through hell."

"Terry, I want an explanation, and it had better be good!"

"Let me show you something." Watson led Scott and Morris behind the bridge to an electrical-control room. He motioned to an opened electrical panel. "Take a look at this. This is the main bridge circuit panel."

Scott and the chief both examined the panel. Several wires had been cut. "What the hell is this?" Scott asked.

"The reason this ship went out of control and nearly smashed into the dredge!"

"Explain!" Scott demanded.

Morris was already searching out the answers. Well trained in marine engineering, his eyes missed nothing.

"My God, Commander," exclaimed the chief. "Look at this!" He was pointing to three wires.

"Somebody came in here and sabotaged the control wiring right after we started down the channel," Watson continued. "We lost control of the ship for several minutes."

"This was *deliberate*?" Scott asked.

"This type of ship uses electrical signals to control the rudder and the engines," Morris replied. "The intercom and the radio are also connected through this panel."

"That's what I'm trying to tell you," Watson insisted. "We were sabotaged! You can see that the intercom and radio circuits were cut!"

"What I'm talking about, sir," Morris continued, "is the steering-control wires. They've been reversed! See, the red wire is connected to the blue wire and the blue wire is connected to the red. This would cause the steering drive to do the opposite from the helm. If the helmsman turned the wheel to starboard, then the hydraulic drive would turn the rudder to port—and vice versa."

"That's what happened. When I called for a course correction to port, instead we turned to starboard. I looked to see what the helmsman was doing, and he was turning the wheel as I had ordered."

"But how did you get away from the dock without noticing this change?" Scott asked.

"That's what really threw me. Everything was normal until we passed Liberty Island. I ordered rudder amidships, and we straightened out as expected. My next course correction wasn't until just above the dredge when I called for twenty degrees to port. Suddenly, we were headed at the dredge. During that straight run from Liberty Island down to Kill Van Kull—which takes about twenty minutes—somebody entered the room, cut the communications, and switched the helm signals."

"Not only that, sir," Morris interjected, "the engine signals are also reversed. See—the wires that control the engine-room telegraph have been rewired. When the bridge changed its control to reverse engine, the engine room got full ahead."

"That's right!" Watson exclaimed. "And with the intercom knocked out, we had no way to talk to the chief engineer to tell him to stop his engine. The ship's captain had to send a runner down to the engineer to tell him to stop the ship. It took five minutes just for him to get down there."

"My God," Scott said, amazed. "But how did you avoid hitting the dredge?"

"I figured pretty fast that the controls had short-circuited, so I told the helmsman to try turning to starboard and the ship turned to port."

"Chief, could one person have done this in just twenty minutes?"

"Sir, I could do this in less than *three* minutes with just a screwdriver and a pair of wire cutters."

Scott looked up and saw that the boarding party from the *Alvin* had entered the bridge.

"Boarding party reporting as ordered," said the officer in charge. "I'm the *Alvin*'s executive officer."

"Good, Lieutenant." Scott returned his salute. "How many men did you bring with you?"

"I have eight guardsmen with M-16s, sir."

"Post two men here on the bridge, two at the pilot's ladder, two in the engine room, and the last two in the crew's mess. I'm going to have the crew gathered in there."

Scott turned to Morris. "Chief, contact the chopper and tell him to go back to Floyd Bennett. We've got things under control here. Then find a padlock and secure this room. Nobody is to go near that panel until the Harbor Police have dusted it for prints. And get the Harbor Police on their way with a crime scene unit."

"Aye, sir."

"Lieutenant, you're with me." He turned to Watson and the ship's captain. "Captain, as of now, you and your crew are under arrest. You're to gather your crew in the crew's mess and wait there until the Harbor Police complete their interviews."

"Yes," the ship's captain answered. His English was good considering he came from Greece as did most of the crew, and he was shaking from the tension. No captain can remain calm when he loses control of his ship.

"Lieutenant, have you got your Morse lamp?"

"Yes, Commander."

"Use it to tell your skipper what's going on and tell him to stand by. Don't use your radio. I think we're being monitored. Then tell your men at the ladder that no one is to board or leave this ship except us or the Harbor Police."

"Aye, sir."

Scott turned to Watson. "I'm planning to move this ship to Governors Island. As soon as Chief Morris gets back and the Harbor Police finish dusting for prints, I'll have Morris correct the wiring of the control panel. Then I'll have the *Alvin* send over two engineers to run the engine room. We'll move down channel to turn around and then come back up. I'll berth her off Castle William."

"Understood. Am I under arrest?"

"No, but you know the drill, old buddy. Your papers are going to have to be suspended as soon as we get back. I'm sure Captain Peters will reinstate them in a few days. You're obviously the victim of someone's treachery."

Aboard the dredge, *William P. McDonald*—1200 Hours

Meanwhile, using the bathroom in her office at the rear of the dredge, Sherry examined her freshened appearance in the mirror. Showered and dressed in new work clothes, she felt presentable once again. She fought to resolutely put the horror of the young man's nearly severed leg out of her mind. Got to focus on the job, she decided as she went forward.

"You okay?" J.D. asked as she rejoined him and Davidson.

"I think so," Sherry answered. "Have you been able to continue the work?"

"Everybody is still pretty shook, but we're getting it back together. We've been pushed back a couple of hours, though."

"Any word about Tim?"

"Not yet. I hope you know just how much Tiny was impressed by what you did."

"He and all of the crew seem exceptionally grateful. Is there something about Tim I don't know?"

"Tim is Tiny's nephew. His sister's boy."

"I had no idea."

"Well, Tiny didn't advertise it. He meant it when he said he considers you part of the crew. He's on the phone with Tim's mother and dad.

"Meanwhile, we've got a new cable installed and are moving ahead with the positioning. Cracker just called up and said it's just about in line."

"With luck, maybe one more pull will get it," Davidson added. "I must confess, Sherry, your rigging plan has worked real well. I'm sorry I doubted you."

"Thank you," she replied. Maybe now, she thought, he'll be more supportive.

■■■■■

"J.D.!" a crewman called. "Cracker says about four inches toward y'all and he'll have the thing set!"

"Okay—easy now." The winch slowly pulled the caisson pipe a few inches.

"Cracker says he's done got it," the crewman called. "Lower the block."

A swift move of J.D.'s right hand and the caisson lowered the last few inches onto the submarine.

"Cracker says bingo. They're ready to weld her on."

"Great news. Tell 'em to burn those rods."

"How long will it take from here, J.D.?" Davidson asked.

"Best guess is about eight hours. Maybe twelve if they have to do much filling."

"Maybe we should try to get some rest."

"Yeah, and some food, too. Come on, let's hit the galley. Cookie makes great coffee."

Aboard the *S.S. Rangoon Expressor*—1245 Hours

Chief Morris entered the bridge and announced that the officers and crew were all accounted for and in the crew's mess. The Harbor Police had arrived and were coming on board.

"Good," Scott said. "Have them get everyone printed and dust the cabinet. Then we'll search for the tools."

"Aye, sir," the chief answered and went to deal with the police.

Scott turned to Terry Watson, standing beside him with sweat still on his face. "Terry, wait here. I'm going to step outside to use my phone. I've got to brief my captain."

■■■■■

As Scott switched off the phone after telling Captain Peters only the minimum possible to foil anyone listening, he saw that Chief Morris was trying to attract his attention. "Okay, Chief. Any progress?"

"Yes, sir. Sometimes we get lucky."

"Let's take a look."

The chief led Scott to the control panel behind the bridge, where a harbor police detective was examining freshly dusted fingerprints. Morris walked confidently, Scott mused, he's really enjoying this detective work.

"Commander," the police sergeant said as he looked up. "We've got several prints. Your culprit did a good job of wiping the cabinet doors and surfaces, but he made the classic mistake of many criminals. He forgot to wipe the cartridges."

"Cartridges?"

"Figure of speech. Many murderers remember to wipe the gun but forget to wipe the bullets. We catch a lot of them by finding their prints on the cartridge cases. We're lucky your perps didn't use latex gloves. In this case, the doors and surfaces were clean, but when he moved the spade lugs for the steering circuits he left his prints on them. We've got partial thumb and forefinger prints."

"So you've identified him."

"Not yet. I've got two men in the mess hall printing every member of the crew right now. We'll have him in a few minutes."

"This is great work, Sergeant! Let's go down and get him!"

The fingerprinting of the crew was in progress when two of the ship's crew suddenly jumped up and ran to the rear exit, where a guardsman with an M-16 rifle was standing. Young and inexperienced, the surprised guardsman, his eyes filled with shock, froze. Two quick hard blows ended the struggle as the men took the rifle and ran from the room.

Scott and Morris rushed to the fallen guardsman, who lay groaning on the deck. He was apparently only slightly injured.

"All right!" Scott shouted. "After them! Chief Morris, form two search teams. Captain, I want a ship's officer to go with each team as guide. Men who speak some English as well as Greek. Lieutenant! Get word to all the boats around this ship to watch for these guys if they try to jump. Let your skipper in on what's happening. Then get back here and take charge of the rest of the detainees."

Scott turned, his fist shaking—his face flushed and sweating. He looked at the bewildered ship's captain.

"Captain, I want to know who these men are and I want their personnel records—pronto!"

Scott and the ship's captain left the mess and headed for the office behind the bridge, where they pulled open a large file cabinet drawer. A few minutes later, the ship's captain surrendered two file folders.

The first was for a Vladimir Rostoff. Scott quickly read the record. Good luck the documents were written in English, the common language used in international shipping. A former seaman with the Soviet navy, Rostoff had successfully applied for work as a deckhand when the Soviet navy was disbanded after the fall of the Communist regime. This was his second voyage with the ship. He had kept to himself and had not made friends with the other crewmen. He had no known family ties.

The second file was for an Alexander Gromeko. He had been a former member of the KGB, assigned to the USSR embassy in Turkey. He too had been cast adrift by the fall of the Soviet empire. He was the radio operator aboard the ship. He had a wife now living in Athens but no children. He had also kept to himself and avoided making friends with the other crewmen except for an occasional conversation in Russian with Rostoff. He was known to be very proficient in English. This was also the second voyage for Gromeko.

Both files contained photographs and fingerprint cards. After a quick review, Scott and the ship's captain returned to the crew's mess.

Sergeant Lyons and eight additional NYPD harbor police officers had come aboard. Scott grimly welcomed the reinforcements—the situation was becoming difficult. Scott was thankful to see Lyons was an excellent leader.

"Commander," the Alvin's lieutenant called. "My chief just radioed that the two fugitives were spotted entering cargo hold three!"

"Good work! Call Morris and tell him to head that way, too. Sergeant Lyons! Bring two of your men, and let's go down there."

The four men, Sergeant Lyons in the lead, ran full speed to the man-sized access hatch at the top of the cargo hold. A patrolman slipped on the wet deck nearly knocking Scott off his feet as they collided. He started to apologize.

"No time for apology," Scott said. "Grab a latch!"

The sound of gunfire greeted the men as the heavy steel hatch swung back and fell against the deck. Peering cautiously down into the semi-blackness, Scott and Lyons could see only a catwalk some eight feet below.

"Don't use the ladder, men," Lyons instructed. "You'll be exposed to fire. Drop down! Go!" Seconds later, two loud thumps were heard as the two officers landed on the metal plates below. "They made it." Lyons could see the officers dive to safety behind one of the many stacks of lumber that filled the hold. Bullets immediately struck the lumber above them. "Our turn, Commander!" Scott hurtled down into chaos.

Lyons joined Scott and the other officers just as another volley of bullets crashed into the lumber, showering the men with splinters and wood dust. Damn air is thick with this stuff, Scott thought, as he labored to breathe through the heavy dust.

As Scott's eyes became accustomed to the dim light, he could see Morris and his team at the far end of the catwalk just entering through the bulkhead door.

"Lyons!" Scott called out over the gunfire. "We've got to put together a coordinated attack. Can you see the Alvin's chief petty officer?"

"Yeah," Lyons answered. "He's on our right His guys have the fugitives pinned against the starboard side."

Scott squeezed around the lumber stack and located the fugitives from their gun flashes. He realized too late that they could also see him as he felt a sudden pain in his left arm. His right hand instinctively gripped the sore area. It was wet with blood!

"Lyons! I'm hit!" His voice was controlled, but tense.

The sergeant reached him quickly and inspected the wound.

"It's just a flesh wound. Gonna bleed awhile, but looks clean." He pulled a bandanna from his hip pocket and hastily wrapped Scott's arm with a tight knot.

They didn't have much time to consider the wound as a loud snap above them warned of an impending avalanche. The steel band holding the lumber stack together had separated, probably from a bullet hit. The heavy boards poured down into the space the two of them had just left an instant before.

Scott could only stare for a moment as the last of the boards smashed onto the pile. He had no doubt how close death had come to claiming what would have been their crushed bodies.

"Now I'm really mad!" Scott said with determination. "Let's get these bastards."

"Look," Lyons pointed out. "Morris is headed for the fire hose cabinet." Scott realized immediately what the chief planned to do.

"They need a diversion. Have your men move to the right and fire several rounds. Tell the *Alvin's* crew to do the same."

Morris didn't have to wait long. The cargo hold reverberated with intense gunfire as the police began the attack. The fugitives responded immediately. Chief Morris quickly jumped across a lumber stack to reach the fire hose cabinet. He nearly snapped off the door handle in his excitement.

He motioned to one of the police officers to open the main water valve as he quietly unreeled the limp hose. High pressure water rapidly filled and stiffened the hose. Morris almost lost his grip as the hose pressed him against a lumber stack. Regaining his control, the chief aimed the nozzle at one of the Russians and, bracing himself against the reaction force he knew was coming, opened the nozzle valve.

The force of the water struck Rostoff on his side, smashing him into the lumber. He dropped his weapon and fell to his knees.

"Get him!" Morris yelled at two police officers who immediately jumped the stunned man and handcuffed him.

Morris saw Scott jump behind a lumber stack as the water stream smashed into the bulkhead, splashing in all directions. Morris quickly managed to regain control of the thrashing hose and redirected the powerful stream toward the other Russian, who had retreated behind another lumber stack.

But Gromeko was unable to fire. The water from the firehose pinned him behind the lumber stack. As the *Alvin's* team moved closer, they heard a shot. Everyone froze. After a few minutes passed, they eased around the lumber to where Gromeko lay, water cascading down on him from the top of the lumber stack.

"Morris!" the *Alvin's* chief called out. "Shut down the water! He shot himself!"

Scott joined the other men at Gromeko's side. The Russian lay dead.

"Damn, damn!" Scott said as he looked at the body.

Checking the two photographs he had brought with him, he confirmed that the dead man was the former KGB agent Gromeko. Scott went back to where Morris and his team were guarding Rostoff.

"Has he said anything?" Scott asked.

"Not a word," Morris answered. "What shall we do with him?"

"Do you speak English?"

No answer. The man stared into space, seeming not to see his captors. Scott examined the man's hard, scarred and expressionless face. Not the face of a man willing to cooperate.

"Can you understand me?"

Again, no reply. Only a sly smile of defiance.

"I don't know if he can understand me or not. Let's take him back to the crew's mess. Maybe he'll talk to the ship's captain. Have the Alvin's crew take charge here. Morris, take Rostoff and let's get out of here."

As the police pulled Rostoff to his feet, he suddenly jerked violently, screamed and gasped. He then slumped and fell to the floor. He appeared dead a moment later as his body went totally still.

"Shit damn!" Scott said. He dropped down beside the limp

figure and placed his hands on Rostoff's chest ready to administer CPR. He leaned down about to blow air into the Russian's mouth when he suddenly stopped. That odor! Burnt almonds.

"Shall I call for para-medics, sir?" Morris asked.

"No. It's cyanide. Probably bit a capsule hidden in his mouth. Now how will we find out who he was working for?"

He turned to Lyons. "Sergeant, we need every scrap of information we can dig up about our two suspects. Call the FBI, Interpol, even the damn Russian Embassy. We must figure out who they were working for."

"Right, Commander," the sergeant answered. "We'll get a thorough background check going. Officers have already gone to the crew's quarters to search their belongings."

Scott nodded, and the men returned to the crew's mess. Several husky harbor policemen followed with the bodies of the two Russians.

"All right, let's get this ship ready to move. Morris, you go to the bridge and fix that panel. Lieutenant, tell your skipper to send us the engineers." Scott sat down at one of the mess tables and laid out his bare arm to allow the medic to properly dress his wound.

Scott and the police questioned the captain and other crew members about Rostoff, but none could supply any further information. Scott pounded his fist against his leg in frustration. The evidence team confirmed that the prints found in the electrical cabinet were those of Vladimir Rostoff.

The police sent to search Rostoff's belongings returned with a screwdriver and wire cutters. They had also found twelve gold coins.

Scott reached for the coins. He felt their weight and threw them back on the table.

"Commander," Morris called from the bridge. "We're ready to move, sir."

"Sergeant, maintain security here. We're going to move the ship." Scott went to the bridge to rejoin the *Alvin's* Lieutenant and the pilot. "Lieutenant, is the *Alvin* ready to escort us back to the station?" he asked.

"Aye, sir."

"Chief, take the helm and signal the engineers. Terry will serve as pilot."

An unplanned parade soon commenced as the steamship, now turned around and headed toward Manhattan, was surrounded by police and press boats. "No way to keep this a secret," Scott muttered as he saw the cameras at work.

He stood on the port side of the ship so that he could see the dredge as they passed. Through his binoculars he could see that the caisson pipe seemed in place. Hoses and thick cables leading down into the water indicated that the welding should be under way.

About an hour later, the ship was abreast of Governors Island, and Scott breathed a sigh of relief as the anchor dropped. He was tired, but rest was still hours away. He rubbed his throbbing arm under the bandage. He'd have to get to a doctor soon to avoid infection.

"Chief, have the coxswain bring our boat up to the pilot's ladder and wait for us," Scott ordered. "Lieutenant, I'd like your chief and a couple of your top guardsmen to remain on this ship to maintain security. I'm going to order the police to provide a security team and patrol boat for tonight. Tomorrow, Captain Peters will no doubt make other arrangements, but this should get us through tonight."

"Aye, sir. I'll inform the *Alvin.*"

Aboard U.S.C.G. Motor Launch—1450 Hours

Half an hour later, Scott and Morris were on board the Coast Guard motor launch headed back to the dredge. Scott hoped that everything was going smoothly. He had been so busy with the steamship that he hadn't had time to contact the dredge.

"How's it going?" Scott shouted up to the dredge deck while Davidson helped secure the launch.

"The second team of divers is down now continuing with the welding," Davidson answered. "They're about one-third complete. Sherry's rigging plan worked great. But we had a bad injury when the bow wave hit from that steamship."

"Oh, no! What happened?"

"Young deckhand Tim Collins was struck by a snapped cable. He's in very critical condition at a hospital in Manhattan. Captain Harris is looking for somebody to hang—maybe us!"

"The guy who caused the accident is already dead. He committed suicide when we caught him and his partner." Scott quickly told the rest of the steamship episode.

"We better go tell Tiny and J.D."

Aboard the dredge, *William P. McDonald*—1518 Hours

Scott briefed the dredge captain and J.D. on the reasons for the near collision, and the subsequent impounding of the steamship.

"You're convinced that this was no accident?" the dredge captain asked.

"Yes. That ship was definitely sabotaged by Rostoff. We know how he did it. What we don't know is why or who paid him."

"Commander," Captain Harris spoke angrily, "I'm just about ready to pull off this job! It's getting too damn dangerous! We've been attacked twice. We've been damaged and people have been hurt! Now my nephew is all torn up and may die! At the least he'll probably lose a leg. Either *you* are going to provide me with real protection or *I* am going to pull my dredge out of here—now!"

"The cutter *Alvin* is coming over here right now and will be with you all night. I'm also ordering more patrol coverage by both the Coast Guard and the Harbor Police. That should give you good protection." Scott stared into Harris's eyes as the dredge captain considered his offer.

"Well, all right—but I want no more crap, understand? Or I pull out of here! My boss is coming up tonight with the company plane. He's bringing my sister and her husband up to see

Tim. He's going to have plenty to say to you when he gets here, Commander."

The veins along the dredge's captain's neck pulsed, and his eyes stared deeply into Scott's. Nothing more seemed appropriate. It was time to leave.

Scott and the others headed back to the Coast Guard motor launch.

"I'm planning to stay on board tonight," Davidson said. "J.D. says I can bunk in his cabin."

"Okay, maybe your presence will help keep Captain Harris from quitting this job. Sherry, are you ready to go? Captain Peters wants to talk to us."

"I guess I've done all I can here today," she responded. "I'd like to talk to Captain Peters. This whole experience has been devastating for me as well as the crew."

Aboard U.S.C.G. Motor Launch—1630 Hours

The Coast Guard motor launch took them at high speed across the nearly calm water. Sherry stood next to Scott at the front of the launch, enjoying the coolness of the fine spray from the bow.

"Let's hope Captain Peters can figure out what to do next," Scott said, watching her face from the corner of his eye. Damn, but she is a good-looking woman.

"Where will the next madness come from?" she asked. "First the explosion yesterday, and now a near miss by that steamship. What next?"

"I don't know, but somebody is sure trying to keep us from touching that sub. Maybe once the boarding party gets in we can clear up the mystery."

"It might just get worse."

"Yeah, it might."

The launch slowed and drifted into the boat slip. Tired or not, Scott led the others on a brisk walk to Captain Peters's house.

U.S.C.G. Station, Governors Island—1650 Hours

"At last," the captain greeted them. "Come in and let's hear it."

They each told their stories while drinking the coffee the captain had ready for them.

"Any more details about Rostoff and Gromeko?" Peters asked.

"The ship's captain said that Rostoff left the ship while they were at the pier to visit some friends in the city, but he had no idea of who or where," Scott answered. "The police are trying to find some leads, but with so little to go on, I don't expect much. Maybe they'll get lucky."

"What amazed me, Captain," Morris interjected, "was the way Rostoff and Gromeko were so quick to kill themselves rather than be taken into custody. It's as if they had specific orders to commit suicide if they were captured."

"I think Gromeko may have been Rostoff's superior," Scott went on, "since he had been a member of the KGB. It's possible Gromeko may have ordered Rostoff to sabotage the wiring as part of some KGB operation.

"Even though the USSR has broken up, some of the operations of the old KGB have no doubt been carried over into the new Russian Security Agency. But, how did the USSR know about this submarine boat, and why would the Russians want to keep us out of the wreck? I'm sure that some government is involved. These attacks are too well planned to be just ordinary criminals. That really scares me. Could we have stumbled onto some clandestine operation of *our* government? This kind of stuff seems like cloak and dagger. Could the C.I.A. be involved?"

"They just might be," Peters replied. He paused as the group dealt with their astonishment. It would get worse. Much worse. "I had a telephone call from Lieutenant Branson just minutes before you arrived. Those two dead divers—they've been identified—CIA operatives. Cuban exiles, Hector Mendoza and his brother Juan."

A minute passed without any response from Scott or his companions, the silence broken only by the rattle of Morris's cup as he nearly dropped it on the table.

"Why were *they* down there?" Scott finally asked.

Peters answered. "The harbor police divers found an explosive device they had placed just behind the sub's sail. It had been covered in the mud until Friday night's blast exposed it. The ATF disarmed and confirmed that it was typical CIA manufacture."

"Friday night's blast was a second attempt to destroy the sub?" Scott was becoming more and more alarmed.

"Almost certainly. I've also talked with the FBI this afternoon. They're sending agents to look at our evidence. This adds to the confusion of who is behind these attacks. If the CIA is involved, it would seem logical that the FBI and ATF would be told to stay away."

"Not necessarily," Morris broke in. "You know the CIA carries out operations without telling any other agency. The FBI has often discovered the CIA doing illegal work. The two agencies have always had conflicts."

"Wait a minute!" Sherry said, her hand held against her head and a confused look on her face. "You said the men on the steamship were Russians!"

"The CIA and KGB have cooperated when it served their mutual interests—especially cover-ups," Scott explained.

"This speculation doesn't get our job done," Peters interrupted "We've got to get into this sub. We'll leave the dead divers, the Russians and the CIA to the FBI and police." He turned to Sherry. "Can we get aboard the sub tomorrow before I lose control of this situation?"

"Yes," Sherry answered. "The welders are still working, but they should finish before two o'clock tomorrow morning. Then the caisson pipe will be pumped dry. The welders should be able to burn a hole through the pressure hull by four o'clock. Once that's done, the submarine will be ventilated until we board at eight."

Peters ran his hand through his graying hair and leaned forward.

"Okay. Who will be in the boarding party, Bob?"

"Myself, Morris, Red, and my coxswain."

"And me," Sherry added.

The men all looked at her with surprise.

"Sherry, we don't know what's down there." Scott said firmly, "You saw the bodies on the video. God knows what else is on board that boat. It may be loaded with unstable explosives that after fifty years of aging could go off from the slightest touch."

"May I remind you that I am the designated representative of the Port Authority?" Sherry challenged, irritation in her voice. "And I'll give you another reason. *Sprechen Sie Deutsch?*"

"What?"

"You are about to go aboard a German submarine. You'd better have someone along who can read German! Me!"

"Good point. You win." Scott sat back in his chair, uneasy but resigned for the moment. The woman had proved her toughness and dedication, so she shouldn't do anything stupid.

Nassau County, Long Island—2320 Hours

That night, Scott found it hard to relax. He lay beside Brenda listening to her gentle breathing as she slept. Exhausted as their latest round of sex had left him, he could not sleep. The events of the past several days kept running through his mind. He tried to make sense of the confusion. This had all started as a simple problem of identifying and disposing of an old wreck, an obstruction to the business of operating a harbor. Now it had become serious, with multiple violence complications by unknown elements. Would there be more attacks to deal with? Maybe the dredge was under attack right now. The telephone could ring at any second.

He was no coward and had been trained as a rescue swimmer, one of the most arduous job assignments in the U.S. Coast Guard. The job often required him to jump into the open sea from rescue helicopters to help injured accident victims into lift harnesses and then wait in the water while the helicopter transported the injured to a hospital. It took guts to remain in the sea while watching one's only means of survival fly away.

But this would be beyond anything he'd ever experienced. Stories of how German soldiers set booby traps to kill Allied troops flooded his mind. A simple trip wire. A pressure plate hidden under a floor mat. Any of these methods could have been set by the crew before they died. One mis-step, one wrong touch, and it would be over. And what of the possible weapon of mass destruction?

The implications of the possible involvement of the U.S. government or the former Soviet or the present Russian government kept intruding into his thoughts. Rostoff and Gromeko could have been ordered by the Russian Security Agency to sink the dredge and stop the effort to board the sub. Why?

Would someone order other operatives to continue the attacks? Rostoff had been a Soviet navy man and Gromeko an agent of the KGB. Both involved in Russian military secrets. But what secrets?

Got to sleep, he thought over and over. Got to sleep.

Aboard the Submarine, *UX-6000*—0800 Hours

Cold droplets of water, condensed from the humid air by the cold steel walls of the chamber around him, struck Scott on his upturned face. He grimaced from the impact as he sought one more look up the long caisson pipe at the blue dot of sky far above him. He shuddered at the realization of the danger he and his companions now faced.

Morris, the coxswain, and he were sixty feet below the surface of the harbor, standing inside a caisson, the metal walls of which held back the cold turbid water of New York Harbor. Air had replaced that water after the caisson had been attached to the sunken vessel and pumped dry. This caisson now allowed him, unhindered, to reach the hull of this long dead World War II German submarine.

Scott stood at the edge of the hole burned out of the steel hull and peered into the blackness below. What was within this silent cylinder of metal that men had been willing to kill to keep secret for eternity?

Now, only a few minutes more, and he and his companions would be the first living persons to tread the deck below in half a century.

Sixty feet above them it was a hot humid day, but the air rising from the submarine below was cold enough to make Scott shiver inside his protective rubber suit. Or was it the dread of what awaited them that caused him to shake? Poison gas? Booby traps? Or worse?

He stepped back for one more look at the sky above, at the blue dot that was their only portal to the living world, and climbed onto the top rung of the ladder leading down to the deck of the submarine below. It was a few minutes after eight.

Scott lowered himself through the jagged hole, a task made more difficult by the heavy air tank strapped to the back of his rubber suit. Good, he thought, the face mask won't be needed. The air below smelled fresh. Checking for bombs and booby traps was tough enough.

Scott switched on the portable lights and fed the power and telephone cables into the crew area just under the hole, while Morris verified that the putrid air had been thoroughly ventilated. The deck sloped to the starboard side, and everything loose had rolled or fallen that way. The coxswain turned the lights toward the pile of bodies—little more than dry patches of skin and bones—that they'd seen through the hot-tap hole.

"Christ," the coxswain said. "I've never seen anything like this."

Morris was about to answer when Scott joined them, a slowly clicking geiger counter in his left hand. Under Scott's left arm was a small orange metal box. Only Scott and Davidson knew its contents. Syringes filled with atropine.

"Don't touch anything!" Scott ordered. "Chief, let's start with a bomb check."

Morris nodded his agreement. He shined his powerful hand spotlight along the central passageway, changing the light's angle carefully to pick up the slight glint or shadow of a slender trip wire. He slowly crept on his knees along the sloping deck, examining each steel plate joint for any sign of ability to move, if only slightly, relative to its neighbor, the signature of a pressure plate. He stopped to mop the sweat from his brow. His training with the bomb squad would prove its value today.

He stopped just within the hatchway leading into the control compartment.

"Commander!" Morris shouted. "I've found a pressure plate!"

Scott move cautiously to his subordinate's side. Morris carefully slid a screwdriver between the plates. He gently began lifting the small rectangle. Sweat dripped from the chief's face as he fought to control the screwdriver. His steady hands belied the tension in his taut muscles. Scott could only watch and sweat.

Slowly, the plate moved upward, a millimeter at a time. Unexpectedly, the steel moved sideways with a jerk. A barely audible snap came from below the moving metal. Scott looked into the chief's eyes. Both men had the same unspoken question on their faces. Why are we still alive?

Morris raised the metal plate just a crack and, aided by his powerful spotlight, peered under the plate. He then lifted the plate and laid it back against the bulkhead. He mopped the sweat from his face with his glove.

"Whew," Morris said at last. "A double fuse type. I don't understand why the primary didn't fire. You can see the chemical back-up fuse is snapped."

"Why didn't the chemical fuse fire?" Scott asked as he watched Morris examining the small cylinder.

"Ha! See the hole, sir? This cylinder contained acid behind the glass diaphragm. When the edge of the plate slipped down, the cylinder bent, breaking the glass. That should have released the acid to attack the thin copper restraining wire. The acid is supposed to dissolve the copper releasing the hammer but—fortunately for us—no acid. The Germans must have been unable to obtain stainless steel, so they substituted ordinary steel and that corroded through losing the acid."

"All right," Scott responded, cutting off Morris's very technical explanation. "So why didn't the primary go off?"

"Same answer. See how the trigger lever is bent? They substituted this thin cut out for the normal forged piece and it didn't hold. Lucky us."

"Yeah, I can see that the explosive charge is big. Would've blown this sub apart."

Morris quickly removed the fuse devices, rendering the

bomb harmless. He then reset the deck plate, and the two men stood. They looked at each other for a moment. Morris shook his head in disbelief at their luck.

■ ■ ■ ■ ■

The preliminary bomb check completed, Scott called up through the hole into the caisson for Davidson and Sherry to climb down.

"Let's check all compartments for bodies," Scott said. "Try to get a count. Red—you, Sherry, and I will work our way toward the stern. Chief—check the forward torpedo compartment and have the coxswain start counting the bodies in here. Take photos first. Have him use a dust mask and gloves when he's moving the bodies. And you, too."

Scott turned as Davidson and Sherry dropped into the sub. "Welcome to World War II," he said. "Morris has cleared the central passageway of bombs. There may be other hidden explosives. Therefore, watch out for booby traps, whatever you do. Anything suspicious is to be brought to my attention immediately."

Everyone nodded that they understood.

The hatch to the torpedo room was open, and Morris went ahead to look for bodies. He pointed his hand-held lantern around the compartment. He didn't see any bodies, only torpedoes, all in their racks, their Nazi markings still visible.

He rejoined the coxswain in his task of separating and counting bodies. He would tell Scott what he'd found in the torpedo room as soon as the commander returned. Scott would not be surprised; he had predicted the weapons would be there.

■ ■ ■ ■ ■

Meanwhile, Scott clambered into the control compartment. It was difficult for the three of them to walk on the steeply sloping deck. They had to brace themselves off the starboard bulkheads. The others joined him as he was looking around with his flashlight.

The room was cold and gray. Intensely cold, Sherry thought, and intensely gray. Death seemed to extrude from every object. She shined her flashlight at the diving control panel. The instruments, still frozen in time with their settings of 1945, seemed to stare back. Overhead and all around, she could see the endless number of pipes, wires, conduits, and more—travel paths for all the contents and energies that pulsed though them—now quiet in their long sleep.

She came face to face with the periscope near the center of the compartment. Somehow it seemed to reach out for her, to transfix her gaze, for she knew that it was here that the captain of this killing machine had stood to plot the destruction of an unlucky surface vessel. She imagined she could hear the sound of a torpedo's high-speed propeller, the explosion of its warhead against the chosen target. The sounds of the crushing and tearing of the ship's metal, the screams of the terrified sailors as their ship slid beneath the surface. At last, the silence of their death.

She began to tremble. Got to snap out of this, she thought, not let my imagination run away with me. This place is spooky enough as it is.

"Are you okay?" Scott asked as he touched her hand.

"Oh...yes...I...sorry, I was just thinking," she responded returning to reality.

"The cold getting to you?"

"I guess a little." She started to move forward. "Oops," she said, bumping into a pair of pipes. "What are these pipes for?"

"That's the snorkel," Davidson answered.

"Why two pipes?"

"One pipe is to bring air inside the boat. The second pipe is to vent diesel exhaust."

"I don't see any bodies in here," Scott said. "Sherry, look here. I think it's the builder's plate." He shined his flashlight on a bronze plate bolted on the bulkhead.

"Yes, it is. UX-6000, Blohm und Voss, Wert Bremen, Stapellauf 24. Oktober 1944, in den Dienst gestallt am: 3. Januar 1945, Schiffseigner: Reichsluftwaffenkommando."

"Okay, smarty, so you can read German," Scott said patiently. "But how about in English?"

"Okay," she answered with a smile. "'UX-6000, Blohm and Voss.' That's the name of the company that built the sub. 'Bremen Shipyard, launched October twenty-fourth, nineteen forty-four, in service watch, January third, nineteen forty-five. Ship owner, Air Force Control,' or 'Command.' Glad you brought me along?"

Scott responded with a forced smile.

"What was that last part?" Davidson asked. "Did you say 'Air Force'?"

"Yes. 'Air Force Command,' or *Luftwaffe*."

"That can't be right! That's nuts! What would the German air force be doing with a goddamn submarine?"

"Mr. Davidson, I only read it. I didn't write it. And please, not so loud."

"Sorry, but this is *nuts*!"

"Look at the bright side, Red," Scott interjected. "This may explain why the German navy had no record of this boat."

"Christ," Davidson sputtered in total disbelief. "Pardon me while I go pound my skull on that bulkhead."

"Let's look in the officers' quarters and see if there are any bodies in there," Scott said as he led them into the next aft compartment toward the stern. The room had a strong odor of mildew from the rotting bed clothes. He pushed open a locker labeled *Kapitan*. He wrote into his notebook the name stenciled below the title: Dorfmann, Heinz R. Inside were several uniforms on hangers. He pulled one out. It was badly deteriorated from mildew, with pieces dropping off. He sneezed. "Damn allergy," he said. "Red, take a look at this! It's a Luftwaffe colonel's uniform! He must have been the boat's commander."

"This is beyond me!"

"Let's check the engine room next," Scott said. He led them through the hatch into the next compartment. Here they found two diesel engines, their throbbing power now silent for eternity, and two generators. Beyond them sat the electric drive motors.

Sherry couldn't help but notice how orderly the compartments had been. Even though trapped down here, she thought, the crew had kept the boat in perfect order. Commendable.

"Hmmm…Well, that leaves the battery compartments," Davidson said. "Let's go take a look." He led the way back to the control compartment. They descended the ladder to the level below and searched the officers' mess. It was also neat and orderly. Scott checked the rear battery compartment, while the others went into the two forward battery compartments. Not much to see, only the rows of large batteries all wired in unison. Again, no bodies. They met back in the officers' mess.

"The officers and crew were all in the crew's mess when they died," Davidson noted.

"Yeah," Scott mused. "But why?"

"Another odd thing. The forward battery compartment should be twice the size of the rear one, but it's not. They're about the same size. There's a bulkhead about half way back."

"Another mystery," Scott answered. "Let's go see how Morris is making out."

In the crew's quarters, Morris was just finishing counting the badly desiccated bodies. Little flesh remained on the skeletons and that was dried and hard. The chief removed his dust mask and wiped his forehead. Despite the cold, the temperature inside the confining suit was hot.

"There are no other bodies back there, Chief," Scott said. "They must all be in here."

"We've counted fifty-four total, sir," the chief answered.

"Fifty-four?" Davidson asked. "Should be fifty-seven."

"No, fifty-four."

"Maybe the Luftwaffe used a smaller crew," Scott suggested. "Or maybe they couldn't find enough men for a full crew so late in the war."

"Maybe."

"But here's a real find," the chief said. He handed Scott several deformed bullets. Small lead balls coated with copper.

Some of them had green paint marks from where they had bounced off the inside of the steel hull.

"What the hell?" Scott was astonished. "Where'd you find these?"

"All around. As we moved the bodies, they kept dropping out."

"Suicide pact," Davidson said. "When they realized that they weren't able to escape, they must have agreed to kill themselves."

"With GI ammo, sir?" the chief asked. "These bullets are standard forty-five-caliber ball ammo. We also found several of these—ejected forty-five-caliber cartridge cases. Used in Thompson submachine guns and in the army's version known as grease guns. As proof positive, this empty M3A1 magazine I found over there. All standard U.S. government issue. I think we've stumbled into a murder scene."

"What?" Scott exclaimed. "U.S. Government Issue?" The others stared in disbelief. "Murder?"

"Yes. If this had been a suicide pact, then at least one of the crew should have been holding a gun or we should have found a gun lying on the deck. But there's no gun anywhere."

"We didn't find any weapons anywhere else either," Davidson interjected. "Certainly no American weapons."

"When you suggested to Captain Peters that this might be one of the Navy's dirty little secrets," the chief continued, "I think you should have said 'one of the *Army*'s dirty little secrets,' Commander."

"My God," exclaimed Davidson, "a German sub run by the Luftwaffe with a crew killed by the U.S. Army. I thought I'd seen everything."

"There's more," the chief continued. He showed Scott a locked trapdoor set in the deck inside the crew's quarters.

"Red," Scott called, "any idea about this trapdoor?"

"No. There's not supposed to be a trapdoor in here."

"It's locked up like a floor safe, Commander," said Morris. "Can't open it."

"Hand me the telephone," Scott said. A moment later he reached J.D. on the dredge. "We've run into a locked door. Can you bring down the welders and tools? You'll have to burn through a deck trapdoor. Oh—and bring down a heavy bolt cutter. I want to open some lockers."

"While we're waiting, let's try to find the damn logbook," Davidson suggested.

"Yeah," Scott agreed. "Let's all search for any papers, letters, et cetera that might answer some questions." Scott quickly made assignments. Everyone headed off as directed.

About ten minutes later, J.D. climbed down the ladder, followed by Cracker.

"It's right in here," the chief said, pointing to the trapdoor. "Curly, hand down the torch." A loud pop and the odor of acetylene announced that the torch was burning.

In a few minutes Cracker had burned away the steel hinges and bolts. The acrid smell of hot metal quickly filled the sub.

"That should do it," J.D. said. "Curly, bring down the crowbars, and we'll lift this door out of the way."

With much banging and prying, the welders soon had the door removed. It fell against the deck with a loud thump. Just as Scott and the others returned Morris shined his light into the hole. A ladder led down to a small space containing machinery.

"Good," Scott said. "You've got it done. Okay, Red, you and Morris go down for a look. That area wasn't ventilated, so you'll need your air masks. J.D., you and Cracker come with me and bring your bolt cutters. I've got some padlocks to cut off."

Scott led the way back into the control compartment. Here they opened a large locker and found it filled with small arms and ammunition. They proceeded to the officers' quarters and cut open two more lockers. They were filled with uniforms and personal items, but no records. Only more of that horrid mildew that triggered Scott's allergy, causing him to sneeze.

When they returned to the crew's quarters, the two men were just climbing out of the compartment below. They removed their air masks and wiped their sweating foreheads.

"So what did you find, Red?" Scott asked.

"A big, empty freezer. Can't imagine what the goddamn

hell it's for!" Davidson said. "I'm going nuts over this damn submarine's being so different from every other Type 21."

They were interrupted by a call from the coxswain. "Chief, could you come to the galley for a minute? There's something in the ventilator duct."

The chief led the way back to the galley. "What are you talking about?" he asked.

"I think it's some kind of a package or something. Behind the grille. I almost missed it. Looked like part of the ductwork at first."

Scott shined his flashlight through the grille. There was something that looked like a wrapped book barely visible. Chief Morris wielded his screwdriver and had the grille off in a minute. He reached up inside the duct and retrieved the object. It was a notebook, all right, inside a thin sealed rubber bag.

"Commander, I believe we've found some written material after all," said the chief as he opened the black cover. The two men quickly scanned the first few pages. German.

"This is a job for our translator." Scott said as he handed the book to Sherry.

Everyone waited as Sherry looked at the first page under the poor light.

"Well," Davidson asked. "What is it?"

"It's a diary," Sherry answered, "written by a man named Heinz R. Dorfmann. It seems to be a record of his involvement in this mission. He writes, 'I believe I must protect myself from criticism should I fail in my mission.' He was apparently very worried about something that was going on. It's going to take some time to figure this out. The book is mildewed and some of the pages are crumbling."

"Okay, be careful not to damage it," Scott responded. "This could be the break we've been looking for."

"I understand, but this is going to be tough."

"Any idea who this author was?" Davidson asked. "Just a crewman, an officer, who?"

"I'm sorry. I just don't know yet."

"Wait a minute," Scott said. "That's the name I saw on the captain's locker."

"That's right," Davidson agreed. "I remember that, too."

"All right, let's finish up. Chief, we need an inventory of weapons and ammo. Also, take more photos. Red, give 'em a hand, will you? J.D., thanks again. You guys can go back up and, please—don't tell anyone about what you've seen. Sherry, let's see if we can figure out more of this diary."

Sherry continued studying the book. Finally she said: "In this part he writes about being told about the high command and Adolf Hitler's decision not to proceed with the development of the uranium bomb. It was expected to take two years and divert too much war production capacity, and, therefore, Reichsmarschall Hermann Göring needed another terror weapon at lower cost. Adolf Hitler would not agree to use chemical weapons."

"Whoa. He gassed millions in the death camps."

"Hitler had been injured by gas during WWI when he was a soldier. He feared that if Germany used poison gas against the Allies—they would retaliate in kind."

"That didn't save the Jews."

"The Jews couldn't fight back."

Their study of the diary was interrupted by the return of the others.

"So, have you two got this thing figured out yet?" Davidson asked.

"Not yet," Scott answered, "but I'm sure this book is damned important. May be the most important item we've come up with. Chief, are you finished?"

"Yes, Commander. We got everything listed and took lots of pictures."

"Okay. Let's head up to the dredge. Give J.D. a call, Chief, and have the chair dropped down. We'll leave the lights down here. We'll come back to remove all the ammo. Right now we need to brief the boss."

The depression that had been descending over Sherry's heart began to lift as the boatswain's chair rose upwards toward the rapidly expanding blue dot. The return to the living world from that awful place of death below exhilarated her. At last, emerging from the long pipe into the fresh air, she found a young crewman waiting to assist her across the gangplank to the relative security of the dredge.

The others came up over the next ten minutes, Chief Morris being the last.

"Have your men close up the pipe good and tight," Scott said to J.D. "I don't want anyone to be able to get in that boat without Coast Guard authorization."

"We got the blank flange all set. We'll set it on top of the flanged end of the pipe and then bolt it down using air-impact wrenches. It'll be one hell of a job to get it off without big equipment."

"Okay. Go ahead and then you can get back to dredging."

"J.D.," Sherry asked, "any news about Tim?"

"Yes. Tim's come to and they've upgraded his condition to serious. The doctors are hopeful that he's going to survive."

"That's wonderful! I've been hoping for some good news."

"That is good," Scott added. "I'm relieved to hear it. Sherry, could I see you in your office?" What he had to say was for her ears only.

U.S.C.G. Headquarters, Governors Island—1150 Hours

Scott and the others arrived back at the Coast Guard station headquarters just before noon. They reported to Captain Peters's office and found him with two civilians in business suits. FBI, I'll bet, Scott thought. The introductions to the two special agents proved him right. They then listened intently to Scott's report.

"Chief Morris, you said you believe that the perpetrators used U.S. Army weapons," Agent Carson said. "Could you be more specific about your conclusion?"

"Yes, sir. The weapon caliber was U.S. issue. Our submachine guns all used the forty-five. The German submachine guns used nine-millimeter ammo. The grease gun would be the logical choice since it's compact with a folding stock. The empty magazine I found was for the grease gun. The Thompson, on the other hand, is rigid and hard to conceal."

"So you believe that the Army is responsible for these murders?"

"Not necessarily. The grease gun was also issued to the other services, including the Navy and Marines. Also, with so many around, a lot of them found their way into the civilian sector. I couldn't possibly say with any certainty who fired the rounds."

"About this diary," Agent Carson said, changing the subject. "Where is it now? It should be placed in the hands of the FBI laboratory."

"Not until the Coast Guard completes its preliminary investigation," Peters responded. He turned to Scott. "Commander, did Miss Edwards indicate how long it will take for her to finish the translation?"

"She hopes to finish tomorrow, sir. With your permission, I'd like to request that the FBI assist us with obtaining information about Heinz Dorfmann, the author of the diary, and Hans Von Kruger, the scientist."

"Good idea. Could the Bureau give us a hand with that, Agent Carson?"

"Certainly. I'll have Washington contact the German Federal Police. I'm sure they'll give us anything they have."

"Thanks. I believe that's all we have for you gentlemen right now. Chief, see that the agents get copies of the photos and inventory sheets. Also, have Marge fax everything to the Secretary's office at the Department of Transportation. Commander Scott, you and Chief Morris are to report to the boathouse at 1300 hours and give the ATF agents whatever help you can with their study of the debris from Friday night's explosion. I'll be calling the Under Secretary after lunch. He hoped to talk with the White House this morning."

Aboard the dredge, *William P. McDonald*—1300 Hours

As Sherry worked on the diary translation, she thought about what Scott had said to her privately before he left the dredge. He thought the information in the diary was the key to this mystery. For that reason, he suspected that the people behind the bombing and the SS *Rangoon Expresser* sabotage would probably do anything to get their hands on it.

He warned her that violence obviously meant nothing to them. It might be safer for Sherry if he took the diary to some other translator.

She had argued that they couldn't know about the diary since it had been found only that morning.

But Scott was still afraid of a leak. "Someone is watching us," he had told her.

He had finally agreed to let her work on it until the next day, but he urged her to keep it out of sight and tell no one what she was doing.

She had felt so brave when she bid him good-bye, but now—as time passed and the full meaning of his words sank in—she began to worry. Well, there was nothing to do but go on. She needed to drink some water. Her mouth was very dry.

She continued her translation. Dorfmann wrote that a scientist, Hans Von Kruger, and his two assistants had been working on *Projekt Energetisch V.C.*, which she interpreted to be "Project Energetic V.C.," whatever that was. Von Kruger had said he was worried by a problem with the method of delivery. This revolved around the failure of Germany to develop a long-range, four-engine bomber. England had been ruled out as a possible target for Project Energetic V.C. due to nearly insurmountable air defense by 1943, which prevented any real chance of getting a bomber through. The V-1 flying bomb had been rejected as being too inaccurate. Being unable to find a good way to use Project Energetic V.C. against England, Luftwaffe Command needed to find a large American target with an unguarded water supply. Dorfmann continued that Von Kruger said that project Energetic V.C. could be upset by *Chlor*.

The target was finally selected when German agents in the U.S. reported that New York City did not chlorinate routinely. Sherry felt a chill when she realized the implications of this information.

U.S.C.G. Boathouse Number Six, Governors Island—1300 Hours

Scott and Chief Morris had finished lunch and reported to the boathouse as ordered. They found the two agents from the Bureau of Alcohol, Tobacco, and Firearms sifting through debris laid out on the floor.

"We're looking at all of the pieces of debris under the microscope to find unexploded bits of dynamite," said the lead agent. He spoke in a tone that reminded Scott of his junior high school science teacher. "When we find the particles that all explosives leave behind, we use spectrographic equipment to determine chemical composition. Since all chemicals contain impurities, we can get a molecular signature of the explosive. The information is then fed into our computer, which compares the impurity mix with spectrographic information from various dynamite manufacturers until a match is found."

"Sounds complicated." Scott was impressed, although he had heard some of the procedure before.

"Well, it is, but we're pretty sure we'll succeed, even with this portable equipment. If not, then we'll have to send the debris to the national lab for more precise analysis."

"Having any luck so far?" Scott asked before the agent could go off on a tangent.

"Yes. I'm sure that we'll be able to identify the manufacturer of the dynamite. We're having a bit more trouble getting the *lot* identified, but we'll get it. Knowing which company made the dynamite and which lot it is should allow us to follow the path it traveled."

"How can we help?"

"You need to concentrate on the details of the boat type.

Then we'll be able to find what it was and where it came from. My guess is that the motor boat that blew up was stolen by the bombers."

"I agree. Okay, Chief, let's go to work."

Morris went back to the main building file room. He searched out catalogs and materials lists of various motorboat makers throughout the world. He also picked up the latest NYPD Harbor Police list of all motorboats stolen along the East Coast in the past two months, since Scott already had his mind made up that the motorboat had been stolen.

Morris returned to the boathouse where he and Scott started trying to match the various pieces to materials used by manufacturers in constructing different motorboat models. This would be time-consuming—the number of manufacturers and boat models ran into the hundreds. The heavy August humidity in the un-air conditioned boathouse wasn't going to help.

"Stupid light," the chief muttered holding up a lamp fixture. "They must have used this lamp on half the motorboats built over the past decade." It would be necessary to match multiple pieces of debris to narrow the selection.

"You can ignore the small craft," Scott said as Morris threw the lamp in a pile. "Hampton estimates that the amount of dynamite used was eight to ten tons, so concentrate on large cabin cruisers."

Several young Coast Guardsmen entered the boathouse and stopped in front of the pile. They were the help Captain Peters had promised. Scott quickly put them to work.

After several hours, they had narrowed the possibilities to a single company and to several models of inboard-engine forty-eight to fifty-four foot cabin cruisers.

Checking the list of stolen motorboats, they homed in on a fifty-two-foot, twin-engine cabin cruiser stolen on Friday evening from a marina near Point Pleasant, New Jersey.

Scott called out toward the other end of the boathouse, "We've identified the boat."

"Good work, Commander. We've got the dynamite manufacturer on the phone. They're looking up the shipping information."

A few minutes later, the agent reported. "The company says that the lot we've identified was shipped on a truck that was hijacked from a truck stop on New Jersey Route 80 Thursday evening. It's time to bring in the Jersey State Police."

"Agreed," Scott commented. "We now know where the dynamite came from and where it went. Now we need to figure out *who* and *why*."

Aboard the dredge, *William P. McDonald*—1600 Hours

Sherry was making slow progress translating the diary. She was so involved that she failed to notice the time. She jolted when her relief engineer, George Wilson, suddenly opened the door and stepped into the office.

"Hey, Sherry," he said. "You working late?"

"Oh! I didn't realize the time."

"Well, you missed the boat, you know."

"Yeah, well it's okay. I'm going in with J.D. and the crew anyway."

"Say, what's that you're working on?" He had been looking at the diary open on the desk.

Sherry quickly closed the book. "George! Go up and check on the dredging progress report, will you?"

"Yeah, okay. Where'd you get that book? Looks like German. Off the sub?"

"George!" Sherry answered in an exasperated tone. "It's none of your business! Now go up and check on that damn report!" Why, Sherry wondered, is he always so nosy? He acts so sneaky.

George shrugged then left the office. Sherry realized that her outburst at him was really anger at herself for allowing the diary to be seen. I'll have to apologize to him tomorrow, she thought, quickly gathering her things together.

U.S.C.G. Headquarters, Governors Island—1630 Hours

Scott and Morris arrived back at Captain Peters's office to find him on the phone. He was just completing his call as they entered.

"That was the Under Secretary," Peters said. "The President has been informed about the boat. He'll make a determination after he gets a report from the NSC as to what agency will take charge. Until then, we're still it. Also, the German embassy has been informed. They're sending up their naval attaché for a look. A Commander Wolfgang Jurgens. He'll be here tomorrow—with a flock of questions, I'd imagine. We're to cooperate with him as fully as possible."

"I'm relieved to hear that the government has left us in charge, sir," Scott said. "I can report excellent progress on the investigation into the bombing. We've identified the type and manufacturer of the boat, and it fits with the harbor police list of stolen boats. The ATF agents have come up with the dynamite source. We've called in the Jersey State cops to run it down."

"Good. I've cleared the SS *Rangoon Expresser* to depart. I'm convinced the ship's captain and crew, other than the two Russians, were innocent of any wrongdoing.

"The press has been calling every few minutes. They're not buying our cover story. Look at the pile of phone slips from my secretary. She's hardly had time to go to the bathroom."

"Anything I can do, sir?"

"Not really. It's me they want. My secretary says she's heard every question imaginable, including if Hitler was living down there. Can you believe these nuts?"

"They can be off the wall, all right."

"Also, the dredge people called. They want to meet with me and the Port Authority managers tomorrow morning out on the dredge. I'd like you and Morris to be there, too."

Fort Lee, New Jersey—1830 Hours

Sherry drove through the late afternoon heat to her home in

Fort Lee. The words of Dorfmann kept passing through her mind. Scott could be right. The diary *was* the key to this whole mystery. She had brought the diary home with her so she could continue to translate that night.

Nausau County, Long Island—1840 Hours

Scott, too, had the diary on his mind as he drove toward Brenda's apartment. Sherry's translation could give him the clues he needed to solve this mystery. Whoever was behind the bombing on Friday night, as well as and the steamship sabotage, was in some way connected to the deaths of the submarine crew.

Somehow these criminals were getting information. An informant maybe? Who could it be? The news stories hadn't begun until after the Friday explosion, so that meant that these people must have gotten their information from someone in a position to know what was going on *before* the blast.

Maybe one of the crew of the *McDonald* had said something in a bar on shore. Maybe someone at the Port Authority. Who? And to whom? He also couldn't get out of his mind the possibility that the CIA or Pentagon might be behind this whole business. If so, they might go to any extreme to stop the investigation.

Sherry Edwards' Apartment, Fort Lee, New Jersey—1900 Hours

Her supper finished, Sherry sat down at her desk to work on the diary.

She turned the brittle pages carefully and read: The Luftwaffe Command was still searching for a means of delivery. Werner von Braun proposed to send a rocket across the Atlantic Ocean to America using a two-stage rocket guided by a human pilot. Such a rocket could drop bombs on New York City, but it was a one-way trip. The plan was approved, but

British bombers had destroyed the rocket factories, preventing completion.

Sherry was horrified to learn that Germany had possessed a long-range six-engine plane which Göring had sent toward the U.S. to see if it could reach New York City. The JU-390 plane did come to within twelve miles of New York City, but it couldn't carry enough cargo to be useful. This brought Göring's staff to the only remaining choice available: a submarine.

She read on: Göring did not trust the navy and feared that Admiral Karl Doenitz would take control of Project Energetic V.C. Therefore, the Luftwaffe Command decided to build its own U-boat and operate it without telling the navy, or even Hitler. That explained why Commander Davidson was so surprised when she read the builder's plate in the sub.

The text continued: The air force had loaded the underseas boat with 11,450 kilograms of V.C. on February 27, 1945. The crew was now aboard the boat, including S.S. Captain Kepler and sixteen S.S. soldiers to protect final delivery of V.C. She was shocked at this information that the submarine had a unit of the dreaded Nazi political police, the *Schutzstaffel*, on board.

The submarine had departed Bremerhaven on March 1, 1945. They had to take a circuitous route to avoid British and American naval patrols, so they had headed north into the North Sea and then south of Iceland.

The voyage had been slowed by the need to remain submerged to avoid detection. During the daylight, the submarine traveled at its maximum depth on electric batteries. The Type 21 submarine was capable of traveling at sixteen knots under water, but the UX-6000 had sacrificed batteries to provide space for the freezer. Therefore, they could run at only ten knots submerged.

Sherry stopped reading to rest her eyes. She leaned back and rested her neck on the chair back. Why this damn freezer? The question kept intruding into her mind.

She resumed: At night, they could rise to periscope depth and raise the snorkel. With fresh air coming in, the diesel engines could be started to produce electricity, and the boat could accelerate to maximum speed.

They were unable to travel on the surface for more than a few minutes at a time for fear of detection by enemy radar. Therefore, the entire trip would be made underwater, and they would be able to travel only two hundred fifty miles each day.

The voyage had been difficult. The only experienced submariners, recruited from the navy, were the chief engineer, the navigator, and one torpedo man. The rest were Luftwaffe men and S.S. troops.

Dorfmann wrote that conflict between himself and the navigator began very soon after departure. They disagreed about almost every decision; it was obvious that the navigator did not trust him. The navigator said he was nervous about the inexperience of the Luftwaffe men operating the controls. The Luftwaffe Command had promised a first-class crew but had not provided one, and this angered the navigator and the other navy men.

All the beds were taken because the boat was carrying its full complement of fifty-seven men.

Sherry stopped and read that part again. Chief Morris had counted only fifty-four bodies. Commander Davidson was right. There were three bodies missing! But where were they?

Dorfmann wrote that the boat had finally reached the lower New York Bay just below the Narrows on March 16, 1945. They had to wait for night before they could start up the channel. They used a special low-powered radio to contact German agents waiting in a small boat at the edge of the bay to meet them.

The agents had arranged a large boathouse so the submarine could be hidden while the cargo, Von Kruger, his two assistants, and the S.S. troops were off-loaded into waiting trucks to make the overland part of the trip. The boathouse would hide the submarine until the men could return after completing delivery of the V.C.

Damn, Sherry thought while tapping her fingers on her chin, what is this V.C. anyway? A chill had clamped itself around Sherry's middle as she considered the possibilities.

She read on: The trip up the channel was to be the most dangerous part of the voyage since the submarine had to travel

submerged at no more than thirty-five feet to stay above the
mud on the bottom. This would allow the submarine to remain
at periscope depth with the snorkel extended.

The agents had informed Göring's staff that there would be
only one section of the channel where the submarine could
be totally submerged—the section that had been deepened for
the mammoth battleship USS *Montana*. The agents planned to
meet the submarine at that part of the channel in a small civilian boat. But first, the submarine had to move up through the
Narrows to this deepened part of the channel. The submarine
would watch for a light signal from the agents indicating
whether it was safe to continue to the boathouse or if they
should submerge if a patrol boat suddenly appeared.

It was at this place that disaster occurred. Sherry read Dorfmann's words with mounting excitement. 'I had been looking
out through the periscope when I suddenly yelled, "Dive! Dive!
American navy destroyer! Danger! Danger!" I knew that
American destroyers had been equipped with new radar capable of detecting periscopes and snorkels even without using
their sonar.

'The inexperienced planesman overreacted and set for a
steep, fast dive. The submarine struck the bottom and plowed
into the mud. We were entombed.'

Dorfmann continued: 'Our repeated efforts to get the U-
boat free were unsuccessful. I tried to get out through the
escape hatch, but the outer hatch was blocked and unusable.
The use of the torpedo tubes to eject men outside the U-boat
was blocked by the mud.

'I was able to raise the periscope to the surface and see out.
I also could raise the snorkel and the radio antenna, which
allowed us to obtain air and to communicate.

'I informed the agents about the problem, but the agents
could not—or would not—help. I sent a coded message to Luftwaffe headquarters in Germany detailing the situation. A message came back that a rescue would be attempted, but it gave
no details.'

Dorfmann told of the endless wait for rescue. They had

food for a month. Air and electricity were available at night when they could raise the snorkel safely and run the engines. Fresh water could be distilled by electricity or with engine-exhaust coolers and vacuum compressors. By rationing the food and water, he believed they could last two months. Conditions were incredibly uncomfortable: the submarine was listing at eight degrees to starboard with the bow down, making walking along the deck difficult at best.

Sherry was surprised—the submarine was now listing at nearly thirty-two degrees to starboard with the bow nearly level. What had caused this shift?

Dorfmann's record continued: 'As April dragged on there was a near mutiny. The three *Kriegsmarine* men wanted to raise the periscope and the snorkel during daylight hours in hopes of attracting the attention of the American patrols. Even capture and internment in a prison camp would be better than dying inside the submarine. The Luftwaffe men were divided, with a dozen of them supporting the navigator. The attempted mutiny ended when S.S. Captain Kepler and his troops backed me. This support has not been without its price. Kepler has now taken charge of the U-boat's log book. I shall confine my private thoughts to this diary.

'20 April 1945. Radio has failed. I now have no way to know what is happening—with any rescue or with the war.

'22 April 1945. The chief engineer informed me that the coupling between the back-up engine and its generator has broken. Worse news is that the spare coupling has a manufacturing defect and cannot be used. This leaves us without any back-up generator should the regular engine fail. Electricity is vital if we are to survive.

'26 April 1945. The last can of sauerkraut served today. Sausage is gone. A few kilograms of flour remain. I instructed the cook to bake the last bread tomorrow.

'27 April 1945. The youngest torpedoman attempted suicide today. A knife was taken from him by his shipmates, who then brought him to me. He told me he wanted to die—he can't stand being trapped any longer. He broke down in tears.

I held this 16 year old boy as I would my own son as his tears ran down onto my shoulder. I could say little to encourage the boy. He is not alone.

'2 May 1945. Broke up three fist fights today. The crew is mentally exhausted and friction between the men is now epidemic. I argued with Kepler about appropriate punishment. I find myself less and less in command.

'4 May 1945. Food nearly gone. Cook reports only 200 kilograms of potatoes left and a few onions. He will make a thin soup and stretch it as long as possible. I have reduced the ration to only 400 calories per day per man. The grumbling of the crew depresses me severely.

'7 May 1945. I continue to look out through the periscope at night. Only a few hundred meters to port are the lights of what I believe is called Staten Island. It is maddening to realize that abundant food is being consumed by the American enemy in their comfortable homes. For this reason, I refuse to allow anyone else to look through the scope—it would only make their bellies hurt even more.

'8 May 1945. Something very strange has happened. I have again viewed the city lights. The city is brightly lighted instead of the subdued level I have seen before. I am certain I saw fireworks in the distance. I have related this to the navigator. He believes the war may have ended. Could the fireworks have been a celebration? I shall have all of the officers look through the periscope this next night. Then, we shall decide what action to take.

'9 May 1945. All of the officers, except S.S. Captain Kepler, believe that war must be over. I ordered the raising of the periscope during daylight to attract the American Navy. Kepler countermanded my order and has relieved me of command. He has placed S.S. guards in the control compartment. I suddenly find myself involved in planning a mutiny aboard my own U-boat. Kepler continues to defy all of my arguments.

'10 May 1945. The soup is nearly gone. Could only issue each man 100 milliliters of the precious liquid. Kepler seized most of the remaining soup and gave his S.S. troops double rations. The rest of the crew is grumbling loudly. Several fights broke out between the S.S. troops and the crew. I tried to stop the fighting, but Kepler ordered his men to beat the crewmen into submission. He now rules through brutality and fear.

'15 May 1945. The regular diesel developed a loud knocking sound last night. The chief engineer believes a piston may have broken. The back up engine-generator remains out of service. I find it difficult to think—I seem paralyzed with the fear of what will happen should the engine fail tonight. The engine is vital to provide our ventilation, fresh water, lights, and heat. Even more threatening is the thawing of our cargo when the battery charge drops too low to power the refrigeration plant.

'16 May 1945. The end for us may be only a few hours distant. The engine failed only minutes after tonight's start-up. The air inside the U-boat can not be ventilated and is becoming thick with carbon dioxide. I struggle to breathe. Kepler has ordered everyone to minimize movement to conserve oxygen. For once, we are in agreement. The batteries are still providing enough electricity to power a few lights. The engineers are trying to remove the good coupling from the failed engine and use it to replace the broken coupling on the back-up engine. I can hear the constant hammering. The crewmen are so weak from hunger that I fear several may not survive this added stress. Many of the young boys are crying.

'17 May 1945. Success. The back-up engine has begun operating. The sweet smell of oxygen rich air has brought back a little hope. Kepler continues to refuse my arguments to raise the periscope in daytime. He steadfastly maintains that his orders require completing our mission or death. I now truly am convinced that we will die at Kepler's hand unless I can find a way to retake command. Direct assault has no chance. Kepler has armed several of the S.S. men with pistols. The crewmen are weak from hunger and unable to do battle.

'20 May 1945. A small good fortune has occurred. The cook happened upon a three kilogram can of sliced peaches. It had fallen behind some trash. I have divided this find equally. Our first taste of food in five days. But, it will not sustain us.

'21 May 1045. Two of the crew, driven mad by hunger and depravation, attacked one of the S.S. men this morning. Kepler had them pistol whipped. I have done what little I can to bind their wounds, but am unable to treat the true problem. I talked with them about honor and duty. The words were hollow and they knew it. They looked at me, without expression, through their pain filled eyes. My heart aches for all of the crew and for my inability to help them.

'22 May 1945. The chief engineer has a plan to jam the snorkel next time it is raised. He will implement his idea tomorrow morning. It must work. I could hardly recognize myself in the mirror. I weighed 85 kilograms when we left Bremerhaven. The gaunt person looking back at me could weigh no more than 50 kilograms. I lay awake at night thinking of Pegnitz, my home. Will I ever see my hometown again with its beautiful forest, its blue sky above, its people? I fear not.

'23 May 1945. The effort to jam the snorkel worked, but Kepler's men beat the chief engineer until he restored power. The snorkel was lowered after only thirty minutes. Not long enough that the Americans would have seen it. I share the crew's despair. Most everyone is sick, weak, and severely depressed. Many of the crew don't even seem to recognize me. They lay where they can, staring without seeing. I spoke with Hans Von Kruger about the cargo. He said: *Unsere kleinen Freunde, die Vibrio Cholerae, benehmen sich anständig im gefrorenen Zustand.*

Sherry began her translation "Our little friends...will behave while frozen."

She stumbled over *Vibrio Cholerae*. She could not translate those words. Then it struck her.

Those two words were not German—they were Latin! They indicated *comma bacillus*. Asiatic Cholera!

Suddenly the reason for the mission of the UX-6000 flowed over her. Germ warfare! The submarine was to deliver to German agents in the U.S. a cargo of deadly bacillus to be poured into the water supply of New York City. Sherry felt her blood freeze. Her hand trembled.

Hundreds of thousands of people would have been stricken. Tens of thousands would have died. The city would have been paralyzed. The entire country would have been in an uproar. My God! she thought. It was monstrous! But what had happened to the cargo? Morris had found the freezer empty. She read on.

On May 25, Dorfmann wrote, the submariners heard the sounds of divers on the hull. Kepler looked out the periscope and saw a small civilian boat with no military or police markings anchored nearby. He was convinced that this must be the rescue that the Luftwaffe Command had promised. They could hear sounds of mud being scraped off to clear the top escape hatch.

Here the diary ended with one last entry. Dorfmann wrote that since he did not know if this was a rescue or capture, he would hide the diary where he was sure it would be undiscovered until he could determine whether he should retrieve it.

■ ■ ■ ■ ■

Sherry felt relief that her long job was over. The full story of the voyage of the U-boat was clear in her mind.

U.S.C.G. Headquarters, Governors Island — 0750 Hours

The sun was already high as Commander Scott arrived at the Coast Guard station that Tuesday morning. He met Chief Morris at the door. Entering the captain's office, they came face to face with a tall, slender man wearing the uniform and insignia of a full commander of the German Federal Navy. Captain Peters made the introductions.

"You are the two officers who visited this underseas boat in the harbor?" Commander Jurgens asked in perfect English.

"Yes, Commander," Scott answered. "Yesterday morning. The boat is definitely a World War Two Type 21. Most of the crew is still on board."

"It is the bodies of the crew that are of most interest to the German government. There are families in Germany who have waited many years for their loved ones to be found. We, too, have our MIA problem. The ambassador instructed me to inquire how soon the bodies will be turned over to Germany, Captain."

"I'm not certain, Commander," Peters replied. "I expect instructions from headquarters today."

"The ambassador wants to have a German mortuary team start the process of identification as soon as possible. You must realize the shock your report had on the government."

"I understand your need, Commander, and I assure you of my desire to cooperate. At the moment, the U-boat has been resealed and will remain so for the immediate future. Commander Scott will supply you with copies of the photos and inventory lists and answer any questions that he can.

"Now, we've been asked to meet with the owner of the dredge, Don Fredericks, and the Port Authority managers this morning. I invite you to join that meeting as an observer. Commander Scott, will you and Chief Morris escort Commander Jurgens to the motor launch? I've got to take an important call. I'll join you in a few minutes."

Aboard the dredge, *William P. McDonald*—0815 Hours

Sherry Edwards was also headed for the *McDonald* that morning. As the service boat pulled up to the rear of the dredge, she saw J.D. standing on the deck. "Morning, J.D.," she said as she climbed aboard. "You waiting for me?"

"Well, yes—and for Tiny. He and Bulldog ran over in the workboat to pick up Don Fredericks. He's Tiny's big boss, you know. He came up last night from Galveston. We're having a big shindig this morning. I understand your boss and the Coast Guard are all coming, too."

"I heard that Bob Scott was coming out," Sherry said, "but I didn't know about the others. Sounds like a good time to keep a low profile. Has there been any more news about Tim?"

"Yes, he's getting better. I know Don Fredericks and Tiny will want to meet with you after the meeting. Fredericks wants to thank you personally."

"Now you're making me nervous."

"You have nothing to worry about," J.D. replied with a smile. "You can do no wrong around here. Not after what you did for Tim."

"Thanks." Sherry returned his smile.

In her office, she fought the usual battle with that old balky copier to make several copies of her translation of the diary.

She stepped into her office bathroom to freshen up.

This office was normally used by the chief engineer,

Frenchy, as his cabin. "Ugh!" she had said when she came aboard the first day and saw the dirt and grime. She was no stranger to dirt, since she often changed the oil in her car's engine and did simple mechanical repairs, but this cabin was seriously filthy. The chief apologized rather sheepishly as he moved into the crew's quarters.

While the copy machine worked slowly, Sherry remembered how her knowledge of cars had made her somewhat of a legend in high school. The boys quickly learned not to pretend that their cars had broken down on a date. She would raise the hood and check out the engine herself before the boy could get his arm around her.

She had been labeled a tomboy by the boys in high school, but she didn't consider herself one, since she had many girlfriends and enjoyed new clothing and trying new makeup and hair styles. And, like them, she enjoyed dating, seldom missing an opportunity to attend parties, but she was not a total party animal. She also treasured her solitude.

She liked curling up at home with a favorite book, or spending countless hours studying her many maps, as she had an intense interest in geography. A good student, she was near the top of every class. She graduated with honors.

Sherry enjoyed mechanical things, and she found the chief's clock collection fascinating. She loved to run her fingers over the beautifully carved wooden figures on them. Geppetto would have been pleased. Sherry looked about her office. Small by landlubber standards, it was perfect for her needs. With curtains over the window, flowers on the desk, and light popular music on her radio, the space felt more her own. Almost feminine. She had a clean bathroom to prove it.

At nine o'clock, her boss, Leon Bishop, a slender man of about fifty, with gray sideburns below his dark brown hair, came into the room. He had been with the Port Authority for twenty-five years, and he was considered a fair and reasonable man to work for. Sherry felt very fortunate to have been assigned to his department. He was supportive of her work and had taken an active interest in the progress of her career.

The two of them went to the captain's office, where they found Harris, J.D., and an older man with gray hair whom Sherry guessed must be Don Fredericks. He was dressed in a dark blue suit with a white shirt and red string tie, and cowboy-style boots, for that native-Texas touch. She was surprised that he was so small—Captain Harris was in such awe of him. His face, partially hidden behind a large white mustache, seemed to be chiseled out of stone. Sherry wondered if he could smile. His lively light gray eyes busily sized people up as they entered the room.

Captain Harris made the introductions. Fredericks reached out to shake Leon's hand. He then turned to Sherry and reached out to take her hand. He looked into Sherry's eyes as he shook her hand, and with a broad smile he said, "I've really been looking forward to meeting you."

"Thank you, sir," Sherry answered, smiling back. Well, she thought, the face can smile after all.

"After we get this-here little confab over," Fredericks went on, "I'd like to talk to you, okay?"

They were interrupted as Commander Scott entered, followed by Peters and the others.

"I asked for this meeting," Fredericks began, "to clear the air about that sub back there and these incidents that happened. I had to come up here to see one of my young men in the hospital with a damn serious injury. I've also had to deal with expensive damage to this dredge. I'm not happy, and I want some answers."

"Mr. Fredericks," Captain Peters began, "the Coast Guard is conducting a full-scale investigation into what may be one of the most heinous crimes I have ever had the unpleasant experience of investigating. The incidents you ask about were criminal acts by persons not yet identified. I regret the injuries and damage your people and you have suffered, but these were surprise attacks. Both the Coast Guard and Harbor Police have increased protection of your people to the highest level. Can I guarantee that no further criminal acts will occur? No, I can't. But I assure you that we are making a maximum effort in your behalf."

"What can you tell me about these jaspers?" Fredericks asked frowning.

"Not much specifically, but we're getting more information. In time we'll nail them."

"Now Russell here," Fredericks said, avoiding the use of Harris's nickname of Tiny, "runs a crew that don't run from any straight-on fight. But this sneaking-around stuff is not the same."

"I understand," Peters responded. "We don't like it either, but now is not the time for men to run. My people and I aren't about to. I hope I can count on you and your people to stand with us."

"I like the way you talk, Peters. American Harbor and Dock Company has no cowards. We'll stand. You can count on that. I would appreciate it if you would tell us as much as you can."

"Yes, you need to know. Commander Scott will brief you now."

Scott itemized what had happened on the SS Rangoon Expresser and told Fredericks about the Friday night explosion, and what had been found aboard the submarine. When he came to the Dorfmann diary, he asked Sherry to tell what she had learned.

Sherry described the history of Project Energetic V.C. and how the Luftwaffe had considered various ways to deliver the project to some target, finally settling on the use of a submarine. She gave Dorfmann's description of the voyage to New York, and his explanation of how the submarine had become entombed in the mud.

Then she read Von Kruger's words about the true mission of the UX-6000.

For a moment, there was stunned silence. Don Fredericks dropped the half-full cup of coffee he had been holding, the spilled liquid pouring onto the floor. Scott glanced toward the old man, who didn't seem to have noticed the mess. His mouth hung partially open, his eyes riveted on Sherry Edwards.

Commander Jurgens spoke first. "This is incredible, Miss Edwards. I cannot believe that the *Kriegsmarine* would have ever agreed to such a mission. It is without honor! Are you certain of your translation?" His face was a mask of disbelief.

"Yes, Commander, within, I estimate, a ten percent margin of error. The choice of New York City was very calculated. The key was the lack of chlorination. Cholera is easily defeated by chlorine, but the Nazis knew that New York City did not regularly chlorinate its water.

"Also, they knew that the water system was only very lightly guarded. They had tools and explosives to break locks, gates—even walls if needed—to get the germs into the head end of one of the two water tunnels where gravity flow would have made injection very easy.

"Once injected into the water, the cholera bacteria would have thawed and become active. With so much pollution added in one shot, there's little doubt that the infection would have spread throughout the water system within a few hours."

She looked down at the transcription and cleared her throat. The room was silent. She continued.

"They selected the winter for several reasons. First, it would give them the maximum amount of darkness to get the submarine into the boathouse where it could be hidden while it was being unloaded. Second, the cold weather slowed the thawing of the bacteria so it would stay frozen long enough to reach the selected water tunnel. Third, they also needed to minimize the dilution factor. They knew that the water consumption by the city residents would be at its lowest in the winter."

Sherry looked at each man in turn as she recited the ramifications of this contamination.

"I called a friend of my cousin who works in Atlanta at the Center for Disease Control and posed this historically archaic scenario, hypothetically, of course."

"Of course," Don Fredericks said. "Good thinking."

"Thank you, sir. Anyways, he said that the effects of cholera are usually felt in about three days, when the body starts purging itself frantically. Most people would die within twenty-four hours of the onset of the disease. So many people would be infected so fast that the hospitals would be overwhelmed before the authorities even realized what had happened.

"Cholera can be treated, but with so much happening at once, tens of thousands would have died before the medical community could begin the battle to stop it. His best guess — half a million, perhaps a million people would have been infected, and between a hundred thousand and two hundred thousand would have died."

For a moment, the room was silent. The men stared at Sherry in disbelief. Then everyone began to talk at once.

After a few minutes, Captain Peters regained control of the meeting. "Gentlemen, please. Miss Edwards, did Dorfmann explain how this decision was reached?"

"Yes. He was convinced that this entire plan revolved around Göring's falling out with Hitler during the last years of the war. Göring knew he needed to do something big to regain Hitler's favor. Von Kruger and his assistants were hired by the Luftwaffe at Göring's order to come up with a weapon. A weapon of mass destruction powerful enough to inflict enough damage on an American target so that President Roosevelt would back away from his unconditional-surrender position and negotiate peace terms.

"Without the nuclear bomb and with Hitler's absolute refusal to authorize the use of poison gas, a biological weapon became his best option. Had the mission succeeded, New York City would have been in chaos and the nation in shock. I believe the President would have been under great pressure to come to terms with Hitler. Much like the Japanese did with us after we dropped the bomb."

Scott could see that Don Fredericks, fresh cup of coffee in hand, was beginning to accept the truth of Sherry's explanation. He and Morris already had.

"May I make a point, Captain?" Scott asked, changing the subject. "We found the boat at a thirty-two-degree list to starboard and too deep for either the periscope or the snorkel to reach the surface, not the eight-degree list Dorfmann mentioned or the shallower depth."

"I can explain that change, Captain," Chief Morris interjected. "When the channel was deepened by the Corps of Engineers for the USS *Montana* project, it was done with stepped sides. The sub landed on the higher step in shallow enough water to have been at periscope depth. But in August, 1945, the corps began to refill that part of the channel. The dredged mud piled up behind the boat and finally pushed it off the step into the present position."

Captain Peters said, "It makes sense to me."

Scott nodded in agreement. "I must raise another question, sir," he said. "Where are the cargo and the three missing crewmen?"

"I have something to report later, but first I'd like Miss Edwards to tell us more about the nature of the cargo."

Scott suspected that the captain was stalling.

"The cargo was some of the most concentrated, toxic, polluted water on earth. It had been frozen into ice. About three thousand gallons. Probably in blocks of perhaps forty to fifty pounds each, wrapped in flexible waterproof containers so that it could be easily and safely handled."

"Thank you," Peters interrupted. "Now I'll tell you my news. I received a phone call just before we left the office from Special Agent Carson of the FBI. He has received word from the Ludwigshafen police that Von Kruger died in Germany. His body was found floating in the Rhine River just north of the Ludwigshafen-Mannheim Bridge on June 26, 1945. He had been murdered."

"Christ!" Fredericks cried out. "This damn-fool story gets more weird by the minute. Miss Edwards just said he was on board the submarine!"

"Obviously he was taken from the submarine alive on May twenty-fifth by whoever removed the cargo and murdered the crew," Scott reasoned. "Captain, how was Von Kruger killed? Forty-five-caliber ball ammunition, I'll bet."

"Right. Remember that Germany was occupied by Allied forces at that time. I think we can safely assume that we know who the missing crewmen were: Von Kruger and his two assistants. The murderers must have needed them to handle the cargo."

"Just how did these murderers get on the sub and over-power the crew," Don Fredericks asked. "If there were sixteen S.S. soldiers on board, they should have been able to defend the crew."

"Captain," Scott interrupted again. He was pleased to finally have his chance to show that he had already figured the answer to this mystery. "Chief Morris and I have speculated on that. I agree that there were enough soldiers and weapons on board the boat to put up a very strong defense, but these men were also very hungry. The way to take the crew was very simple: You appear to be the rescue team that the Luftwaffe Command had promised. You enter the sub carrying not weapons but containers of food. A few reassuring words of German and that entire crew would have believed that you were there to save them. They would have gathered in the crew's mess to eat.

"The invaders probably found out who Von Kruger and his two assistants were while everyone else was eating and got them to one side. Then they whipped out a couple of hidden grease guns, and in seconds it was over. After that, they cleaned out the freezer, took Von Kruger and his assistants to show them how to handle the cargo, and they disappeared."

"Disappeared where?" J.D. asked. "And why?"

Scott smiled. He was really hitting his stride as the "great detective."

"Chief Morris and I have developed five possible scenar-ios. The first is that a cover-up by the surviving Nazis was car-ried out for the purpose of hiding the evidence. They would have crossed the Atlantic, found the sub, removed the cargo, and shot the crewmen to silence them. This scenario is almost impossible because transportation out of Germany for Ger-man nationals was carefully controlled by the Allies. For them to have arrived in New York with weapons is a very long shot. Maybe they could have bribed some Allied officers to aid them, but I don't buy it.

"The second scenario is that the sub was discovered by some U.S. military people who didn't know that the war had ended and therefore shot the crew thinking they were defending our country. But when Truman announced V-E day on May seventh, the entire country went wild. No U.S. troops could have been ignorant of the end of the war unless they'd been on another planet. It's too farfetched. Any U.S. troops would've surely reported the find.

"The third scenario is that one of the Allied governments found out about the sub and its cargo and decided to go after it for its own germ-warfare research. That government would have sent clandestine forces to murder the crew and steal the cargo for return to the nation involved. This scenario is a strong possibility, but it has a weakness. When the war ended, Göring and most of the surviving Luftwaffe senior officers fled from the Russians and were captured by the U.S. Army. I'm not convinced that any Nazi with the necessary information fell into Russian, British, or French hands.

"The fourth scenario is that some Nazi survivors wanted to use the cargo to continue the fight against the Allies. But they would have run up against the same transportation problems described for the first scenario. In addition, they would have had to find a way to transport the frozen cargo back to Germany, and all transportation to Germany was under the direct control of Allied forces.

"This scenario has two other serious flaws: First, why would such a Nazi force shoot its own crewmen? If their purpose was to continue the war, they needed additional fighters. The second flaw is that if you're still carrying on the war, then why not finish the original mission and attack New York City with the cholera? It makes no sense to do anything else.

"Therefore, Morris and I have concluded that none of these first four scenarios hold up logically. We have settled on the fifth scenario. This whole business revolves around money. This was a crime of profit. Those invaders needed to get that cargo somewhere in order to trade it for money. If we can figure out who would want such a deadly cargo, then I think we'll know who these killers were."

Scott sat back, arms folded, a look of satisfaction on his face.

"It would have to be some government, wouldn't it?" J.D.

asked. "Would any private party be interested? What about some terrorist group?"

"The damn Russians!" Fredericks exclaimed.

"Maybe, but I don't know for sure," Scott responded. "The only thing that makes any sense — since no outbreak on this magnitude has occurred anywhere these past fifty years — would be germ warfare studies or development. Remember that the men who sabotaged the steamship were both former Soviet navy and KGB members. There is a very strong possibility that the KGB or its predecessor, the NKVD, may have been the customer and is now trying to stop our investigation in order to continue the cover-up. I could even believe that our own government, through the OSS, the predecessor of the CIA, could be involved. The OSS may have chosen to kill the German crew rather than capture them in order to keep their own involvement a secret.

"As to the question about terrorist groups, I don't believe the information about the sub would have been likely to have reached such people. The time frame is too short for them to have learned about the weapon and organized its capture."

"Well, it's interesting to speculate," Peters broke in, "but this part of the investigation is beyond Coast Guard jurisdiction. The final phase of our work will be the ultimate disposition of the submarine and its contents."

"If I might comment at this time, Captain," Jurgens spoke up. "This entire story is incredible. The German government of today knows nothing of these alleged events. If it happened as Miss Edwards has told it, then there are many questions to be answered. The German ambassador is waiting for my report, and I know he has already made an appointment to see your President tomorrow. I must be able to tell him when we might gain access to the U-boat."

"Yes, of course, Commander. Leon and I discussed setting up a barge alongside the caisson pipe with a small crane to remove the cover and lower people and tools into the sub for the work that must be done. Leon, are the arrangements going forward?"

"Yes, Captain," Bishop answered. "I've got a crew work-

ing now to load the barge with a crane, compressor, generator, and office trailer with portable toilet facilities. They should
have it all tied down by noon so that everything can be picked
up this afternoon. Once the workboat brings the barge over to
the caisson pipe, the welders will secure it. I also plan to put
Harbor Police on board around the clock to control who gets on
the barge or down to the sub."

"Excellent. Mr. Fredericks, are your men ready to do their
part?"

"Yes. Russell and J.D. are all set."

"Okay then, I guess that's it. Unless there is something else,
I think we're wrapped up."

As the meeting broke up, Commander Jurgens stepped to
Sherry's side. "*Fraulein Edwards*," he said, "*es ist offensichtlich,
dass Ihnen die deutsche Sprache geläufig ist. Waren Sie in Deutschland?*"

"*Danke, Herr Oberbefehlshaber,*" Sherry answered. "*Ich war
in Frankfurt.*"

"Please forgive me. I needed to test your ability with German."

"That's okay, Commander," Sherry answered with a smile.

"You did a fantastic job," Scott said to Sherry. "We're about
to shove off, so I'll talk with you later." She responded with a
broad smile.

Leon came up to thank Sherry. "Good job. You made us
both look good."

"Thanks, boss."

He pulled her aside where they could speak privately.

"J.D. tells me that Don Fredericks has asked to see you
alone after we go. A little advice: He's one of the richest and
most politically powerful men in the entire country. He speaks
for most of the big money in the oil business. He can pick up
the telephone and talk to any politician in the country—
including the President. But as long as I have known him, he
has always seemed a fair man. A word from him to the Governor can make or break a career. My best advice: Be polite but
don't say anything you don't really mean. He respects people
who stand on their own feet."

"Thanks for the advice."

"Sherry," Captain Harris said, beckoning, "would you sit here." He motioned to a chair beside his desk. "Mr. Fredericks," he continued. "We'll be down in the galley, if that's okay."

"Sure thing, Russell. Thanks for staying, young lady. I've really been looking forward to us getting to know each other."

"Me too, Mr. Fredericks."

"Let's get rid of that. You just call me Don."

"I'll try, but I'm not sure if I'll be comfortable with that."

"Oh, now—don't let all that big-shot stuff impress you. I'm impressed by you, young lady. May I call you Sherry? You're smart, beautiful, and a right capable woman. In all my years, I haven't seen many ol' boys or gals your equal."

"Thank you, Don." Sounds like he's after something, she thought, but nice compliment.

"There, see, that wasn't so hard, was it? I want to thank you for helping Tim. You sure enough saved his life."

"I would have done that for anyone."

"Yes, I do believe you would, but you done helped a young man who means one awful lot to me. You see, I married late and me and my wife never had any children of our own. So we, well, sort of adopted Russell and his sister. Russell never did marry, but his sister did, and I've always looked on Tim as a kind of grandson. That boy means more to me than just about anything. So, I owe you an awful lot."

"You don't owe me anything."

"Russell done said you'd say that. He's quite taken with you, you know."

"I'm surprised he would say that about me. He never seemed to like me."

Don laughed. "That Russell! He's just a big pussycat. He gets so tongue-tied around a pretty girl. I swear, that's why he never got married. Every time he sees a pretty girl, he gets all damn-fool flustered and falls over his own dang tongue. What a character! He just *seems* not to like you 'cause he can't talk to a pretty girl. Believe me, you just give him a big smile, and you'll have him quaking in his boots."

"I find that a bit hard to believe." Sherry shook her head and laughed.

"It's true—believe me. But, really, I'd still like to do something for you."

"Thanks, but I can't accept any gift from a contractor. It would be a violation of Port Authority policy."

"Well now, you don't need to worry about your job. There's a job waiting for you in Galveston anytime you want, and at double your present salary. You'll love Galveston, I know you will."

"I don't know what to say." Sherry began to shift in her chair and pulled at her pant leg. She then poked at her hair with her right hand as her left hand squeezed the arm rest.

"'Yes' would be nice. You'd be a great addition to AH and D. We can always use a good engineer. I know you'd find the work rewarding."

"I'm really pretty happy at the Port Authority, and my family is here. Would you let me think about it?"

"Sure. Well, why don't we go on down and see if Cookie has our grub ready. Here's my card. I've written down the number to the private line in my office. You ever need anything, you call, promise?"

"Sure, and thanks," Sherry answered as she accepted the card with a smile. Might be useful, she thought. She put his information in her purse. He offered his arm, but she politely refused.

As they walked along the catwalk, Don explained to Sherry. "Ol' Charlie, J.D., and me are the only ones left from the original dredge crew. We helped Cap'n Billy McDonald slap her together back in the ol' days."

"That makes me wonder why J.D. isn't the captain."

"Well now, I do dearly love ol' J.D.—like a brother. But sometimes he doesn't like to push men as hard as needed. That stuff I told you about Russell being a pussycat only applies to pretty girls like you. A man—now that's different. If some man gets out of line, Russell will pound him right through that floor plate without so much as a howdy-do. It takes a strong will to control a bunch of rowdies like you find on a construction crew like this one. When Russell gives an order, it's assholes-and-elbows time, and you can bet a million on that."

"*That* part I've seen," Sherry said with a chuckle.

"I hear ya," Fredericks answered with a laugh. "Oh, I almost forgot. I'd sure appreciate if you would join me and Tim's parents for supper tonight. Tim's mother wants to thank you personally. How about seven thirty at that fancy hotel J.D. put us in. Don't that beat all!" he laughed. "I done forgotten the name of the damn place."

"I'd be happy to meet Tim's mom and dad."

Aboard U.S.C.G. Motor Launch—1610 Hours

U.S.C.G. Captain Peters circled the harbor in the Coast Guard motor launch, conducting a guided tour for Commander Jurgens. Jurgens could see that Peters was very proud of the job his command was doing in operating one of the world's busiest harbors. They arrived back at Governors Island late in the afternoon.

"I have certainly enjoyed this tour, Captain," Commander Jurgens said as he disembarked, "and I appreciate your cooperation in sharing the information on the U-boat. I shall inform our ambassador of your courtesy."

"I'm to call the Under Secretary at 1630 hours. I'll ask permission to turn the bodies over to the ambassador for his disposition. I'm sure he'll agree."

U.S.C.G. Headquarters, Governors Island—1800 Hours

It was still hot as Captain Peters left his office. He was not in a good frame of mind. "Damn stupid decision!" he muttered.

The orders from Washington were unfavorable. He hated the thought of breaking the bad news to Scott and Chief Morris. They were his best friends, always ready to support him. But this news would be tough to swallow for sure.

Ron Peters had joined the Coast Guard almost thirty years ago after graduating from junior college in his home state of Ohio. He and Scott had first served together on the old cutter *Nelson*. It was Peters's first command as a skipper; Scott had been third officer. He was a fresh young ensign, and his easy manner made him a pleasure to work with.

Thankfully, Chief Morris was an experienced petty officer, and he had helped both the new skipper and the young ensign to operate the cutter successfully. The three of them developed a strong friendship that Ron Peters still treasured.

He had lost contact with Scott and Morris for a time when he was assigned to Chesapeake Bay. It was there that he met and married his wife some fifteen years ago. She and the two wonderful sons she had given him were the center of his life. Like most career military officers, he found that balancing the demands of the service with the demands of fatherhood was never easy. Based on the pleasant home life he and his family enjoyed, he felt he must have succeeded.

He had been named Captain of the Port of New York some eight years ago and had managed to get both Morris and Scott assigned to his command. Peters knew that Scott was having serious family difficulties, and he was only a little surprised when Chief Morris told him about Scott's moving in with his girlfriend. Such personal difficulties had a way of derailing an officer's career, and he told Scott that the promotion review board did not look fondly on officers who could not control their family situations—no matter who was at fault.

Morris had not married, and both Peters and Scott kidded him about it from time to time. He always answered that he had just never found the right girl for an "old coastie." But Peters had noticed that the chief and his secretary seemed a bit more than just friendly coworkers, and he began to wonder if maybe the old bachelor was about to fall. Even Scott had commented that something seemed to be going on. They joked with the chief a little, but he steadfastly denied everything.

Peters stopped on the shore and looked west toward Liberty Island. He enjoyed the view of the great statue as the sun moved lower in the evening sky.

He enjoyed playing ball with his two sons and could still hit a baseball over a hundred yards—much to the envy of the older boy. He regretted that the pressures of command were giving him less and less time with his family. Well, he thought, I must be getting home. The younger son would need help with his algebra again. I'll let Scott and Chief Morris enjoy their evening before I give them the bad news.

Aboard the dredge, *William P. McDonald*—1930 Hours

Cracker was not happy. Neither was his friend Curly. They had planned to go to Newark with some other crewmen after work. But Frenchy told them that they would have to stay on board for some emergency work. Their comments were not pleasant to hear, but the chief engineer didn't care. The number four engine was down with a cracked piston, and the rear engine mount on number five was broken.

The two welders, dragging the welding gear, found him and Bear unscrewing the bolts holding the cylinder head on the top of the number four engine. Frenchy stopped and stepped down to show them the work to be done.

"Over here," the chief engineer said as he directed them to the rear of number five. The heavy metal cover normally over the flywheel was already removed, exposing the spinning flywheel and the coupling between the engine and the generator. He pointed toward a small space between the flywheel and the floor plates where a man could crawl in under the engine. "You gonna have to hang through that hole to reach that mount."

"So shut it down and I'll get started," Cracker responded.

"No way. You gonna have to do it hot."

"Say what? Are you fucking nuts! Shut it the hell down!"

"No way. With number four down, can't maintain full production with only four engines running. Tiny ain't going to cut back with us behind schedule!"

"You're crazy, Frenchy! How am I going to work down

there with that flywheel rotating inches over my head? Those teeth will rip my ass to pieces if I get too close!"

"Then don't get too close, dummy!"

"Hey, why me, dammit?"

"Because you're the lead ironworker! There's the damn iron, so get your ass in there and lead it, fuckhead!"

"How am I going to weld that mount with it vibrating all over the goddamn place!"

"Clamp it, Cracker, clamp it! Come on Bear, let's go find that spare piston!"

The two welders stared after them. Cracker muttered, "That stupid, web-footed jerk! If he unzipped his pants, his goddamn brain's would fall out!"

"Well, let's get 'er done," Curly responded obviously very happy that he wasn't going in that miserable hole.

"That's damn easy for you to say. You ain't the one who's putting his ass next to that fuckin' wheel!"

"I'll watch your back and make sure you don't get too close."

"Oh, great! Thanks a lot!"

With a great deal of difficulty, Cracker worked his way down the hole. Curly handed him the heavy C-clamps to hold the engine mount in place so it could be welded. He then carefully fed the welding leads in, staying clear of the big, rotating flywheel. A bright arcing light showed that Cracker had started the welding. Curly looked up and saw Bear, sweat pouring down his face in the heat, coming back up the center aisle pushing a hand truck carrying the new 18-inch diameter piston for number four engine.

"Hey, Curly," Bear said, "how's our ol' buddy doing?"

"Hey, Cracker," Curly yelled down the hole, "Bear wants to know how you're doing."

"Tell that dickhead I'm having a goddamn fuckin' blast! Me and Sherry are kissing, and she's all over me. Now, now Sherry, you're gonna have to wait till later. Can't you see I'm too busy to screw you now, baby?"

"Man, oh man," Bear said with a laugh, "I believe our good buddy is having a hell of a good time in there."

"Up yours, Bear!" Cracker shouted back, as Bear and Curly laughed at his discomfort.

■ ■ ■ ■ ■

The explosion near the Brooklyn side of the harbor happened just before nine p.m. Jet fuel burns fiercely, and here was an entire bargeful on fire, lighting the harbor from Governors Island to the Narrows. Billy McDonald, the grandson of the man who had built the dredge, and Cookie ran to the window on the second level just off the galley to watch the spectacle.

The patrol boats assigned to guard the submarine and dredge were now needed at the site of the fire. No one on the dredge had noticed that they were suddenly without any police protection.

But this had been anticipated—planned, in fact—by the five men on the black-painted speedboat that was very quietly approaching the *McDonald*. To maintain the element of surprise, they shut off the speedboat's engine before reaching the side of the dredge facing away from the fire and drifted the last hundred yards. They slipped aboard unseen, and J.D., his attention on watching the fire, was completely unaware of their presence until he felt the hard, cold muzzle of an automatic pistol in his back.

"What the hell?" J.D. said.

"Shut your mouth if you want to live!" the gunman said quietly in a thick Slavic accent. "Now turn round slowly."

"What do you want?" J.D. asked as he faced the gunmen. He looked quickly for a way to escape, but saw none.

"You show us Sherry Edwards' office and open door. Do it and you might not die."

J.D. saw that he was facing five heavily armed men all wearing black clothes and black ski masks. He had to believe they were professional killers. He had no choice but to do as ordered. He led them down the rear passageway to Sherry's office and unlocked the door. He watched as the gunmen entered the office and began to tear it apart. Can't do a damn thing, J.D. thought, with a gun in my face.

"What are you looking for?" J.D. asked.

"Keep quiet, American. And you know what's good for you, you do it!" The muzzle of the pistol in his hand swung hard.

J.D. moaned in pain, his cheek torn open by the blow. He saw his own blood dripping on the deck.

■ ■ ■ ■ ■

Billy happened to glance down from watching the fire and saw the gunmen take J.D. prisoner. For a moment, he couldn't get his legs to move. But, then they did—fast! He hurried up the stairs to Captain Harris's cabin, and banged on the door until he heard the dredge captain yell, "Come in—Billy, what the hell's the matter?"

A few words from the young deckhand was enough.

Harris quickly understood. "Damn! We've been invaded. Go get the boys. Get 'em up here—fast! Run, dammit!" His face hardened and the veins on his neck started to pulse.

The dredge captain grabbed his keys and opened the gun cabinet in his office.

When Billy and the other men arrived a few minutes later, Harris ordered, "Everybody grab your gun and ammo!" He quickly explained the situation. "They sound like real bad asses to me. I ain't giving them a chance—we're going to bushwhack the bastards. Forget the lousy cops—there's no time. Load up with heavy shot! We're not shooting rabbits, by God!"

"Here, Bear," Harris said as he handed him Frenchy's old .41 caliber six-shot revolver and a box of ammo. "Take this to Frenchy! You two take cover in the engine room so you can watch the rear door. If those men come through that door, y'all blast 'em! All right, the rest of you follow me!"

The dredge captain led them down the right-side deck, jumping over piles of supplies, toward the rear of the dredge, where they could take cover behind a large reel of steel cable. Sweating and breathing hard from exertion and tension, they tried to calm down. The dredge captain could see down through the rear passageway to Sherry's office. J.D. was leaning against the bulkhead obviously in pain, blood dripping from his torn cheek. One gunman was barely visible beyond him.

Harris instructed the others in a quiet voice. "Listen: get set, and when I yell 'now,' everybody comes up together and fires at once. I'll take the first one. Slim, you hit the second. Cracker, take out number three. Curly, you get number four, and Billy, take the last guy. They have to come this way to get back to their boat. Now watch out for J.D. Aim, dammit, but don't hesitate!"

They didn't have long to wait. The gunmen, having finished their search, started up the passageway. Each was carrying a submachine gun. J.D. was being pushed along in front by the first gunman, who was pressing the muzzle of his pistol into J.D.'s back.

The crewmen quietly pulled the hammers on their guns back, sweat forming on their faces.

Harris waited until J.D. was right in front of him and just beyond the line of fire. The gunmen were only a few feet away.

He took a breath.

"NOW!"

The crew rose as one. J.D.'s eyes flashed as he recognized what was happening. He threw himself face down as his crew's guns went off with a shattering roar nearly simultaneously— an instant before the gunmen could bring up their weapons. The look of grim determination on the dredgemen's faces mirrored their deadly work.

The high velocity metal bullet and shotgun pellets entered the chests of the first three gunmen with ejection of blood and flesh from the massive wounds. The gunmen's eyes went wide open and wild from the devastating pain as the metal shredded their lungs, hearts and blood vessels. Their mouths dropped open as if to speak, but no words came—only screams. Collapse to the deck of the three bodies came a few seconds later. They would move no more.

Curly's single load of lead pellets struck the fourth gunman in the left shoulder, spinning him around and into the bulkhead. Billy's target was the farthest away and he lacked a clear line of fire. His shotgun pellets barely struck the last gunman, tearing the left side of his face open.

It was not enough. The gunman's finger completed its pull of the trigger and his automatic nine-millimeter submachine gun returned a rapid chattering burst of a dozen rounds. Most of the soft lead bullets struck the steel cable, but two of them found their targets. Billy went down with a scream of pain. Curly fell beside him.

Down the passageway, J.D. now lay against the bulkhead, still bleeding from his torn cheek.

With the determination learned from years of gunfights, Harris fired a second bullet toward the fourth and fifth gunmen as they dived through the rear door into the engine room. Blood dripped from his lip. He fought the pain and didn't show any notice.

Cracker frantically pumped a new shell into his twelve-gauge and fired at the fleeing gunmen.

Both missed. Both cursed. The sound of Bear's forty-five told the dredge captain that the two gunmen were now in the engine room.

"Damn!" Harris said, surveying the situation. "Billy, where'd he hit you?"

"My left shoulder," Billy responded. "I think it's broken."

"Okay, kid. Rest easy while I check Curly."

"Just nicked my head," Curly said. "Sure messed up my hair."

"Yeah, looks like he just grazed you." Harris hastily checked the wound. "It's gonna bleed for a while. Lucky he hit your hard head. Otherwise he might have hurt you."

"Oh, yeah, thanks a bunch."

"J.D., you okay?" Harris called.

"Just my cheek. No bullet hits." He rose and stumbled toward them.

"All right. Can you help Billy? He's got the worst of it."

"Yeah, I think so. Let me get the spare first aid kit from the storeroom."

The dredge captain picked up Billy's shotgun and several spare shells.

"Look, kid, I'm gonna leave you my forty-four. You can handle that with your one good hand, okay?"

"Yeah, okay," Billy responded grimacing from obvious pain.

"All right. J.D., I'm gonna leave you boys here to guard the engine-room back door. Pick up one of those automatics, and if those bastards come back out that door, y'all blast 'em, you hear! Cracker, Slim, you're with me! We've got to go help Bear and Frenchy!"

At a dead run, they hurried up the right side of the dredge until they reached the engine-room side door right by engine number one. They found Frenchy crouched beside the front of the engine. The dredge captain could see Bear across the center aisle behind generator number two. They crept up beside Frenchy.

"Where are they?" Harris asked. He had to yell to be heard over the roar of the engines.

"They're over back of engine number six. Can't tell how many."

"There's just two of them now. We killed the other three out back!"

As if the engine noise wasn't enough, a salvo smashed into the side of the engine block, breaking into fragments that ricocheted around the room. Frenchy answered with two quick shots. Hell, Cracker thought, the gunfire could barely be heard over the roar of the damn diesels.

"Cracker," Harris ordered, "you and Slim work your way down toward number five. Don't let them see you until you can get a good shot. I'll move over to cover Bear!"

If Cracker had been unhappy before, he was really pissed now.

"Of all the crap," he muttered. "All I wanted tonight was to go get boozed up and chase some good looking pussy. What do I get? Crawling on my belly in this stinkin' filthy oil, gettin' my ass shot to fuckin' hell!"

"Shove it up your ugly nose, Cracker," Slim, the dredge's electrician, said in a loud whisper obviously tiring of Cracker's bitching. "I ain't enjoyin' playing snake either, jerkface."

After a few minutes of stealth, they reached their positions, Slim behind engine number five and Cracker at the end of number three. Slim could peer around toward engine number six. The gunmen were barely visible, leaning against the generator beyond the engine. Slim could just make out one left foot. Not a good target, Cracker thought. He'd have to wait and hope one of them moved back toward the bulkhead.

Cracker also peered around number three. He couldn't see much, but he'd be able to cover the center aisle if they tried to move toward Frenchy. Nothing to do but wait.

■ ■ ■ ■ ■

The dredge captain crossed the center aisle and came up beside Bear behind generator number two.

"Welcome to fun town," Bear greeted him. "Keep down! They can see us from that corner if you go above the casing."

"You've been drawing most of the fire?" Harris asked. He dabbed at his swollen lip, hit by a bullet fragment, with a rag.

"Yeah. They can barely see Frenchy."

A barrage from the two gunmen interrupted them. The high-velocity bullets smacked into the steel bulkhead behind Bear and the dredge captain with loud clanging sounds, bursting into tiny fragments that flew off in all directions. "Damn" and "Ouch" were heard as some fragments found flesh, nicking and cutting the men's skin. A second later, they heard Cracker fire twice.

"Tiny," Frenchy yelled, "one of them has moved up back of four!"

"Did Cracker hit him?" Harris called back.

"I don't think so. I just saw his hand back of generator number four."

"Damn. They're trying to get up on us, Bear!"

■ ■ ■ ■ ■

Cracker was cursing himself. When the two gunmen opened fire at Bear and the dredge captain, Cracker saw one of them come around the end of number six and duck behind generator four. For an instant, he had been in Cracker's field.

"Take that, bastard!" Cracker shouted as he squeezed the trigger.

The shot missed. He quickly pumped a fresh shell and fired again, but the gunman had managed to get behind a heavy chain block. The lead pellets simply bounced off and fell harmlessly to the deck.

"Cracker," Slim called, "did you get him?"

"No, dammit! The damn chain block got in the fuckin' way!"

Cracker realized that the gunman knew where he was. Nothing to do but pump another shell and hope for another shot. He didn't have long to wait.

Suddenly, the gunman came around the chain block and fired at Cracker. Cracker pulled back as the bullets smacked into the engine block above him. The air about his face was full of lead and rust particles, making it impossible to breathe. The gunman rushed toward Cracker.

He didn't see Slim coming around engine five, an error Cracker could see the man would soon regret as Slim shot him in the leg.

The gunman fought to maintain his balance, but he couldn't. His right foot caught on the welding cables that Cracker and Curly had been using to repair the engine mount, and he fell, with a sickening scream, toward the uncovered spinning flywheel of the huge engine.

It took but a moment for the teeth to do their murderous work. Bits of flesh and blood flew across the engine room covering every surface with spots of red. The disemboweled corpse ripped apart, the head and shoulders being flung against the bulkhead, the legs being slammed into the deck and separated. The remaining torso jammed onto the flywheel to rotate with it while the arms wrapped tightly to the driveshaft.

The two dredgemen were unable to turn their eyes away.

Cracker didn't have time for remorse. The last gunman came around the end of engine number six. The chattering of his submachine gun brought Slim and Cracker back to reality.

He fired a short, unaimed burst in their direction, the bullets striking the bulkhead behind them.

Slim's shotgun exploded again, but the shot missed.

Running full speed, the gunman headed toward the door to the electrical-switch room, firing short bursts at Frenchy and then at Bear, forcing them to take cover.

Cracker, his legs finally able to move again, took off after him around engine number three. Reaching the center aisle, he took a shot at the fleeing gunman but hit only the closing door as the gunman burst through into the electrical-switch room. "Lousy son of a bitch!" Cracker shouted as he determinedly ran after him.

Slim came around the end of engine number three following Cracker. He slowed to break open his double barrel and stuff in two fresh shells.

"Tiny," he screamed, "Cracker's fired his last shot! His gun is empty!"

"Oh, my God!" Harris responded and ran after Cracker and the gunman. But the electrical-switch room was empty. The stairway door was just closing and Harris heard a single pistol shot ring out from behind the door.

He crashed through the door, shotgun at the ready. The gunman was on the fourth step, frantically shoving a fresh magazine into his submachine gun. Cracker lay on the deck holding his right knee. The dredge captain could see that the welder was experiencing intense pain as agony etched his face. The sound of the submachine gun's bolt being yanked back as the gunman turned toward Harris was unmistakable.

The dredge captain didn't wait. The shotgun exploded, the muzzle less than four feet from its target. The lead pellets struck the gunman at the top of the neck just below the chin. An eruption of blood and brain matter followed the metal against the stairway bulkhead.

Harris watched with satisfaction as the gunman's dead body dropped back against the stairs, his gun clattering to the deck.

Cracker looked up at the dredge captain. "Thanks, Tiny."

Harris pulled the shotgun's pump reload, ejecting the spent

shell and shoving a fresh shell into the firing chamber. He looked at the fallen gunman as if deciding whether to shoot again. "Don't mention it." He spat against the wall.

Slim stepped through the door a few seconds later.

"Can you get up?" Harris asked Cracker.

"If you give me a hand, I'll try."

Slim and the dredge captain helped Cracker to his feet. They half carried him to the crew's quarters where he was laid on his bunk.

"Let's get everybody in here," Harris told Slim. "Charlie! You in here?"

"Yeah, Tiny," Charlie answered.

"Get up to the radiophone! Call the damn cops and get them out here on the double! Tell 'em we got wounded! Slim, go get J.D. and the boys. I'll get Frenchy and Bear."

■ ■ ■ ■ ■

"Okay, everybody listen up!" Harris began, when the crew finally gathered together. "Now, we've got a big problem. If this business had happened in Texas, we'd be considered in the right without any questions, but we're in Yankee land and they've got some damn funny ideas up here. These people don't understand a man defending his property by shooting somebody. I figure the cops will be swarming all over us in a few minutes. They all figure we're nothing but a bunch of redneck good ol' boys, and they'll be looking for any way to get us.

"So, everybody must tell the same story or we could have serious trouble. Now, y'all get this straight. We ordered them to put down their guns! They fired! We fired! They missed! We didn't! Now get it straight, and I don't want to hear any other words."

"You think they'll question each of us?" Billy asked.

"Yeah, Billy," Harris said calmly. "Listen, everybody did good, and I'm damn proud of the way nobody chickened out. This was tough and dirty, but these bastards attacked us and we defended ourselves as men should.

"All right, we've still got to keep this dredge running. Frenchy, shut down engine number five. I know the cops are going to want to get what's left of that guy out of there."

N.Y.P.D. Harbor Police Headquarters—2120 Hours

The frantic radio call from the dredge was received by the communication center and immediately relayed to Lieutenant Otis Branson, the watch commander. He immediately notified the Coast Guard duty officer and then dispatched two patrol boats to the dredge, climbing aboard the first boat as it pulled away from the pier.

"Been a busy night, Mike," he said to his sergeant, who was standing beside him.

"Yeah, that's for sure," Sergeant Lyons answered. "This on top of that fire is a bit much. Anything more on that story about the men seen on the barge just before the fire broke out? Sounds suspicious to me."

"Sure does, but no word yet. Our detectives are handling that right now with the fire marshall. They'll let us know if anything comes up."

"What exactly did the dredge operator say about this shooting?"

"Just that there were several men killed. We'll know in a couple of minutes."

"I'll get the men ready to board," Lyons responded as the patrol boat arrived at the boat tie-up.

Aboard the dredge, *William P. McDonald*—2145 Hours

Captain Harris met the Harbor Police boat. It was obvious that he was not pleased to see that the lieutenant was black.

"I'm Lieutenant Branson, Harbor Police. Are you the dredge captain?"

"Yeah, that's right. Where the hell were you when we needed you?"

"We responded as quickly as possible to your call, Captain," Branson replied coolly to the dredge captain's obvious hostility.

"I mean, where was the damn police protection you were supposed to be providing when we were invaded?"

"We've been busy tonight, Captain. You saw that barge fire. Now, I want the story on this shooting. Where are the bodies I heard about?"

"The first three are on the other side of the dredge. Follow me."

"'The first three'?" Branson asked in surprise. He was becoming annoyed with the dredge captain's attitude. Branson was a large and powerful man in his sixteenth year with the Harbor Police. His black hair, beard, and mustache covered many scars. He was known to be a fighter—with both his fists and his wits—and had subdued many suspects who resisted arrest. He had fought his way up through the ranks of the Harbor Police and had made many enemies along the way. A sharp dresser, he was considered to be a "tough dude" by his subordinates. "Just how many people are dead here?" he asked.

"Five." Harris answered as they came up to the three dead gunmen lying on the floor just past Sherry's office.

"Did you say 'five'? Just what the hell has been going on out here?"

"A goddamn war, that's what! We were invaded by these bastards!"

"Sergeant, get the Crime Scene Unit up here right away. Captain, I want your people in one place so we can question everybody. Also, have all weapons placed here for tagging as evidence."

"Most of the crew is in their quarters, including the wounded, and just when are the wounded going to be removed to the hospital?"

"The rescue helicopter is on its way, and your wounded will be sent immediately. Now show me the other two bodies."

The dredge captain led the police into the engine room and to the side of engine number five. The remains of the man's body lay grotesquely on top of the flywheel.

"My God!" Branson reacted in horror. "I've never seen anything like this. How did it happen?"

"The engine was operating at the time. He fell on the flywheel."

"Fell? Or maybe was pushed or thrown."

"What are you trying to say, nig—Lieutenant!" Harris snapped back.

"I would caution you, Captain, you and your people have some serious questions to answer—and this is not the South, mister!"

"We defended ourselves because you weren't here to do your damn job!"

"Captain, your attitude is your worst enemy! The more you're uncooperative, the more I'm going to dig, mister! Now be smart and show me that fifth body!"

The dredge captain wisely did not answer but strode off toward the electrical-switch-room door with the police following him. Branson could see that the dredge captain was seething, but the lieutenant was determined to get a complete story and didn't care what anyone felt.

"Who shot him?" Branson asked.

"I did. He shot Cracker and was about to shoot me!"

"This Cracker is one of your wounded?"

"Yeah, he got it in the knee and needs to be in a hospital, dammit!"

"All right, Captain!" Branson was holding his anger. "Sergeant, where is the rescue chopper?"

"I'll check on it, sir."

"Now, Captain, I want the whole story of who did what, when, and where. I want to know who shot who and why and how."

"We ordered them to drop their guns, they fired, we fired, they missed, we didn't."

"That's your story?"

"Damn right!"

"Well, I'll tell you, Captain: As an experienced police officer who has seen a lot of shooting scenes, I think you and your people opened fire without any warning and murdered these men. And then you chased this man in here and shot him while he was trying to get away from you. Right?"

"No way! I ordered them to lay down their guns and they fired, dammit!"

"It's thin as fart gas, Captain! My experience says that's flotsam, and you know it!"

Just then, Sergeant Lyons returned. "The chopper is here, Lieutenant. They're loading the wounded guys now."

"Thank you, Sergeant. Let's get set up for the interviewing of everyone else on board while the CSU does its job. We could use an office."

"All right," Harris answered grudgingly. "My office is up these stairs. I'll show you."

Branson followed him to his office.

"Yes, this will do nicely. Now, bring up the first of the crew who participated in this shooting. Sergeant, call headquarters. Tell them to get NYPD to assign guards at the hospital to those injured men until we can get there for questioning."

Aboard the U.S.C.G. Motor Launch—2155 Hours

Commander Scott stood by the motor launch's railing transfixed by the enormity of the burning fuel barge. The towering flames were both terrifying and beautiful at the same time. The heat of the fire struck his face with uncomfortable intensity even across a half mile of water.

Called back to duty when the fire began, Scott and Chief Morris had rushed to investigate, but there was nothing they could do. Hell, Scott thought, there was nothing anybody could. Even the fire boats could barely get close enough to pump powerful streams of water from their monitor nozzles into the inferno. They watered, not to put out the fire, but rather to keep the steel sides of the barge from melting, which would release burning oil to float across the water and spread the flames into nearby piers.

Scott grabbed the railing as the motor launch bucked across the wake left by a passing steamship. He wondered what had happened aboard the dredge. The police call was brief, but it had left little doubt that a gun battle had occurred. He would know in a minute as the motor launch reversed its engines and slowed to a gentle bump against the side of a NYPD Harbor Police patrol boat.

Scott quickly clambered across the boat and jumped over the small intervening gap to land aboard the *William P. McDonald*.

Aboard the dredge, *William P. McDonald*—2200 Hours

"Dammit!" Don Fredericks was saying to the officer at the police check point. "I've got to see about my boys."

"It's all right, officer," Scott said as he stepped beside Fredericks. "This man is with me." The two of them went quickly to the crew's quarters.

"Sergeant," Scott said as they reached the quiet of the switch room, "is Captain Harris under arrest?"

"No, sir, not at this time. We are detaining him for questioning."

"That being the case, Mr. Fredericks and Captain Harris should be free to talk with each other privately."

"Yes, but I can't let him leave until the detectives finish questioning the crew."

"Then if you'll excuse us, we'll go in and talk with him."

As they brushed past the police guard, Fredericks called. "Russell! What the hell happened here?"

"Mr. Fredericks," Harris said, "I've been worried bad! I was afraid you wouldn't be able to get out here. These cops are crazy!"

"Scott here helped me get past the guards. Now tell me what the hell happened out here."

The dredge captain summarized the attack. Since Scott was listening, Harris continued to alter the truth, insisting that he had tried to get the gunmen to surrender before shooting.

"Sure sounds like self-defense to me," Fredericks said.

"The problem is that the cops don't want to believe me. That lieutenant's got his mind made up that I didn't warn them but fired first. He keeps talking murder."

"The difficulty that you have here is New York law," Scott interjected, "which says that you may not use deadly force to defend your own life if you have any reasonable way to escape the danger. Just looking around, I can see why the police are questioning what you did. The law would have been satisfied if you and the other crew members had barricaded yourselves in here, for example, and waited until they left."

"But what about J.D? They had him at gunpoint. They were going to kill him!"

"The cops could argue that you couldn't know that for sure. The intruders might have only held him hostage until they reached their boat, then let him go."

"I couldn't take that chance! I *had* to believe that they would shoot J.D."

"I'm afraid that argument won't sell in New York. Up here that's called vigilantism."

"What the goddamn hell was I supposed to do—stand back and let them kill him?"

"You should have called the police. The use of deadly force is an option only to save your own life—and then only if no reasonable means of escape can be found. Also, you and your crew may have problems if the guns are unlicensed. That's a pretty serious charge in itself."

"I was hoping you were on our side," Fredericks spoke up.

"I can't be on anyone's side. I will talk with Lieutenant Branson and at least get him to understand your side of the story, but I can't interfere with his investigation. I hope your lawyers get here quickly."

"I need to use a phone to call my vice president, Joe Johnson," Fredericks grumbled.

Captain Harris spoke up. "There's one up in the galley."

■ ■ ■ ■ ■

The two men entered the galley to find Cookie sitting alone at one of the tables.

"Cookie!" Fredericks said, glad to see a friendly face from the past. "Get me the phone."

"Yes, sir, boss," Cookie answered as he rose from his chair, a big smile on his round face. He was gregarious, helpful, and very popular with the crew. His smooth skin belied his sixty-two years, though his close-cropped beard was white. He was always filled with an infectious enthusiasm for life. A moment later, he laid the phone on the table.

"Thanks. Bob, I really 'preciate your help tonight. This whole business has me some upset."

"Me too," Scott said. "I feel somewhat responsible for leaving your people unprotected in order to cover the fire. Just not enough police to cover everything."

"I realize now that you were in a bind," Fredericks went on. "I'm just pissed that these damn cops can't seem to understand it."

"I know, but I hope the Richmond County DA will be able to apply some common sense."

"I'm going to step out on the engine-room roof where I can have some privacy."

Fredericks headed for the ladder that led to the roof hatch. He climbed up and with some difficulty released the latch. He then swung the heavy hatch cover out of the way and climbed out on the roof. He covered his ears as he was greeted by the tremendous noise coming through the exhaust stacks. He remembered, from the days when he had been captain of the dredge, that there was an indentation in the wall where he could get away from much of the noise. He reached his goal, switched on the phone, and dialed a number in New Jersey.

"Jerry! Don here. Get your damn co-pilot up. I want you two to get your butts back to Houston. Pronto. I want you at Hobby in three hours to meet Joe Johnson. What? Well, kick that broad out of there and zip up your damn pants. Now move it! The only sound I want to hear is the sound of the door hitting you in the ass on your way out!" He pressed the END button, checked for an available signal, and dialed a number in Houston.

"Johnson." The voice came weakly from the small phone.

"Joe, it's Don. I'm sending the plane back to Hobby. I want you to round up the lawyers and get them out to our hangar. I want Jerry to get loaded up and back here before I see the damn sun. Three of the boys are in the hospital, so Russell's going to need some help. Round up Kendall and a couple of the boys and bring them, too."

"Kendall just got back."

"Yeah, I know. But with Cracker out, Russell's got no lead ironworker. Tell Kendall to forget the unpacking and get his ass out to the hangar. And tell Jerry to have cars waiting at Teterboro and send everybody over to the hotel to meet me. I'll set up some rooms."

"Okay. Sounds like it's getting messy up there."

"You don't know the half of it! These fuckin' cops are plumb loco. Russell and the boys blow away some rotten sons of bitches who needed killing, and now these stupid assholes are trying to make our boys out to be murderers! I'm mad! Real mad! They want a fight—well, they have picked on the wrong outfit! It's take-names-and-kick-ass time, and they are gonna find out! Ain't no way they are gonna kick this ol' boy like a dead chicken laying in the road!"

"Okay, I understand. Anything else?"

"No. I'll call you in the morning." Fredericks switched off the phone. He looked toward the Brooklyn shore, where the fuel barge was still burning brightly despite the efforts of the fire fighters. With so much fuel on board, it was probably going to burn all night. He turned away and retraced his steps to the galley, where Scott was waiting for him.

"My lawyer will be here in the morning," Don said. "He'll sure enough get things straight. I want to thank you for your help. I hope you're not making trouble for yourself."

"I don't think so. Now why don't we get going. We're going to need some sleep tonight."

Aboard the U.S.C.G. Motor Launch—2245 Hours

The Statue of Liberty, lit more brightly than by its usual spot-lights, reflected the light from the huge fire. Fredericks and Scott stood together by the boat's rail, not saying anything. Their eyes were riveted to the flames towering skyward from the burning fuel barge. The efforts of the fireboats pumping tons of water and foam had failed to dampen the incandescent scene.

Finally, Scott spoke. "It's hard to believe that tomorrow it will be only one week since your dredge hit that U-boat. So much has happened."

"Yes, I know. I'm just unable to understand these damn-fool attacks. You reckon that fire was set by the same jaspers that hit Russell?"

"Yes, I do. The big question remains who is behind this group of hit men? I believe the answer lies in knowing who entered that boat in May 1945 and removed that awful cargo. Those same people are trying hard to stop this investigation, probably before we find out who they are and can arrest them for what they did in forty-five."

"You make it sound as if we're still at war."

"In a way, we are. Your men on the dredge are soldiers on the front. Nobody expected your dredge to hit the submarine. It just happened."

"So my boys have sort of been drafted?"

"I suppose you could think of it that way."

After dropping Fredericks at the fireboat dock the patrol boat headed toward Governors Island.

Scott sighed. It had been some night.

Fifth Avenue Hotel, Manhattan—0715 Hours

Bradley Dexter fought sleep as he sat up on the bed. He had managed a couple of hours sleep on the plane coming up from Houston—thanks to the luxurious comfort of the private jet—and a bit more at the hotel. Slowly waking up as the hot shower revived his skin, his mind raced with questions about why he had been rushed to New York with no prior notice. Joe Johnson had been able to provide only the barest of information as he actually shoved Dexter onto the plane. "No time!" Johnson said strongly.

Dexter was a partner in one of Houston's most prestigious law firms. He was also one of the top criminal defense lawyers in the country. A tall, slender man of fifty, his light reddish hair was only beginning to show signs of balding, and his large sideburns were just starting to gray. He dressed quickly, as he knew Don Fredericks expected to join him for breakfast. Then he would get all the facts about this shooting.

"Howdy, Brad," Fredericks greeted him at the restaurant. "Thanks for coming."

"Joe didn't give me a chance to say no," Dexter said.

"That sounds like Joe okay," Fredericks answered. "I told him to get you up here pronto." He briefed the lawyer on the events of the previous night. "That cop kept saying my boys could go to jail for this. Can they?"

"Second-degree murder is serious prison time. Now, you say none of the attackers survived?"

"No, nary a one." They paused to watch the waiter pour coffee.

"Was the dredge equipped with any kind of automatic-video or sound-recording surveillance system?"

"No."

"So the police are suspicious, but they have no actual witnesses. That means that they will have to depend on physical evidence."

"What does that mean?" Dexter watched as Fredericks looked, with disdain, at the home fries on his plate. Knowing Fredericks's preference, Dexter suspected his client was wondering don't these folks know 'bout grits?

"They'll look at the angles of the bullets. Things like the relative positions of the shooters and the victims. Distances. They'll try to find any evidence that your crew fired from hiding without warning, et cetera." Dexter sliced through the sausage link smoothly. He was quite satisfied with the home fries.

"What really bothers me is that my boys defended themselves and killed some scum that needed killing! So what's the big deal, dammit!"

"New York is very scared of vigilantism. They fear armed mobs roaming the streets shooting supposed bad people on the weakest evidence. So they step on anyone who appears to be acting like a vigilante."

"You figure they'll try the boys for murder?" Fredericks cradled his coffee cup between his hands, his voice rising in protest.

"It depends on the evidence. If they can find physical evidence—say, that the gunmen were shot in the back or from above—or if one of the crew says the wrong thing, then they probably will." He bit into the jellied toast. "Hmm. Very tasty."

"What if Russell didn't warn them jaspers like he said?" Dexter could see that Fredericks suspected this was true despite what Captain Harris had said the night before.

"Whoa! I don't want to hear it!" Dexter answered strongly. "I am an officer of the court. I cannot and will not knowingly participate in perjury."

"All right. I get the message. What's your first move?" Fredericks set the empty coffee cup down.

"I need to see the scene and talk to the police. I must know everything the police know. Then, I'll talk with the crew and get their stories."

U.S.C.G. Headquarters, Governors Island—0810 Hours

Bob Scott sat back in his chair as he studied a stack of documents that had just arrived from Special Agent Carson's office. The FBI report concerning mercenary activity in the metropolitan area was thorough.

Carson's note made it clear that the bureau's mindset was that the presence of the group of gunmen killed aboard the dredge the night before was related to the submarine. Lieutenant Branson's office agreed. Scott was convinced. He read on:

'The criminal organization of eastern European exiles has been connected to a lengthy list of crimes and violence, especially strike-breaking. They usually deal with strikers by terrorizing the leaders. If the strikers continue to resist, then killings start and the union finally collapses.

'People who want to hire mercenary soldiers usually do so through advertisements in *Soldier of Fortune*–type magazines. This particular group has run such ads, and the sting operation is trying to contact the killers by answering one of their ads.

'A letter has already been sent by Agent Carson to make the initial contact through the post office box given in the ad. We have discovered that, to avoid detection, the killers use intermediaries to place the ads and rent the boxes. The intermediaries then pick up the mail and go to a pay phone at a specified time to wait for a call from the group.

'To foil the police, the intermediaries don't approach the pay phone until the last minute, making wire taps and bugging impossible. They also change pay phones frequently to frustrate police surveillance.

'Once the intermediary reports mail received, he is given instructions to go to a drop point. Only when they are satisfied that he is not being observed will they complete the contact.

'At the drop point, they normally employ a homeless person—expendable and unlikely to be missed—to make the actual contact, so that if the police move in, the contact person has no useful information. He would have nothing but two envelopes: one containing payment in cash for the intermediary; the other empty and addressed to a second post office box.

'The contact person is simply told to hand the first envelope to the intermediary and take the mail from him. The mail is placed in the second envelope and dropped in a mailbox. The mercenaries carefully watch this step to ensure that no police surveillance takes place. They pay the person a small amount of cash to make the contact and promise a large payment when the task is done. Instead, they usually kill the homeless person to ensure his silence.

'This final address is of a box rented by one of the mercenaries using a false ID. They seldom use each box more than a few times before changing to another. If the leaders of the mercenaries believe the letter genuine, they then hire a lawyer to investigate the letter writer.

'If satisfied that the writer is not a plant, the lawyer sets up a meeting to discuss the job the writer wants done. Only then does the lawyer arrange a direct meeting with the mercenary leaders. If they think anyone might betray them, he is killed.

'By using this painstaking method, they have successfully avoided discovery by the police.'

Scott looked up from his reading as Chief Morris entered his office.

"I heard we're joining the FBI task force," the chief commented.

"Yes," Scott replied. "The boss tells me we're to meet with them this afternoon. Everybody's convinced mercenaries are behind the attacks. The question that remains is who is behind these mercenaries."

"What about the sub?"

"Captain Peters was very evasive when I asked him. Something is going on, but I don't think he wants to tell us."

"I noticed that too. He seems depressed about something. I hope he'll get around to telling us what's bothering him soon."

FBI Headquarters, Manhattan—1547 Hours

Chief Morris pulled the Coast Guard staff car into a visitor's parking space at the Federal Office Complex in downtown Manhattan. Scott followed Morris's lead to the lobby where they found the directory.

"Fifth floor," the chief announced.

They entered an office with floor to ceiling windows, floor to ceiling blinds, and a large oval table. Special Agents Carson and Woodruff were already there waiting for the other members of the task force to arrive. When Lieutenant Branson and Sergeant Lyons finally joined the group, everyone quieted.

"Okay, we're all here now, so let's begin," Agent Carson said as he shuffled some papers. "Our purpose is to investigate and identify the criminal conspiracy behind the various attacks revolving around the UX-6000 and the people involved. We need to find out who is behind the attacks and why. We must also find out who murdered the crew of the submarine in 1945 and removed the cargo of cholera bacteria.

"The most puzzling aspect concerns the cargo and the two missing crewmen who were taken from the submarine along with Von Kruger. We know that Von Kruger was murdered in Germany, so I'm of the belief that these other two men may have also ended up in Germany. But before we get to that, please give Agent Woodruff your attention. He'll review the criminal activities of this past week."

Woodruff passed out copies of a criminal summary beginning with the hijacking of the interstate truck in west New Jersey on Friday afternoon. This was followed by the report of the theft of the cabin cruiser *Mary Ann* from the marina in Ocean County and its use in the blast on Friday night. The attempt to smash the dredge with the steamship *Rangoon Expresser* was detailed, along with the shootout on the dredge Tuesday evening.

"Some additional information has been received since this report was written," Agent Woodruff continued. "The New Jersey State Police have reported finding the hijacked truck in an abandoned building in Atlantic County. They lifted several latent prints, which our fingerprint people have just reported match the prints of three of the men who were killed aboard the *McDonald* on Tuesday night. The bad news is we haven't tied them to any names or other identifications.

"The director believes this task force should proceed along several lines of investigation," Woodruff went on, "and you've been divided into three teams to do the assigned work. The first team will be researching all pertinent U.S. government files dealing with the capture and interrogation of Reichsmarschall Göring in forty-five.

"The director believes that someone learned about the submarine through those interrogations. We must find out who visited Göring after his capture and why. We need to know what they learned and what they did with the information. This will be a tedious job, involving sifting through thousands of pages and running down various leads. We decided to ask you, Commander Scott, and your chief to go to Washington and work those files."

"Understood."

"The Attorney General is making the necessary arrangements and procuring clearances," Carson added. "We want you to stay in close contact with us. Please call in every day to report your progress."

"Very well. When do we start?"

"I'd like you to report to the Superintendent of Official

Document Storage tomorrow morning. My secretary is making the travel arrangements for you now."

Scott half raised his hand. "I must ask a very serious question."

"Go ahead, Commander."

"Is there any possibility that some part of our own government is behind this?"

"The director doesn't believe so. When this began, the Washington office of the FBI began calling every other agency. So far, nothing has come out."

"Even the CIA? The Pentagon?"

"They claim to be as pure as newborns."

Morris had to stifle his laugh. He hadn't forgotten the two dead divers.

"Okay," Scott responded. "We are ready to get started."

"Good. Now, the second team will be the German Federal Police. Lieutenant Mueller, we are asking you to return to Germany and scour all police files from 1945. The German police operated under Allied Military Police supervision during the occupation, but I understand files were turned over to your agency after the occupation ended."

"Yes," Mueller replied with a strong accent.

"The big problem is that we don't know who the two assistants to Von Kruger were. The first problem is to determine their identities. I understand that your agency has access to the Luftwaffe files."

"Yes."

"Then you will need to go through them and search out anything on this Project Energetic V.C., especially the personnel records."

"Yes. I've been told that I will have whatever manpower may be needed."

"I assure you, Agent Carson," Commander Jurgens broke in, "of the complete cooperation of the German government. They are as eager to solve this crime as you."

"I'm sure that they are. I understand you have a medical identification team on its way from Germany, Commander."

"Yes. They left Frankfurt this afternoon. They will be landing at JFK in a few hours."

"The submarine is to be opened tomorrow and the bodies brought up," Carson continued. "Now, turning to the third team," he said. "This will be the largest endeavor, as we are going to use a maximum sting effort to smoke out this mercenary army. NYPD is committing at least ten officers and four detectives to assist us. And the New Jersey State Police will be providing several men starting tomorrow—along with the ATF people—so we should have enough.

"Any further questions? If not, let's get started. The U.S. Attorney wants these people found, so let's push it hard. Stay in close touch with me and Woodruff. This meeting is adjourned."

As the meeting broke up, Scott approached Carson and handed over the Dorfmann diary. "As promised."

"Good. I want to get this down to Washington as soon as possible. A lot of people have been asking to look at it. Let me get your travel itinerary."

Nassau County, Long Island—1850 Hours

Scott finally reached Brenda's apartment. He had been delayed for fifty minutes by a terrible jam on the expressway. Another tractor trailer accident. What a nightmare the damn road was. He entered the apartment and found Brenda watching TV.

Standing beside her chair, he leaned down to kiss and embrace her. Her scent, her warm moist breath instantly stimulated him. She responded by wrapping her arms around his neck. Scott straightened up, lifting her petite body out of the chair.

"Oh, lover," she whispered, "I've been needing this!"

"Me too, baby, me too," he said, kissing and hugging her. He released her and stepped back to admire her outfit.

"Do you think the dress is OK?" she asked.

"Looks fine," Scott answered as he gazed at her.

"I made reservations for eight thirty, and we're going to have to jump to make it."

Scott hurried to shower and change into slacks and a sport jacket. "Am I to know where I'm taking you for dinner?" he asked as they walked to the car.

"I wanted to go back to that little restaurant on Eighth Avenue where we had our first date. I'm feeling romantic."

"Then we *are* going to have to hurry."

"You don't mind?"

"Of course not. Anything you desire." He bent down to kiss her.

"Hey, now! You promised to behave!"

"Isn't that behaving?" he joked.

She answered with a smile.

Once in the car, Scott put on a tape that he knew Brenda would enjoy. She sat next to him with her head against his shoulder.

"You know you're making me hot enough to boil," he said after several miles.

"You can handle it," she laughed and squeezed his arm. "And I'm not moving, so you're just going to have to stand it. I love being held by you and I'm not missing one second of your touch."

"You're gonna catch it later, you know."

Both Scott and Brenda were so preoccupied that they had failed to notice a dark blue sedan following them. As they traveled uptown through Manhattan, the car continued to follow a short distance behind. A tough trick in the island's traffic.

Shortly before eight thirty, they arrived at the restaurant in Midtown. Scott couldn't believe their luck—a parking space. Scott glanced up, after opening the door for Brenda, to see a blue sedan stop immediately alongside his Oldsmobile. He tried to look into the vehicle, but the windows were smoke tinted preventing any vision of the occupants. Damn double parkers, Scott thought, I ought to call a cop. He guided Brenda into the restaurant.

Eighth Avenue Restaurant, Manhattan—2035 Hours

Scott watched Brenda sipping her wine at the restaurant. She was very poised no matter what she was doing, he thought.

"Are you looking at me again?" she asked.

"Uh-huh. I love to look at you."

"Why?"

"Because you're the most wonderful girl on the planet, and I am so lucky to have met you and fallen in love with you."

"Is that so? You're sure that I've fallen in love with you?"

"Uh-huh."

"Well, okay," she responded, "maybe I have. So, what do you think we should do about it?"

"Get married."

"I think you've got a small problem, my love."

"Yeah, I know. I heard from her lawyer this afternoon. I told him I wouldn't contest the final divorce settlement. But even so, it will take some time."

"How long?"

"Wish I knew. All I can do is ask for an early court date. With the courts all backed up, it could still be many more months."

"Tomorrow wouldn't be soon enough." She looked sad at news of the long wait.

"I know, baby, but I'm afraid we've got no choice. These things take time and, sadly, lots of money. Gonna be tough to do on my salary." Scott was downcast at the thought of the cost. A new car would no doubt be cheaper. Picking up the check just placed on the table, he wondered if a new car might not be cheaper than dinner.

"Well, at least you'll have a place to stay. I love you so much I can hardly stand it, but I'd wait a thousand years if that's what it takes."

"That means more to me than you could ever know," he replied as he caressed her hand. He then handed over his credit card to the less than friendly waiter.

"Oh, darn, now you've made me get all weepy, y'know. I'd better go fix my face."

"Your face is perfect." Scott soothed her. Doesn't really matter, he thought, since we're ready to go anyway.

"Well, let me go check it anyway. Oh darn, where is my makeup? Must have left it in the car."

"I'll go get it, baby." He stood beside the table—ready to go. He signed the credit card slip and retrieved his card.

"No, lover. You wouldn't know what to look for. Just give me the keys and I'll get it."

"I'll come with you. I wouldn't want you to be molested by some unsavory character."

She laughed and said with an impish smile, "As unsavory as you!"

Scott followed her out the door of the restaurant.

"Oh, just wait there," she said with a laugh. "See—except for you, there's no unsavory character out here."

"I'll watch anyway. Besides, I like to watch over you."

"See what I mean!" she taunted as she leaned down to unlock the door and release the latch. "You're—"

Scott didn't really hear the explosion. He was blinded by the intense flash. Everything went black.

Midtown Manhattan—2115 Hours

Detective Sergeant Alan Hillerman and his partner, Tom Dunn, were stopped on Fifth Avenue near the Public Library. It had been a tough shift for the two Midtown detectives. They had already been to a very bad domestic-violence scene that evening and were trying to enjoy some coffee before going back to the precinct. Hillerman had laid his head back against the seat, eyes closed, trying to understand why a man would stab a woman he claimed to love. His thoughts were interrupted by the radio calling for them to go immediately to a car-bomb scene on Eighth Avenue. He noted the time as 9:18 p.m. Detective Dunn had the tires squealing and siren wailing as the unmarked car got under way seconds after the call came in.

"Did he say Forty-eighth Street?" he asked Hillerman over the roar of the engine and wailing siren.

"No, Forty-fifth at Eighth Avenue." He grabbed the seat as the car swerved to pass slow-moving theater district traffic.

The two detectives steeled themselves for what they knew would be a tough scene. Any bombing was bad. The bomb made the scene difficult to sort out. And then there would be the torn up people. The dead. The injured.

Hillerman and Dunn had been partners for nearly three years. Hillerman was senior, having earned his detective badge some ten years before. Dunn, at twenty-eight, was a strong man whose élan made up for his inexperience. Hillerman was very pleased with his partner and the two of them had quickly come to trust each other with their very lives.

Hillerman had joined the NYPD after a tour with the US Army Military Police. His record as a detective had been excellent and he was considered the best on the Midtown squad.

The past month had been eventful for Hillerman. He had taken the examination for promotion to lieutenant and done well. He hoped to receive his silver bar before the year ended. That and his excellent relationship with his girlfriend, Jill Engels, had buoyed his spirits to a high he could not remember.

Eighth Avenue was usually noisy, but tonight it was particularly loud. Sirens of fire trucks, police cars, and ambulances filled the night. Flames from burning cars cast their glow on the scene of terror. The front windows of the restaurant were gone. Their shattered glass had riddled the faces and bodies of patrons.

Patrolmen Sanders and his partner were the first to arrive at the restaurant. They jumped from their patrol car to stop the gathering onlookers from entering the area. The patrolmen could hear screams for help but knew their immediate task was to secure the perimeter. The fire and rescue people would arrive in a few minutes, and the crowd would only delay them from helping the injured.

Patrolman Sanders was relieved to see several patrolmen arriving to help. Inside, the restaurant was chaos, with people crying and screaming. Nearly everyone had been cut by the flying glass, and the rescue people worked quickly to sort out those requiring hospitalization to get them loaded into the ambulances.

The firemen were already working to extinguish the flames as Hillerman and Dunn arrived. They passed through the police line and began a search for bodies.

"Hey, detectives, over here!" one of the firemen shouted.

The two detectives hurried to him. "What you got?" Hillerman asked.

"Some guy, he's under this car. I think he's dead. Help me pull him out, will you?"

With the two detectives' help, the man's body was pulled out from under the car where it had been wedged. Hillerman studied the man's battered and bloodied face. "Hey, I think I know this guy. See if you can find any ID."

Dunn went through the man's pockets. "I got his wallet," he said as he began to search through the papers. "Looks like he's in the Coast Guard."

"My God!" Hillerman choked through his suddenly dry mouth. "It's Bob Scott!"

"Yeah, you're right. That's what his ID says. You know him?"

"He's my cousin's boy friend. Oh, God no! Was Brenda here? Tom, get EMT quick. I've got to find out about Brenda." Hillerman's panic was now in control. Dunn couldn't remember ever seeing his partner so agitated. His eyes wild and wet.

In moments two of the EMTs arrived and began to check Scott over. "It looks worse than it is," the technician said. "I think he'll make it." They loaded Scott into an ambulance.

"There should have been a girl with this guy," Hillerman said frantically to anyone who would listen. "Did anybody see a girl?"

"Yeah, got a sponge?" said Officer Sanders. "Try the wall!"

Hillerman looked in the direction Sanders was pointing. He could see bits of flesh and blood on the bricks. A body had been slammed against the wall by the explosion. He glanced down at the remains of a mangled, shattered female body lying in the black plastic bag. His heart stopped cold as the sound of the zipper being closed reached his ears. For only the second time in his career with the NYPD, his stomach contents landed on the street.

"Here, have some water," Dunn said as he helped his partner.

"My first cousin." Hillerman finally was able to speak. "A wonderful young woman."

"Hey, suits!" Patrolman Sanders called. "The Crime Scene Unit is here. You're wanted!"

"Okay?" Dunn asked. "We've got to get back to work." The two detectives went to meet with the CSU leader.

"Looks like the bomb was under the Olds," the police technician said. "Probably two to four pounds of C-four. You can see the wires ran to both doors. No matter which door was opened, the wires would touch like a switch and that was that. Whoever did this wanted these folks real dead, that's for sure."

"Will you be able to identify the type and source of explosive?" Hillerman asked.

"I think so, with time."

"Okay, get on with it. I want these bastards bad."

The work of the Crime Scene Unit would take a while. The various pieces of debris would be inventoried, measured, photographed, and finally bagged. Every piece that might have any value in the investigation needed to be preserved.

As the work progressed, a patrolman shouted at Hillerman and Dunn. "Hey, detectives! Over here! We got you a customer!"

"What have you got?" Dunn asked as they hurried over.

"A real live volunteer, a citizen willing to come forward with information."

"Must be an out-of-towner," Hillerman muttered as they walked toward a man standing by the police line.

"Hi. I'm Detective Sergeant Hillerman and this is Detective Dunn. You have something to tell us?"

"Yeah, I saw a car double-parked by the one that blew up."

"First, could I get your name and address please," Dunn requested. He quickly wrote down the information.

"This car you saw," Hillerman asked, "why did you take notice of it? Did you see who was in it?"

"The car stopped for just a few minutes and the driver stayed behind the wheel while the other guy got out and slipped under that Oldsmobile. Then he got back in the car and they drove off."

"What kind of car?" Dunn asked.

"I don't know that model. It was a dark blue sedan."

"That's a lot of cars. Anything special about it?"

"No, that's why I wrote down the license number."

"You wrote down the plate number?" Hillerman asked excitedly.

"Yeah, here," the man replied as he handed the detective a slip of paper. "I was dialing the police from the phone over there when the bomb went off."

"Tom, there is nothing like dumb luck. Get this plate on the air fast! Now, sir. Can you describe the occupants of this car?"

"Two men dressed in black outfits with black boots and ski masks. That's all I really saw."

"You didn't see their faces?"

"No, not well at all."

"I thank you for your help. I may have some questions for you later. Here's my card. If you think of anything more, please call."

Dunn caught Hillerman's attention as he returned from the radio car. "I got an APB going out—but some bad news."

"Let me guess—it's stolen."

"You got it. Five'll get you ten it'll be wiped clean when we find it. We're dealing with real pros, Alan."

"Yeah, looks that way all right. So why here? This car? My cousin?"

"Hey, Detective," a patrolman called from a radio car, "they got that car you're looking for. In Queens."

"How 'bout the men?" Hillerman called back.

"Yeah, two men dressed in black. Might be your perps."

"Tell 'em we're on our way there. Get a location, will ya? Come on, Tom."

"East end of the Fifty-ninth Street Bridge!" the patrolman yelled as the detectives ran to their car.

"Burn some rubber, Tom," Hillerman said. The car shot forward, lights flashing and siren wailing. As they approached the bridge, Alan raised the watch commander on the radio. The car had stopped near the Queens end of the bridge. The suspects were in a small store exchanging fire with officers surrounding the building. The air was thick with bullets, the watch commander had reported.

"We need those two for questioning," Hillerman said as the car rolled across the bridge. "I hope they get 'em alive."

East End Queensboro Bridge, Queens—2235 Hours

"We'll know in a minute. There's the scene ahead." They pulled up alongside several other police cars. Rotating lights on the cars flashed over the scene, adding to its macabre appearance.

"Where's the watch commander?" Hillerman yelled at the first officer he saw.

The patrolman pointed him toward a lieutenant behind one of the cars.

"Lieutenant, we're Hillerman and Dunn from Midtown. What's the situation?"

"I'm Roberts, Queens South," the lieutenant answered. "They're pinned down. We've called for them to lay down their arms and surrender, but so far we're only getting return fire. I've got two guys wounded so far. What's with these perpetrators?"

"We think they're the two who bombed a car on Eighth Avenue. Killed two—a woman outside and a patron inside the restaurant—and injured twenty or so more. We need these guys alive, Lieutenant."

The air shook with rapid repercussions as the police and the suspects exchanged fire.

"I'm making no promises, Sergeant," Roberts answered.

Turning to a patrol sergeant, he ordered, "Hit 'em with some gas, Sarge."

Two patrolmen fired tear gas into the store. A burst of automatic fire was the response from inside. The gray mist from the tear gas canisters quickly filled the store and wafted out of the shattered window.

"These guys aren't going to give up, Sergeant," Roberts shouted. "We're going to need more backup."

Just then an intense burst of automatic fire came from the store. Hillerman and Dunn dived for cover as they heard the sound of bullets passing over their heads.

"They're making a break to the right!"

All the police seemed to be firing at once in response. Someone yelled, "I got one!"

"He'd better not be dead! We need him alive to answer questions," said Hillerman.

"More gas!" yelled Roberts.

Gunfight fire continued as gas canisters exploded around the remaining suspect. Then the firing from the store stopped. Everyone waited apprehensively.

"Is he hit?" Roberts called out. "What's the situation?"

"Can't tell, Lieutenant," one of the sergeants called back.

"Hold your fire. Try the bullhorn."

One of the sergeants called to the suspect to throw out his gun and surrender. No response.

"I think he's down for good!" a patrolman called out.

"Sarge, try to move in," Roberts yelled.

The sergeant and two other patrolmen crept carefully up to the front of the store. They took cover behind a low wall below the windows. Hillerman and Dunn watched, their muscles tensed and mouths dry. Still no response. The sergeant was finally ready for the rush.

He sniffed the air. The tear gas hadn't cleared. He signaled to the other officers to put on gas masks. The three officers moved quickly, guns at the ready. They stopped, breathing hard and rapidly, in front of the store's sales counter and again waited for a response. The sergeant signaled that he believed that the suspect was dead or incapacitated.

The two patrolmen moved to opposite ends of the bullet-riddled counter. On a signal they rushed around back while the sergeant came over the top. The second suspect was lying, apparently dead, on the floor. The man's body had no heartbeat and was covered with blood. The officers glanced at each other's eyes The sergeant very carefully raised his helmet over the top of the store counter into the police floodlights, then very slowly he stood up.

"It's over, Lieutenant!" the sergeant shouted. "He's dead!"

"All right, get the CSU in here!"

"Damn it, Lieutenant!" Dunn said. "We needed to question that suspect." They followed the lieutenant into the shattered store.

As they peered down at the two men, the lieutenant responded, "It would have been a waste of time, Detective. We know these people over here. They won't talk. The few we've arrested look at American cops like we're a bunch of Sunday school teachers. These guys have dealt with the KGB, for God's sake. You didn't have a chance of getting anything."

"What do you mean—'dealt with the KGB'?" Hillerman asked.

"After the breakup of the Soviet Union, Eastern Bloc military types packed up and came through the golden door looking for work. Who should they run into on the way but their friendly neighborhood private army recruiter. So they join up to do anything somebody is willing to pay them for."

"So these guys are former Russian soldiers?"

"Russian, East German, Polish, Hungarian—who knows. Paid killers, assassins, bombers, thieves, drug peddlers—you name it. Nothing but trouble!"

"Can you give us any leads on who might have hired them?"

"No. We've got a lot of them in Queens, but who's running them is still a big question. We know some of the conduits between the buyers and sellers, but you can't get anything out of them. The closest we've gotten was with some stings by the feds. They got a lawyer to arrange a contact with a supposed leader. The mercenaries smelled a rat and broke off contact before the feds could move in."

"Did they get anything from the lawyer?" Dunn asked.

"No. When they went back to get him, he was dead. His reward for letting the feds get so close. You can get more from Agent Carson at the FBI Manhattan office."

NINE
Thursday
13 August

U.S.C.G. Headquarters, Governors Island—0600 Hours

Captain Peters awoke just before six o'clock. He was still tired, but he had to get to the hospital and find out about Scott. As the last of the shaving cream flowed toward the drain, the telephone rang. It was Morris calling from the hospital.

"How's Bob?" Peters asked.

"He's still in ICU. The doctor's best guess is that he'll be conscious by noon. They say for you to come to the hospital around fourteen-hundred hours. I'll stay here until then if that's okay with you."

"Okay. Call me if there's any change." Peters replaced the handset and shook his head in disbelief. "My God," he muttered.

Midtown Hospital, Manhattan—0810 Hours

Jill Engles, Brenda's close friend, was fighting to keep her composure. It had been a terrible night, and now she and Hillerman were on their way to the hospital to see Bob Scott. Hillerman had held her much of the night trying to console her, but the blessed relief of dreams would not come. Her blue eyes, dull and red from crying, contrasted sharply with her otherwise immaculate face. She pushed her unbrushed hair back from her cheeks, but it wouldn't stay.

They entered the hospital room to find Scott being examined by a doctor. Chief Morris looked up at Hillerman, his face showing the effects of sitting for long hours in a stiff-back chair.

"Good morning, Doctor. I'm Detective Sergeant Hillerman. How is he?"

"He's making progress," the doctor answered. The doctor paused to adjust his stethoscope. His brown eyes finally made contact with Hillerman's face.

"Has he regained consciousness?" Hillerman looked deep into the doctor's eyes trying to gain any unspoken information that the man might give with a quick movement. But the doctor's face and eyes remained without expression.

"Yes, about six o'clock in ICU. We brought him up here about an hour ago. He's asleep now."

"I need to talk to him. Will he be awake soon?"

"Difficult to say. Maybe an hour. I don't want to wake him. He must come out of it on his own." The doctor raised his finger to his lips as a sign to remain quiet.

"Understood."

Well, nothing to do but wait, Hillerman thought as he and Jill sat down. He held Jill's hand trying to console her as she fought to control her emotions. Their wait was less than expected, when a weak moan came from Scott.

What's that blob? Scott wondered looking through his fuzzy eyes. A nose. Eyes. Oh—it's a face.

"Chief?" Scott asked weakly, sounding very confused. But he had finally made out the face hanging over him. A tired face in need of a shave.

"Yes, Bob, it's me. How are you feeling?"

"I don't know. What happened?"

"Are you in bad pain?"

"I'm not sure. I feel doped up. Sorta woozy-like."

"Yeah, I can imagine. You were badly messed up by a car bomb. Alan and Miss Engles are here."

"Alan is here? Does he know what happened?" Scott's spirit rose at the mention of his good friend's name.

"Hi, Bob." Hillerman stood by the bed. "We dragged you

out from under what was left of a car last night. Thought you were dead at first."

"I don't remember. What do you mean? Under a car?" I never went under any car, he thought. Where the hell am I anyway? I must be in a damn hospital.

"You must have been thrown there by the explosion." Hillerman's voice trembled.

"Explosion? I don't understand. Where's Brenda?" Is everyone crazy? Scott wondered. He couldn't remember ever seeing tears on Hillerman's face.

"Somebody put a bomb under your car last night while you were in the restaurant with Brenda. We think you were the target. We don't know why yet."

"Explosion? Car? I don't understand. What are you saying? Where's Brenda?" His confusion was turning into agitation. He struggled to move against limbs that seemed to weigh tons.

"I brought Jill with me to talk to you." The detective's voice broke.

Scott slowly turned his head and looked toward where Jill stood on the other side of the bed, her hand resting lightly on his wrist. He could see from her reddened eyes and tear-streaked face that she had been crying. She reached down, took his hand between both of hers, and gently squeezed.

"Hi, big guy," she said, trying to be upbeat. "I am so sorry."

"Jill, what's going on?" Oh no, he thought, she's not crazy too.

"It's Brenda," Jill said in a quavering voice, tears welling in her eyes. "She's dead."

"What? What are you saying?" Scott labored to breathe. His chest seemed locked in solid stone.

"It's true. She's gone." Tears rolled down her cheeks and dripped onto the bedspread.

"I don't understand. How? You're mistaken!" His eyes moved rapidly from face to face, his head jerking without control. He started to pull at the tubes and wires connecting him to a variety of drips and monitors.

"I wish she were," Hillerman broke in. "Brenda was killed when she opened the car door. The door was wired with a switch that set off the bomb."

"Bomb? My car? This whole thing is nuts! Where is Brenda?" He seemed to be trying to get out of the bed. Morris restrained him.

"It's all true, Bob," Hillerman insisted. "Brenda is dead. If it's any comfort, I'm sure that she didn't suffer. She died instantly." He wiped the wetness from his face with a tissue from the nightstand. He handed Jill another tissue.

"But what bomb? There was no bomb in my car!" Scott looked frantically from one to the other.

"Two hired killers were seen around your car while you and Brenda were inside the restaurant. We believe they put the bomb under your car and wired the doors. Unfortunately, Brenda was the one who set it off." The detective's voice finally regained its strength.

"Oh my God! She's really dead?" Scott choked out the words, falling back onto the pillow as he began to accept the truth. He started to cry. "No, God, no."

"Chief," Hillerman said, "better call the nurse."

Hudson County, New Jersey — 0940 Hours

A short time later, Sergeant Hillerman and his partner headed west through the Lincoln Tunnel to meet FBI Special Agent Carson in New Jersey. It was early but the air was already warm and sticky. Detective Dunn drove the unmarked police car through the heavy traffic.

"Did Carson tell you much about this deal?" Dunn asked.

"No, but Lieutenant Roberts told me that he and four guys from Queens are joining us. We're going to be running some sort of import-export business that's having labor problems. The scam is for us to contact these mercenaries and hire them to break the union."

"Should be interesting. What's our part?"

"Don't know yet. We'll find out pretty soon. It's not far from here."

Heading south from the tunnel, Hillerman sat back to think about the war he and Dunn had stumbled into just the night before. He was still finding it hard to believe that this one group of mercenary soldiers could have been involved in so much killing and destruction. One bad bunch, he thought. He had read the FBI report right after the gun battle in Queens.

His meeting with Agent Carson the night before had been hastily arranged. He still wondered why Carson was so eager to meet him that the meeting was held at midnight. He didn't want to leave Jill alone, but the FBI was extremely demanding.

Carson had studied the detective's face for only a moment, then insisted that only Hillerman could make the planned sting operation work. He hadn't explained why. But the FBI agent did tell him that he and Dunn would be the ones to finally meet the mercenaries face to face. If they were discovered to be police officers, however, the mercenaries would kill them. Not a pleasant thought, Hillerman mused.

Now they were at the location given him by Agent Carson.

Carson was waiting for them in the business office. "Welcome to the New China Import Company, detectives," he said. "I trust you're ready to go to work." The agent waved his hand at the dingy surroundings.

"Yes," Hillerman answered. "How do we fit in?" A quick look about the small office revealed unpretentious furnishings against walls of peeling plaster.

"You're the bosses, the owners."

"That'll be a problem since we don't know beans about the import business."

"Fortunately, you'll have a good teacher. The real owner will work with you and tell you what you need to know."

"How did you get him to do that?"

"Easy. He owes about half a million in back taxes to the IRS. Didn't take much persuasion. He jumped at the chance to have us get the tax evasion charges dropped and cut a deal on payback in exchange for his cooperation. Let's go out to the warehouse and meet the others."

The detectives followed Carson to the rear of the building, where they found several officers moving a group of boxes. Dressed in work clothes, they didn't look like cops. A young businessman was instructing them on handling the merchandise. Carson made the introductions.

Hillerman immediately understood why he had been chosen to impersonate the boss. They might have been twins. Well, a lot alike for sure. A few dabs of makeup would complete the duplication. Carson made the introductions.

"Wow, you do look a lot like me!" Lewis said, eyeing Hillerman.

"We'll have to compare family histories," Hillerman responded.

"I thought this business was supposed to be broke," Lieutenant Roberts interjected. "Where'd all this stuff come from?"

Carson reassured him. "Our friends at Customs were kind enough to loan us a bunch of seized shipments of illegal Chinese-made goods."

"I thought the ATF and Jersey cops were joining us," Dunn commented.

"They are. The ATF agents are in Atlantic City right now tearing that hijacked truck apart, looking for clues. The Jersey cops are over at the union hall learning to be organizers. They're going to play the bad guys that you're trying to hire the mercenaries to stop from unionizing your workers."

"You got the union to agree to this?" Hillerman was surprised. This FBI cop really does seem to know his stuff.

"Sure. They want these guys found as bad as we do!" Carson leaned against the stack of boxes. He looked quite pleased with himself.

"So, what's the drill?" Roberts asked.

"Lieutenant Roberts, you and your guys are the warehouse crew. You're to load outgoing trucks with the merchandise and unload incoming trucks."

"You're selling this stuff?"

"No. It'll be the same stuff over and over. You'll load the company truck with these boxes and drive it out to a terminal in western New Jersey. The truck will be unloaded and the boxes reloaded into a delivery van. The delivery van will drive the stuff back here and you'll unload it for reuse."

"This is carrying recycling a bit far."

"Well, if we do it right, it'll look like we're just buying, selling, shipping, and receiving."

"You want us to start loading this truck then?"

"Yes, according to this shipping order I've made up." Carson handed a piece of paper to the police lieutenant.

"Okay, we'll get started." Roberts quickly scanned the list.

"Good. Hillerman, let's you and me go back to the office, and I'll show you what you need to do."

As they walked back to the office, Hillerman asked Carson about the contact letter to the mercenaries.

"The letter was given to the postal inspectors this morning and they carried it to the Bronx and put it in the post office box to be picked up. They'll call us as soon as the intermediary makes his move." Carson paused and pulled a cigarette from a gold colored case.

"Are you going to follow him?" Hillerman stopped and moved a piece of broken asphalt off the driveway.

"No. We don't want to spook him. We want the letter to reach the mercenaries. If we try surveillance, it might screw things up." The flame from the lighter was quickly sucked into the end of the cigarette. Carson coughed and put the lighter back in his pocket.

Midtown Hospital, Manhattan—1310 Hours

Captain Peters swung the hospital room door open, arousing a dozing Chief Morris. Scott was still sleeping off the sedative.

"What's the word on our friend?" Peters asked.

"Pretty rough, sir. The nurse had to sedate him after we told him about the death of his girlfriend. Hit him awfully hard." Morris had to stifle a yawn.

"Do you think he'll wake up soon?"

"The nurse said the drug should wear off about now."

Their conversation was interrupted by a movement in the

bed. Peters leaned over as Scott opened his eyes and looked up at him. Another face, Scott thought.

"Captain, I didn't know you were here, sir," Scott said. He was thankful that his vision was improved.

"I got here just a few minutes ago. How's it going?" Peters replied.

"I'm not sure. I'm so dopey I barely know my name."

"You got pretty banged up. I think you're the only officer in Coast Guard history to be knocked out of action by an Oldsmobile fender."

"I hope you'll excuse me if I don't laugh." Scott hurt too much.

"I was sorry to hear about Brenda."

"Thanks and thanks for coming to see me." Scott tried to smile, but his face felt like stiff cardboard.

"I'm really hiding out. The enemy is in the harbor." Peters waved his hand toward the water.

"Sir?"

"The U.S. Navy has arrived. The arrogant bastards steamed up the channel this morning, flags waving and bands playing. There're enough Navy unintelligence officers in the harbor to cover it from the Battery to Liberty Island. The President got talked into turning the sub over to Navy Intelligence. What's worse, he also signed an order transferring our station to Navy control for the duration."

"Oh, no, you mean we're under the Navy!" Scott winced.

"Not us three. I managed to convince the Under Secretary to get us assigned to the FBI task force. It should keep us out of Ledbetter's grasp for a while."

"You mean *Captain* Ledbetter?" Morris broke in incredulously. "The skipper of the destroyer that struck our cutter back in eighty-one?"

"That's him. Jerome Ledbetter. He still blames us for the accident. I still remember, painfully, our treatment by the Navy board of inquiry."

Scott remembered too and was sure that Morris hadn't forgotten either.

"Why, that son of a bitch!" the chief sputtered. "Sorry, sir. I remember the lies Ledbetter told when he put the blame on you, captain."

"That's okay, Pat. You're right. He is one real S.O.B."

"Did you say the three of us, sir?" Scott asked. "I'm a bit messed up at the moment."

"Morris and I can handle it. But I put you down to keep you free of our Navy brethren." Peters smiled at his achievement.

"Thanks. But I've got to find out who killed Brenda."

"Feel better first. Are you going to be able to handle this?"

"Yes. I'm past the first shock," Scott said, his mind taking hold. "Now I'm getting fucking mad. I want to find out who made me into a damn target. Brenda should not have died. The damn KGB wanted *me* dead, not her. They must have been involved because of Rostoff and Gromeko."

Mercenary Hideout, Queens—1330 Hours

The voice at the other end of the telephone was very familiar to Mikelovich. The powerful voice of Senator Samuel Tifton calling from Washington, D.C., on a scrambler circuit.

"Are you certain that bastard is dead?" Tifton demanded. "I can't afford any screw-up. Do you understand me?!"

"The police report says that he died at the hospital," Mikelovich answered. "His girlfriend was killed when the bomb went off." The Russian leaned against the concrete block wall.

"You will get into that hospital and find that Coast Guard bastard's body. I want absolute confirmation. Nothing less, by damn!"

"I have lost seven men. I need replacements."

"All right. I've already started that moving. I've made arrangements with our Cuban allies. Seven recruits are on their way to Mexico today. Arrangements are set with my inside people at the Border Patrol to leave that section below

Del Rio unguarded on Sunday night. I've also told two CIA operatives to silence the listening devices and put a get away car on that back road. Should be routine."

"You still want me to attack dredge? Need big gun."

"Damn right and I especially want you to find that Edwards bitch and kill her. She may have learned more than she's already told. I want her silenced. I don't give a damn what it takes. The Cubans are providing you with an 82 mm recoilless rifle. It's coming across with your replacements. Use it!"

"I understand."

"You'd better. I'm the only man with the power to get weapons, and replacements across the border. One word from me and you're burned. Now do as you're told!" Click.

Hudson County, New Jersey — 1420 Hours

Hillerman was helping Lieutenant Roberts check the merchandise loaded on the company truck. Bunch of nonsense, he thought. He looked up to see his partner come through the warehouse door.

"Alan! Carson wants to see you!" Detective Dunn announced.

"Yeah, okay. Be right there." Hillerman handed a box to another policeman and started toward the door.

"I sure hope these G-men know what they're doing," Dunn said as he and Hillerman walked toward the office. "Personally, I'm not feeling very secure with this whole setup."

"I think Carson's pretty sharp. Remember, he's been after these guys for three years. We just got into this, so we're the rookies."

"I hope you're right, partner."

In the office a police woman in plain clothes acted as receptionist.

"He's in the back, guys," she greeted them. "Go on through."

The rear office, a dingy room, buzzed with the noise of an air conditioner laboring in the bottom half of the only window.

The window's top half, blocked by plywood that kept out the sun, only added to the dinginess. An old gray-colored metal coat cabinet, loose squeaky doors included, blocked the room's open door from prying eyes.

Carson and Frank Lewis were discussing the loading orders for the next truck as the detectives came in.

"Come in, men," Carson said. "Frank, would you excuse us, please."

"Sure," Lewis answered and left the room.

"The postal inspectors have called. The intermediary picked up the letter about 11:15 this morning. So we're on our way."

"When do you think we'll hear from the perps?"

"Based on our last sting try, I figure that you'll get a phone call from some lawyer on Monday, most likely." Carson snuffed out his cigarette in a well used metal ash tray.

"If you've tried this before, why didn't it work? Why do you think it'll work this time?"

"That wonderful face of yours. Last time we got everything rolling and the agent acting as the businessman talked to the lawyer and set up a meet. He goes to the lawyer's office to meet him and suddenly the guy denies everything and practically throws our man out on the street. Were we ever caught flat-footed! Couldn't figure it out.

"But then we discovered that the mercenaries had sent a woman to get a look at the real businessman and take his picture with a tiny, concealed camera. When our man showed for the meeting, the lawyer knew it was a trick and denied everything. But this time it won't be a problem. In fact, we're not going to stop them from photographing Lewis if they choose to since you look so much alike. I figure it'll convince them that you're the real thing." The agent drew another cigarette from his tobacco case.

"Agent Carson." Dunn was puzzled. "I don't see why you don't just follow the letter. It would lead you right to these guys, wouldn't it?"

Hillerman had wondered about that, too. These feds always seem to do everything the dumb way.

"We've tried that—back when we first started this investigation. We tailed the intermediary and watched him make the contact. Then we followed the contact and watched him drop the second envelope in the mailbox. Spent that night going through one monster pile of mail. But we found it! Steamed it open and checked the letter inside. It was ours all right.

"We had the postal inspectors put it in the addressed box. We watched that box for two days but the letter was never picked up. We believe they had an informant in the post office who let them know we were watching the box, so they never showed. The renter of the box used a phony name and address so the trail went nowhere." Carson flicked the small blue lighter and sucked the flame into the end of the cigarette.

"These guys are sharp."

"I've arranged for the Jersey cops to raid us about three o'clock this afternoon. One of our union contacts is on good terms with a couple of news hounds. I've had them leak to the press that the union organizers are coming here and there might be violence. We're not going to resist—other than verbal protests by you, Alan, as the boss. They will come in with some strong-arm stuff, bust up some boxes, break a windshield, et cetera. If all goes well, we'll make the six o'clock news." He tossed the blue lighter to the side of the desk.

"That should help convince the mercenaries that this is real. What do you want me to say as a protest?"

"Just yell about this being private property and they have no right to be here. That sort of stuff." Carson smiled as if to say 'gotcha.'

Aboard the dredge, *William P. McDonald*—1435 Hours

Sherry was finding the afternoon heat oppressive as she climbed up the ladder at the rear of the dredge. When she reached the deck, she found a sweating J.D. standing at the railing looking through binoculars.

"What are you looking at?" she asked.

"I was looking at the barge by the sub," he answered. "The Navy is bringing those bodies up."

"Any up yet?" She wisely moved into the shade at the side of the dredge.

"Yeah. They just brought up the second one a minute ago. Why did the Navy suddenly get into this deal anyway? Where's Captain Peters? I thought he was in charge."

"That's quite a story. I heard a good bit about it when I visited Bob Scott at the hospital."

"How's he doing?"

"Mending physically, but I could see he's really sick over Brenda's death. I hope he'll be able to cope with his loss. I really hate to see him suffer."

"I think you're a bit sweet on him." J.D. chuckled.

"Why do you say that?" She didn't think she had been so obvious. "We're just friends."

"I got eyes." J.D. snickered.

She was surprised at his perception. Just what kind of man was he? she wondered. "Were you ever married?" He seemed to know a lot about relationships for a bachelor.

"Once. A long time ago." He set the binoculars on the deck and joined her in the shade. "Had two kids."

"What happened? If you don't mind talking about it."

"I guess not. Just too much time apart. When you work in construction, you have to travel a lot. Sometimes you can't get home for weeks at a time. My wife got interested in another man and told me she wanted someone who was home all the time. So I walked away."

"I'm sorry." She was also very hot and ready to get inside an air-conditioned space, but J.D. was proving to be interesting.

"Well, it was for the best. She's happy now. I'm married to this old dredge. This is my home till they beach me." J.D. stroked his chin. He looked skyward.

"That seems true of some of the others in the crew."

"Yeah, most of us are roamers. We just follow this old dredge around. Spend our off-duty time playing cards, drinking, chasing broads." He looked back at Sherry.

"Some life." Sherry smiled and stifled a laugh.

"What can I say? Satisfies us, I guess." He laughed softly for a moment.

"Can I get into my office today?"

"Yeah. Tiny called that police lieutenant this morning and got permission to clean up. I'll see if I can get someone to help you if you'd like."

"Maybe later. I'd better sort through the papers myself. I'll let you know." I sure hope the air conditioner wasn't damaged, she thought.

After removing the police tape, Sherry opened the door onto a big mess. Files and papers were strewn everywhere. An hour later, she had the room looking almost normal again. Oh no, she thought with exasperation as the cellular phone began buzzing in the middle of washing her hands.

It was her boss, Leon Bishop. "Just wanted to let you know that something very strange just happened. That assistant of yours."

"George?"

"Yeah. He called in and said that he's quitting. Without notice, no less. Damn inconvenient! Strange, too, don't you think?" Bishop sounded puzzled.

"He's been out sick."

"Well, yeah. He did call in sick the last coupla days, so that's what I thought, too. But the quitting. Very unexpected for a career guy."

"You got a point. Maybe we should let the Coast Guard know about this." Suddenly, her suspicions were aroused. George knew about the diary.

"You think it's significant?"

"I don't know. But there've been some odd things happening. Got to wonder why."

"I'll see about finding a replacement. Can you manage on your own for a few days?"

"Sure. I'll be okay." She rubbed her chin in puzzlement. With Bob Scott in the hospital, she decided that Special Agent Carson needed this information.

Her fingers soon found his card.

"What can I do for you?" Carson asked.

Sherry told him about George Wilson and shared her suspicions.

"You're thinking that Wilson may have told whoever is behind these attacks about the diary?"

"It does seem to fit."

"All right. I'll have some agents pick him up for questioning. Thanks. Perhaps it'll come to something."

Sherry returned to the enormous task of straightening her office, but her mind was elsewhere.

Manhasset, Long Island—1820 Hours

Hillerman made the six o'clock news all right. He and Jill sat on the couch in Jill's apartment watching the TV. The news program showed three large rough-looking men take clubs and strike the import-export company van and several cartons. Broken glass flew across the driveway at the New Jersey business. A quick cut brought a close-up of Hillerman's face protesting the action as the intruders continued to threaten. Good street theatre, he thought.

"I can't really explain everything we're doing," he told her as she curled up in his arms, "but there's a lot of lawmen determined to solve this nasty situation. You've got to have faith in us."

"I do, and I want them caught. Brenda was my very best friend ever. But I don't want you to get hurt."

"I won't."

"You know you're kind of cute on TV. In a burly sort of way."

"Stop that. I'm just doing my job." He pulled her closer. He didn't want her to see his face grinning at the thought of himself on TV. Yeah — fifteen seconds of fame. And all of it a lie.

Aboard Amtrak's Metroliner, Southbound—2048 Hours

Chief Morris returned to his seat from the rest room at the end of the coach. The rapid acceleration of the metroliner made walking difficult and he had to grab a seat back to steady himself. When he sat down, Captain Peters yawned, waking from his nap.

"Welcome back, sir," the chief said. "Did you have a good nap?"

"Yeah, I guess so. Where are we?"

"We just pulled out of Baltimore. Be in D.C. shortly."

"That a newspaper you've got there?"

"I picked it up at the back of the car. One of those supermarket tabloids. Look at the crazy picture on the front page."

The picture was an artist's rendering of a very old Adolf Hitler climbing out of the submarine found in New York harbor. The headline said, "Hitler Found Living on Secret Sub in Harbor." Peters laughed.

"Where do these nuts come up with this stuff?" asked the chief.

"I don't know, but at least they got the nationality right this time."

For a few minutes the two men looked silently out the window at the passing lights and listened to the sound of the wheels rushing along the track. Peters began to laugh.

"What's so funny, Captain?"

"It's one of those crazy ideas that just suddenly pop into my head from time to time."

"Sir?"

"What did those Germans do with all of the garbage while they were trapped aboard the submarine? They must have had a lot of empty cans and other stuff. Where did they put it?"

"I found it when I went into the bow of the boat. They had stuffed it all into the torpedo tubes!"

"I should have thought of that!"

The two men laughed as the train rushed through the darkness of the Maryland countryside toward Washington's Union Station.

Washington, D.C.—0810 Hours

The morning was hot, and Morris mopped his forehead with his handkerchief as they climbed the steps to the Archives Building. "Whew, it's gonna be a scorcher, Captain!" The business suit he wore chafed worse than his uniform.

The superintendent was waiting for them.

"Mrs. Sloan will assist you," the superintendent said. "The document-storage boxes were brought up from the warehouse yesterday as soon we received the Attorney General's order."

A pleasant woman in her mid-forties, wearing a light blouse and skirt, took them to a basement office. Two tables and chairs sat next to a very large stack of document-storage boxes.

"Oh, my God, sir," the chief exclaimed. "There must be a million boxes in here!"

"Only a hundred and sixty, actually," said Mrs. Sloan.

"Well, I guess we might as well get started," Peters said. "I'll take the first box. Chief, you start with the second."

They set the boxes on the tables. Mrs. Sloan cut the wire seals and swung the tops back.

"This box has files from August 14, 1945, to the nineteenth, Ron," Morris said. "That's after the sub was invaded. Should we bother with these?"

"Yeah. There's a chance Göring talked to somebody about

185

the U-boat at some time during his captivity. Don't want to miss anything."

"Aye, sir. It'll take months to read all of these papers."

"Think of the bright side, Pat. It's air-conditioned in here and we don't have to deal with Ledbetter."

"You're on. Oh, good Lord, listen to this one. Some Army captain is complaining because Göring's special chocolate order hasn't arrived on time. My heart bleeds!"

"Actually, that's interesting."

"You're kidding!"

"Think about it. Why would the Army care about fancy chocolates for Göring unless he told somebody something of value in exchange for preferential treatment?"

"I hadn't thought of that."

"Keep digging."

Aboard the dredge, *William P. McDonald*—0950 Hours

Sherry was in her office on the dredge working on the final plans for the disposition of the submarine UX-6000. Her meeting with Captain Harris and J.D. had gone well that morning.

The two men told her that Bradley Dexter convinced the Richmond County D.A. to drop all criminal investigation of the gun fight. The D.A. and the police had decided that the killings were justified as self defense.

Everything seemed to be going right for a change. Well, most everything, she thought as she swatted at the bothersome fly again. Thankfully, the dredge captain was warming to her and their relationship was becoming close. It could be time to deepen his obviously growing feelings to her. She knew he could be a powerful ally to her job success.

Her cellular phone rang.

"Sherry!" It was Scott calling from his hospital room. "You've got serious trouble."

"Bob? What's wrong?"

"Half an hour ago, I got a call from Special Agent Carson,"

Scott said. "The FBI found George Wilson in a dumpster on Third Avenue! He's dead! Shot full of holes!"

"What!" She suddenly forgot how to breathe.

"That's not all. A few minutes ago, I talked to your boss and Sergeant Ford of the Fort Lee police. Your apartment was ransacked this morning after you left. Trashed completely."

"I don't believe it!" She gasped for breath.

"You *must* contact Sergeant Ford right away. The police have been trying to call you. They want you to meet them as soon as possible."

"Oh, my God! This is crazy!"

"I just told Captain Harris. He's coming down to your office right now. He wants you to stay on the dredge for the next few days so that he can protect you. I agree. These people may be after you like they were after George. As soon as Captain Harris gets there, he'll tell you the plan for guarding you. Then get in touch with Sergeant Ford."

Sherry looked up to see the dredge captain and J.D. coming in the door. Her face turned ashen as the blood drained away. Her breath labored, and she needed to hold onto her desk for support.

"I can see that you've talked with Commander Scott," Harris observed, his hand resting on the holster carrying his spare Magnum revolver. "I've armed the crew with the extra guns."

"Oh, Tiny, I'm scared to death! Poor George." Her face was taut, her mouth parched. "What do I do?"

"For once, listen to me as captain of this crew. If you'll follow my instructions, I'll get you through this okay. Understand?"

"Yes." She tried to swallow.

"I want you to move into my cabin tonight and stay there for the next few days. I'll be sleeping *here* so that if those bastards come looking for you, they'll meet my bullets instead. J.D. will be right next to you in his cabin with his nine-millimeter and shotgun, so if they get past me, they'll still be in trouble. I'll also have a couple of other men standing watch fully armed."

"But I don't have anything here. No nightclothes, not even a toothbrush."

"I know. I'm sending you to meet Sergeant Ford so you can get some of your things while you're in Fort Lee."

"You want me to drive to Fort Lee?"

"No. I'm sending you in our van. These murderers might know your car and be watching for you. So I'm having Cowboy and Bear drive you up."

"When?"

"Right after you call Ford. J.D. and Bulldog will handle the workboat. I'm going to line up Cowboy and Bear. You make that call."

The dredge captain stepped out into the passageway as Sherry telephoned Sergeant Ford. Cowboy and Bear came out the rear engine room door. Bear wore his .45-caliber semiautomatic and holster, and he carried his pump-action twelve-gauge shotgun. Cowboy wore his .357-caliber revolver and carried a semiautomatic .270-caliber carbine. Both were large and powerful men experienced in combat.

Cowboy was in his late forties, with a full head of hair and large brown eyes. His nose was bent at an odd angle from being broken in numerous barroom fights. A mellow man and slow to anger, if harassed long enough he would finally rise and deliver a smashing blow.

Bear was larger, only forty-two, and had brownish hair that curled around his clean-shaven face. His brown eyes danced with enthusiasm for life. His scarred hands showed the effects of a lifetime of hard work. Both men were popular with the rest of the crew.

"All right, you two," Harris said to them. "You drive Sherry wherever she has to go—and whatever happens, you guard her! If anything happens to that girl, I'd better find you two bastards in body bags, you hear?"

"Yeah," Cowboy answered. "I reckon you said it plain enough."

Sherry emerged from her office obviously still shaken.

"All right, J.D. and Bulldog are ready to move out. Y'all be damn careful now."

Aboard the Workboat—1000 Hours

She stood by the railing trying to regain her composure as the powerful engine drove them toward Port Newark. She still couldn't believe that the people behind the attacks now wanted to kill *her*. First they tried to kill Bob Scott, and now they had succeeded with George Wilson. Maybe she *was* a target. Shivers went through her despite the warmth of the sunny morning.

J.D. joined her.

"How you hanging in?" he asked.

"About like jelly. I'm shaking badly."

"You've got a lot of friends, and they're going to look out for you. You know you can count on me and Tiny."

"Yes, I know. That's what's holding me together." She reached over and placed her hand on J.D.'s.

He gave it a gentle squeeze with his other hand. She appreciated his show of support.

The stubby bow of the workboat thrust the turbid water aside as it neared the service dock. J.D. called Bear and Cowboy over. "Now you bubbas listen up! When you get ashore, remember that you're going to be subject to local gun laws. These Yankee lawmen have some crazy ideas about guns, so keep them hidden out of sight and bring them out only if you have to.

"All right—Bear, you drive. Cowboy, you're riding shotgun. When you're coming back, call us about half an hour from the dock, and we'll come back in for you."

Fort Lee, New Jersey—1040 Hours

The trip to Fort Lee was without incident. As the van pulled into the parking lot at Sherry's apartment building, they could see Fort Lee police cars at the curb. She stepped out and approached a police sergeant waiting by the door. She hoped her shaking hands and pale complexion wouldn't be obvious.

"Miss Edwards?" he asked. "I'm Sergeant Ford. Follow me, please."

Sherry was unprepared for the devastation she found in her apartment. Amid the piles of torn clothing lay the ruined contents from the emptied drawers. Her heart was numbed to see the fish from the smashed glass tank lying stilled among the soaked debris. Smells of spilled cosmetics added false pleasantry to the chaos.

"Oh, no!" Sherry cried at the sight. "Those damn people!" She raised her hands to cover her cheeks as if to block out the scene.

"What people?"

"Sergeant, I don't know what I'm allowed to tell you, but I think this is related to a string of murders, bombings, and other attacks this past week." She lowered her hands to her breast.

"What are you talking about?"

"You've stumbled onto a federal investigation. I'm not free to discuss it with you. Talk to Special Agent Carson at the Manhattan FBI office."

"Can you tell me what's been stolen here?"

"Sergeant, I assure you, these people weren't here to steal anything except maybe my life and a diary."

"This is getting damned interesting! Let me see if that phone is still working?"

Sergeant Ford called Agent Carson at his office. Sherry waited with deepening sorrow at the loss of her belongings until he had obtained whatever information Carson was willing to provide. She picked out the few usable articles that remained and filled a small overnight case. She stood up and turned toward Ford.

"Carson says to let you go without further questioning. We're going to close up this apartment for now until the feds and the state cops can comb through this mess. Do you have a place to stay?"

"Yes. Agent Carson or Commander Scott can reach me." Let me out of here, she thought.

Sherry returned to the waiting van carrying the bag. Her facial expression left no doubt as to her frame of mind.

Cowboy could see that she must have been through a difficult meeting with the cops through her sickened expression.

"I thought you were gonna get a bunch of clothes?" Cowboy asked.

"There's not much to get. They destroyed almost everything!"

"Let's head back then."

Washington, D.C.—1320 Hours

Chief Morris and Captain Peters were just finishing lunch at the cafeteria in the Archives building.

"I'm still a bit confused by these files, Ron. Neither of us has found anything earlier than August forty-five. Where was Göring before he was moved to the prison block at the Palace of Justice in Nuremberg?"

"He was captured in May by U.S. troops near Salzburg. On the eighth of May, I believe. He should have been turned over to G-2 for interrogation. I'm pretty sure he was held by Army Military Police at a prisoner-of-war camp until they moved him."

"That's what's bugging me. We've never seen any paperwork of that first month. If he told someone about the boat, he probably did so during that first week or ten days after he was caught."

"Agreed. Let's get back to it. The answer has got to be in one of those boxes."

On their way back to the office, Mrs. Sloan stopped them. "Captain, you're to call an officer in Virginia as soon as you can. He said it was urgent. Here is his number."

"Okay. Pat, you go ahead. I'll be along shortly."

Chief Morris returned to the office and, pulling another file folder, started reading the papers. Oh, good Lord, he thought, more complaints about Göring's diet, and now he's griping about his uniforms not being cleaned regularly! What a dandy! The chief read on.

The captain rejoined him a half hour later. He seemed a bit rattled.

"Problems, sir?"

"Yeah. Ledbetter moved faster than I expected. I spoke with a lawyer on the Judge Advocate General staff. He's been named to represent me to answer questions raised by Ledbetter."

"Good Lord! A court-martial, sir?"

"No. A review board instead. I'm to be ready to answer the questions on Monday at Governors Island."

"I really find it hard to see what they could question. You haven't done anything to justify this."

"Well, that doesn't seem to matter to the Navy. I called my secretary at the station, and she confirmed that Ledbetter's been going through all of the files. I also called Bob."

"How's he doing?"

"Better. He's sitting up, and they've been having him do some walking. He thinks they plan to throw him out of the hospital on Sunday."

"Where will he go then?"

"If he's able to walk and do some light work, I'm thinking he might be able to join us with this research."

Aboard the dredge, *William P. McDonald*—1330 Hours

Cowboy jumped aboard the dredge with the tie-up rope to secure the workboat. As Sherry climbed the ladder, she was surprised to see Cracker sitting in a chair with a shotgun in his lap.

"Well, this is a surprise. I didn't think you were ready to leave the hospital yet," she said.

"I'm convalescing, Sherry. What do you think of my new job? I'm a security guard." He rocked back and forth in the chair, a big smile on his face.

"So you're going to shoot unwelcome guests."

"Either that or club them to death with my cast." He laughed and raised his plaster sheathed leg.

"So what're Kendall and Curly doing?" She looked toward where the two workmen were raising a piece of steel bar.

"Oh, Kendall keeps trying to make everybody believe he's a welder."

"Hey, Kendall!" Curly shouted, "Did you hear? The mouth is running!"

"Yeah, I heard! He's still trying to learn how to light a torch!" He quickly tightened the C-clamp to secure the bar for welding.

"Really, what *are* you guys doing?" Sherry asked.

"Tiny wants a fence along the side here," Cracker answered, "to help keep people from coming aboard so easy-like."

"Tiny's taking no chances," Curly added. "Not after Tuesday night." His hand moved in front of his eyes as Kendall struck a bright arc.

Cracker remembered suddenly. "Oh, Sherry—Tiny wanted you to go right up to his office when you got back."

"Okay, just as soon as I put my case in my office."

"No, girl, that ain't the plan. You're supposed to move up to Tiny's cabin right now. He's already moved into yours." Cracker smiled and snickered loudly.

"Come on, Sherry. I'll carry your stuff for you," Cowboy offered. "Let's go see the man!"

When Sherry and Cowboy reached the dredge captain's office, Sherry noticed that her files and other materials had indeed been brought up. J.D. was filling a box with some of the dredge captain's things.

"Good! You're back," Harris greeted her. "Any problems?"

"Couldn't get many things. Most of my stuff at the apartment was trashed."

"Uh-huh. I'm not surprised. They're telling you what they plan to do to you when they catch you. It's happened to me a coupla times in the old days."

"I can't believe somebody really wants to kill me." She was still groping for some other answer.

"Well, they do." He nodded at Cowboy. "Thanks for taking care of Sherry. Go help Bulldog move the steering anchors, will ya?" As cowboy left, he turned to Sherry. "Okay, now while you were ashore, J.D. and I were on the phone with Scott and with that FBI cop, Carson. Carson is convinced that George must have told those killers about you before they shot him. He thinks you're a definite target, and Scott does, too. So, you're going to stay out here for now so I can protect you. The cops won't do anything to protect you since you're not a witness they need. J.D., will you see if that holster fits?"

"Holster?"

"Yes, holster and pistol. You're about to begin your training in self-defense."

"A gun?"

J.D. reached around Sherry's waist and buckled the belt carrying the holster and pistol. She tried to back away, but there was nowhere to go. "Tiny, I've never even touched one in my whole life!"

"Take it easy," J.D. said as he continued adjusting the holster. "The magazine is empty. I just want you to get used to the feel of the holster right now."

"Oh, guys—I can't do this!" Her eyes were wide with her amazement at the sight of the deadly tool.

"You can and you *will*!" Harris said strongly. "You've been able to live a nice sweet life till now. But there are nasty men out there who want you *dead*! So—like it or not—you are going to have to change. You don't have any options!"

"Cops carry guns! *I'm* not supposed to." But Sherry was beginning to accept the inevitable.

"You've been very fortunate to live in the suburbs most of your life. I'm sorry to have to shove it in your face, girl, but you have suddenly woke up down here in the gutter where the tough life goes on. Now it's kill or be killed!"

J.D. broke in. "You can't count on having a cop around when you need one. You have no choice. You must be able to defend yourself."

"But...I don't know anything about guns. I've never had one in my hands. Never!"

"It just so happens that J.D. was an instructor of weapons and tactics when he was in the Marines back in the fifties. One of the very best! Tomorrow morning, target practice!" She could see that the dredge captain was not going to accept any protest.

"Do I really have to wear this now?"

"Yes! I want you to get used to the feel of it. That stays on except when you're in the head or asleep!"

"Damn!" Sherry muttered, then sighed with resignation.

"Sherry," J.D. said softly, "you're going to have to trust us. You have no choice."

"I just can't believe I could ever shoot someone."

"The best thing is to avoid a gunfight. But if you can't, then the biggest difference between surviving a gunfight and ending up dead is the willingness to pull that trigger. Most people hesitate and as a result end up dead.

"Forget all that fast-gun business you see in the movies. It's not the first one to pull his gun who wins—or even the one who's the best shot. It's the one who grabs his gun and pulls that trigger first with adequate accuracy. That's the one who walks away. I intend to train you to have that determination."

"All right. Let's give you some time to settle in," Harris said, "then we'll get together for supper about six-thirty. Okay?"

"Okay—and thanks for caring." Sherry stepped directly in front of Harris and quickly surrounded the big man with her arms. Taken by surprise, Harris responded with his own awkward embrace. They swayed together for a full minute. She rested her forehead against the dredge captain's chest as he lifted her five foot-six inch frame just off the floor. She felt secure for the first time in many hours and didn't care what J.D. or anyone else might think.

Finally, Sherry was alone. She sat down on the dredge captain's bed and looked around. The cabin consisted of two rooms. The office was more spacious, the walls decorated with pictures of ships and construction apparatus above several filing cabinets, a bookcase, and a large gun cabinet. A large desk and high back swivel chair dominated the center of the room. This was nothing like her apartment had been. That had been a happy place.

She got up to explore further. The holster and gun felt heavy at her side. The bed-sitting-room contained a bed, night stands pushed against the rear wall, and two large comfortable chairs at the other end. A cabinet containing a television and sound system was against the wall opposite the chairs, and plenty of video and audio tapes. Tiny's private space, Sherry thought, a lonely place for a socially weak man, a man who almost never went ashore.

She picked up a chess set from the chair and looked down at a volume entitled: *Outlines of Roman History* by H. F. Pelham. She pulled at her chin, surprised yet impressed, as she stared at the book. She turned and put the chess set down on a table as she pondered just what kind of man this dredge captain might be.

Through a connecting door a large bathroom joined, as a shared space, with the first mate's cabin. The cabin's doors in turn opened onto a catwalk at the front of the dredge, just behind the control cab.

The rooms were very masculine, but she resigned herself to make the best of the situation. Already she missed her apartment, but the dredge captain and J.D. were right: that part of her life was destroyed. Opening her suitcase, she tried to settle in. I need to show strength right now, she thought, biting her lip a couple of times to keep from crying. She spent some time getting organized, and a bit after six o'clock, she sat down to watch the news on TV.

■ ■ ■ ■ ■

Back in the cabin after supper, Sherry unbuckled the holster and set it on the nightstand. She stood by the bed for several minutes and stared at the gun, hoping it would go away. It wouldn't. There were many unfamiliar noises to deal with as she lay down.

Even though the cabin was somewhat soundproofed, the roar of the diesel engines was still noticeable. The vibrations were continuous as the operator kept the cutter head digging. Left, then right, then left again. Sherry knew that the dredge would dig away forty tons of mud every minute, enough to fill a huge tractor-trailer truck every thirty seconds, even as she slept.

She looked up at the ceiling, her mind racing over the events of the past few weeks. Just being in this room, in this bed, proved how much her relationship had changed with Harris. His hostile attitude, which had prevented any prior relationship, had softened and become very warm. She knew he desired her and, Sherry had to admit, that could work to her advantage. She even liked the idea. She found his size and hardness—fascinating.

Soon the engine noise seemed to draw her mind away from the mad events of the day. She kept focused on the drumming...drumming...drum...She drifted off to sleep.

Washington, D.C.—0710 Hours

The muggy, oppressive heat bore down on Washington as Chief Morris and Captain Peters left the hotel for the drive to the Archives building.

"What did Carson tell you, sir?" Morris asked as they walked to the car after the captain's telephone call.

"The German Federal Police have identified the two assistants who left the boat with Von Kruger: Kurt Bruning and Johann Meyer—both science technicians. The German medical team has finished identifying the bodies from the sub and are positive that Bruning and Meyer were not among the dead. Now the police are trying to find out what happened to them. Since Von Kruger was found murdered in Germany, it may be that the other two suffered the same fate. At least, that's my theory."

"Okay, so now we know for sure who the three men were who left the boat. But the cargo? Anything yet about where the *cargo* went?" Morris remained convinced the cargo would be the final key.

"No, not yet, but I still believe with you and Scott that it went back to Germany. We need to prove our theory of course. I still think we're going to find the answer to what happened to it somewhere in those boxes."

As they drove toward the Mall, the chief asked about the

captain's meeting at the Judge Advocate General's office the afternoon before.

"It wasn't very encouraging. Ledbetter is questioning every document. Answering all of the issues he's raising could take weeks."

"That man is one vindictive bastard!"

"It's more than that, Pat. There's something else driving this so-called investigation. Can't prove it, but I feel it. Almost sinister."

Aboard the dredge, *William P. McDonald*—0715 Hours

Sherry awoke just before seven. After she showered and dressed, she reluctantly buckled on the gun belt. Just in time, she thought as J.D. knocked. She put her hard hat on and joined him on the catwalk.

"I'm glad to see you're in uniform." He quickly, but not very subtly, inspected her holster. "Ready to learn to use that gun?"

"I guess so. I needed time to think about it. I realize I'm going to have to do it whether I like it or not."

"Sleep okay?"

"Better than I thought I would with all the noise and tension."

"Good. Let me ask you something."

"Ask away."

"When we were moving your stuff I saw a picture of you with a trophy and a bow. What was that all about?"

Sherry chuckled. "Oh, that. That's an old picture."

"But you won a trophy for archery, right?"

"Yeah, but firing at targets, not people."

"But you won a trophy, so you're good."

"A long time ago."

"Same talent with a gun, really. That's great. And I'm glad you're well rested. You'll need all your strength today. I'm planning to push hard."

"No mercy, huh?"

"Not a bit!"

Midtown Hospital, Manhattan—0745 Hours

Scott looked up from his magazine as Hillerman entered the hospital room. A broad grin appeared on Scott's face as he recognized his close friend of nearly ten years.

"Good to see you sitting up," Hillerman said. "Getting stronger?"

"Yeah," Scott answered. "Been walking some. I'm determined to get back in this investigation. Must find Brenda's killers."

"Dunn and I will get them. I guarantee we won't stop until we do."

Scott knew that Hillerman meant every word. He had come to know the strength of the man. They had sailed and hunted together and faced death or serious injury several times. Scott remembered how they had been caught in a severe squall while sailing and had to fight to survive when a huge wave struck their ketch. Hillerman's strength and guts saved Scott's life when he pulled him back aboard the nearly capsized craft.

The two men had become as close as brothers. They trusted each other implicitly, and when Scott confided to Hillerman that his marriage was failing and he wanted to meet other women—Hillerman arranged for Scott to meet Brenda.

"I'm gonna kill 'em, Alan," Scott went on. "I swear it."

"I know you loved Brenda, but I'm the cop remember. This is my job now and Brenda was my cousin. I loved her as the sister I didn't have. I'll never forget her way of brightening a room when she entered."

"Those bastards destroyed all that! I'll never forgive what they did if I live a thousand years. She was more than wonderful. That special way she tossed her head. Her playful smile and the way she'd tease me. No way I'm staying out of this."

"Leave the fight to me. You're headed down to D.C. on

Monday. You do the brain work and figure out who's giving the orders. I'll find the damn mercenaries."

Washington, D.C. — 1140 Hours

Morris was getting hungry. It had been several hours since breakfast, and the work of studying file after file was very tiring. Not to mention damn awful boring. Oh, my God, he thought, not another complaint about Göring's food and laundry. "Oh, wow!" the chief suddenly cried out. "Captain! I've found it!"

"What?"

"Read this! A memo sent to the Monuments, Fine Arts, and Archives office complaining about vandals stealing art objects from Göring's train. He was promised that his property would be protected in return for information about a secret submarine attack on New York City!"

"Well, well! This is proof of what we've suspected—some U.S. Army people *did* find out about the UX-6000 from Göring. Good work, Chief!"

"The date on the memo is about right: 7 June 1945. It would fit our presumed timetable."

"Right. Let me call Carson with this. Fax that memo up to his office."

Since it was Saturday, the FBI support staff had the day off, so Carson answered the phone himself.

Peters said, "We've found a memo that appears to prove our theory that Göring did trade information about the U-boat for special treatment. It's being faxed up now."

"Very good. I was about to call you, Captain. I just finished talking with Lieutenant Mueller. The Ludwigshafen police found a file on Johann Meyer from 1945. He died in a hospital in Heidelberg on June 11, 1945, from—get this—cholera!"

"Cholera! That's it then. As we've been theorizing all along, the cargo *was* taken back to Germany!"

"It sure looks that way. But why?"

"As Morris and Scott suspected from the beginning, this is

a crime for profit. That cargo was sold to someone who wanted it real bad. The *who* and *why* may lead us to these murderers."

"Agreed. Continue to search for who talked with Göring during those first days after his capture. Those are the most likely suspects."

Peters slammed the phone down triumphantly. "Meyer died in Germany," he told the chief, "from—get this—cholera. Our theory is proving correct."

"I knew it! These murdering bastards did all of this for money! And they tried to kill Bob to continue to cover up what they did in 1945!"

"There's little doubt now. Keep digging!"

Aboard the dredge, *William P. McDonald*—1200 Hours

Sherry returned to the galley after showering and changing. She had overcome her fear of guns and could master using one after all. Hell, she thought, I'm doing just great. She joined Captain Harris and J.D. at their table to have lunch. Cookie served her a chicken salad sandwich. It smelled great.

Harris greeted her. "J.D. tells me you're picking things up very well. I'm pleased."

"J.D. is proving to be quite a trainer."

"It's easy when I have such a good student," J.D. responded with a broad smile.

"What's next, J.D.?" Harris asked, interrupting the mutual admiration society.

"Identification and decision making. I plan to use rotating cardboard targets. Could use Cowboy to turn them."

"Yeah, no problem. I'm sure Bulldog's done with him by now."

"This will be much tougher." J.D. turned to Sherry. "This part of your training is more involved with when and when not to shoot. All cops have to go through this—and it's very hard." J.D. obviously did not share the dredge captain's total lack of respect for law-enforcement officers.

"Shooting the gun well and accurately is only a part of

firearms responsibility," Harris put in. "Now you have to learn *when* you should fire. If you make a mistake and shoot an innocent person, you could find yourself facing charges of murder. In this gun business, there is no 'Please excuse my mistake.' You can't make a mistake. Not even one."

■ ■ ■ ■ ■

An exhausted Sherry lay on the bed in the captain's cabin to rest for an hour after lunch. She looked at the ink stains on her fingers from the fingerprinting by Sergeant Lyons, who had come aboard the dredge after lunch to complete her application for gun permits. Fingerprinted, huh, she thought, now I'll fit in with the ex-cons in this crew. She had washed her hands several times, but still some of the ink remained.

She reflected on the events of the last two days. Her life had changed so much she couldn't believe what was happening. She still hadn't called her parents—she didn't want them to worry.

On the catwalk outside the cabin, Captain Harris and J.D. watched Cowboy complete the target setup for Sherry's next practice session.

"There's not much time," Harris said. "The *Hercules* will be here in fifteen days to pull us out of here. That's not going to change. Sherry will have to go back ashore the day before we leave. We can't protect her any longer than that. She's got to be ready to defend herself in less than two weeks. Can you do it?"

"I think so. She's pretty capable."

"You're not forgetting that you won't be able to train out here while we do the submarine burial job? I'll need all hands to install the extending gear on Monday."

"We'll stop the training on Monday, but I plan to use the pump room on Tuesday for indoor training."

"I'll let you have Cowboy and Bear as much as possible, but the dredging has to come first."

"Understood. Time to get back to it."

"Bear down hard, J.D. She's got to be ready to leave our protection when the *Hercules* enters the harbor."

■ ■ ■ ■

At the front of the dredge, Cowboy had set up several full-size cutouts on rope operated turntables. Sherry would not be able to see the target until it was turned toward her and as Cowboy quickly manipulated each turntable, she would have only one second to decide whether to shoot.

J.D. signaled Cowboy to pull the first target. Sherry was confronted with a child holding a teddy bear. Sherry held her fire.

"Good," J.D. said. "Next!"

The next target was a thug holding a pistol. She gasped at the realism and fired.

Three rapid explosions rent the afternoon air. The thunder of the diesel engines kept anyone off the dredge from hearing the gunfire.

"Very good. Next!"

The target was a woman carrying a package.

Sherry fired. But only one bullet as she quickly realized her error.

"No, no, no! You just shot an innocent bystander! You'll go to jail for that!"

"I'm sorry."

"'Sorry' don't get it! Next!"

A teenage boy holding a knife suddenly appeared.

Sherry fired. Her rapid three-shot pattern did its deadly task.

"No, no, no! You can't shoot a person holding a knife unless he charges at you. You're guilty of excessive force!"

"You're not making this easy!"

"It's *not* easy! Do it again! Next!"

As the afternoon wore on, Sherry's responses improved until she was able to identify each target accurately and quickly. J.D. let her sit for a short rest while he went to speak with Cowboy.

"You got our little surprise ready?"

"It's right here."

"Push it out after the boy-chasing-the-ball target. You got your revolver loaded with blanks?"

"Yep."

"Give her one second and then fire at her through your peephole."

Resuming her combat stance, she sighed with resignation as Cowboy turned the first target. It was a man with a gun aimed right at her nose.

Her gun exploded rapidly again.

"Good! Again!"

The image of a boy chasing a ball came into view.

Sherry held her fire.

"Good! Next!"

Suddenly a lifelike mannequin dressed as a thug with a pistol was in front of Sherry. She gasped in surprise and hesitated.

The sharp blast of Cowboy's revolver completed Sherry's misery. Her mouth hung open and her eyes stared without focus.

J.D. stepped to her side. "You're dead," he said softly. "You hesitated."

"Oh, dammit!" She pouted in disgust.

"You must be ready for anything! Cowboy! Mix 'em up and do it again!"

Five more times the tables were turned and cardboard yielded to lead when without warning the mannequin was again pushed out. Cowboy reached for his revolver but before he could pull his trigger, Sherry's first bullet crashed into the mannequin followed by two more. The mannequin fell to the deck.

"You did it!" J.D. yelled. "You just saved your life!"

Cowboy again mixed the targets, and Sherry repeated the practice. Once again, the mannequin was pushed out unexpectedly only to be downed by her quick triple pattern.

J.D. stopped the practice. "You're not finished!" he said.

"What do you mean?" she sputtered holding her weapon between her breasts.

"You've knocked him down, but do you know if he's dead?"

"I hit him twice in his chest!"

"A man can take a lot of punishment. You've probably given him a fatal wound, but he can still pull a trigger. He could still shoot you. There's an old saying, Sherry: 'Two in the chest and two in the head makes them very goddamn dead.'"

"What are you saying?"

"When you shoot a man, finish him! Don't leave him able to recover and pursue you and try again to kill you. KILL HIM! NOW! DO IT!"

"I'm a Christian, J.D.!" He wants me to become a murderer, she thought, even if it is a mannequin—I don't like the idea at all.

"And I want you to be a *live* Christian!" KILL HIM! DO IT!"

Sherry finally bit her lip and raised her gun. Two sharp reports and two bullets flew. The mix of styrofoam and fast lead proved explosive; the head disintegrated.

"Good! Very good! Cowboy, put another head on that thing, and let's do it again!"

South Manhattan—1720 Hours

The news that Commander Scott was being released from the hospital brought Chief Morris back to Manhattan. He was eager to discuss what had been discovered in D.C. Still weak, Scott sat in the front passenger seat as the chief steered the Coast Guard staff car toward the Whitehall Street ferry landing.

The chief said, "You know, I just can't stop turning over in my mind the question of who wanted that cargo so bad. Do you think a reward was offered for it?"

"After Germany surrendered, there was a mad scramble by the Allies to grab, steal, buy, or beg anything of military value that they could find.," Scott answered. "It's possible that Operation Overcast found out about that cargo and went after it. But why kill the crew and then take the cargo back to Germany? It doesn't fit."

"No—but what if somebody *else* in the U.S. Army found out about the cargo and realized that the Army or the Soviets would pay big money to get it. So they make a real fast trip across the Atlantic, find the boat, grab the cargo, haul it back to Germany, and use Von Kruger to sell it to whoever agreed to buy it."

"That makes some sense, all right."

"And then, we come along and find the sub and discover what happened," Morris surmised. "So the same ex-Army people who pulled off this caper are still around and hire mercenaries to stop our investigation."

"That seems to fit. Now figure out what Overcast would want with that cargo."

"The war with Japan was still going on. Maybe they wanted to dump it on Tokyo and start an epidemic of cholera there."

"It never happened, Pat, so your idea seems wrong. Maybe the Army germ warfare people wanted it?"

"Maybe. Or maybe the Soviets for their germ warfare program."

"Yes, maybe," Scott responded with a quizzical look. "Let's take a look at the Overcast files. Could Carson get them for us?"

"I'm sure he could. I'm surprised you would be willing to add to that mountain of boxes you've already got."

"That's a problem, all right, but we need to follow the cargo. The files may have names of the merchants and black marketeers."

Their conversation ended as the Governors Island ferry arrived and the staff car was quickly loaded. Morris leaned back and closed his eyes. Thank God, Morris thought, Scott will be with us on Monday. Maybe he can figure this mystery out.

Aboard the dredge, *William P. McDonald*—1945 Hours

Captain Harris stroked his chin as he studied the chess board. "You are a devious woman," he finally said. "You're after my rook." He glanced up at his opponent, Sherry Edwards, who was lying face down on the bed, legs bent upward at the knees, her head braced in her hands.

"Oh, I'm after much more than that," she replied. She looked up at the dredge captain with her green eyes staring deeply into his. She smiled impishly as she watched him squirm. She crossed her symmetrically perfect bare calves at the narrow ankles. She moved her left hand to push her bishop forward. "Check, Captain."

She was enjoying watching Harris sweat, both over the game and his view of her scantily dressed body. She had invited the dredge captain to join her for a game of chess and he had quickly agreed. She was a bit amused at his effort to clean up and put his best appearance forward. He reminded her of an awkward schoolboy arriving for a first date.

"Damn," he exclaimed. "I think you've got me." He glanced again at her legs. She was enjoying her power, men were so predictable. She quickly rose from the bed and approached the nearly immobilized man. He tried to reach for a smoldering cigarette from the ash stand, but his shaking hand only knocked the butt to the deck.

"You've lost. Time to pay," she said hoarsely. She smiled at the shocked look on his face as she slowly moved her hand to the top button on the thin taut blouse. The cloth separated quickly as the button was released exposing the smooth rolling tops of her large breasts. The dredge captain's mouth dropped open as his eyes locked intently. He gasped, he couldn't move. She had him and knew it. He would be so easy, she mused.

"Why me?" Harris asked, barely audible.

"You're the perfect choice," she answered softly. She moved her hand down to the next button releasing her blouse to gap open even further.

"There's lots of ol' boys on this dredge who'd go mad to screw you."

"They're too eager and single. I usually pick men who are married." Then, she thought, when I finish with my fun, I can send them home to their wives. She unbuttoned the lower buttons—the blouse swung completely open.

"I'm not married." His breath was quick and shallow. He pulled at his collar.

"Yes you are. To your job and this dredge. I'm sure that when the tugboat comes to pull this equipment to Boston, you'll go with it." She reached up and slid the bra's shoulder strap free to fall into the crook of her left arm. Harris's brow was wet; sweat dripped off his nose. His fingers dug into the chair's armrest.

"You know I must."

"I'm counting on it." She slid the right strap free.

"I always figured you'd want that guy, Scott. The way you and him always look at each other."

"I like Commander Scott very much." But when he told me that he was leaving his wife, she remembered, I knew I couldn't use him and then send him away. He would take my heart, and I can't allow that. She reached behind her and unhooked her bra's back strap. "I'll just keep him interested until I decide to have him."

"Why?" Harris could barely speak.

How can I answer such a question, she wondered. How do I tell him that I once loved a man very deeply. We were planning to marry, but he was killed in a terrible traffic accident. I mourned for months. I've never known such heartache. I swore I would never let a man get so deep in my heart again. So, now I pick a man I can use whenever I need sex and then end it at my choosing. She moved her hands forward—the bra sliding free and dropping to the floor. She finally replied, "because I feel like it."

She watched with amusement as Harris froze, his eyes fixated on her smoothly curving breasts, her fully erect nipples. She placed her hand behind his head and with steady, firm pressure, pulled his open mouth over her nipple.

"Let's see if you know what to do with it," she whispered. She held him firmly to her breast as he suckled like a newborn.

After several minutes she withdrew and stepped back. "Now it's your turn to undress." She reached down and unbuttoned her mini-skirt and let it drop away.

Harris worked his fingers as rapidly as he could but seemed to find it difficult to control the buttons. He finally tore his shirt away and dropped his pants. Sherry sat down on the end of the bed and gasped. Her back trembled as her muscles tightened. Her mouth went dry, her eyes staring at more than she had been prepared to see. Much more.

"Whatever possessed this crew to call you Tiny?" she said hoarsely. She knew it was too late to turn back now.

His huge hands cupped around her buttocks as she gasped out. I don't know if I can stretch enough, she feared as he began his penetration. She bit down on her lip as pain and yet pleasure engulfed her.

She looked up at the muscular giant above her through glazed eyes. His lightly bronzed skin, coated thinly with sweat, glistened in the lamp light. His powerful muscles rippled with his every move. Muscles, she'd been told, capable of lifting a 400 pound barbell overhead. Now, all that strength is being used by him to force his thick penis far deeper than any previous man had ever gone.

Her well developed leg muscles quickly matched his rhythm, and her hands grasped his elbows to add all her strength to his. Her heavy breasts impacted against his forearms with each powerful thrust. His moving, heaving chest stroked the sensitive tips of her teats, adding ripples of intense tickling to the rush of pleasure thundering into her mind. Her nerves seemed on fire as waves of intense euphoria surged providing forcefully exquisite sensations beyond her many experiences. His breathing was coming hard and fast as he increased his thrusting even faster.

She heard her own cries and moans as her body lapsed into powerful spasms of erotic relief. Pulses of joy exploded into a sudden flood of hot liquid deep within. Deep, deep, deep. She passed out.

■ ■ ■ ■ ■

Sherry stepped out of the bathroom wearing her pink bathrobe. The shower had felt good, and the chance to straighten her makeup and hair was even better. She smiled at Harris as she approached the small table where he sat stirring a fresh cup of coffee. Vapor rose from the cup he had prepared for her. She stepped to his chair and kissed him for several minutes.

"Thanks, Tiny," she said as she broke free and backed to her chair.

"I should be thanking you," he replied. "If you only knew how much I've wanted you ever since you first came aboard."

"You had a strange way of showing it." She added some creamer to her cup.

"You drove me crazy. You're the most beautiful girl I've ever seen. More beautiful than any playmate photo. I just couldn't think around you." She lifted the cup and took a sip. He continued, "If I had only known what you're really like. Did you know that all the crew think you're frigid?" She set the cup down.

"Now you know the truth about me. And I know the truth about you, my dear captain—you're a fraud."

"A fraud?" He jerked his hand, spilling some of the hot liquid over the lip of his cup.

"You're not the big ignorant oaf you pretend to be. You're actually very intelligent, sensitive, and an excellent lover. You rang bells I didn't even know I had. Shall we keep each other's secret?" She reached across the table and lightly stroked his hand with her fingertips.

"You've got a deal." Their eyes locked in deep contact.

She stood up and stepped immediately in front of him. A quick move of her hand and the sash holding her robe fell away. A quick shake and the robe was at her feet.

"Now," she said. "Let's get back to bed. You've got a lot of work to do. I happen to like being the cylinder in a hot engine." She reached down and lifted his hand to her firm breast. It was to be a long night.

Washington, D.C.—0912 Hours

Mrs. Sloan led the forklift into the basement office where Chief Morris and the recovering Bob Scott were already at work on the Göring file boxes.

"What's this?" Scott asked.

"The first pallet of Operation Overcast file boxes, as ordered by the Attorney General," Mrs. Sloan answered.

"The first?"

"That's right, Commander. There are seven more pallets coming over from Virginia. They'll be here by lunchtime."

Scott could only respond by shaking his head in disbelief.

"Now you can see the magnitude of this job," the chief said to Scott as Mrs. Sloan left. "The Göring file is a hundred sixty boxes by itself."

"Yikes! Didn't the Army have anything to do except fill out forms and memos after the war?"

"Guess not, sir. You want to chase the Overcast stuff while I keep after Göring?"

"Probably best. You're already into that stuff." More boxes or not, Scott was very happy to be out of the hospital and finally able to assist in the search for those who had hired Brenda's killers.

Hudson County, New Jersey—1020 Hours

Alan Hillerman and his partner hurried into the office of the import-export business to meet with Agent Carson.

Carson said, "The mercenaries have hired one Pedro Vargas, attorney, to check you out. His office has been sending out requests for information on Frank Lewis. Also, Frank told me that he saw a strange car near his house yesterday and he thinks he was photographed."

"So what's the drill from here?" Hillerman asked.

"We'll have to wait for Vargas to make contact. If it works like last time, he'll probably call this afternoon. So you're going to have to sit by the phone and wait. Did you get that Frank Lewis history memorized?"

"Yeah, I'm ready."

"Good. Remember: don't answer his questions like the data's fresh. Some things—like your mother's maiden name—you should answer quickly, but less significant details—like what your math grades were in high school—should be hemmed and hawed over. Say something like 'How should I remember that?' Then say, 'Probably was a C, maybe a B.'"

"Understood. What about a wire?"

"No. These guys will search you and use a radio-signal-strength detector. They'd pick up a wire. No gun or recorder either. It will be safer that way. Now, we're going to cover you as best we can. I'll have agents inside the building and photographers in cars around the building. We'll snap everyone coming and going all day, then you can point them out for us later. Any questions?"

"You're going to be able to pull me out fast if they suspect I'm a cop, aren't you?"

"We'll have directional mikes on the room where Vargas usually meets with clients. I'll also have men on the nearby rooftop with telescopes trained on the window. If anything goes down, we'll be there in sixty seconds."

"I'll be dead in sixty seconds!"

"I can't give you instant cover without tipping them off to

our presence. It's the risk you're going to have to take." Hillerman thought, what risk are you feds taking? Then he thought of Brenda.

■ ■ ■ ■

The policewoman signaled Hillerman to pick up his telephone.

"Mr. Lewis, my name is Pedro Vargas." The voice was precise and slightly accented. "I'm an attorney-at-law. I've been retained by some individuals you've asked to meet. They are ready to meet you this afternoon at two o'clock at my office. This will be your only opportunity, and I will not be able to reschedule. You must come alone. Do you understand?"

"Yes. I'll be there. What's the address?" Hillerman wrote it down. It was the building in the Bay Ridge section of Brooklyn that Carson had located and placed under surveillance that morning.

A moment later Carson entered the room. "Right on schedule," he said. "What did I tell you?"

"You were right about the address, too."

"Okay, let's move. You'll take Lewis's company car. It has a phone, so we'll be able to maintain contact in case you have trouble en route, but don't use it unless you must in case they've figured a way to listen in."

"You think that's really likely?"

"Don't underestimate these people. They're first-class pros."

"I know. That's why I'm damn scared."

"A little fear right now would be in order, fella."

A very nervous Hillerman drove Frank Lewis's car out the gate and headed south toward the Holland Tunnel. The trip to Bay Ridge in Brooklyn would take at least an hour and could easily take longer if traffic got tied up. I hope this is a good omen, he thought. The traffic moved smoothly, and he was able to reach Vargas's office with a few minutes to spare.

Pulling into the nearly full parking lot, he could see that he had picked up a tail. When he entered the second-floor office of the attorney, he'd never felt so vulnerable in his life. His stomach hurt—more than a little.

A shriveled, elderly man was waiting inside the front office, holding a photograph. He's a lot older than I'd expected, Hillerman thought. Hell, I don't know what I had expected. The man studied Hillerman's face for a moment, then locked the door.

"A few questions," the man said with that precise voice Hillerman heard on the phone. What was your father's mother's maiden name?"

"My paternal grandmother was a Swenson," Hillerman answered with false assurance.

"And your maternal grandmother?"

"Uh, I gotta think. She was a Tarrelson."

"Where did you buy your first house?"

"Plainfield."

"And the next house?"

"Uh, we moved to Montclair."

"What was the name of your high school football coach?"

"Oh, that was Ramsey."

"What position did you play on the football team in your sophomore year?"

"I was a tackle."

"Okay. I'm satisfied. Please be seated while I speak to the others. I'll be just a minute."

Hillerman sat and waited. But then, what else could he do? He watched Vargas enter the rear office and close the door. His stomach really hurt now. Several minutes went by before the lawyer returned, accompanied by a man carrying a submachine gun.

"You must submit to a search," Vargas said.

The gunman slung his weapon around his neck by its strap.

"Yes, very well," Hillerman said, hoping that his tone of feigned impatience masked his fear. He stood for the pat down by the gunman.

Next was a check with a radio-field-strength meter. Hillerman hoped that sweat wouldn't register on the meter. The man was finally satisfied that the detective was clean.

"Please come in, Mr. Lewis."

Hillerman felt the cold eyes of two men sitting behind a table as he entered the room. Neither said anything or offered any welcome. From the position of their hands, Hillerman suspected they had guns in their laps.

"Mr. Lewis, I won't be introducing these men—per their instructions. Please address this man as Number One and the other gentleman as Number Two." Hillerman's eyes followed the old lawyer's finger. "Both men have seen your letter asking for help against union activists. Do you want them killed?" Vargas asked.

"Killed? No. I just want them to back off. I need you to just rough them up a bit."

"No, Mr. Lewis." Number One joined the exchange. He told Hillerman in a heavy Slavic accent that he knew the leaders of the union in New Jersey and that unless the mercenaries struck hard and fast, they would not back off. At least one of the leaders had to be killed in order to convince the union to stop their organizing efforts.

"I didn't know it would come to that," Hillerman said, hesitating. The sweat building in his armpits didn't help his demeanor. His eyes darted quickly from face to face. Got to remember what these men look like, the detective reminded himself.

"If these men are to help you, Mr. Lewis," Vargas interjected, "you must let them proceed in their own way. You do understand?"

"Yes. Agreed."

"Then you will bring one hundred thousand dollars to this man in two days or no deal," Number One responded as he pointed toward Vargas.

"Also, Mr. Lewis," Vargas added, "you are responsible for *my* fee. Bring one hundred *twenty* thousand dollars—in cash—I charge twenty percent."

"Isn't that a lot for legal fees!"

"This isn't exactly 'legal,' Mr. Lewis. I must charge commensurate with my risk exposure."

"Well, this is more than I had expected." He paused and appeared to be considering his options. "But I'll do it to save my business."

"Then I'll look forward to seeing you in two days."

Hillerman left the office convinced that he had just met the leader of the band of hired killers who had murdered Brenda. He was still trembling as he reached the lobby. He hurried from the building and drove quickly toward Manhattan. The rearview mirror revealed that he was being followed again. This is a very careful bunch, he thought. It would be impossible for him to contact Carson en route with them behind him—they would see him use the phone. He had no choice but to drive straight back to the import company.

Carson had not returned, and Agent Woodruff was the only task force member at the office.

"How did it go?" Woodruff asked as he set his can of ice cold Pepsi down on the table.

"I'm still alive," Hillerman answered. He briefed the agent on the afternoon's meeting, then asked, "Where is Carson?" He looked again at the can of soda. I sure could use one of those right now, Hillerman thought.

"Right now, he and the others are following everybody who left that building after you did. They couldn't be sure who you met with, so they split into teams and followed everybody. Carson and your partner followed three men who looked the part. He'll want you to look at all the photos that were taken."

"How long do you think he'll be?"

"Maybe an hour. He should be calling as soon as they decide if they got anything."

Washington, D.C.—1415 Hours

Chief Morris placed another file box on his table. He looked over at Scott, who was reading a page from another box. "Find anything interesting yet?"

"Just looking at this report on nerve-gas development," Scott replied. "The Germans had come up with some awful stuff."

"Doesn't sound like our missing cargo though."

"No, but there is a comment about checking on a secret quantity of toxin near Heidelberg."

"Hmmm...didn't Meyer die in Heidelberg?"

"Yes. May not be related though."

"Commander!" Morris suddenly squawked. "Look at this! I think I've found the visitors' log for Göring's first days in detention."

"That's great. What are the dates?"

"Military Police Prison Interrogation Center, Augsburg, Germany, the twelfth of May, 1945, to the twenty-first of May, 1945." The chief was very excited.

"Whoa! Göring was arrested on May eighth. You're missing four days."

"No, not really. Captain Peters told me that Göring was held at Fischorn Castle for three or four days before the Army moved him to the interrogation center, so this could be from day one for all practical purposes. Hey, wait a minute! The first date someone came to interview the Reichsmarschall was the eighteenth of May 1945."

"Hmmm. Chief, look at this. I think someone cut a couple of pages out of this book." Scott ran his finger along the binding.

"Hey, you're right. A neat cut—almost at the binding. Only about a quarter of an inch still here. The damn visitors' book and the names we need have been cut out—I don't believe it! Nuts!" the chief flung the book down onto the table with a thump.

"Easy, Pat. Maybe something can be worked up with what we've got." Scott picked up the book to study it closer.

"What do you mean?"

"Look at these other pages. See how they used both sides of each page? The book was probably laid out flat and open.

So, the guys who signed on page five would have been able to see who signed on page four."

"Oh, come on, sir. Who's gonna remember a name he might have seen fifty years ago?"

"Probably no one. But someone might remember something notable like, say, a part of a unit or group within the Army. Contact Army Records and see if any of the people on page five are still around somewhere."

"They're all probably dead by now." Morris was still not believing this idea.

"Some, no doubt. But look at this name. A second lieutenant in 1945. Probably around twenty-five years old or even younger. He might be no more than seventy-five today. Very likely still with us. Call Army Records. Find out about all the names on this page."

"A damn long shot!"

"Granted...Now, here's another possibility. When this book was laid open exposing pages two and three for signing— before those pages were removed—page three had to be lying on top of page five. So when the signatures were made on page three, there was almost certainly an impression made through to page five. I wouldn't be surprised if the FBI lab could bring out those impressions and read them."

"From a fountain pen?"

"Look at the ink lines on page five. No smudges or uneven width like you'd expect from an army issue fountain pen. These lines are ball point quality. The man in charge of keeping this book probably purchased one. Ball points were available in the forties."

Hudson County, New Jersey—1650 Hours

Hillerman and Woodruff were waiting when Carson and Dunn entered the office.

"We think we followed your contacts," Carson announced. "Take a look at these photos, Alan." He laid a half dozen photos on the desk.

"That's them okay. This one was called Number One." Hillerman pointed to the first picture. "And this one is Number Two. The third man appeared to be a soldier." Hillerman felt those stomach pains at seeing those faces again.

"Good. We guessed right. The way they acted, I was pretty sure they were our suspects. We followed them almost to La Guardia Airport. We think they're using a building near the airport as a safe house. I left Lieutenant Roberts and several of his men to set up surveillance."

"You don't think they spotted the tail, do you?" Hillerman asked.

"No, I'm sure they didn't. We did a lot of handing off with Roberts's guys and with a chopper. They were looking, though. They went around a couple of blocks for no reason and stopped several times, checking out every car. They're pros—for sure."

"I've got to take a hundred and twenty thousand dollars to them on Wednesday at two, all in cash."

"All right. I'm sure we can get some confiscated drug money from DEA or Customs. I've already asked for a radio-equipped attaché case."

"Whoa!" Hillerman held his hand in front of him as a sign to stop. "That's not a good idea. They checked me with a field-strength detector today."

"This case will send out a signal only when you activate it. So if you see a detector, just don't send a signal. It'll be your call."

Washington, D.C.—1700 Hours

Scott looked up, expecting to see Chief Morris returning from the fax machine. Instead, Captain Peters entered the room. "Captain! Good to see you, sir. What happened?"

"It was very odd," Peters answered. "Ledbetter only presented a few minor discrepancies. My lawyer handled them easily. After the hearing, Ledbetter petitioned to extend the investigation. My lawyer is mystified. Seems that Ledbetter only wants to delay my return to command."

"Why?"

"Don't know. It looks like that's what somebody is telling him to do. Haven't been able to figure it out. What's been going on here?"

Scott filled Captain Peters in on the discovery of the visitors' log and the missing pages. Their discussion was interrupted as an excited Chief Morris came into the room. He said quickly: "Of the twenty-three names on page five, there are fifteen ex-Army guys still with us. But they're all over the planet—except for two living in the D.C. area. The first one is now a retired brigadier general living near Fort Myer. The other is a retired master sergeant living near Andrews. I got addresses and phone numbers."

"Call them and make appointments," Scott said. "We'll show them that log. Maybe—just maybe—one of them will remember something."

"I'm on it!"

"I need to call Carson," Peters said to Scott. "I'll ask him about your idea of having the FBI lab try to read those impressions."

"Sure. I want to follow up on this item I found about Heidelberg," Scott said, scanning the Overcast files.

■ ■ ■ ■ ■

"Bob!" the chief said as he reentered the room. "We have an appointment with General Milton. Sergeant Elders is out of town. His daughter expects him back day after tomorrow."

"That's great. You got directions?"

Thirty minutes later at General Milton's, Chief Morris placed the visitors' logbook on the coffee table in front of the general.

"Is this what you wanted me to look at?" The general looked puzzled.

"Yes, sir," Scott said, opening the book. "As you can see, your name appears here on page five. Notice that the first two sheets have been carefully cut from the book. We're hoping that you can remember something that you might have seen on the facing page—a name, perhaps."

"Good heavens, Commander! I haven't seen this book for fifty years. How could I remember? See, I was just a young shavetail in those days. Part of M.F.A and A. We were trying to find all the artwork that Göring had stolen."

"I understand the difficulty, sir. I'm hoping you might remember some detail. Maybe a unit name or section."

"Well, let me think. Hmmm, I'm sure that there were some names on the facing page, all right." He squinted as if trying to see the past. Then his eyes popped wide. "Hey wait a minute! Yes, I do remember one thing about that page: the names on it were almost all OSS! I'm sure of that because I had wanted to be assigned to the OSS, but I got turned down! So it caught my attention."

"Any of the names come to you, sir?"

"No. I don't think I can do you any good there. I didn't really look at the names other than to see that almost all of them had OSS identification beside them." He shook his head in frustration. "Does this help?"

"Yes, sir! It certainly does. I thank you very much."

Scott and Morris went straight back to the Archives building. They were jubilant. The general may just have given them the key to the mystery.

"The OSS, sir!" Morris commented. "Incredible! Then these guys were all Army Intelligence."

"Right, Chief. They would have been informed of Göring's capture before nearly anyone else."

"How are we going to get those names?"

"We'll have Carson get us the OSS files. That's not going to be easy, though."

"Why not?"

"The OSS became the CIA in forty-six, so those files will be under CIA control."

Morris wasn't really all that surprised. Those two dead divers were CIA operatives, weren't they?

Aboard the dredge, *William P. McDonald*—1715 Hours

Sherry stepped out of the dredge captain's office to see what was happening with the conversion work. She nearly collided with J.D., who was walking briskly along the catwalk.

"Ah, there's my loafer," he joked. "We'll get you back to work tomorrow."

"Loafer! I'll have you know I've just finished a big stack of reports. Besides, I deserved some time off after what you did yesterday."

"You mean that little gunfight?"

"Little! You guys were supposed to be using blanks! I nearly died when those forty-five slugs hit right by my head!"

"Wanted you to know what real bullets sound like. Will you ever forget it?"

"Never!" Her face tightened into a frown as she shook her finger in front of J.D.'s grinning face.

"Good. Then maybe we won't have to do it again." He smiled as he stopped by the control cab and pushed the door open. "Hey, Charlie! Time to get with it! Loafing is over!"

"Well, it's about time you ol' boys done got finished," Charlie retorted as he continued packing fresh tobacco in his pipe. "Talk about loafing and fooling around!"

"Yeah, yeah. Push the pump start, and let's go."

"I take it the Navy finished emptying the submarine this afternoon." Sherry commented.

"Yep," J.D. responded. "All done. They'll set the charges right after we get the hole finished. Wednesday morning this sub will be history."

"Thank heavens. Maybe I can get my life back."

"I wouldn't count on that. Burying this old sub may not end the threat against you."

"It's got to end sometime." Hopefully, not with my death, she thought.

"All we can do is continue your training and get you so strong that you can defend yourself. You did very well with the concealed weapons training yesterday. Tomorrow you're going to work on martial arts and bomb recognition."

"My mother was right. I should have been a housewife."

J.D. laughed and clapped her on the shoulder.

Aboard the dredge, *William P. McDonald*—0650 Hours

"This dad-burn weather ain't helping," Charlie muttered to himself as he fought to keep the dredging of the burial trench going. A powerful arc of brilliant electric light struck the bridge tower again, and Charlie grimaced as the windows shook from the roar of thunder. Accompanied by heavy rain and wind that caused choppy waves, the storm had worsened Charlie's task. The sun came up before the storm finally cleared.

J.D. and the dredge captain were already discussing the day's schedule when Sherry arrived for breakfast.

"I wanted to ask about going ashore soon," Sherry asked. "I need to clean out my apartment and make arrangements for a new place."

"Yeah. J.D. and I thought about that, too," Harris answered. He smiled warmly at her.

"Later this afternoon would be okay," J.D. suggested. "We'll be coming to the end of the deep cut and there should be a couple hours before we start the tear-down of the extension gear."

"Okay. The tear-down will be a lot easier," Harris replied. "So I could spare you and maybe Cowboy."

"We'll go ashore around four."

■ ■ ■ ■ ■

A short time later, Sherry and J.D. joined Cowboy, who was a martial arts expert, in the pump room. He looked forward to showing her how to inflict pain on an attacker.

He showed her every combination of sudden and close attacks. Sherry proved a capable student, able to deliver quick blows that would cause pain and damage. A few times, Cowboy had to admit, she hurt him damn bad.

Satisfied that she had mastered the lesson, he picked up a package and opened it.

"J.D. had this special handbag made up for you. It's to provide you with a shield against a threat we ain't covered yet—the nasty ol' boy with a knife. If an attacker comes up at you with a knife, and you try to hit him with your elbow or foot, you're just gonna get stuck with a knife in your side while you're swinging into him. So, now you gotta learn to use this purse as a shield and a weapon."

"How can a purse stop a knife?"

"This one has a sixteen-gauge-steel plate under the flap. It'll stop any knife and most small caliber bullets. And that shoulder strap has been reinforced with a steel cable that attaches to the plate. Nobody's gonna break that off.

"See here—the top of this bag has a false zipper you can shove your hand through quick to reach your gun. So, the plan is to use the shield to stop the knife and maybe knock it outta his hand.

"If you're walking along with your hand inside the bag on the butt of your gun, you can see that the shield is between your hand and his knife. You move the bag to stop the knife and pull the gun all at the same time. Okay? Now I'm gonna be jumpin' out at you like before, but now I'm holding a knife. Don't worry, it's got a rubber blade. Okay, let's go!"

Washington, D.C.—0930 Hours

Scott looked up from a pile of file folders as Morris came back from the telephone.

"Any luck, Pat?"

"Aye, sir. I talked with that retired major, and he agrees with the general that the names on page four were definitely OSS. But he couldn't come up with any of them. I talked with two other ex-Army men, but they didn't remember anything."

"Sergeant Elders is still out of town?" Scott continued his questioning.

"Yeah. I'll try him again tomorrow. Where is the captain?"

"He went to talk to Carson. Should be back in a minute."

"Finding anything?" the chief asked, showing he could ask questions too.

"Another reference to searching for biological agents and a report about a large amount turning up near Heidelberg. Overcast personnel had been assigned to locate and secure it."

"Think it's Göring's cargo?"

"Don't know yet, but it's possible."

Morris glanced up to see Captain Peters returning. "Hello, sir. Any news?"

"Carson checked," Peters replied. "The OSS personnel files are in CIA custody—as I suspected. They can't be released except by direct Presidential order. The Attorney General's working on it, but it may take a couple of days.

"Carson also reported that the German Federal Police have found out what happened to Bruning. They had trouble locating his file because the French military police, who were supervising the Ludwigshafen police during the occupation, had misspelled his name. But they've straightened it out and now tell us he was also found shot dead in Ludwigshafen in June, 1945."

"Then all three of them died in Ludwigshafen or Heidelberg. Why there?" Morris continued his questioning.

"Remember that the report on Meyer was actually from the Ludwigshafen police."

"But he died in a hospital in Heidelberg. Why not in a hospital in Ludwigshafen?"

"I can answer that, Pat," Scott broke in. "Ludwigshafen was one of the most heavily bombed cities in Germany. The

British bombed it nearly every night and the Americans bombed it nearly every day. There wouldn't have been a functioning hospital in Ludwigshafen in June of '45. But Heidelberg wasn't bombed at all, so it would have been the nearest place to Ludwigshafen with a working hospital."

"Why was Ludwigshafen so heavily bombed?" Chief Morris asked.

"Because that was where the Germans made synthetic gasoline and rubber—Oh, my God! How dumb can I be! That's it! I just realized where our missing cargo was taken!"

"What are you talking about, Bob?" Peters asked.

"Captain, call Carson back! Tell him to call the German Federal Police as soon as possible! Have them get the Ludwigshafen police to search their files from '45—find out who took charge of the synthetic rubber factory. I'd bet a million dollars it was the damned OSS!"

"Have you lost your mind? What the hell are you talking about?" Peters looked completely baffled.

"Synthetic rubber! To make airtight synthetic rubber you have to freeze the chemical reactors! That's why everybody ended up in Ludwigshafen! They needed to keep the cargo *frozen*! They needed that synthetic rubber factory to supply enough refrigeration!"

"But Bob, you said that Ludwigshafen had been bombed around the clock." Chief Morris pulled at his chin, his eyebrows arched.

"Yes, but the Germans kept rebuilding that rubber factory as fast as the Allies could knock it down. It had the highest priority of all German industry—the army needed airtight rubber for their truck tires. They kept that factory running right up until the French First Army overran and captured it."

Peters was finally convinced. "Okay, I'm on my way," he said as he headed for the door.

Scott shouted after him, "Find out who in the OSS signed the orders! I'd bet another million he's one of our perps!"

Aboard the dredge, *William P. McDonald*—1230 Hours

After lunch Sherry went to the dredge's machine shop along with two of the crew.

"Okay, ma chérie," Bear began, pointing to a collection of devices on the workbench. "What I'm gonna tell you 'bout is how to know a bomb if you ever come to find one."

What followed was a tedious intricate lecture on bomb making. As Bear explained the three components of a bomb (the explosive, the detonator, and the trigger) and went into exhaustive detail about the various types of explosives (dynamite, gunpowder, plastic, TNT, and on and on), Sherry's mind started to wander. She was tired and suffering from information overload. She found herself wondering how Bear came to know so much about building bombs. Come to think of it, what did she really know about Bear—or any of the others? I must be getting paranoid, she thought, mentally giving herself a shake as Bear asked if she remembered the bomb Cowboy had pulled out of her car's tailpipe.

"Sure, I'll never forget it." She was certain of that—she nearly fainted when Cowboy set it on her desk after the dredge captain sent him to check on her car.

"Well, they're easy to spot. All you need is a flashlight to look up the pipe to see them."

"What do I do then? How do I get it out?"

"You don't do nuttin'. You call the cops and let them handle it. That's true of every bomb we'll show you. You don't touch any of them. That's what the bomb squad is for."

For the next two hours, Bear and J.D. showed Sherry every triggering method used by bombers. They showed her how to use her flashlight to spot the hidden killers. A piece of tape and a tiny thread across door-posts and over latches would reveal if someone had tampered with them. Bear showed her an ignition-switch bomb, triggered when the driver turned the key to start the car.

He showed her a real terror, a trembler-switch bomb—the most dangerous since it can be totally contained within a simple box. Any innocent-looking package could, when picked up, explode.

He showed her a floor-mounted bomb that could be set behind a closed door. The best defense against this was to set a mirror so she could look at the back of the door without opening it. A drill, a peephole mounted in reverse, and she could see the mirror behind the door.

"Bear," J.D. finally interrupted the lesson. "We're going ashore in a few minutes. The workboat's going to be tied up later."

"Yeah, okay. Chérie's ready for a break." Bear smiled as he gave her name its French pronunciation.

Hudson County, New Jersey—1300 Hours

Hillerman joined Carson in the rear office. Woodruff had just delivered the attaché case filled with money. One hundred thousand dollars in stacks of one-hundred-dollar bills. Hillerman sucked in his breath, he had never seen so much cash. An additional twenty thousand dollars was in a separate envelope.

"This is a combination-lock case," Agent Carson began. "Look here. There are three numbered wheels you use to unlock it. The first wheel has only two positions that do anything. If you dial a six, you'll unlock the case but silence the transmitter so no message will be sent. Use that position if you feel any danger that they may detect the radio. Understand?"

"Yes."

"Now, if you set that wheel to five, then the case will also unlock, but when you swing it open, the radio will come on and transmit a coded message. To select which code will be sent, you have to turn the other two wheels to get in two numbers between zero one and nine nine. Okay so far?"

"Yeah. What are these codes?"

"Woodruff, give Hillerman that list, would you?"

Hillerman studied the code list for a moment.

"You're going to have to memorize that list. There are thirty-six working possibilities. We'll have a receiver in a van across the street. If you send a code, we'll know it immediately, and we'll move in accordance to the code you send. Understand?"

"Yes."

"Scared?"

"You have to ask?"

"You should be. Let's talk about tomorrow. Our surveillance team at the hideout is pretty sure that this group has between twelve and fifteen members. We've got a telephone tap on the line going in, and we have reason to believe that this contract concerning the sub is the only job they're involved with at this time. So we're pretty sure all of them will be waiting at the hideout when the leaders are meeting you at two o'clock.

"I've met with the Queens Borough commander and have arranged a force of two hundred NYPD to surround that building tomorrow. State troopers from New Jersey and New York will also be joining us. At Vargas's office, we'll have twenty NYPD and six FBI to back you."

"How about my partner?"

"Dunn will be with me and Woodruff. We'll also have the Brooklyn SWAT guys. So you're going to have a lot of backup within sixty seconds. Any questions?"

"No. Just a statement — sixty seconds is too long."

Northeastern New Jersey—1640 Hours

Bulldog pulled the workboat up to the service dock at Port Newark. Cowboy, J.D., and Sherry climbed onto the dock.

"You okay?" J.D. asked her.

"Yeah," Sherry answered. "It's just that it's been a while since I've been on solid ground."

"It has at that."

"OK, let's run a bomb check. Cowboy, check the front. Sherry, check the back. I'll get the doors." A few minutes later, J.D. was satisfied that the van was clean. "Let's roll. Cowboy, you take the wheel. I'll ride shotgun."

Cowboy headed for the turnpike and Sherry's apartment in Fort Lee. His eyes kept glancing at the traffic behind them in the rearview mirrors. "J.D.," he said as they passed Giants Stadium, "there's a brown sedan behind us. I ain't sure, but I think that ol' boy is tailing us."

"Okay. Let's find out. Change lanes and slow down." Cowboy moved to the right lane between two slow-moving trucks.

"He's doing the same." Cowboy could see the sedan move behind the truck behind the van.

"All right. Take the next exit." J.D. looked already convinced.

Cowboy pulled off and passed through the tollbooth. Why do I always get the surly one, he thought as he handed the unfriendly face the payment.

"He's still behind us," Cowboy observed in the mirror.

"Okay. Make a U-turn and go right back up on the turnpike."

Cowboy complied and with another toll ticket in hand, he speeded up onto the turnpike. His stomach tightened when the brown sedan did the same.

"What do we do now?" Cowboy asked.

"I-Eighty is just ahead," J.D. said after consulting a map. "Take the westbound exit and head toward Paterson. There's a state police barracks in Totowa. We'll pull off there and try to shake our tail. Then, come back to I-Eighty eastbound to get to Fort Lee if we shake 'em."

"Sure enough."

"You okay, Sherry?"

"So far. You think they're after me?"

"Uh-huh."

Sweetheart, Cowboy thought, without a doubt.

About twenty minutes later, a relieved Cowboy pulled into

sanctuary, the parking lot of the New Jersey State Police barracks.

"Turn around," J.D. said as he watched the sedan drive away. "Let's wait a few minutes and see what happens."

They didn't need to wait long as two New Jersey state troopers came out of the building and headed for their patrol cars. The two patrol cars started quickly and Cowboy had to move the van fast to get between them.

"Well, as them truckers say, 'we is in that ol' rocking chair,'" Cowboy said with a chuckle.

"Yeah. Try to stay between the cops. Our tail may assume we've arranged a police escort and break off."

"Sure enough. Well looky here, would you? Our two cops are both going up this-here eastbound ramp."

"What luck! Any sign of our tail?"

"Nope. Looks like them ol' boys have figured we're covered."

For about five miles, Cowboy managed to remain between the two police cars. J.D. kept watch, but the brown sedan was nowhere to be seen.

"You want me to follow him?" Cowboy asked as the first police car signaled for a turn.

"No. Let's go on to Sherry's place. I think we've lost our tail."

Been quite a trip, Cowboy thought as he turned into the parking lot by Sherry's apartment.

■ ■ ■ ■ ■

Sherry sighed as she and J.D. confronted the locked door to her home, her former refuge. J.D. checked the door for signs of tampering. Satisfied, he unlocked the door and swung it open.

The apartment was much the same as Sherry remembered from Friday. She shook her head in despair. "Well, I'll start picking through this pile. Could you carry some of the bigger stuff down to the Dumpster?"

"Sure. I'm real sorry about this, Sherry."

"Yeah, me too."

A job it was. After two hours of boxes filled and boxes emptied, a clean empty apartment emerged from the chaos. Sherry was thankful some of her things were salvageable and felt her spirits lift as she packed several boxes. It was time to leave.

Walking several yards behind J.D., Sherry suddenly felt she was being followed. Glancing over her shoulder she couldn't believe her eyes. A man wearing a black baseball cap and sunglasses was rushing toward her with a knife in his hand.

She dropped the boxes she was carrying and swung her purse to strike the knife. Her aim proved perfect as the knife flew from his hand. Surprise showed in his eyes. As he lowered his hand, his shirt fell open allowing Sherry to see a small pistol in his belt. His hand was moving toward it, and there was no doubt as to his intent. Sherry pulled the bag around and swung it against the man's head.

J.D., hearing the thump, turned in time to see the man falling. He rushed back to Sherry's side as she replaced the bag on her shoulder.

"What the hell happened?"

Sherry explained as J.D. bent down to examine the man on the ground.

"Is he hurt badly?" she asked.

"He's breathing. Let's get out of here!"

■ ■ ■ ■ ■

"Got bad news," Cowboy announced as he guided the van down the road. "I done seen that brown sedan again a few minutes ago."

"Damn! Are you sure?" J.D. asked.

"Yep, and they are now behind us, 'bout three cars back."

"That explains where the guy who jumped Sherry came from."

"Can we lose them?" Sherry asked.

"I doubt it," J.D. answered. "Cowboy, see if you can mix with traffic. Maybe we can confuse them."

For the next several miles, before they got to the turnpike,

Cowboy tried various tricks to lose the brown sedan. "J.D., there's just two ol' boys in the front," he said. "I don't see nobody in the back."

"Yeah, and the one in the passenger seat is definitely carrying a submachine gun."

"What do you think they're going to do?" Sherry asked. Her face was taut with wide open eyes.

"They're waiting for a break in the traffic so they can pull up alongside and rake us with that gun."

"What can we do?" Her mouth was dry and her voice hoarse.

"Well, if we do nothing, they'll eventually get their chance. That car is faster than this van. We're going to have to pull a surprise. Cowboy, I'm going to take out their radiator. Sherry, practice is over. You're going to have to give me suppression fire."

"Damn. All right."

"Get out your piece and lock and load. Turn around in the seat. Aim straight out the back window. When Cowboy presses the back window switch to open it, you'll be able to fire before that guy in the passenger seat does.

"Put four or five rounds through the top of his windshield. That will make him duck down and let me hit their radiator. You understand what you're supposed to do?"

"Yes," she answered as she pulled her pistol out and prepared it for firing.

"Take the next off ramp. There's almost no traffic going that way. We'll nail them there."

Cowboy headed for the exit. As expected, the brown sedan also left the stream of traffic for the exit. He watched as the gap between the cars began to close. At fifty yards, he pushed the switch to drop the International Suburban's rear glass.

"Fire!" J.D. instructed. A cacophony of sound blasted the air. "Floor it! Sherry, get down!"

The van leapt forward. J.D. kept the carbine aimed at the sedan, which pulled onto the shoulder and stopped. Steam poured from under its hood.

"You okay?" J.D. asked Sherry.

"Shaking badly!"

"You did just great! You can sit up now."

"Say now," Cowboy said with a laugh, "I do believe them ol' boys done gone and got themselves a heap of car trouble!"

J.D. joined with the laughter and said, "Yeah, you could say that."

"Is it over?" Sherry asked, wondering whether anyone was going to call the police. Surely someone must have heard the gunfire or seen the brown sedan disabled by the side of the road. They weren't in Siberia, for God's sake! They were in Hudson County, New Jersey!

"I think it's over. We'll be long gone when they get going again."

"Do you think I hit those men?"

"Nah. You put those rounds right near the top of that windshield—right where I asked you to put them. Good shooting."

"Them ol' boys will be picking glass outta their hair for a week," Cowboy broke in.

"I've never shot live bullets at people before." She lowered her eyes to the floor of the van.

"I know. Maybe you'll never have to do it again. Hand me the cell phone, Cowboy. I'd best call Tiny."

New York Harbor—1800 Hours

Bulldog and Baby Face, a deckhand, were waiting at the dock with the workboat when Cowboy pulled into the parking lot. Sherry needed no urging as she and the two men jumped aboard the boat, and Bulldog immediately had the engines at full throttle.

As the workboat moved east toward Liberty Island, a small, high-speed boat pulled along the port side. The three friends, enjoying coffee in the small cabin, jumped up and looked toward the stairway at the sudden sound of gunfire and breaking glass.

"What the hell?" Cowboy shouted.

The three of them flew up the steps. Bulldog laid on the deck, beneath the uncontrolled wheel, covered with blood. Just outside the wheelhouse, Baby Face moaned, lying in a bloody puddle. He wasn't moving.

"Oh, my God!" Sherry reacted with every muscle tightening, her eyes wide open and wild. She put her hand over her open mouth.

"How's Baby Face?" J.D. shouted as he examined Bulldog. "Bulldog is out cold!"

"He's bad!" Cowboy answered. "Don't look good at all."

"Cowboy, see if you can find out where those shots came from. I'll take the wheel."

"Come on, Sherry. There's nothing you can do for Baby Face. He's had it! Look!" Cowboy's arm shot straight out, pointing toward a fast moving craft. "There's the shooters. In that speedboat!"

"They're coming back, Cowboy!" Sherry shouted.

Cowboy responded by opening fire with his carbine. Crack! Crack!

The speedboat whooshed about and headed back toward the slower lumbering workboat. My God, Sherry thought preparing her pistol, these bastards are trying to kill me! Her blood suddenly went cold as she realized that Cowboy had stopped firing.

"Son of a bitch! I'm jammed!" he shouted.

The distance between the two boats was rapidly closing. Sherry raised her gun and took aim. She remembered J.D.'s words: the pistol is effective only to seventy yards. Wait for it, she thought. Wait for it!

She could see one of the three men in the speedboat aiming a long, pipelike weapon at the workboat. Another man steadied him while a third man handled the controls.

Sherry's HP-35 spoke four more times that afternoon. A twentieth of a second after leaving the muzzle of the pistol the first bullet struck the forehead of the man holding the pipe.

The man fell forward, lowering the front of the pipe. Unfortunately, his brain had already sent a signal to his finger to pull the trigger, and as he fell, his forearm muscle completed its contraction. The weapon fired. The rocket-propelled grenade, no longer under human control, struck the bottom of the speedboat and exploded.

Sherry gasped as the speedboat disappeared in an enormous fireball, debris flying off in all directions. The horror worsened as the shattered bodies of the men hurled high into the air.

"Yippee! Wow, what a shot! Great shooting, girl!" Cowboy cheered.

"My God! What happened?" She staggered back and lowered her pistol.

"You just done saved our butts! That's what! A couple of seconds later and that grenade would've been right in our laps!"

"Cowboy!" J.D. shouted, "come take the wheel. I need to look after Bulldog."

Cowboy and Sherry hurried to the wheelhouse. Cowboy grabbed the controls, and J.D. and Sherry cleaned the blood from Bulldog's face and applied bandages to the wounds.

"You did real good, Sherry," J.D. said as he worked. "I thank you for saving our lives. When Cowboy's carbine jammed, you and your pistol were all there was between us and death. I couldn't go below for my gun and still control the boat. You came through like a soldier."

"I'm still trying to understand what happened. How bad are Bulldog and Baby Face?"

"Bulldog should make it. I think Baby Face is dead."

"Oh, God—no."

"Yeah. No pulse. Nothing. It's not a game any more, and the radio's shot to pieces. All we can do is get to the dredge."

Aboard the dredge, *William P. McDonald*—1840 Hours

It was near suppertime when they reached the safety of the big dredge. They climbed up the ladder to the rear to find the dredge captain waiting to greet them.

"What happened?" Harris asked, seeing the damage. No

one on the dredge had seen or heard the firefight five miles away.

J.D. quickly told him everything including Bulldog's injuries and Baby Face's death.

"Slim!" Harris shouted, "go tell Charlie to call the cops and get a medevac chopper on the way! Sherry, I'm proud of the way you handled yourself."

"I'm still scared," she responded. "I've never been so scared."

"You should be. Facing a person holding a gun is damn scary! But sounds like you didn't flinch. You stayed at your post and pulled that trigger when the chips were down. That's all that mattered. You overcame your fear and did what had to be done. Good job." He wrapped his arms around her and held her to him for several minutes.

Sherry could hear the crewmen behind her snickering and commenting on the show of affection. She didn't give a damn, she felt secure for the first time in several hours.

Try as she might, Sherry could not understand why everyone was acting like she was a hero. Didn't they know that she had just killed three men? Didn't they care about Baby Face?

"Now go up to your cabin and relax for a while. Later, we'll get together for supper," Harris continued. "You're really one of us now."

Manhasset, Long Island—1900 Hours

Alan Hillerman's mind wasn't on his driving. He had been trying to decide what he would tell Jill that night. He knew that he would be facing serious danger the next day when he carried the money to the meeting at Vargas's office. Time to find out if I've got an actor's skills, he thought as he practiced putting on a happy face.

The sound of the vacuum greeted him as he entered. Jill looked up and shut off the machine.

"So, did the mighty prince slay the mean old dragon today?" she joked.

"Ha! Well, he didn't eat me!" Hillerman joked in return. "That's about all I can say."

"That's something anyway. So, what did you do today?"

"Oh, the usual. Chased down some wild hookers and then punished them by making love to them all day long."

"Oh, sure! I can see that, all right."

"Yeah, fat chance. The nearest I got to any wild ladies was the drive down Canal Street."

"Well, then, maybe I'll forgive you. How about some dinner, sport?"

"Surprise! I stopped and picked up a bucket of chicken."

"Oh, you are a prince after all!"

After dinner, he held her close and tight. So tight, she thought as she struggled to breathe, something must be wrong.

FOURTEEN
Wednesday
19 August

Aboard the dredge, *William P. McDonald*—0720 Hours

Sherry dipped into her breakfast cereal as the dredge captain discussed the day's work with J.D.

"What's the schedule on the sub's burial?" Harris asked.

"Supposed to be around nine o'clock," J.D. answered.

"Let's just shut down for a coffee break about fifteen minutes before and let the boys watch. They'll just stop for the show anyway."

"Yeah, you're right. Okay, I'll pass the word."

"Have you got any plans for Sherry? Is she able to continue training after yesterday?"

"I plan to take her out back for shotgun training. Shoot some skeet. You told me earlier you can go on, right Sherry?"

They both saw the hard look in her eyes was affirmative.

■ ■ ■ ■ ■

Sherry put the empty shotgun down for reloading.

"Hey, it's about time for the big show," J.D. announced. "Let's go watch the Navy."

From the front of the dredge, they could see that the barge had been pulled away from the caisson pipe where it had been tied for several days. Barely floating, J.D. thought, must be half the Navy standing on it.

"I'm really looking forward to this," Sherry said looking off into the distance. "It will be good to say good-bye to the sub—especially after the way it's wrecked so many lives."

"Well, this'll put that pigboat so deep nobody will ever have to worry about it again," Harris replied.

Their conversation was cut short by a rumble from below the surface of the water. Then smoke and steam blew out the caisson pipe. The first explosions had come from the small shaped charges that blasted holes through the steel hull.

"How long will it take to fill the sub with water?" J.D. asked.

"Maybe three to five minutes," Sherry answered.

The continuing stream of vapor pouring from the caisson pipe left no doubt that the submarine was filling rapidly. Water rose through the open bulkheads, into the now empty battery compartments, past where the bodies had lain.

Charlie was in the control cab ready to pull the caisson pipe away from the submarine as soon as the second blast severed the weld.

"They just called," Charlie yelled out the window. "Start pulling in thirty seconds."

A much larger blast suddenly shook the dredge. A geyser of water and smoke burst from the top of the caisson as the pipe began a violent dance, then crashed back into the water.

"Pull it, Charlie!" Harris shouted.

The cable quickly tightened. Slowly, the long steel thread reeled in the caisson pipe like a big fish.

A moment later, a tremendous explosion broke the surface. Deep below, out of sight of human eyes, large explosive charges pushed the UX-6000 over the edge and into the trench. A huge curtain of water, mud, and smoke rose high into the air. Several minutes later the water calmed.

"Well, I guess that's that!" said Harris. "We'll fish the caisson pipe out of the drink and load it on the barge."

"How can the Navy know if the sub is in the trench?" J.D. asked.

"See that motor launch moving in?" Sherry answered. "They're going to do a magnetic-sonar run. In a few minutes they'll have a picture of how things lie. There's too much mud stirred up for divers to see anything right now."

"Let's get these bubbas back to work," Harris said and shouted down to the deck. "Show's over!"

Washington, D.C.—0915 Hours

Scott and Morris looked up from their files as a smiling Captain Peters came into the room.

"Good news, sir?" Chief Morris.

"Yes! Our police should be as fast as the Germans. We've got a name. Carson just heard from Mueller that the Ludwigshafen police have found an order to the French military police commander, written in May '45, directing him to hand over the synthetic rubber plant for 'special testing.' The order was signed by Major S. P. Tilton, OSS!"

"Then we've got 'em!" Scott said with elation.

"Carson has already contacted Army Records and they're trying to locate his file. Carson also notified the FBI main office, and they've issued an all-points bulletin."

"Hot damn!" Morris shouted. "Then our job is done!"

"Not so fast," Peters said. "We don't know if Tilton is alive *or* if we can find him. We don't know if he was really involved or was merely a patsy. We don't know if he can or will give us the names of the men who entered the UX-6000."

"So we keep digging?"

"Yes. What time did Elders' daughter say he would be home?"

"About 1500 Hours."

"Okay, then give him a call. We'll keep digging in case Tilton turns out to be a dead end."

Queens, New York—1015 Hours

Agents Carson and Woodruff pulled up to the maintenance

hangar at La Guardia Airport, joining a great many police vehicles already there. Inside were nearly three hundred forty police officers from federal, state, and local agencies milling about, coffee cups in hand, as if attending a reunion.

Agent Carson signaled for attention. "Okay, everybody! Please gather around! I'm Special Agent Carson, FBI. I will be directing this operation as agent in charge for the Bureau's Manhattan office. Now, let me lay out the details of the raid. We're going to be rounding up about fifteen of the most murderous and well-armed mercenaries I've ever encountered. They have been active throughout the tristate area committing murders, bank robberies, hijackings, bombings, beatings, and just about anything else you can think of.

"We have tracked them to an abandoned warehouse near here that they are using as a headquarters and armory. The building has doors on only one side. Our main force will be approaching from the west against those doors.

"The building is in the middle of a large parking lot, so there's no way to approach it without being seen. You'd have to run across a hundred yards of paved surface without any cover, and with what they have inside, it would be suicide. ATF Agent Bates will tell you about the firepower we believe these people have in that building. Agent Bates."

The weapons listed by Bates were shocking—even to experienced police officers. Heavy machine guns, antitank cannons, rocket-propelled grenades, and much more. Even weapons capable of blasting entire houses to bits a mile away. The officers glanced at each other in disbelief.

NYPD Captain O'Toole listened and shuddered. Bullets that could penetrate three-quarter inch steel plates or pass through an entire automobile and still kill a man? Good, God! He had never faced such potential terror. And now he must lead his fellow NYPD officers against such arms?

"Agent Carson, what are we supposed to do?" Captain O'Toole asked. "I mean, this job is for the Marines!"

"I agree with you, Captain O'Toole, and that's exactly why I've requested help from the military. First Army will be providing five tanks with full crews to aid us. They're scheduled to arrive about five o'clock. Our job is to surround and contain the criminals until the tanks are delivered."

"Why not have the tanks here now?"

"Too much chance of being seen. No, we contain first, then bring up the big stuff for the final attack. Remember this: Our surveillance team tells us they're certain there are no women or children with these mercenaries.

"We have no concern about killing these men if they resist. We are going to call on them to surrender. But if they don't, then I intend to pour fire down on their heads!"

"My God!" Captain O'Toole called out. "We've got civilians around here. You start firing those tank guns and, well, the shells could go right through that building, several houses, and end up in some baby's crib two blocks away!"

"Yes. That is why you must first evacuate all of the houses for a quarter mile around the building. But you can't start the evacuation until we surround the building, or you'll give us away. You'll have two hours to get it done. The Transit Authority will supply you with about a hundred buses."

"That's a lot of people to move—maybe ten thousand. What about crowd and traffic control and the damn press?"

"The Housing and Transit officers will assist you with that work, Captain, after they move the people. You'll also have to use some of your other men—perhaps half—to work those areas. This brings us to disposition of manpower.

"You're to cover the rear of the building. There are no doors or windows on that side, but once things get going, I'm expecting these criminals to use explosives to make an escape hole. So your men are there to keep them bottled up. I would suggest fifty men plus Lieutenant Roberts and his six, who will join you as we move in.

"The rest of your manpower plus the Housing and Transit officers will give you about two hundred men for crowd, traffic, and press control. Okay?"

"All right. It's a little thin, but we'll do it."

"Captain Reynolds, I want you to split your state police

officers down the middle. Put half on the north side and half on the south side. The main force of federal officers will come from the west and advance behind the tanks. Any questions?"

"How are you going to tell these guys to surrender?" asked NY State Police Captain Reynolds. "We're going to be too far for a bullhorn."

"We're going to simply call them on the telephone after everyone's in place. The phone company has supplied us with their number."

"Now, I'd like to discuss timing. We have Lieutenant Roberts and six NYPD officers maintaining a covert surveillance on the building. My most recent communication is that all is quiet and our quarry are in the building except for the two leaders and two gunmen who left early this morning.

"The leaders are most probably headed for a meeting in Brooklyn that's the first phase of this operation. You'll have to remain at the staging area until the first phase is complete. Once we've bagged the leaders, the hideout is to be surrounded and the civilians evacuated. Any questions?"

"Why not use armed helicopters to fire down through the roof instead of using these tanks?" Captain O'Toole asked. "I'm worried about those cannon shells skipping all over town."

"The tanks are to be equipped with low velocity cannon rounds. Choppers will be made available if we need them, but we know they have some anti-air missiles in that building, so we won't use gunships until we know it's safe.

"Any other questions?" Carson looked around. "If not, then Agent Woodruff and I are leaving for Brooklyn. Agent Fisher will be in charge here until we return. The airport kitchen is making some lunch for you. That's all."

Washington, D.C. —1100 Hours

Scott opened another file folder. Chief Morris leaned back in his chair and yawned after finishing yet another stack of memoranda.

"You know, sir," the chief said, "they invented the floppy disk about forty years too late."

"You've got a point," Scott responded. "Hmm....Well now, what the hell have we here?"

"Find something?"

"I do believe I have. I've found a memo from Overcast Headquarters to Field Search Group Five dated the seventh of June, 1945. 'Authorized to pay eight hundred thousand U.S. dollars to three German nationals for information concerning the location of a cache of biological agents involving cholera. The Weapons Technology Committee is satisfied that these agents can be of immediate use to U.S. forces in the war against Japan.' How about that!"

"This confirms our suspicion. I'm more certain than ever that this was a crime of greed."

"You're right. Do you realize what eight hundred thousand dollars was worth back then? That would have been about six million in today's money....So after Von Kruger and his two assistants turned over the cargo and collected the money, our perpetrators would have killed them and taken the cash."

"Yes, that's exactly what must have happened. Is Ron still on the phone with Carson?"

Peters walked in and Scott handed the captain the paper.

After reading the memo, he said, "Great. The proof we needed. Chief, take this to the fax machine and send it up to Carson's office."

Bay Ridge Section, Brooklyn—1145 Hours

Hillerman picked up the attaché case with the money. A hundred twenty thousand was pretty heavy, he thought as he placed the case beside him on the seat. He drove Frank Lewis's car toward the Holland Tunnel, watching in the rearview mirror to see if he was being tailed again. Yeah, he thought, there they are. Nothing to do but drive on to Brooklyn.

Carson and Woodruff had already arrived at the operations

command truck a block away from the building where the meeting was to take place. Everyone was in place. Detective Dunn and another detective were in the parking lot, dressed as mechanics and trying to look like they were working on a broken-down car. The Brooklyn SWAT team had been secreted in an empty office just down the hallway from Vargas's. They looked like a crew of painters, carrying boxes of wallpaper and paint, as they came up the stairs.

More than a dozen very hot uniformed officers were inside the un-air conditioned rear of a truck parked in front of the building. Several others were on top of nearby buildings with rifles, scopes, and directional microphones. They were ready to move when their radios, connected to Carson and Woodruff, barked the order. The radio in front of Carson came to life as officers on the rooftops confirmed that the two mercenary leaders had arrived and were inside Vargas's office.

"Well," Carson said, "nothing to do but wait."

"Yeah," Woodruff answered. "That's always the worst part."

The quiet of the command center was broken again as the radio reported Hillerman's arrival at the Bay Ridge office building. The two mercenaries, who had been tailing Hillerman, parked at the curb. Two plain clothes police officers surreptitiously took up positions to keep them under surveillance. Vargas and the mercenary called Number Two were waiting for Hillerman. Another patdown and radio check. Damn guys take no chances, Hillerman thought.

"You're right on time, Mr. Lewis," said Vargas. "Please step into the back office."

Number One was waiting behind the table. This is it, Hillerman thought, fear gripping his tensed body as he set the attaché case on the table. Number Two set the radio-signal detector beside it and moved the control switch. He sat down beside Number One with his very intimidating submachine gun hanging by a strap around his neck.

"Please open the case, Mr. Lewis," Vargas instructed.

Hillerman set the wheels and lifted the lid. An instant—it

took no more—and he knew death had come. The radio detector's needle swung suddenly to the right. It had not been switched off as Hillerman had thought. Number Two jumped to his feet.

"Signal! He's a cop!" he shouted.

The knife in his hand appeared as if by magic as he grabbed the case from Hillerman. He slashed the lining, the transmitter was in his hand in an instant. Hillerman had not managed a breath.

"Pig!" Number Two screamed and raised his gun.

There was no time for Hillerman to react. He could only watch as the bullets struck into his chest, his blood being blasted out toward his murderer. Waves of intense pain reached his brain almost instantly and began to shut down his conscious mind. His eyes ceased functioning and his legs collapsed under his dying body. His last thought was of Jill, that he would never hold her again.

"Shots fired!" Carson's radio barked.

"It's going down! Move in! Move in!" Carson shouted.

"We just got code five-one-one," Woodruff responded as the two agents dashed out of the truck.

The second floor hallway was bedlam as the SWAT team rushed toward the door of Vargas's office. The first two officers carried a battering ram. They quickly smashed open the locked door. Immediately behind them were two full body armored officers carrying twelve-gauge automatic-action shotguns. They jumped through the open door ready to fire.

As they crept toward the rear office, a burst of gunfire came from the room. One officer jumped to the far side of the open door, landing in a crouch with the shotgun aimed through the door.

Number Two turned and pointed his gun at the SWAT officer, who responded with a blast, striking him with such force that his arm was nearly severed. Blood splattered every surface. The wounded man spun toward the window, his gun flying.

The other shotgun-carrying officer stopped at the near side

of the door and aimed almost at the same instant as the first officer had fired. Number One could see that he had no chance. He raised his hands.

The SWAT team medic, his revolver in hand, swiftly entered the room to check on the casualties.

■ ■ ■ ■ ■

Carson and Woodruff ran up the stairs and struggled through the crowd of officers now piling into the front office.

"Make way—FBI!" Carson shouted, pushing through the men into the rear office. His eyes were met by the sight he had most feared. The medic was kneeling beside Hillerman, who was lying motionless in blood soaked attire. The medic looked up, his eyes meeting Carson's. Nothing needed to be said.

Carson looked over to where Vargas lay. The medic checked the lawyer and shook his head. Vargas would practice law no more.

The police swiftly had the two mercenaries' weapons and had handcuffed Number One. Number Two was unable to offer any further resistance.

"All right! Read 'em their rights!" Carson shouted. "And use the damn card—I don't want any technicalities here!"

"Carson," the Brooklyn NYPD lieutenant called, "bad news, I'm afraid. My guys lost those two in the car that tailed Hillerman."

"Damn! Lieutenant! I want those two, dammit!"

"I got eight cars and a chopper on it. I'm still hoping for a sighting. They were last seen on Atlantic Avenue heading east."

"Get them, Lieutenant! Get them NOW!"

■ ■ ■ ■ ■

Detective Dunn arrived in the office as the two mercenaries were being removed. He looked at Carson and Woodruff and knew the worst even before he looked at Hillerman's body.

"I'm sorry, Tom," Carson said. "I'm truly sorry."

Dunn looked at Carson but couldn't answer. Do you truly

care, fed cop, Dunn thought, even a little. He knelt beside his partner's body, tears welling in his eyes. He was able to tell Jill later that evening, as he held the sobbing woman, that Hillerman had not suffered. He had died almost instantly.

Outside the Mercenary Hideout, Queens—1440 Hours

Carson reached FBI Agent Fisher and was relieved to hear that the police were already surrounding the hideout of the remaining mercenaries. "We'll be at the operations command center in about ten minutes," he told Fisher. "Tell the phone company to switch their phone now."

"I sure hope things go better in Queens than they did in Brooklyn," Woodruff muttered as he drove the car at high speed toward Queens.

"I'm with you. I can't believe the Brooklyn cops lost that tail."

The hideout was already surrounded when Carson and Woodruff arrived at the operations command-center, a trailer two blocks from the warehouse. Nearly two hundred officers, with buses and ambulances, were evacuating the surrounding houses.

"Captain O'Toole," Carson said. "What's your best estimate of evacuation time."

"About two hours. The Police Commissioner and Mayor are on their way here."

"I'll deal with them. Any word on the tanks?"

"They're on the way. Should be here about five—as planned," Fisher answered.

"Then we have about two and a half hours to finish the evacuation and start negotiations. As soon as the people are out, Captain, I'll call those mercenaries, so keep me posted on your progress. Tell all the officers to stay out of sight until I make that first call. We don't want to spook them and start any shooting until these houses are empty."

■ ■ ■ ■ ■

Anna Koslov was one of the homeowners being evacuated. She protested at having to leave her black labrador, Oscar, behind, but the police did not have room or time to take pets.

She looked back at the small, well-kept house with apprehension as she boarded the waiting bus. The small garden that she had spent so many hours tending bloomed with flowers, the envy of many of her neighbors. She worried about Oscar being alone as the bus began moving down the street toward the temporary shelter.

Washington, D.C. —1500 Hours

Chief Morris placed a call to retired Master Sergeant Elders.

"I'm calling to ask you about a visitors' logbook you signed back in '45 when you went to see Reichsmarschall Herman Göring. Do you remember that?"

"Lord! I never would have believed that anyone would call about *that*. Yes, I remember signing the visitors' log. Why do you ask?"

"The first two sheets, which contained pages one through four, were cut out—we think to hide some names. Your name was on page five. The names we're interested in were on page four. We believe that the book was laid open, so you would have been able to see the names on page four. We're trying to get a lead on those names. Can you help us?"

"Whew! No, I don't remember any names—but wait! You should be talking to Sergeant Yancey Curtis. He was the Military Police sergeant of the guard. That logbook would have been in his charge. Call him, why don't you?"

"He and I became good friends after the war. I've got his phone number and address around here someplace . . . Yeah, here it is. He's retired to Florida. A little town near Pensacola. Call old Yancey up. He's a barrel of laughs."

Chief Morris wrote down the number and address and placed the call.

He said to Curtis, "I hope I can get you to think back to '45 when you were sergeant of the guard for Reichsmarschall

Göring. I've been told that you were in charge of the visitors' logbook. We're trying to find some names of early visitors who would have signed the first four pages of the logbook. Those pages have been cut from the book. We believe the people on those four pages may have been with the OSS. One of the names may have been a Major Tilton. Can you help us?"

"Why, those rotten bastards! Yeah, I can believe they'd pull a stunt like that. They gave me such a hard time about signing the book. What an argument! But the S.O.B.'s name was Tifton, not Tilton. I'll never forget Major Tifton if I live a thousand years! What a prick! I'd love to see him pulled down."

"We have agents looking for him. What I need are the names of some of the people with him."

"He was always with three or four other OSS types. A Captain Erickson— Douglas, I think. Then there was a first looey, Sam Bernard. The other guy was a second looey. He didn't act so damn arrogant. His name was—give me a sec . . . Vince Brogano! Yeah, Vince Brogano. Oh, a Navy guy a couple of times, Commander Rolland Ledbetter. Me and the other MPs referred to them as the Asshole Pack. I still burn every time I see Tifton on TV."

"He's on TV?"

"On the news. He's that big-mouthed senator from California." There followed several seconds of silence. "Chief? You still there?"

"You're pos...positive?"

"Absolutely."

■ ■ ■ ■ ■

Near the Mercenary Hideout, Queens—1520 Hours

Betsy screamed out and fought to loosen her hands from the transit policeman's grip.

"Mommy! Mommy!" she cried. "I want to get Sam!" She pulled against the officer's hand with all the strength her four year old body could muster. Tears ran down her rounded cheeks and her blonde hair bounced as she shook her head in frustration.

"Betsy!" her mother said firmly. "We can't get your teddy bear. Sam will be here when you come home."

"I want him now!"

"I'm very sorry about this," Betsy's mother apologized to the officer struggling to put the child on the waiting bus. "Is there any way I could get her toy?"

"No time, ma'am," the officer said firmly. "Sorry. Please get on board."

Betsy's mother could only glance back toward the family's small two story house. The freshly painted shutters seemed so inviting. She could only hope that she and Betsy would soon be able to come home to their security, to be surrounded by the things of their lives. To return to Sam the teddy bear.

■ ■ ■ ■ ■

"Agent Carson, I'm the police commissioner for the City of New York," said a large, burly man wearing an obviously expensive tailored suit with a large diamond pinky ring on his left hand. "The Mayor is on his way. I want to know what you're doing. I'm receiving some unnerving reports."

Carson explained the plan to capture the remaining mercenaries. What is the matter with this arrogant bastard? Carson wondered.

"Commissioner, I remain in charge of what is a federal operation. I expect you to provide us with the support we need from your department," Carson said with his voice rising in pitch and volume.

"I see that His Honor has arrived," the Police Commissioner said looking out the open door. "We'll be back to finish this discussion." He turned and moved toward the door.

"Of course. However, I'm proceeding as planned." Carson's voice returned to its normal pitch and volume.

"The lousy politicians are getting jumpy," said Woodruff. "What do they expect us to do—invite these perps to a picnic?"

"You know politicians. They're always worried about what the goddamn press is going to say. Besides, some of these mercenaries may be voters or contributors to their campaign funds."

"Yeah, I can believe that."

Their conversation was interrupted by the telephone specially connected to the hideout.

"Don't answer that," Carson ordered. "Is the caller ID working?"

"Yeah, a number is coming through. They're trying to call Vargas's office."

"The phone company fixed it so that no matter what number they try to call, it'll end up on this phone. They also blocked all incoming calls except us. They'll talk to us or nobody."

About fifteen minutes had passed since the Mayor's arrival. Carson could see that the two officials were having an agitated discussion. They had been joined by the deputy chief of police and the Queens borough police commander. Finally, the men came up the steps into the command center.

"Agent Carson," the Mayor began. "I've been discussing the situation with the police commissioner. We're both quite concerned about this attack plan you proposed. It appears very risky to both of us."

"Mr. Mayor, the perpetrators in that building are equipped with powerful military weapons that can do terrible damage to this neighborhood if they open fire. The police have no weaponry capable of hitting back. Therefore, I've convinced both the Governor and the President to provide heavy military equipment to counter the arsenal in that building."

"Do you intend to use these tanks?"

"Not if they surrender. My plan calls for a demonstration to try to get them to come out. We'll be using that telephone to discuss the situation with them just as soon as Captain O'Toole tells me the surrounding houses are empty."

"And if they choose not to surrender?"

"Then I will release Commander Scott to move forward

with a strike force of federal officers and Coast Guardsmen behind the tanks. The tanks will return fire if the mercenaries shoot their heavy weapons at the strike force."

"That will result in many deaths, " said the commissioner. "The press will call us murderers. They will rip us apart, Your Honor."

"I disagree," Carson countered. "This is not a hostage situation. Everyone inside that building is a criminal. Even if we kill them all, the press can't make much of it."

"Ha! You really don't believe that," sneered the commissioner.

"I hasten to remind you, Agent Carson," said the Mayor, "that we have judges and juries to deal with such questions. Law enforcement officers are required to capture perpetrators alive for trial whenever possible."

"I'm not arguing the point, Mr. Mayor. That is exactly what I hope to accomplish. But I can't be certain what they'll do, and we must be prepared for the worst. I would also remind you, sir, that these officers now surrounding the building will be getting tired long before midnight and will need to be replaced by fresh people."

"Agent Carson! I am not about to sacrifice lives to save your budget! That is unacceptable!"

"Then, Mr. Mayor, I would suggest that you start arranging for hundreds of relief officers if this is to be a protracted siege. Put that in your own budget and balance it."

"I find your arrogant manner intolerable! I intend to discuss this matter with the Governor and the President. Let's get back to City Hall, Commissioner. This matter is not yet settled, Agent Carson. You would be well advised to take no action until the Commissioner or I return. Do you understand?"

"Yes, Mr. Mayor. I apologize if I seem arrogant, but I have to think about these officers' lives and the lives of the civilians we've been evacuating. I intend to proceed with my already approved plan, sir."

Carson rolled his eyes toward the ceiling in disbelief as the mayor turned away.

He was brought back to the immediate problem as the telephone began ringing.

"Our quarry is trying to ring Vargas again," said Woodruff.

"I'm not surprised. They must be getting pretty nervous by now."

The door slammed, and Captain O'Toole entered the trailer to report that the evacuation was nearly completed. It was time for negotiations to start.

"Okay. Let's call and give them the bad news," Carson said as he dialed the number supplied by the phone company. His face was a mask of smugness.

"Hello. This is Special Agent Carson of the FBI. I'm calling to tell you that you are surrounded by police and federal agents and that you and all those with you are under—." His smug look vanished. "He hung up!"

The phone rang again.

"This is Special Agent Car—. He hung up again!"

"Maybe he doesn't like your voice," Woodruff suggested. The joke wasn't quite appreciated as Carson glanced at his fellow agent with arched eyebrows.

It rang again.

"Look, we've had the phone company change your phone to ring here no matter what num—Damn! He hung up again!"

"Hard to negotiate when one side is doing all of the talking. So far, they're still dialing Vargas's number." Woodruff's eyes remained focused on the caller I.D.

Carson picked up the phone again.

"It's your FBI again, fella! I'm the only person you're going to talk to, so it's time to talk to me. Stop hanging up and start talking—." Click. "This guy is something else!"

"That time he dialed a different number."

"Get the phone company to run it."

Several minutes went by. The radio came on as Captain O'Toole reported that a man with binoculars had just been seen on the building's roof.

"Shall we fire at him?" O'Toole asked.

"No! But let him see some of your guys!" Carson

answered. He hoped that seeing the surrounding force would convince them to surrender.

Several more minutes passed.

"I'll call them again," said Carson as he dialed the phone. "It's Agent Carson again. Are you ready to talk to me? Don't hang up now. We saw a man on your roof a few minutes ago, so you know by now you're surrounded.

"Why don't you start by telling me your name....No? Well, then, I'll just call you Number Three since we've already arrested Numbers One and Two at Vargas's office. Oh, it's true! I know you've been trying to dial Vargas's office. Your situation is hopeless. You have only one chance—lay down your guns and surren—." Click. "Well, here we go again!"

"Hung up?" Woodruff asked, not really needing to.

"Yeah. I'm afraid Roberts may be right. These guys are not going to give up without a fight."

"Captain Reynolds wants to see you," Agent Fisher called in through the door.

"Agent Carson," Captain Reynolds began. "I've been talking to O'Toole and the borough police commander, and we're all worried about the deployment around this building. With only fifty men on each side, we're spread pretty thin, especially if this goes on after dark. I've got only one officer for every fifteen feet. If these guys rush us, I doubt our line will hold. We're going to need to double, maybe triple, our personnel if we're going to hold these lines tonight."

"Have you discussed this with the superintendent?"

"Yes. O'Toole's been talking to the borough police commander. The story's the same everywhere. It's going to be rough enough just maintaining the present force around the clock. Everybody has manpower shortage problems. The officers are working overtime as it is."

"I understand. To ease your mind, Commander Scott and his Coast Guardsmen should be here in a few minutes."

A mile from the building five heavy tanks, carried by truck transporters built to handle the sixty-ton loads, eased to a stop in the now traffic-free city street. They were halted to avoid being seen by the mercenaries.

When informed, Fisher yelled, "Carson! The Army has just arrived, and the Coast Guard is right behind them."

■ ■ ■ ■ ■

"How shall I deploy, Commander?" Chief Morris asked as the trucks carrying the volunteer guardsmen came to a stop. It had been a fast afternoon coming up from Washington, followed by arming and transporting this military force to Queens.

"We're to go in with the tanks," Scott answered. "Fall in alongside the Army while I meet with Carson."

■ ■ ■ ■ ■

"Agent Carson, I am Lieutenant Berry, 308th Tank Battalion, reporting as ordered, sir."

"Thank you, Lieutenant."

"May I ask about our objective, sir?"

"Yes. You may have to help us attack and capture approximately fifteen heavily-armed men who are occupying that warehouse across the parking lot."

"That building over there, sir?" The lieutenant looked surprised. "I don't understand. That's an ordinary civilian structure. I thought this target was a heavy concrete blockhouse." He appeared confused.

"Does that make a difference?"

"It certainly does! Agent Carson, you don't seem to understand the firepower of a long-barrel, 105 millimeter high-velocity gun. A few rounds and there won't be a building over there. Just a pile of rubble!"

"You were supposed to bring *low*-velocity ammunition, Lieutenant."

"We did, sir, but low-velocity ammunition only reduces muzzle velocity so the shell has less penetrating power. The high-explosive charge inside the shell is still just as powerful. A round of hypershot would penetrate that building and probably a dozen houses."

"Actually, I'm not planning for you to fire your heavy guns. We need your tanks to shield our men from the heavy weapons the mercenaries are believed to possess."

"What heavy weapons?"

"Here's the ATF list."

Berry scanned the list. His eyes opened wide under arched eyebrows. "What the hell is going on here?"

"Didn't the general brief you?"

"Sir, commanding generals don't waste their time briefing lieutenants. I was told by my colonel to bring these ground assets and report to you."

"We have surrounded a group of mercenary soldiers in that building. As you can see, there's no cover in the parking lot surrounding the building, and no way anybody is going to run across a hundred yards without being blown to hell. So we need your armor to protect our officers from their firepower as we cross that open space. I was assured by your general that your tanks can stand up to their weapons."

"It depends on how the weapons strike the vehicle. Against the frontal armor, the P-27 is no threat and even the T-21 is only a minor threat. But if they hit a track, the vehicle will be stopped. Then while it's immobilized, they can move and set up to strike the side or top and penetrate the thinner armor, killing the crew inside."

"Can we prevent that?"

"Certainly, sir. The instant they open fire, my crews will open up and level that building before they get a second chance."

"That's exactly what everybody around here does *not* want."

"I don't see any way to avoid that result if these ground assets are to be utilized."

■ ■ ■ ■ ■

The return of the Police Commissioner, accompanied by a female officer, interrupted their discussion. Commander Scott, his M-16 rifle slung over his shoulder, followed them into the room.

"This is Lieutenant Cynthia Williams of our hostage negotiation team," the commissioner said introducing the tall black woman. "The Mayor insists that every effort be made to talk these perpetrators into surrender before any attack. I insist that Lieutenant Williams be provided opportunity to commence negotiations at once."

"Certainly, Commissioner. There's the phone." Why should I object, Carson thought, I hadn't made any progress.

"Agent Carson," said Lieutenant Williams, "have you accomplished anything yet?"

"I'm afraid not. So far, I talk and he hangs up."

"Perhaps he will be more receptive to me."

The lieutenant dialed the number and waited for an answer.

"Hello, this is Lieutenant Cynthia Williams, NYPD. I'm a police negotiator and I want to discuss—." Click. "He hung up!" She looked surprised that the man at the other end did not make demands, as had always happened in past contacts with gunmen.

"Welcome to our nightmare, Lieutenant."

Fisher entered the trailer and handed Carson a slip of paper.

"The phone company identified the other number our perps tried to call. It's a cellular number subscribed to by a George Smith, who has a post office box address here in Queens."

"Who is George Smith?" asked Williams.

"Apparently an alias used by one of our perps. Shows a little imagination, though. They could have used *John* Smith like everybody else."

"Hmm....Let me give that a try," said Lieutenant Williams as she dialed the number. "Hello, George Smith? This is Cynthia. No wait, don't hang up, George! Let's you and me talk. You are George Smith, aren't you? Well, if you're not, then why not tell me your name....All right, then, we'll just pretend that you're George, okay?

"Look you gotta believe me. The police have you surrounded. Hundreds of officers. So you can't get away. If you
don't come out, then we're going to have to come in and get
you. Surely you can understand that, can't you? Damn. He
hung up again."

"Frustrating, isn't it?" said Carson. Ha, he thought, it was-
n't just me after all.

Suddenly Captain O'Toole's voice came over the radio.

"They're opening a small hole in the rear wall! Good Lord!
Get down!"

The drumming sound of machine-gun fire was unmistakable. Bullets sprayed across the parking area, hitting the pavement and thudding into the walls of the houses beyond. The
police dived for cover.

An instant later, a small slit opened in the left truck access
door and the heavy drumming sound was now heard in the
front of the building.

"Get down!" Scott yelled as bullets smashed through the
wall of the trailer just over Lieutenant Williams's head. She
dropped to the floor, joining the men who also fell to cover.
The firing continued for several minutes. Finally it stopped.
"Let's get out of here!"

As they ran out of the trailer, the firing resumed. Bullets
struck two houses nearby with shattered glass flying in every
direction.

The negotiators dived behind a retaining wall. The bullets
whined overhead.

"Is everybody okay?" Scott asked.

They were, but their respite was short-lived. A powerful
explosion ripped apart a nearby house, showering them with
flying debris of all descriptions.

Anna Koslov's worry over her small house, her dog, Oscar,
and the well-tended garden no longer mattered.

"My God! A P-27 round," yelled Lieutenant Berry.

More violent explosions damaged several houses. Then
silence. Betsy would never hold her teddy bear again.

"Why did they shoot?" asked the commissioner. "None of
the police fired at them."

"A demonstration," Carson answered. "Probably in response to Lieutenant Williams's threat that the police would move against them. I was afraid we had put the command center too close, but I wanted visual contact. Fisher, get in touch with Reynolds and O'Toole and ask about injuries."

■ ■ ■ ■ ■

It was about five-thirty when the trailer containing the operations-command center was pulled back out of the line of fire using a winch truck to minimize exposure. The telephones and electricity were reconnected. The electricity to the mercenary hideout had been cut and the water shut off. Carson called an impromptu meeting.

"Agent Carson," the commissioner began, "you've heard both Captain O'Toole and Captain Reynolds report that enough police manpower has been obtained for the next three days to provide round-the-clock coverage. The arrival of the Army and Coast Guard gives us enough military force to contain any breakout attempt.

"Therefore, there is no urgency to proceed against that building. We've cut their electricity and water, and we control their telephone. We should wait for these factors to have the desired effect. Meantime, I want Lieutenant Williams to continue with negotiations."

"I don't know about that, Commissioner," Lieutenant Williams responded. "My last try brought on all that shooting."

"Don't blame yourself, Lieutenant," Scott interjected. "That was bound to happen when our intentions were made known. But Commissioner, Agent Carson erred earlier when he said that this situation was different from Waco because we have no hostages—no women or children. We most certainly do have hostages—over ten thousand of them: the people we evacuated this afternoon. Plus thousands more potential hostages still in homes within the mile-wide range of the T-21."

Scott continued keeping his stern gaze on the commissioner. "How do you propose to keep all of those people out of their homes for an extended period of time? And if those criminals should open fire indiscriminately and destroy some occupied houses and kill innocent people, then I wonder how the Mayor would deal with the publicity. His political opponents might accuse you and him of incompetence at the very least and murder at the worst!"

"I am outraged by your arrogance! You damn feds come into my city and usurp my authority. Now, you expect me to lick your boots. Man, am I ever pissed!"

"Sir, evacuation of all of the houses for a radius of one mile around that building is simply not possible. You would have to move about fifty thousand people. Where will you move them? How would you feed them and house them? It's just not possible, and you and the Mayor must know that. So the only practical way to handle this situation is Carson's plan. We have about three hours of daylight left. I don't intend to waste them!"

Agent Carson shook his head in agreement with the FBI's appointed military leader.

The commissioner looked contemptuously at Scott, who was standing beside the desk in his black flak vest and bullet resistant helmet still holding his rifle.

"I thought pit bulls were kept in cages," he finally said. "I want Lieutenant Williams to try again!"

"Fine," Scott agreed. "Lieutenant, tell them about the army's tanks. Tell them the tanks are ready to be used. Come out now or face the consequences."

She dialed the number, reminding herself that the most important duty of a negotiator is to defuse a situation with calmness, then build rapport with the criminal.

She had to establish a first-name, friend-to-friend conversation and attempt to build trust with the criminal. Since the mercenary answering the phone had not spoken and would not give his name, Williams could only try to draw him out by calling him George. Using this alias would show the mercenaries that the police knew a lot about them, and therefore their situation was hopeless.

"George, it's Lieutenant Williams again. That shooting was

not very smart. You just made things worse. We've had the Army bring in some big tanks with huge cannons. Unless you and your comrades come out and surrender, we're going to have to let the Army start those tanks.

"He just hung up again!"

"Put out the word—quick!" Scott yelled. "Get everybody down! I've got that feeling!"

A minute later, a powerful explosion ripped a vacant house to shreds. A few seconds later, a second blast destroyed another house. The wreckage began to burn.

"A T-21 shell, Commander?" asked Carson.

"Very likely. High-explosive antipersonnel, probably."

"Another demonstration?"

"They want us to know what they've got, for sure. Well, Commissioner," Scott pressed. "Just how much more do you need to see? How do you plan to answer accusations of allowing criminals to fire indiscriminately with reckless disregard of human life and property? In fact, the media people must be straining at their leashes already after hearing these explosions. Good thing we established a temporary restricted air space already, or we'd have news helicopters too.

"Now you've got two houses on fire, and there's no way to bring in fire fighters with those guns blazing. So the fires are going to spread. Are you going to let Queens burn down? I'm sure the owners of those houses are going to be screaming about their property.

"How are you going to explain not using the tanks to end this quickly? You had better make a decision. The press will be all over City Hall."

"Dammit! All right! Proceed!" the commissioner agreed. His face was taut with sweat rolling down his cheeks.

"That's what I've been waiting to hear," said Scott as he reached for his radio.

"Scott to Berry, you are ordered to move your platoon forward. You are hereby authorized to respond to opposing fire as required to protect your command. Scott out."

A minute later, the tanks began to move.

Lieutenant Berry's tank moved first down the narrow

street, screened from mercenary eyes by a row of houses. Walking behind each of the rumbling steel monsters, guardsmen and federal officers—dressed in bulletproof vests and helmets with face shields—inched forward.

The tanks had moved only a few yards when Scott, breathing hard after his run, joined Chief Morris walking beside the lead tank.

"At last, Chief!" Scott shouted over the roar of the engines. "At last!" His determination to even the score for both Brenda's and Hillerman's deaths was openly apparent.

Scott could see the wider avenue ahead where this single file restriction would end. A left turn and the tanks could move three abreast, a much more satisfactory arrangement. Come on, he thought, let's get there. These murdering bastards will wish they'd never heard of me.

Scott looked toward his friend marching beside him. He realized that his determination to destroy these criminals was troubling the chief. "You want these killers dead so bad," the chief had said, "you're denying the danger."

Scott knew that the MI Abrams battle tank was equipped with reactive armor packages capable of stopping powerful antitank shells. But he also knew that when the impact came, a cloud of deadly fragments would burst in every direction, including theirs. If that weren't enough, there was the rest of the weaponry in enemy hands.

They reached the avenue at last. Scott quickly directed the tanks into a rank of three to be followed by the other two. The guardsmen and federal officers then grouped behind the tanks. Scott clambered aboard Lieutenant Berry's tank and moved behind the turret, within speaking distance of the young army officer.

A wave of Scott's hand and the force of men and machines moved up the avenue. Ten minutes. Ten minutes until the force would be exposed to the enemy's view.

Scott could see inside the slow-moving tank through the open hatch. The gunner was sitting in his seat, waiting for the order to fire. Scott glanced at the soldier who had loaded the heavy cannon, standing at the side of the turret to avoid being hit when the cannon's breech recoiled. He cradled the next high explosive cartridge in his arms like a baby, ready to quickly shove the round home the instant the spent casing ejected. Scott remembered his own training aboard large Coast Guard cutters when he had fired the main cannon. The gunner and loader must become a team with the cannon so as to load, aim, and fire every five seconds with deadly accuracy.

The waiting was the worst part, never knowing if an enemy weapon might overpower the armor and bathe the inside of the turret with white hot metal. Scott knew that if that happened they would all die a horrible fiery death in there. There would be no escape. To live together, work together, and die together was the unspoken fate of tank crewmen.

The radio in Scott's hand crackled to life.

"O'Toole to Scott. The mercenaries are opening more slits in the rear wall again. It looks like they're opening a hole in the roof, too. Over."

"A hole in the roof? To shoot from, you mean? Over."

"Can't tell, but—Look out! Get down!"

The sound of heavy .51-caliber machine-gun fire filled the air, joined by a second sound: a heavy *thump* followed by a powerful explosion.

Captain O'Toole screamed into his radio, "We are under heavy fire! They've got a mortar in there! Just blew up a house—all to hell dammit! Over."

"Scott to O'Toole. Understood. Get your people under cover! The tanks are moving down the avenue now! Out!"

A second mortar shell landed between two police cars behind the police line. The explosion lifted the cars in a momentary dance, ended by their violent impact with the ground.

"Captain!" screamed Lieutenant Roberts, "I've got two guys hit!"

Another explosion ripped the row of houses behind O'Toole's men.

"Roberts!" O'Toole shouted back. "Get everybody under heavy cover! Those bullets are going right through the cars! They'll kill anybody on the other side!"

Their brief exchange was interrupted by another explosion. A police car a few yards away was blasted to destruction. Lieutenant Roberts felt a sharp pain as a piece of the vehicle's shattered windshield struck his hand.

"Damn!" Roberts yelled. "That shot came from the slit on the right!"

"O'Toole to Scott. We are taking rocket-propelled-grenade fire from a P-27 as well as heavy machine-gun and mortar fire. I think they're trying to clear us out of here so they can escape out the back. Over!"

"Understood. I'll have Reynolds pull some of his people over to your left and right corners. Pull your people away from the center toward your corners. That should keep them out of the main zone of fire. Over."

"Roger—son of a bitch! They just blew a hole in the back wall! Big enough for several men!"

"Get your sharpshooters to put fire on that hole! Don't let them get away, dammit!"

"Where are those damn tanks! We're in trouble here!"

"Pour on the rifle fire. The tanks are almost there! Scott out!"

As the distance between the tanks and building shrank, the killing range of the T21 would soon be reached. Scott's hands began to sweat as he looked toward the building. In response to the known danger, Scott had instructed the gunner to load the main gun with a round of high-explosive ammunition. He now understood why the general sent this unit instead of the M1A1 Abrams. That model's 120-millimeter gun would have been too powerful.

Suddenly, the slit in the left garage door opened again. The flashes of a machine gun joined the sound of bullets striking the armor. Even though the machine gun was no threat to the tanks, it soon became clear that the bullets would ricochet off the armor into the men on foot. Several were struck.

Scott's position on top of the turret quickly became the

mercenaries' center of attention. Even he didn't have that much courage, and dived off the back of the vehicle in undignified haste. Only then did he realize that his exit was late. His left hand instinctively moved to a gash on his right arm as blood dripped to the pavement below his feet.

Even before Scott's sudden exit, Lieutenant Berry's finger pressed the trigger of the triple barrel gatling machine gun. The sound of forty bullets every second was more a constant scream than a chatter. The stream of bullets shredded the metal garage door in seconds, revealing the Soviet made .51-caliber heavy machine gun still firing from behind its armored shield.

Scott glanced at the guardsmen walking beside him. So young, he thought, their faces distorted with fear as they gripped their M-16 rifles. They'll fight, Scott knew, I'm proud of these 'coasties.' They didn't have to come. This is an FBI operation—not an official Coast guard action. They could have said no, but to a man, they answered Captain Peters's call without any dissent.

"Now, Berry! Now!" Scott shouted into his radio.

The slit on the center garage door of the hideout suddenly opened. Scott found he was looking straight down the muzzle of a Soviet-made T21 Tarasnice antitank gun. Berry needed no further prodding.

"Front-rank gunners!" Berry yelled into his microphone. "Target center door! Two rounds each! Fire!"

A second later the T21 fired. Its 82-millimeter antitank shell struck Lieutenant Berry's tank on the right side of the turret and exploded against the armor. Less than a hundredth of a second later, the crushed, shattered pieces of the shell fell away from the tank.

The exploded reactive armor bore mute testimony to the contest waged. The armor had won.

The blasts from the 105-millimeter guns were so strong that most of the men behind the tanks lost their intentionally unfastened helmets. Windows of the adjacent houses disappeared in shards of glass. The shell from Berry's tank penetrated the center garage door and exploded against the rear wall, which disappeared in a cloud of smoke and dust. The debris rained down as far away as Captain O'Toole's officers, who were lying behind the cover of a low masonry wall. Where the shells from the tanks on either side of Berry hit the front of the mercenaries' building, the wall simply disappeared.

The empty cartridge, spewing acrid gunpowder smoke, shot out of the open breech, as the cannon reached the end of its recoil. It fell onto the steel plate below with a clang. The soldier responsible for loading the cannon moved with precision as he shoved the fresh loaded cartridge home.

"Up!" he shouted as the breech closed. The gunner's trigger finger was already moving.

The roof of the building had been lifted off what remained of the walls and flew upward. Before it could fall back, the second salvo of 105-millimeter shells exploded nearly simultaneously. The roof was again lifted upward in hundreds of pieces flung in all directions. Moments later, flames began to shoot up from the piles of debris.

Two figures emerged from the smoke and dust. They stumbled forward with weapons in their hands. Scott raised his M-16 and took aim. The rifle bucked only slightly as the bullets took flight.

The small, high-velocity .223 caliber copper-sheathed bullets impacted the chests of the two mercenaries. Scott watched as spurts of blood flew outward from the impacts. The two men staggered for a moment, but their bodies soon fell to the pavement.

Scott lowered his rifle, and for a moment, he simply stared at the stilled flesh. The heat and waves of deafening sound from the hideout's exploding ammunition soon forced Scott and the other officers into hasty retreat.

There was no further response from the remains of the building.

Newark International Airport, New Jersey— 0010 Hours

Scott stepped through the door of the security office at Newark
International Airport. Still wearing his body armor, bullet proof
helmet, and bloodied bandage on his arm, he knew he must be
a fearsome sight to the airport police officer at the duty desk.
Other federal officers piled into the small space in front of the
duty desk as Scott identified himself.

"Are they still in the gate waiting area?" Scott asked.

"Yes," the officer answered. "I've got two men maintaining
surveillance."

"How many?"

"Three elderly men. Why are you looking for them?"

"Murder, conspiracy, and more. Are they sitting with the
other passengers?"

"Yes. That's a big problem. If they resist—what about the
innocent people?"

"After we're in position, I want you to have Douglas Erickson paged. We'll nab him at the courtesy phone. I feel sure that
when he fails to rejoin the other two, they'll come to look for
him and we can grab them. With luck—no shooting will be
needed."

"If they see you dressed like that—they're bound to know
something is wrong."

"I'll have the FBI agents make the approach. No one
should notice them in their suits—they'll blend right in."

Scott quickly reviewed the passenger manifest and handed out copies of passport photos of the three fugitives. So arrogant, he thought. These men actually used their own names instead of aliases!

He and Morris waited in the small alcove. Scott glanced at his watch. It was 12:20 a.m. The three FBI agents stood near the courtesy phone trying very hard to be invisible. A moment later, the announcer paged Douglas Erickson to come to the courtesy phone.

Scott could just see past the partition corner into the main passageway. And then he saw him. The slender older man walked with a youthful step and appeared to be physically strong. He stopped at the phone and picked up the hand set— the last act of a free man. Handcuffs snapped around his wrists.

Morris held open the door leading to the airport staff stairway as the FBI agents firmly led the protesting man away. Scott listened as one of the agents read the Miranda warning. Erickson stared at Scott with contempt. A quick search found no weapon.

"The mercenaries are dead, you bastard!" Scott said, staring right back. "Just give me any excuse!" His right hand rested on top of the nine-millimeter pistol at his side.

"Take it easy, Commander," one of the FBI agents cautioned. "Our perp has an appointment with the U.S. Attorney."

Erickson was forced to sit on the steps, both wrists chained to the steel handrail. He said nothing.

The three FBI agents returned to their positions by the courtesy phone. Scott's plan anticipated that one of the two remaining fugitives would soon come to the phone to search for Erickson. Better be soon, Scott thought looking at his watch, the flight to Athens would board in twelve minutes. It just took five.

The second fugitive stepped into the passageway and peered toward the phone. He looked confused. He hesitated, then walked slowly toward the phone, still looking around for Erickson.

Two steps later and the man found himself handcuffed and

searched. The warnings were read, while Scott looked at the passport photo to reaffirm his recognition of the face of Vince Brogano. The FBI agents found a stiff plastic knife—deadly and not detectable by the airport metal detectors. They left Brogano in Chief Morris's charge, and with Scott at the lead proceeded directly to the gate area. Scott thought it would be safe to capture the third fugitive when he was separated from the others.

This was ex-Navy Commander Rolland Ledbetter. The face of the man waiting in the cushioned seat was a match with the photo. The armed men made a rapid approach. Ledbetter looked up when Scott and the others suddenly appeared. The other passengers froze as Ledbetter was pulled from the seat and handcuffed.

"Captain Peters certainly wants to meet you," Scott said firmly as they left the gate waiting area.

■ ■ ■ ■ ■

"Yes, Captain," Scott said into the telephone in the airport police station. "We have them—all three."

"Have the FBI take them to Manhattan," Captain Peters responded. "Then you and Morris come to Washington immediately. The FBI's jet is waiting for you."

"Any progress finding the Senator?"

"Not yet. Carson has every agent out looking for Tifton. We're quite sure he's still in the area."

"We've got to catch him. He's behind everything, sir. He's the top man."

"I know. I'll look for you two within the hour."

Washington, D.C.—0130 Hours

Scott looked over at his friend, Chief Morris, seated in the rear of the FBI car. As the vehicle passed through the empty streets of the nation's capital, both men fought sleep. The FBI driver turned into the parking garage at the J. Edgar Hoover Building. Only ten hours had elapsed since Scott and Chief Morris had left Washington for New York. And now they were back again.

The message from Agent Carson about the fourth fugitive had reached Scott just minutes before the FBI jet landed. Stanley Bernard had been arrested near Valdosta, Georgia, after a high-speed auto chase. The FBI agents were already en route back to Washington with Bernard in handcuffs. Now to find the criminal's boss.

■ ■ ■ ■ ■

Scott was thankful for the opportunity to clean up and have his wound checked again before rejoining Captain Peters and the others.

"We got a lead, Commander," Carson said as Scott took a place at the conference table. "Senator Tifton is a major stockholder in a photographic studio company. We just found out that there is a townhouse in Arlington owned by that company. Grab a shotgun. We're leaving immediately."

Scott settled into the rear seat of the staff car beside Captain Peters. Their conversation quickly turned to the involvement of Captain Jerome Ledbetter of Naval Intelligence.

"He's restricted to his quarters, Bob," Peters said. "The Judge Advocate General staff is starting an investigation into why I was relieved of command. The fact that Jerome Ledbetter's father was involved with these conspirators has thrown that action into serious question. We'll question the father, Rolland Ledbetter, tomorrow."

Scott looked out the side window of the staff car as it crossed the bridge into Arlington. The Potomac was black, with only the lights of the two cities visible. The car turned onto the empty residential street leading to the photographic studio. Scott gripped the shotgun a little tighter as the building came into view.

Arlington, Virginia—0220 Hours

Scott pressed the doorbell button. After a moment, he used his fist to pound loudly on the green wooden door. Nearly two minutes passed before the door swung open a few inches against its security chain. The face of a man appeared in the small opening. Too young to be the senator, Scott realized, as he held the warrant up for the man to see.

"Police! Open up this door!" Scott ordered. "Now!"

The man hesitated for a moment. The view beyond Scott was filled with federal and local police officers. The man finally released the chain. Scott shoved the door open, sending the man against the wall.

"Where's the Senator?" Scott demanded.

"I'll let him know you're here," the shaken man answered.

"No you won't! Lead us to him!"

Again, the man hesitated. The menace of Scott's shotgun only inches from his face finally brought motion. With Scott and his captive in the lead, the line of officers surged toward a door at the rear of the short hall. Scott pulled the door open, and they went quickly down the stairs.

Scott realized that he was standing at the side of a video studio. He could see mats laid on the floor where half a dozen young men and women were engaged in various sexual activities. On the far side was a tripod mounted video camera. Bright lights lit the scene and momentarily blinded the police. Scott, his eyes shielded from the lights by his upheld left hand, finally made out a face behind the video camera. The face of the U.S. senator from California.

"Senator Tifton!" Scout shouted. "You're under arrest!" Scott paid no attention to the young people scurrying to retrieve their clothing. His gaze was riveted on his quarry. "Come out from there! Now!"

"How dare you come in here!" the senator shouted back. "Get off my property." He stepped back toward a desk behind the camera. His hand moved rapidly toward the top left drawer.

"Stop!" Scott leveled his shotgun directly at the old man. Oh no, Scott thought, he's going for a gun. Should I fire or wait? He could hear the other police officers moving into the studio behind him and the metallic clicks as they drove cartridges into their firing chambers. Surely the old man can see that he has no chance, Scott wondered. "If you aim a gun toward me, I'll fire!" Scott warned.

The senator withdrew his hand from the drawer. The object he held was not a gun—it was an oval shaped steel ball—a hand grenade.

"You're that asshole Scott!" the senator said. Scott realized that his grey Coast Guard bulletproof vest, his name stenciled in white ink on the right side, revealed all to the old politician's eyes. "I thought the mercenaries had killed your butt!"

"They're all dead or in jail. You're going to be joining them, dead or alive. The choice is yours."

"I don't think so." The senator's other hand moved to the restraining pin and its pull ring. His finger quickly secured the ring and pulled it and the restraining pin from the handle. Only the senator's other hand restrained the spring lever, keeping the hand grenade from exploding. "At least I finally get to kill you—you stinking water cop!"

Scott's throat couldn't pass air as he watched the deadly bomb drop from the senator's hand onto the floor at Scott's feet. The released spring lever flipped outward igniting the time fuse as the grenade landed.

Instinct took over as Scott, dropping his shotgun, grabbed one of the mats and threw it over the grenade. Four more mats immediately joined Scott's as fellow officers reacted. Two FBI agents tipped a heavy table up against the side of the mattress pile. A flurry of diving men landed on the floor against the walls. The mattress pile-up had taken four seconds—the time fuse took five.

The muffled explosion rattled the room. Scott moved his hands away from his ears to cover his face from the falling debris of disintegrated mattresses and ceiling tiles. He quickly rose, wiping his face and struggling to breathe in the particle filled air. He retrieved the shotgun.

"Is everybody okay?" Scott called out. None of the officers appeared hurt and Scott turned his eyes toward the side door that he had seen the senator move through as the grenade landed on the floor. "Come on, dammit. Let's get the bastard!"

The door was only a few feet away and Scott reached the sheet metal faced panel first. He feared the senator might be just behind the door—gun in the old man's hand.

Scott decided to kick the door open to minimize his exposure. He raised his right leg, but paused when a sound came through the door. The sound Scott recognized as an electric garage door opener.

Scott's well aimed, powerful kick broke the latch, and swung the door open revealing a one car garage. Scott jumped through the door, shotgun raised for firing, and found his way blocked by a shiny Mercedes. On the opposite side of the car stood the senator, a pistol in his hand.

The garage door had reached the top of its travel and come to a stop. Scott glanced toward the open door and was relieved to see two police officers standing immediately outside the garage, guns raised. Now, Scott thought, this miserable bastard must see that he is trapped.

"Drop the gun, Senator," Scott ordered. "It's over." Scott and several other police officers worked their way around the front of the car, keeping their guns aimed at their quarry. The senator backed up against a workbench that ran along the side of the garage. He looked at Scott, anger filling his eyes with hate, then glanced at the officers stepping through the open garage door.

The senator's hand directed the pistol's muzzle upward and as Scott and the others watched, their faces taut, eyes open wide, he raised the gun against his own temple.

"Don't do it!" Scott ordered. "You must stand trial."

The senator smiled in defiance. Everyone held his breath. The click of the hammer striking the firing pin without the expected explosion caught everyone by surprise—especially the senator.

"Grab the damn gun!" Scott ordered as he and the police leaped forward. The senator stumbled back against the work bench, his right hand, still holding the pistol. Scott immediately swung the shotgun, smashing the butt down onto the senator's hand, crushing the bones against the hard steel of the pistol. Scott could hear the bones cracking. As the old man screamed out, Scott slammed the shotgun against the senator's knee, the weapon bouncing off the bone with a snapping sound. Scott found himself screaming "You bastard!" as his fist shot forward, driving into the senator's face. The sound of the senator's nose breaking was pure pleasure to Scott. The old killer slumped back onto the work bench screaming in agony.

He would harm no one again.

U.S.C.G. Headquarters, Governors Island—0830 Hours

Sherry was happy to be getting off the workboat at Governor's Island that morning. The weather was pleasant, and she had begun getting her life together once more. With the death of the mercenaries and the arrest of the conspirators, she had come ashore the day before to arrange for a new furnished apartment. It felt good to be on her own once again. She was preparing to leave the *McDonald* the next day and move into her new home.

Captain Peters greeted her and her dredge companions as they entered his office. "Thank you for coming," Peters began. "I asked you all to join us so that we could bring you up to date and, frankly, to thank you for your part in supporting us in this complex situation. Now I'll turn the explanation over to Commander Scott."

Scott nodded and turned to the others. "I too want to express my gratitude. One way I felt we could do this is to bring you up to speed on the particulars of what we now know." No one spoke, so he began: "Doug Erickson had hired Yuri Mikelovich and his mercenaries to break strikes against his trucking company. Those same mercenaries were then hired to help with the coverup over the sub business. They had planned to kill both Sherry and me and steal the Dorfmann diary."

"Was it this Mikelovich who tried to blow us up?" Captain Harris asked.

"Yes. The explosives used were from one of Erickson's own company's trucks that he arranged to be left unguarded in western New Jersey so that Mikelovich's men could hijack it.

"The mercenaries then took the truck and explosives to the Jersey shore, put the explosives on a cabin cruiser and sailed it to the site of the submarine. George Wilson told Erickson that a marker buoy had been left. The mercenaries were to scuttle the cruiser on top of the sub and set off the dynamite to crush the sub and end the investigation. You can imagine their surprise when it turned out that the marker buoy had been moved."

"Do I understand correctly that you've arrested everyone who was involved?" Sherry asked.

"We've arrested all of the conspirators—except for the two mercenaries who managed to evade an extensive police manhunt. I can't say, Sherry, that the threat to your life is ended. I doubt that those two remaining mercenaries will pursue you now that Erickson and Mikelovich are in custody, but there is always a possibility that they'll try to kill you out of revenge."

"Just who is in jail? The news reports said a U.S. senator was arrested."

"The senator is Sam Tifton of California. One of the most corrupt public officials I've ever encountered. We arrested him in a studio taking pornographic videos. The FBI is still digging up a big volume of kickbacks and payoffs from defense contractors, drug dealers, and more. The men we entrust the leadership of our nation to should be of high character. Not like this man.

"His involvement with his video activities worked to our advantage. He hadn't heard the news of the attack on the mercenaries and was completely surprised when we arrested him. His accomplices, however, were all trying to escape.

"One of them, Sam Bernard, has been telling everything and is trying to turn state's evidence for a deal. He had been a first lieutenant in Tifton's O.S.S. unit, and he says he was reluctantly involved in the original crime. How he managed to convince the voters in Georgia to elect him Attorney General last year is beyond me.

"I will now read a portion of the confession Bernard gave me and the FBI the day after his capture. This part is about the events that occurred inside the submarine on 25 May 1945.

"This transcript is in Bernard's own words."

It started when the U.S. Army formed special intelligence units to go behind German lines in France. That's when the other three officers and I first came together. We were to direct French resistance fighters and collect information. The intense danger we faced hardened us into a close relationship under the command of Major Tifton. We obeyed his orders without question. But I guess you're more interested in what happened stateside, right?

Okay. Capturing the submarine had been much easier than we had anticipated. The Germans welcomed the five of us with enthusiasm. The submariners obviously believed that we were there to rescue them and dug into the offered food like ravenous animals.

Lieutenant Brogano's limited ability with German calmed the crew when he said that the five of us were from Berlin. His request of the submarine's captain to identify the three special weapon specialists obtained instant cooperation. We had agreed that these key Germans were necessary for the safe handling of the dangerous cargo.

I want one thing understood up front. Killing those sailors who had been trapped inside that immobile underwater steel prison for weeks and weeks was unnecessary. Totally unnecessary. I wanted to capture them, not shoot them. I never would have gone down there if I knew that. Those poor guys were so hungry that it was easy to lure them together with the promise of food. But the only thing they dined on, unfortunately, was U.S. Army lead. I swear—double swear—that I did not know the major's intentions. I repeat—I did not know! When the guns began to fire, I was as shocked as those poor krauts.

Taken by surprise, the Germans were unable to take cover. They had no chance. The bullets struck with such force that bits of blood-soaked flesh and bone flew from the bodies, coating every surface, including the clothing and skin of the murderers.

Everything seemed covered with blood. The bulkheads, the deck, the furnishings—all dripped with the red liquid. Made me sick, physically nauseous.

Even after the guns went silent, it still wasn't quiet in that tomb. Moans and cries kept coming from the heap of dying men. I forced myself to watch as the major walked slowly forward, his feet slipping on the blood-soaked deck. Pistol raised at the ready, he silenced the human sounds that came from the pile. Only then was it over.

I remember him then—our commanding officer, Major Sam Tifton—turn toward those of us still alive. Even then, the major's face had a hardness in the many creases and furrows that lined it. No one doubted his resolve.

"Bernie," he said to me, "get the hose set up and wash this blood out of here." That's what he said. Then he told Vince to get the welding started.

While I set up the hose, I watched as the major turned and moved, through the murky light cast by the only bulb that had survived the bullets, toward the three surviving German crewmen. They had been taken aside and handcuffed to a pipe.

"One of you speaks English," the major demanded. "Come on! I know it! Fatso Göring told me so." Even in that weak light you could see that hard face was filled with anger and hate.

I watched as the three Germans looked at the major with terror-filled eyes. I knew that the major was not known to be patient, and I pleaded with my eyes for the three survivors to cooperate. The sound of the bolt on the sub-machine being cocked convinced them.

"Bitte, bitte," the older German blurted out. "Ya, I sprechen sie English." Tears flowed down his cheeks, and he shook against the handcuffs.

"All right," the major said. "You will open the cargo freezer and the three of you will prepare to remove the stuff."

Captain Doug Erickson had the keys in his hand in an instant and in a moment started the prisoners toward the bow of the submarine. The still hot sub-machine gun that he had used as he stood firing alongside the major was hanging on his neck by its strap. The Germans stumbled along the sloping wet deck trembling, the muzzle of the captain's weapon only inches from their backs. Then they were gone.

We had less than an hour to set the monorail. Welding cables quickly pulled down the temporary caisson pipe that connected the sunken submarine's top hatch with the surface of the water some fifteen feet above. I still remember squinting in the dimness of that one bulb when—whoosh! A brilliant arc of light almost blinded me as Vince quickly attached the support brackets to the underside of the submarine's hull overhead.

The work went quickly since the pieces had been prefabricated from plans the major had stolen from the navy's intelligence files. As you figured out by now, the major isn't one for following protocol when it's inconvenient.

Lieutenant Brogano had been trained with ironworking skills to enable him to destroy steel bridges, thereby frustrating German war transport. He used those skills to install the vital monorail needed to remove the cargo. U.S. Navy Commander Rolland Ledbetter lifted the pieces of inverted T-shaped track as Brogano shoved the connecting bolts into place.

Ledbetter—I never really much cared for him. He had been a late addition to our group. A very necessary addition, I might add. Since he commanded the New York Coast Guard Station for the wartime navy, only he could manipulate the orders to keep the Coast Guard from investigating our impossible-to-hide activities. Think about it—we pulled this off right under the noses of the officials of America's largest city. I heard Major Tifton say he was thankful that the commander proved so easy to corrupt. Maybe that's why I didn't like him.

Anyway, with the monorail completed, it was time to move our deadly cargo. Spooky stuff. It waited below, packed in hundreds of cardboard boxes stacked in the freezer. Each box weighed twenty kilograms, and the three Germans moved them easily. They placed them in the cargo baskets that hung from the monorail's rolling hoist, handling the boxes with great care. Meticulous care. They knew that only a thin rubber membrane separated them from a horrible death. Four hours after the five of us had "invaded" the trapped submarine, the cargo was completely off-loaded, much faster than we had expected.

After that, the major ordered that every piece of paper be gathered and removed least some important evidence about the cargo be overlooked. Erickson saw that I was shaking as I filled several laundry bags with papers.

"Bernie," Erickson asked me. "What's wrong with you? You okay? The job is going on schedule."

As God is my witness, I stopped and looked him right in the eye. "Did you have to kill them?"

"What the hell were we supposed to do?" he said. "Invite them to a picnic? For Christ's sake, you've killed krauts before. What's bugging you now?" He was so damned smug and proud.

"That was war," I answered him. "This is murder. The war ended three weeks ago, dammit. Now you sit there looking so damned relaxed—I can't believe it. Have you no feelings left?"

"Don't let the major hear that," he warned me. "Just think about the money we're going to get for this job. Nobody gives a damn about a bunch of krauts anyway."

I think now back to when Erickson and I had parachuted into France before D-Day. He berated me because I had held back whenever it was necessary to kill. And he was right. I'm not a killer. Several times Erickson had to step in and fire the fatal bullets.

That's why he always referred to me as the "weak link," even in front of the others. Even to my face. Especially to my face, the cold bastard. Erickson and the major even discussed leaving me out of this caper. Now, I wish they had.

When I asked Erickson if he was worried about the police, he laughed. "The major and Rolland have everything arranged," he said. It seems the Corps of Engineers was supposed to pump dredge spoil over the sub the following month, shove the damn boat into the deep channel, and bury it under a million tons of mud. It was never supposed to be found again.

Erickson, the arrogant fool, spoke with such confidence. Now look where we are.

Funny, the things that stick in your mind. I remember the fresh cool air with a touch of brine as I stepped off of the lift at the top of the caisson pipe. Night had come during the stay below and the lights of the surrounding city cast a gentle light across the water. The weather had remained calm with just a light chop on the water. If it weren't for all the death down below, I might have thought it beautiful. But I was still trying to keep my lunch down.

Erickson, on the other hand, I could see felt good about himself and the job we had just completed. "A good execution of a good plan," he had said. "The major will be pleased." I knew that meant a lot to him. You see, the major was his mentor. Kind of strange, since he had just celebrated his twenty-seventh birthday and the major was only thirty at the time.

"We're done, Sam," I overheard Erickson say as he stepped to the major's side. He was so proud of being chosen as the unit's executive officer and the major's trusted friend. "What about the three Germans?"

"They have to be our front to get the money. We'll kill 'em later."

"Fine with me."

My blood ran cold. They were so casual.

Vince welded the hatch shut. Since the sea cocks wouldn't open, we couldn't flood the boat. So we set booby traps. But, of course, you know that.

On the way back to shore, while I still fought being sick, Erickson and the major were already planning their futures, if you can believe it. Erickson was going to use his share of the dough to buy a fleet of trucks. Start a motor freight line. We all know what happened to major—I mean Senator Tifton. The krauts in the sub weren't even cold and the major—I can still see the stub of cigar bouncing between his teeth as he spoke—said: "Maybe I'll be president someday." He came pretty damned close, didn't he?

Scott paused and set the confession down in front of him. He looked up, extended his hand, and poured a glass of water into a plastic cup from the chrome plated pitcher that had been sitting at the center of the table. He replaced the pitcher and raised the cup to his lips and drank. Everyone watched him, unable to say anything, as they tried to cope with the words of the written confession.

Scott then began again:

"The man who directed the mercenaries to attack us was Douglas Erickson, a former captain in Tifton's unit and his very willing supporter. He pushed the others to go along with whatever Tifton wanted. We caught him, Vincent Brogano, and Ledbetter trying to board a flight to Athens at Newark. They expected that we would cover the other New York airports, so they thought they could go to New Jersey and not be seen. We had every route covered.

"The arrest of former Navy Commander Rolland Ledbetter has revealed that the depth of their influence led right into the National Security Council and naval intelligence. It was Rolland Ledbetter who had his son, Jerome, convince the President to relieve Captain Peters and turn the investigation of the sub over to naval intelligence. With the son in charge, Tifton and Erickson expected to control the results of the investigation. But they didn't have a way to control the FBI task force and that's what brought them down.

"We also have the two mercenary leaders locked up. Mikelovich, who was called Number One, is in jail. The mercenary we know as Number Two is in the hospital under heavy guard. We are still trying to determine his identity."

"Any information concerning the mercenaries?" J.D. asked. "Who were they? Where did they come from?"

"We have identified only Mikelovich positively. He was a soldier in the Soviet army in the cold war. The reason we were able to learn about him was that the Russian authorities have been searching for him. They jumped when we sent his prints to Moscow for their help.

"The others we've sent were not people they've had any interest in, so they've been foot-dragging. But Mikelovich was different. He's a fugitive from Russian justice.

"Seems he killed a local man while he was stationed in

Poland with the Red Army. Then he raped the man's wife and daughter. He is under a death sentence in Russia, and they want him back.

"We believe that the others are all ex–Eastern Bloc soldiers and will be identified when those governments decide to get around to it."

"Why did they kill George Wilson?" Sherry asked.

"George was killed when he realized how far Erickson was prepared to go. He had gone to see Erickson and demanded more money. Erickson refused and told Mikelovich to silence George."

"This Erickson is crazy!" J.D. broke in.

"Yes. Even Bernard said that Erickson had gone beyond what the others in the group wanted. He ordered Mikelovich to try a second time to get the diary and kill Sherry. The reason that they didn't try a second time to kill me was that the NYPD had put out a false report that both Brenda and I had been killed, and the mercenaries believed it."

"What will happen to those men you've arrested?" asked Sherry.

"They will all stand trial. The U.S. Attorney's Office is still writing up the charges. None of them will ever see the outside of a prison again. On top of that, the New York State district attorneys are busy writing up their own lists. And if that's not enough, they'll still face charges in New Jersey and Connecticut. And the Germans want a piece of them, too."

"Whatever happened to the cargo of the submarine?" asked J.D.

"Captain Peters, Chief Morris, and I went to Washington to go through a mountain of files. We found a paper trail leading from the purchase of the cargo by the U.S. Army to its shipment to the Pacific, where the plan was to air-drop the frozen blocks onto Tokyo's watershed.

"The mission was canceled because on July twentieth the first atom bomb was tested in New Mexico and a decision was made to use this new weapon instead. Biological weapons were not really trusted in those days, and so the Navy was ordered to melt down all of the blocks of cholera and mix the germs with chlorine bleach to destroy them. They dumped the dead cargo at sea."

"Did you ever figure out why the two divers were murdered?" Sherry asked.

"Yes, Bernard cleared that up. The first diver had been trapped on top of the sub when a wall of mud broke free and slid over the man. His brother, the other diver, tried to free the trapped diver but couldn't. The free diver returned to the boat where Mikelovich was waiting.

"They argued extensively. The diver wanted to summon the police to rescue his brother, but Mikelovich refused. They began to fight with fists when one of Mikelovich's men shot the diver. They then chained the diver to a weight and threw him overboard to sink down and join his trapped brother.

"Mikelovich cut the two air hoses and left the scene. You must realize that the two divers were not part of the mercenary army and Mikelovich considered them to be expendable.

"This brings us to the end of my report."

"Sherry," said Captain Peters, "I wanted to thank you especially for your help with my unfortunate situation with the Navy. I've always believed that the use of political influence is improper, and I've always tried to avoid it. Morris's contacting you on my behalf was a big surprise. I'm grateful for the results."

"I did what I thought was necessary, sir," the chief responded, "and I would do it again—no matter what."

"So, the President did help after Don Fredericks called him?" Sherry asked.

"Yes. He rejected the board's report without comment. It's as if it never happened. Captain Ledbetter is under investigation for falsifying information."

Harris and Scott moved to the other side of the office where they could speak without being overheard.

"Commander," Harris began, "I wanted to talk to you about Sherry. I still worry about her being attacked by the last two mercenaries. I've trained her hard, and she's pretty proficient in self-defense. She can handle a gun as well as any man—better than most. She can punch out most guys' lights, and she knows more about bombs than your average cop. But we're about to pull out of here. The tugboat *Hercules* left Miami last night. It'll be here Thursday to pull us to Boston.

"So, whether I like it or not, Sherry has to come back on shore—on her own again. I'm sure she can handle almost anything, but, well, I still worry. I'd feel better if I knew that somebody was looking out for her."

"I'd enjoy that duty very much," Scott answered, "but it sounds like you care for her yourself."

"More than you could possibly know. She's the best thing to ever come into my life. I want to stay here and protect her, but I can't, and she insists that I go to Boston."

"I'll do everything I can, rest assured."

"I'd appreciate that very much. Thanks."

Sherry approached. "And just what have you two been talking about?"

"Oh, a very pretty and wonderful young lady," Scott answered with a broad smile.

"And just what lies has Tiny been telling you about me?"

"Just about how terrific you are with a gun, as well as all your other accomplishments."

"Yeah, what a great Saturday-night date I'd be! Look at me! Ugly old work boots, baggy pants."

"You look fantastic! I'll be first in line, if you'll let me."

"Well, I'll take it under consideration," Sherry responded as she moved to Harris's side and gave him a gentle hug of affection. "But first I've got to get moved into my new apartment."

"We're going to miss you a lot," Harris sighed.

"I'll never forget you guys either—a bunch of cutthroats who no doubt saved my life. I'm not sure whether I should shoot you for pounding me so hard or kiss you good-bye."

"Can we vote on it?"

"Well, I'll think about it, Tiny."

"So, Commander, what do you think of Sherry as a lean, mean, fighting machine?"

"She's wonderful!"

"Well, I'll tell you this: If she's ever attacked by a mugger, he'll end up in jail or a hospital. She'll chop him to pieces—no doubt about it."

"Oh, listen to you!" Sherry responded.

"Hey, everybody!" J.D. said as he joined them, "it's time to get back to work. Let's go before they throw us out into the street."

As they left the building, Scott and Sherry dropped behind. "I hope you'll let me spend some time with you," Scott said as he rubbed his injured arm.

"Sure. I'd like that very much. How is your arm?"

"Getting better." He waved a hand in dismissal, and then said," So much has happened in these past weeks. I'm still trying to sort it all out."

"What did happen out there in Queens? Sounded like World War III."

"Felt like it, too. It's a scene I can't dispel from my mind. Maybe never. The carnage was beyond anything I have ever experienced. After the second salvo of cannon shells destroyed the mercenaries, the resulting fire was hotter than any blast furnace. The flames towered into the sky. The stores of ammunition and explosives added to the heat and thunder.

"Fire ringed the scene as houses around the mercenary building joined in the expanding conflagration. My God, I had thought, the entire city might go up. There was nothing to do but wait and watch until fire fighters could safely be brought in. Did you know that the press named me Commander Butcher that day?"

"I saw that in the newspaper," Sherry answered. "I'm sorry."

"Well, to hell with them. What do they know about the emptiness that can occupy a man's soul? I feel no remorse. The mercenaries are dead, and that's all that matters.

"I just wished those O.S.S. officers had also burned in that hell. They're men who abused their positions of trust and power for their personal gain. I hate them for what they did to me and Brenda. I hate them for dishonoring the millions of good men and women who fought that terrible war and destroyed Hitler. Those bastards stole, not only that cargo, but diminished the value of the heroic efforts of their fellow soldiers, sailors and marines. The miserable scum."

His left hand rubbed his healing bullet wound. It still hurt. A few inches to the left, and he wouldn't have any more problems. Such is luck. "One question I've been wanting to ask—how did the Germans come up with all of that cholera? Did Dorfmann say anything about that in the diary?"

"Yes. I did find that, and I translated it into my notes, but it was so horrible that I ripped the page up and threw it away."

"Heavens! Why?"

"It was so horrible, I just couldn't speak the words. I didn't want to talk about it."

"And now? Can you tell me what you found?"

"It's still hard, but maybe, if you really want to know, I could tell you."

"I'd like to know. It's the one piece of the puzzle I'm still missing."

"Von Kruger and his assistants had a laboratory in Berlin and were ready to begin to produce the cholera for the mission as 1944 was coming to a close. In mid-December, the lab was destroyed by Allied bombing, and Von Kruger reported to Luftwaffe command that the project could not be completed.

"Luftwaffe command would have none of it and ordered that another way be found. They put the problem into S.S. hands, and the decision was made to take the small remaining supply of cholera and infect the water supply of one of the concentration camps.

"There were over thirty thousand people in that camp, and they all got cholera. The guards forced them to vomit and defecate into buckets that were then collected. Then—and this is the true horror—as the people died, which most of them did, the guards drained the blood and other body fluids and collected them.

"Then, all of these collected fluids were strained and then concentrated, using vacuum distillation—similar to the type used to make evaporated milk—until three thousand gallons of very concentrated cholera medium remained. Von Kruger and his assistants mixed the special chemicals they had discovered to keep the cholera in a state of suspended animation, a condition that could be maintained nearly indefinitely, as long as the solution was kept frozen and concentrated.

"These chemicals were to dissipate once the cargo from the submarine was dropped into the water tunnel in New York. The blocks would melt and be diluted by the water moving to the city. The cholera would then reawaken and be ready to infect the people of New York City by the hundreds of thousands. The story still gives me nightmares, Bob."

"Unbelievable!"

"Yes—and now you and I are the only two people outside of the highest levels of the federal government who know the whole truth."

"But the diary still exists."

"Oh, sure. You turned it over to Agent Carson. Have you heard anything about it since? Anything on the media? No! All you hear is the same cover story about a chemical-process tank being dug up, and how the Navy has neutralized the danger.

"The destruction of the mercenaries has been handled as a separate and unrelated event. The government will never admit that they have the diary. It'll be buried in some file in the back of some warehouse—and the truth with it."

"Now the mayor and police commissioner are denying that the attack destroying the mercenaries ever happened. A gas explosion they claim. They've even got the media to retract their stories. I tell you Bob, the big lie is the way for them to protect the image of the city. All the politicians are jumping aboard the cover-up."

"Yeah, you're right. It's the thing that they do best."

"And now I have to walk around with this armored purse packing this, this *cannon*. Look inside and what do you see? Anything a normal woman would need? An automatic pistol, ammo clips, my badge as a special auxiliary policewoman so I can legally carry a concealed weapon, gun permits, and ID card. I barely have room for my car keys and lipstick!"

"At least you can defend yourself."

"Oh, yes. I sure can. J.D. did a terrific job of training me.

His record with the Marine Corps was so highly respected that the police accepted my training as fully equivalent.

"Now I can shoot the buttons off of your uniform at sixty yards and never singe so much as a hair. I'll be continuing to train after I come ashore. I'm joining a weight-lifting club to build strength and a martial arts school to learn karate. I'll also be using the police firing range to keep my aim sharp."

"You seem to be getting your life back in order."

"That's what I've got to find out. Do I still have a life here? I still have friends and family here. I still have a job I like and a good boss I enjoy working for. Now I have to rebuild my home—my sanctuary—in my new apartment. Replace the things I lost and make it a place I can feel comfortable in."

Scott nodded. "I've got to get my life back together, too. I'm staying at the Governors Island BOQ right now, which is a little better than camping out. I'm still trying to sort out my feelings about Brenda. I've got to finish my divorce and try to build a new life."

"Seems we're both going to be busy finding ourselves. Maybe we can help each other."

"I'd like that. Yes, I would—very much."

As they continued toward the pier, Scott instinctively reached out and took Sherry's hand. They walked along holding hands without speaking.

Then Sherry said, "A dollar for your thoughts. Aren't I extravagant?"

"Oh—I'm sorry." He pulled back from his musings. "Your perfume...your touch...so much like Brenda's. For a few moments I was with her again....I hope you don't mind. I was at peace again."

She squeezed his hand.

"Thanks. You're a good friend."

They reached the pier and could see that Harris and J.D. were eager to depart.

"Well, I'd better get aboard, Bob."

Scott gave her hand a last, gentle squeeze as they looked into each other's eyes. Damn, she thought, do I really want to do this? He's so weak and vulnerable—I could take him in a minute. But I can't. He'd go straight into my heart. Straight in. Sherry pulled away and turned her eyes from his distractingly handsome face. "You know, when you consider the lives destroyed by that submarine—both now and back in '45—I think opening that boat opened a portal into hell itself."

"Yeah, maybe. But it also opened up some friendships."

She smiled. "Yes. Yes, it did," she said, giving him a peck on the cheek. "I guess some good came out of it after all." She stepped aboard the workboat as J.D. loosened the rope and the boat began moving.

"Hey, Sherry!" Scott shouted. "When will I see you again?"

"Not today! I've got a dredge to run. Call me later." She blew him a kiss then turned away.

EPILOGUE
September 10 1995

Otto Dorfmann shuffled his left foot against the wet green grass as he waited for the eulogy to end. The rain had been thankfully brief, and he hoped the priest would soon finish. Unlikely, since he knew the old churchman was a windbag.

Dorfmann's eyes settled onto the gray painted metal coffin laying upon the red nylon straps. He rubbed his tired face; there had been little time to sleep since the letter from the German Ministry of Defense arrived. The news of the discovery of his father's remains after so many years had brought much turmoil.

The government had offered a military guard of honor, but as the only surviving child of the U-boat captain, he had refused. He wanted a simple, private, family ceremony for the father he didn't remember. He had been only four years old when his father's submarine went to sea.

He thought back to the stories of those days that his Uncle Kurt had told him. How his father had been told that his entire family had died on the train destroyed by American bombers, the train carrying him, his mother, and older sister. How he, the son—unidentified amongst the survivors—had been placed in one of the hundreds of orphanages to await his fate along with the tens of thousands of other children who had been torn from home and family.

It had only been by chance that his uncle had found him and brought him back to the family's hometown, Pegnitz, in southern Germany. He had now lived his life and raised his own family in what had been his parents' house. He glanced up for a moment at the factory building beyond the cemetery where he, his two sons, and most of the residents of Pegnitz worked producing high quality chemical pumps, which had earned the community its well deserved reputation.

The gentle click jarred Dorfmann back to reality as the straps began the lowering of the gray box into the grave, the final resting place of the U-boat captain, next to his long dead wife and daughter.

Dorfmann glanced at the small group of onlookers. None showed any emotion. He was not surprised. Almost no one remembered much about this ancestor. It had been too long. Whatever acts had defined his life now were too distant to hold any meaning.

Dorfmann could only wonder what his life might have been had his parents and sister survived the horrors of that war. He remembered nothing about that time and only knew of those events from his uncle's stories. Yet, he still felt cheated.

The gray box now lay at the bottom of the hole dug in the yellow-orange soil. The ceremony thus ended, the small family group began to depart. Dorfmann reached down and clasped the small hand of his grandson. He wiped away some sudden tears with his other hand as he thought of how his own sons had been cheated from the wonderful pleasure of knowing their grandparents. He turned away from the grave and walked with his grandson toward the cemetery's wrought iron gate.

COMING FROM ANDOVER PRESS

The Capital Murder Trial of Thomas Koskovich by Peter W. Schneider. Nonfiction. The true crime history of the infamous New Jersey pizza thrill murders. Follow the story of the jury as the sixteen men and women are selected from over a thousand jury candidates to hear and view the evidence against the accused. Learn the full facts of the police investigation that led to the arrest of Thomas Koskovich, and read the full confession made by the accused the night of his arrest. Read as the prosecuter lays out the facts of the night of the murders, how the accused teenage killers selected their victims, lured them to their killing ground and proceeded to carry out their plan to experience what it feels like to kill somebody. Follow the jury as they listen to numerous witnesses called by the prosecuter and the defense team as the lawyers argue to win their cases. Join the jury as they assemble to consider their verdict in an emotionally charged jury room and hear the reaction in the courtroom as the decision is handed down.

Bayou Death Stalk by Peter W. Schneider. Fiction. Return to the time in Louisiana when oil investment money flowed freely attracting criminals, corrupt government officials and greedy union bosses to extort their illicit payoffs from contractors and oil companies. The author, who himself worked for an oil company, has assembled some of the facts of that time into a single story. A story of a construction company being hired to build new harbor facilities only to be stopped by murder and extortion. The company turns to a strong leader. A woman who has a reputation for finding a way to win. Follow the beautiful Sherry Edwards as she confronts the gangsters, defeats them and leads her construction crew to complete her assigned project. A task complicated by her own romantic involvements as her every movement is watched by assassins determined to bring about the woman's early death. A story far closer to truth than fiction, far closer than many in Louisiana care to remember.

Join us on the web:
www.andoverpress.com
E-mail us at:
pschneider@nac.net